Sue & John —

Thanks for the
you enjoy it
to our friendly family debates!

E. M[signature]

THE LIBERTY GROUP

Eric Myerholtz

authorHOUSE®

AuthorHouse™
1663 Liberty Drive
Bloomington, IN 47403
www.authorhouse.com
Phone: 1-800-839-8640

© 2010 Eric Myerholtz. All rights reserved.

No part of this book may be reproduced, stored in a retrieval system, or transmitted by any means without the written permission of the author.

First published by AuthorHouse 8/17/2010

ISBN: 978-1-4520-6138-2 (e)
ISBN: 978-1-4520-6137-5 (sc)
ISBN: 978-1-4520-6136-8 (hc)

Library of Congress Control Number: 2010911742

Printed in the United States of America

This book is printed on acid-free paper.

Because of the dynamic nature of the Internet, any Web addresses or links contained in this book may have changed since publication and may no longer be valid. The views expressed in this work are solely those of the author and do not necessarily reflect the views of the publisher, and the publisher hereby disclaims any responsibility for them.

Thank you to:

*Mitch, Marty and Mark – for being such supportive friends
My parents and brothers – for teaching me so much
Elizabeth, Emily and David – for being the
best kids any father could wish for
Linda – for being the love of my life*

Chapter 1

Mitch wiped the sweat from his face as he tore through the unfamiliar streets. He knew who had sent his pursuers, and being caught was not an option. Running for your life was an experience no one should ever face, he thought, and the unfamiliar streets only compounded the complexity of the situation. Mitch had never been to Charleston before, but it seemed to him half the United States was in South Carolina today. This was actually a good thing, allowing him to use the crowds for cover. He turned a corner and found himself at the end of a large outdoor market. Mitch took the time to grab a T-shirt from a booth where a vendor was occupied by another customer and threw it on, followed by a baseball cap obtained from another little table. A pair of sunglasses completed the ensemble, and he tried to act as if he hadn't just been running and hiding for the last twenty minutes. He stood in the middle of a larger group of tourists waiting in line for one of the many horse-drawn carriage rides through the historic part of the town. He caught sight of his pursuers now; they were entering the market about two blocks down, scanning every which way for a glimpse of him.

Mitch wound his way to the front of the line and used a departing carriage as a shield to continue walking away from the area. He needed to find a place to think. He exited the other end of the booths and turned onto Market Street as the carriage continued straight ahead. Mitch walked a short distance down the block and saw a line of people gathered outside of Hyman's Restaurant. He noticed a second entrance to the left of the line, walked in, took the stairway up, pausing shortly on the landing to see if anyone was following him up the street before continuing to the dining room on the second floor. He grabbed the only empty table he saw, sat down, and picked up a menu, hiding his face.

"We usually don't let people pick whatever table they want," a soft, southern-accented voice told him. "In fact, the hostess is bringing a couple up right now to sit there. If you haven't noticed, we are a little busy."

"I will give you fifty dollars to let me stay here for an hour. I'll order whatever; I just need time!" His pleading eyes must have registered with her (or she needed fifty dollars). She plopped down a bowl of boiled peanuts and met the hostess as she entered the room, indicating there must have been a mistake.

"This gentleman was just seated a few minutes ago, and I've already taken his order and put it in." The confused hostess took the other patrons away, and the waitress turned back to him. "I'll bring you a beer; you look like you could use one."

"Diet Coke and a large glass of water, please."

"No problem."

Although she was absolutely right about the beer, it was more important to keep his reactions and thoughts as focused as possible right now. Mitch also needed to keep himself hydrated—running through the streets in this humidity was draining him quickly. He was a distance runner (his tall, lanky form being tailor-made for the activity) but most of his training had been in the dry Arizona heat, not this oppressive, muggy weather. He downed the water before she could ask him if he knew what he wanted to order. He requested more water and glanced beside her at a whiteboard full of combo platters offering three, five, or seven items from a list.

"I'll take the buffalo shrimp, the deviled crab, and the Charleston salmon and grits." The waitress walked away, and he took in his surroundings. This looked like a great place to have a fun time with the family, if only that were the case today. The table was adorned with little gold plates listing the names of famous people who had sat there. He read "Billy Joel" on his table. How about that. Mitch's mind went back to a conversation he had with his seventeen-year-old daughter, Lynne, about four months ago. She had wanted tickets to see *Movin' Out*, the musical based on Billy Joel's work. Had that really only been last May? That was the night before this whole mess started.

Mitch peered out the window and saw his two adversaries standing in the street, shaking their heads, and talking animatedly to the occupants of a parked vehicle. After about a minute of discussion, the two men got in the car, and Mitch watched it drive away. He let go a slow, long exhale. *Safe, at least for now.* He thought back to that day four months ago and wondered what he did to play himself into this predicament. He loved athletics and used sports analogies in his columns often. He could not help thinking, as he sat in this unknown town, that it was the bottom of the ninth and he was down a few runs.

Chapter 2

Four Months Earlier

Mitch's two dogs forced him from his peaceful slumber with their whining to get outside. He kissed is his wife, Marie, softly so as not to wake her and eased his 6'2" slender frame out of bed. As he walked by his kids' rooms, he realized they, too, were still sleeping soundly. He continued downstairs and over to the back door, opened it, and the two canines eagerly bounded outside. This was a very typical weekend morning for Mitch. Soon, the dogs were scratching at the door to come in to be fed. After they ate, he grabbed his sandals, the dog leashes, and his cell phone and headed out for the morning walk.

The larger dog (an Australian shepherd named Sydney, even though the breed had nothing to do with Australia) was acquired a few years ago as a puppy and pretty much obeyed every command Mitch gave it. The smaller dog was a mixed breed Marie had found searching a rescue society online page, and it didn't listen so well. Mitch and Marie had been married eighteen years, and recently, the cat they purchased upon returning from their honeymoon had passed away, leaving Marie feeling a huge void in her life. Her answer was to get a second dog—a friend for Sydney that was already named Sage. As Sydney and Sage sniffed every smell they could on their walk, Mitch felt his cell phone buzz. He deftly put both leashes in one hand and retrieved his phone. "John" was displayed on the screen. His boss. What could he want to talk to him about this early on a Saturday morning?

"Good morning," Mitch answered. "Assuming I wasn't sleeping in? Good thing this phone didn't buzz on my nightstand and wake Marie up." Mitch always kept his phone on vibrate—that way, he never had to worry about it going off in a meeting or during church.

"Yes, I was assuming you would be up and about by now," John replied. "What are you doing?"

"I'm walking my dogs. What are you up to? I figured you would be busy on a golf course somewhere this morning." John was an avid golfer, one of the reasons he came to Phoenix. Mitch and John were both quite accomplished on the course and often had some great matches against each other.

"I'm actually on the way to the club right now, but there is something I need to discuss with you, and I thought maybe we could get together for lunch today. Are you free, or do you have kids' activities keeping you busy?"

"I can probably make something work. Ed has a guitar lesson, but I can meet you sometime around one o'clock."

"Great—how about BW-3's on Fourth Street?"

"You know I can't say no to wings," Mitch replied. "See you there. Do I get any hint about what you want to talk about? My articles a bit too much for you lately?"

"It's something I think you'll be excited about."

"A raise?" Mitch asked hopefully.

"Of course not, but the possibility of more responsibility with none of the perks," his boss quipped back.

"Great. See you at one." Mitch hung up the phone and continued his walk, contemplating what this conversation would be about. Mitch had been a conservative political columnist for the *Arizona Republic* for ten years, after starting his career as a sports writer. In the past year or so, his weekly columns had been picked up by a few online publications as well. John Manos was a senior editor at the paper. He and Mitch had worked together for five years, with John moving to the *Republic* from the *San Francisco Chronicle*. Prior to the *Chronicle*, John had worked at the *Los Angeles Times*. Mitch and John initially seemed to struggle with their professional relationship. John understood Mitch was hired to write conservative articles, but he had difficulty trying not to inject his own opinion (which more often than not was almost the opposite of Mitch's) or at least to tone down the conservatism Mitch presented. Mitch considered this editorial license to be his boss overstepping his bounds, and there were a few tense moments between the two. After about six months, they developed an understanding and, for the most part, had become respectful colleagues and even fairly good friends. John was about twenty years older than Mitch and was at a different stage of life; his kids were married with children of their own. John and his wife, Janice, were fully acclimated now to being empty nesters. They had moved to Phoenix when their youngest had entered college, knowing they wanted to be somewhere warmer than the Bay Area when they retired.

    Mitch assumed John was kidding about the responsibility comment. Mitch reported to John, but "reported to" basically meant he turned his articles in on time and John read them, made suggestions, or continued his efforts to tone Mitch down. No one reported to Mitch, nor did he want that. He enjoyed his writing and had no intention of ever becoming an editor. His articles had received several local accolades recently, and Mitch was being quoted at times by some conservative talk radio hosts, so he knew his writing was being read nationally, at least by some. Thinking about this call from his boss as he walked his dogs home, Mitch realized he was really happy with what he had right now and hoped whatever John wanted would not change his routine dramatically.

Mitch and Marie lived in a wonderful four-bedroom house in a quiet area of Phoenix, overlooking a golf course. They had the required swimming pool in the back (necessary as Phoenix registers over one hundred degrees about 33 percent of the time, but to a guy who grew up in northern Ohio, it seemed perpetually over one hundred). The house also had a decently sized yard for the Phoenix area. Their friends even joked about the park they had next to their house, referring to their green space. As Mitch walked in the house, he unleashed the dogs and could hear the television. The front room was more of a living room, with the family computer and a few sports collectibles Mitch had accumulated over the years. Passing through this room, Mitch entered the kitchen and turned right. The kitchen had an open feel, with the family room off to the side. Jane was up; he knew it was her before he even saw his middle child. Jane was the early riser of the kids. She went to bed earlier and awoke earlier—almost always. Jane was fourteen and finishing her eighth-grade year. She had Mitch's brown dark hair and his height (as she was 5'10") but everything else about her appearance was similar to her mom's. Her blue eyes were all Jane's though, as both Mitch and Marie had green.

"How are you this morning, sweetheart?" Mitch asked as he walked over and kissed her on the head.

"I'm fine," she replied, not looking away from one of the numerous *Law and Order* reruns played on a variety of cable networks. Mitch glanced up and saw what she was watching.

"Do you have to watch this on Saturday morning?" he said, longing for the days when he would watch *Mulan* or *Beauty and the Beast* with her.

"There's nothing else on," Jane replied.

"A hundred channels of cable and she can't find something else to watch," Mitch mumbled to himself as he headed back to the kitchen.

As he prepared a bowl of cereal for himself, he flipped on his computer to catch up on the overnight news. Putting the first spoonful of GoLean Crunch in his mouth, he read the headline on the Yahoo! network and set his spoon down. Jack Kemp had died early that morning. Jack Kemp was one of Mitch's conservative icons, and he had quoted Mr. Kemp on many occasions, especially regarding supply-side economics. He had never had the honor of meeting the man but felt as if a friend had died. Jane heard the spoon clink on the counter and asked him what was wrong.

"A man I respected very much passed away" was his reply. "I didn't know him personally, but he was a great mind." Jane, unsure of what to say, returned to her show. When her dad said someone was a great mind, this meant it had to do with politics. She knew her father needed to be politically minded for his work, but she also knew she did not need to be. Although she was just fourteen, she intended to be an archeologist and wanted to live in Greece. These were her goals at this point, and those goals did not require an opinion as to what side of the congressional aisle was best for her.

Mitch read the article about Jack Kemp and looked for more information scanning the other headlines. "How did they leave out some of his best quotes?" Mitch questioned aloud without the expectation of an answer from his daughter. He had always thought Kemp could win an argument with a turn of phrase. Two of his favorites were "There are no limits to our future if we don't put limits on our people" and, in reference to liberal Democrats, Kemp had said, "They don't understand that you can't create more employees without first creating more employers, that you can't have capitalism without capital, and we can't expect people to defend property rights when they're denied access to property." Mitch silently said a prayer for Mr. Kemp's family.

Hearing the water turn on upstairs jolted him from his Jack Kemp thoughts. He knew this meant Marie was up, and he started making her a pot of coffee. Mitch had never developed a taste for the stuff himself, but he felt one of his husbandly duties was to have a cup ready for Marie when she awoke (as he was almost always awake before her). Over the years, he had learned how strong (industrial strength—European style) she liked her coffee and could make it to her satisfaction. Mitch felt it was one of the small things he could do for her to offset his incessant snoring. A few minutes later, he gave her a kiss as she entered the kitchen and handed her the cinnamon hazelnut flavored java.

"Good morning," Mitch said.

"Good morning to you—thanks for the coffee," Marie replied. Marie was medium height, with dark brown hair and beautiful green eyes. To Mitch, she looked more beautiful every day. He knew he was quite biased, but he also knew that she had certain qualities that many women envied, such as her youthful appearance and her incredible metabolism. One true story Mitch told in an almost bragging fashion at times was how Marie, the day she returned from the hospital after having their first child, put her pre-pregnancy jeans on with no problem. Every day, he counted his blessings that he fell in love with his best friend, who just happened to be gorgeous as well.

Mitch and Marie had gone to the same high school, but Marie was two years younger than her husband. They had not started dating until Marie was a senior, with Mitch already a sophomore at Bowling Green State University. Mitch and one of his high school friends, Al Miller, were roommates at the college, which was only about thirty minutes from Marie's house. Mitch still remembered how Al's grandfather had been mayor of Bowling Green while they were in college, and he had the good fortune of meeting Ronald Reagan in 1988 when Reagan did a campaign tour through the town for George H. W. Bush. Mitch thought back to that day several times a year, knowing that seeing Reagan and the presence he commanded helped shape his future. That and, of course, much of the reading he had done on the great individuals who had founded the country.

"What's on your schedule today?" he asked his wife.

"I think I am going to meet my friend Stephanie for lunch. How about you?"

"John called and wants to meet me for lunch as well. I'm going after Ed's guitar lesson."

"That's a little strange; he doesn't usually call you in on the weekends," Marie commented. "Maybe we'll be at the same place."

"I don't think so, not unless you and Steph will be enjoying spicy wings as well."

"BW's, huh?" Marie knew what "wings" meant. "Did he say what he wants to talk about?"

"No, just that it was something that would be exciting."

"A raise?" Marie asked, her voice inflecting hopefulness.

"That's what I asked. No luck."

* * * * *

Mitch contemplated what his boss might want as he drove to lunch, having dropped his son back at home after his guitar lesson. He and John had talked several times recently about the struggles of the newspaper industry, and Mitch wondered if this was somehow connected. The truth was newspaper circulation for most large-city publications had experienced a long, slow decline for the past twenty years. More concerning was that this trend was increasing, with some papers dropping 5–10 percent in the last couple of years. The *Arizona Republic* had not been immune to this phenomenon. Daily subscriptions had dropped from 467,000 to the current 413,000 in just five years. The Sunday subscriptions, the day when most of the ads appeared and when circulation was typically much higher (two reasons why Sundays accounted for the largest percent of revenue), had dropped from 587,000 in 2004 to the current 463,000. These types of declines were being experienced throughout the United States. The *Los Angeles Times* had lost over 250,000 daily subscriptions and over 340,000 Sunday deliveries over the same five years. Some papers, such as the *Seattle Post-Intelligencer*, had recently ceased their newspaper production altogether and had gone to strictly an Internet publication.

Obviously, most newspapers have an Internet site, and many industry experts claimed the reduced hard-copy sales levels were being offset by the increased use of the Web site version, which also sold advertising. The problem was that Internet revenues had been flat over the past few years while print advertising had declined sharply. Most newspapers (and the industry in general) blamed the Internet as well as the consistent availability of news shows on cable. (People preferred to watch television instead of reading.) Mitch privately mused if newspapers in general had not become as liberal as they had, maybe circulation would not be declining. He had debated with John recently that cutting back was leading to lower circulation.

"Do you think fewer people are subscribing because we are offering less in the paper?" he had asked John.

"Mitch, how can we continue to produce a paper like we did twenty years ago when we are only selling a fraction of the advertising we did then?" John had replied.

"Advertising revenue will follow subscriptions. If we increase subscriptions, we will be able to sell more advertising. However, we cannot increase subscriptions if we continue to reduce staff and cut back the product we offer. If pizza places did what we are doing, they would be putting half a pizza in a box and asking consumers to pay the same price. How many people are going to buy half a pizza at a full pizza price? That's what we are offering, half a newspaper. Who wants to pay for that?"

In their debates, Mitch typically used a business example; it's what he knew. John was in no mood for this.

"You're a columnist—you don't see the numbers. You don't know what we're dealing with."

"That's true, but I know a thing or two about quality, and our quality, as well as the quality of newspapers across the USA, has suffered considerably. Did you see what the *Los Angeles Times* did? Good thing you got out of there when you did. They cut seventy-five newsroom staff—the second cut already this year. That staff was close to what, 1,300 when you were there. Now they have maybe 700. Is the Los

Angeles population down almost 50 percent? Is there 50 percent less news now? How can they expect to report the same quality and quantity of news with half the staff when more is happening now than ever before?"

"But, Mitch, people turn on the cable networks to get the news. They just don't read as much."

"We don't have to accept that; most cable news networks are national. You might hear a snippet of a story about your area, but nothing in depth. Even the local television news stories are at best two or three minutes long. You cannot get any amount of detail from that, nor obtain the necessary information you need to form any kind of opinion. We are allowing this country to have a fast food mentality when it comes to news. Does eating fast food provide a good healthy diet? Obviously not. Just as reading fast news does not give a healthy amount of information. People need *quality* newspapers to provide that!"

"Well, why don't you become a newspaper administrator instead of a columnist and set everything right, if you have all the answers?"

"You wouldn't want that; you'd lose your best columnist!" Mitch joked.

John cracked up at that point and let the debate go.

* * * *

As Paul and Gus drove to the restaurant, they discussed the proposition they were about to drop on Mitch.

"Are you sure this is a good idea, Gus?" Paul asked. "I hesitate to bring someone like Mitch Bartter into our planning. Don't you think we could accomplish this project ourselves by creating a pseudonym?"

"No, I definitely do not," Gus replied. "Mitch just may be the most important piece!" Gus knew Paul was not thinking everything through with that suggestion.

"We need all the support we can get, not just financial," he continued. "I want people to be emotionally invested! That will help allow us greater flexibility. This Mitch Bartter character is really developing a following, and I think he is our best bet, although I am contacting others as well to complete the overall project. Mitch should see this as an opportunity to further his career, build a national reputation. Hopefully, his mind is focused on these personal advantages enough to somewhat cloud his judgment. Plus, there is more to the story, but I do not have that all outlined yet; you'll have to trust me."

"I think it is a bit of a risk," Paul replied. "John says he is quite bright and not so determined on reaching a bigger audience. He may dig into who you are and what you are after."

"I'm not concerned. He won't find anything on me I don't want found. However, he is very passionate about the message he puts in his columns. He will view this with the potential to share this passion with a wider audience. He truly thinks he can change some people's minds out there. That should play right into our hands. Also, Mitch loves to refer to the Constitution and the fact that the United States is just that, a group of states. He is a big states' rights guy. If necessary to try to convince him to join our cause, throw in some big government bashing."

Gus didn't think much of opinion columns or those who wrote them. Actually, Gus didn't think very much of too many people. Gus Reed was an independently wealthy sixty-year-old, having inherited millions of dollars when he was very young and invested quite wisely over the years to amass a fortune closing in on a billion dollars. Gus informed everyone that his wealth had come at a hefty price, though. Gus's mind wandered to what he had once confessed to Paul. Gus had a twenty-two-year-old girlfriend named Kathy at the time of the inheritance, and the newfound wealth resulted in a very short engagement and an extravagant wedding. The two of them spent most of the next six months traveling and enjoying life when she became pregnant. Gus was ecstatic with the news, but his young bride was very apprehensive. Things in her life had changed so much, so quickly her head was spinning. Kathy's plans had not included being married and having a child by the time she was twenty-three.

The pregnancy went well, and they were soon the parents of a beautiful baby girl who they named Casey. Postpartum depression hit Kathy hard, though, as well as her realization that she did not love Gus and had probably been blinded by the money. She told him as much as she was packing her bags.

"What about Casey?" Gus was imploring. "We can make this work."

"You're missing the point; I don't want to make this work. I thought I loved you, but I think I let your money influence my judgment. I'm not ready to be tied down with a family."

"What do you want to do? You don't have to be tied down; we'll get a nanny. You can go to school, work, whatever you want." Gus was begging at this point.

"There is only one problem with that—you'd still be here." The cold words hit him like a sucker punch from a heavyweight champ. His tone turned nasty.

"I suppose you'll be going after half my money now?" he spat at her.

"Again, as usual, you're not listening to me. The money has messed me up. I don't want it." She stopped and thought for a second. "Well, I do need a little to set myself up and go back to school. I'll offer you, right now, a divorce settlement of $250,000. Call your attorney and get him over here, even handwrite the documents if you desire, but I just want out!"

Still reeling from the conversation, Gus did call an attorney. In the meantime, Kathy had thrown her things into her car, stating she wanted to drive to a friend's house before the attorney arrived. Kathy was killed in a car accident on the way, leaving Casey in the care of Gus.

Gus related to Paul that as the years went by after that, he punished himself for so foolishly falling for Kathy, someone who had planned to walk out on her own child. He, however, never got too far in the punishment, because Casey became his pride and joy. He gave her all she could want, and the two of them were very close. Casey unfortunately contracted bone cancer in her late teens and lost her battle in 2001. Gus had never remarried or even dated seriously. He had poured his energy into his investments, several causes he deemed worthy, including the plan he and a friend had hatched during their college days, and obviously his daughter. The eight years since Casey's passing had been very lonely, and his bitterness over the major events in his life had created a very jaded individual.

His sharp mind and sense of vindication had resulted in the rebirth of his college thoughts, and he set in motion a very elaborate plan a few years ago. As events unfolded in the first few years of the twenty-first century, this plan accelerated and began to take serious shape.

Gus smiled to himself at the details of the history he had provided to Paul, who was one member of a small but dedicated team assisting him. Paul and one other person knew more of what Gus was planning than the others, but even they had been left in the dark about some of the final touches, which Gus was just now setting in place. He had duped several others to his cause, and Mitch would be the keystone, playing the biggest role.

"Do you think he will jump on board right away?" Paul's question jolted Gus back to the present day.

"Absolutely," Gus replied. "You know what we have been setting in place over the last year. He will look at this as an opportunity to be part of something big. This will be a new venue away from the ones already pilloried by the liberal press. Tell Mitch he will be part of the voice, advertising and promoting the information and bringing in new members. It will be tailored to the audience Mitch reaches each week. You will tell him a well-financed group was very unhappy with the results of the 2008 presidential election, as well as the last few congressional elections. Business leaders from all over the country are financing this project to promote conservative values. We want

Mitch to be an integral part of this education process. Stroke his ego a bit—everyone likes that. We like how he communicates his ideas, his straightforward yet non-condescending approach, and we feel he will bring many readers to our pages. Don't mention money. Our Web site will work on loosening purse strings when people visit it. I plan to be in the booth beside you; you have the microphone on your lapel?"

"My Notre Dame pin," Paul stated.

"You a Notre Dame fan?" Gus asked.

"No, but Mitch is," Paul said with a smile, knowing Gus would be impressed.

"Nice. Doing a little research on your own now?"

"Hey, I can have a good idea every now and then."

"That pin is great. I'll be able to hear the whole conversation."

"I'm still concerned Mitch will see through this eventually and be a bit of a loose cannon," Paul confessed.

"I'll try not to be offended at your lack of faith in my plan," Gus said genially. "If it helps set you at ease, we will be monitoring all of Mitch's communications. We'll know if he is on to something. Besides, don't we have some dirt on him yet?"

"No. This guy appears to be clean as a whistle. He may have rented a porno once, but I can't even prove that. He didn't even have any childhood indiscretions I could find. By the way, how are you monitoring his communications?"

"Don't worry about those details; I have them under control. You just worry about convincing him to join our cause today. I'll have Charlie look into setting a trap or two to impugn his character. I want some blackmail security if I need it."

Paul shook his head in disbelief at Gus's meticulousness.

"You are well financed and obviously motivated," Paul said aloud, impressed by Gus.

"Paul, you have known me long enough by now to realize you should never doubt my motivation or my willingness to do whatever it takes to accomplish this goal. I will not fail, and I will remove all obstacles in my way through whatever means necessary. Please, never underestimate the financial resources at my disposal as well. Although I have worked hard to keep my wealth a secret, suffice it to say that money will not be a problem."

"I thought you said Mitch would help bring in the money?" Paul questioned.

"I did, but that is as much to set everything up as it is to finance us. Believe me, you will understand eventually." The conversation ended as they pulled into the restaurant.

* * * * *

John arrived first and saw Paul was already sitting in a booth. He indicated to the hostess he was heading to meet a friend and slid in next to Paul. The two men served on a local nonprofit board together. John knew Paul was an attorney, but he had never really talked to him about his client base. They had both served on the board for several years and had developed a mutual respect.

"Nice to see you again, Paul, although you were pretty vague about what you wanted to meet about and why you wanted Mitch. I was unaware that you even knew him."

"I don't," confessed Paul. "But I have read his articles for a few years now, and I think he could help our cause, assuming of course it does not conflict with any of his current obligations for the *Republic*."

"Well, I guess that will depend on what you have in mind," John replied. "Here he comes now."

Mitch walked into the restaurant and scanned the room. The Buffalo Wild Wings was configured like so many others across the country, with the counter and hostess station just inside and to the right, a large open area with booths along the walls and tables in the center. Every inch of wall was occupied by either a massive television screen or some sports paraphernalia. Several smaller televisions were also mounted in strategic areas, showing different sporting events or trivia games. Off to the side of the large room was a bar area, with more varieties of beer on tap than most pubs.

Mitch spotted John quickly, but was surprised to see he was not alone. John hadn't mentioned he would be meeting with another person as well.

"Hey, John," Mitch said as he reached the table. "Hi—Mitch Bartter," he said to Paul, holding out his hand. Paul stood as well as he could in a booth and shook Mitch's hand.

"Paul Gregory."

They all sat down, and John quickly indicated it was Paul who had requested their presence for some unknown reason and turned the conversation to him.

"Why don't we order, and then I'll end the intrigue," Paul suggested, as the waitress had just walked up to the table. After all asking for different combinations of boneless wings, Paul began his explanation.

"John, I obviously do not know where you stand politically, but Mitch has recorded his beliefs in the paper every week for the last ten years. I know you are just the person I need to assist with a very exciting project. You, like many Americans, could not have been happy with the election results last November. I am affiliated with a relatively new organization that is working to ensure a different outcome in future elections. It is called the Liberty Group."

"And how are you planning to ensure these different outcomes?" Mitch interrupted.

"We are in the process of establishing a master Web site with links to state-specific pages—ultimately, one for each state. We want to establish contacts in each state to be leaders of their portions of our movement. This will be a true grassroots organization, with localized leadership reporting to the overall group. These state and local leaders will be in charge of commenting on issues specific to their counties and cities with direction from the top on national issues. We hope to be the voices of reason that bring more of America back to our cause."

"And what is your cause?" Mitch asked.

"Our cause is the American cause. We want to see the America that the Constitution envisioned, not the government gone wild version we are experiencing now. Without trying to overstate it too much, we want to be the John Adams, Thomas Jefferson, and Thomas Paine of our day. Our leadership group feels you are just the person to organize the opinion articles of the master Web site."

Mitch sat wide-eyed at this point. "It is ironic to me that you mention several of our founding fathers. As you describe what you want to accomplish, for some reason, I am reminded of the Sons of Liberty groups that organized in colonial America before the Revolutionary War."

"You have deducted that our name wasn't just a random choice," Paul noted.

"What, you mean like Sam Adams and company?" John questioned.

"Sam Adams was one of the leaders," Mitch explained, "along with Paul Revere, John Hancock, Patrick Henry, and many others. They, too, set up regions—Sam Adams led the New England portion."

"We hope our state Web sites will act as sort of our Liberty Poles," Paul added.

"Excuse me, 'Liberty Poles'?" John asked.

"Oftentimes, in the different regions, members or patriots would erect what they called 'Liberty Poles' or 'Liberty Trees,'" Mitch continued. "These locations would then act as a gathering place where individuals could speak their opinions and raise awareness as well as draw more members to their causes."

"We believe what has happened in the first few months of this presidency and this session of Congress can be viewed with the same disdain with which the Stamp Act was viewed back then," Paul stated. "The patriots believed their individual rights were being eliminated, and they responded with organized opposition. We believe our individual rights are also now being taken away."

"Is that what got the Sons of Liberty going, the Stamp Act?" questioned John. "That act happened a decade before the Revolutionary War, didn't it?"

"Essentially, it is what is believed to have triggered the organization," Mitch explained, having studied American history extensively. "Like I said, Sam Adams led the Boston-based group, forming officially around August of 1765, although a group called the Loyal Nine with similar traits had existed for some time before that. By late fall of that year, a group had established itself in New York, and by December, alliances had formed between groups in Connecticut, New York, and Massachusetts. When the Stamp Act was repealed, the groups did not have as much vigor, if you will, but the representatives stayed in contact, and as other acts were passed, the group continued to gain members and led some fairly high-profile incidents. The Sons of Liberty were believed to have been responsible for quite a few of the tar and feathering occurrences around that time."

"Instead of tar and feathers," Paul quickly interjected, "we will use the Internet, hold rallies, things of that nature. Who says you need a candidate to give a speech?" He took a deep breath and seemed to be selecting his next words carefully. "We have digressed a little off topic with this history lesson. The point is we have quietly put together a very well-planned and well-financed agenda to oppose what we believe to be a quickening march toward socialism and away from the freedoms on which our country was founded. We feel more Americans will agree with us, and we need to get the message of our organization to as many people as possible. We feel you can help us, Mitch, with this and other aspects. By incorporating references to our group in your articles, you will raise awareness of the Liberty Group and bring people to our Web site and to our meetings. They can then find their individual state groups and get connected from there."

"That sounds all well and good," Mitch stated, "but I am a small-time columnist. Why not go to someone with a wider audience, like Rush, Sean Hannity, or George Will?"

Paul smiled and continued on. "We actually have thought about this long and hard. Our leadership believes that, although there are nationwide established venues, such as the individuals you mentioned as well as others, having a new voice fits our group better. You've seen all the criticism Rush has taken lately. He's brilliant, but too many in the mainstream discount him. Also, right now, we are an unknown entity. No offense, but even though you have had a small amount of national exposure, you, too, are a relative unknown. We feel this is a strength for us. Anyhow, if we do this correctly, the national talk show hosts on both radio and television will be discussing us soon enough.

"Also, and I can't emphasize this enough, we like your style. You try to remain above what I call the gutter fray. I know that sounds like a sales pitch, but you have always expressed your ideas in a manner ... how should I say this? A reader who does not agree with your Republican views at least will think about what you have said. You are not insulting. You have a commonsense approach."

"Thanks for the kind words. I do try to set forth educated opinions and point out the flaws in other arguments, as opposed to just name calling and fear mongering. However, I do not have Republican views; I have conservative opinions. I am a conservative, not necessarily a Republican. I have criticized many Republicans in my columns over the years." After contemplating the situation for a few seconds, he inquired, "So, you basically want me to mention your group and Web site in a few articles. That's it?"

"Not even close. Much, much more. If John acquiesces, we want you to supply a weekly article for our Web site, maybe more. In addition, we want you to contact other writers throughout the United States to see if any of them would also be interested in writing articles for our site. We would pay them on a per article basis, in most cases more than they make writing for their current newspapers. John has said you have some pretty extensive contacts with writers all over the country from various conferences and seminars you have attended. As I said earlier, we want to establish groups in every state if possible, but we will start with pockets of the country if we have to. We also want you to be a part of the leadership group, which luckily is based here in Phoenix. We want you to come to our meetings and be part of our strategy planning. We are really hoping you'll join our team!"

"Your responsibilities to the *Republic* would remain as they are," John quickly added. "We would also request that the articles you submit to the *Republic* be different than the ones for the Liberty Group. Essentially, you will be doubling your writing workload."

"Don't sugarcoat it for me, John. Geez, I was just getting excited."

"We will be paying you as well," Paul added, wanting to entice Mitch further. "We are well financed and should be able to augment your income nicely. John has mentioned you have three kids, one of whom is approaching college soon, if my memory serves."

"It's okay, Paul; I was just kidding a little with John there. I am very intrigued. It does sound a bit redundant though, what with groups like the Heritage Foundation out there spreading the word, so to speak. Also, there are publications that have online information and articles every day. The American Spectator and National Review Online, for instance."

"A good point, but again, we hope to organize this at the state level and even break the states into regions. We want to lay out our agenda in a very methodical way. This will be a long-term endeavor. Also, as I said, those groups are well established and have already been discounted by much of the biased media."

John flinched a bit at Paul's choice of words. As an editor, he had a hard time swallowing all the claims of liberal bias—especially working for the *Republic*.

The waitress brought their food and Mitch dug into his mango-habanero-flavored boneless wings. The group was silent for a few minutes as they all ate and thought about what had been said.

"How is the organization set up, and who is funding this?" Mitch inquired. "I'm no businessman, but I can't see how this is gaining them any monetary advantage.

The Liberty Group

"We have established a corporation," Paul responded. "I am one of the vice presidents. There is one other VP and a CFO, and we report to the president, who is the 100 percent owner. Our financiers wish to remain anonymous; even I am unaware of who they all are. I believe our president knows who is providing the startup funds. We have incurred significant upfront costs but plan to recoup them with advertising on our Web site. If you and your writer friends bring enough hits to our site, we will be able to sell more advertising and forward our cause to an even greater extent. We meet weekly to discuss issues in different states and national items to which we want to respond. It has been quite hectic these last few months. We feel we are ready to go live, and your articles will be a key part. We are also hoping the team of writers you put together from around the country will create a national, but local feel. We obviously hope you have some contacts in the larger cities and states with significant electoral votes—New York, Florida, Texas, Ohio, North Carolina, etc. We have someone from California we will introduce you to as well. You will be our correspondent in charge. We would not ask you to edit any of the content; we are giving these columnists free reign, with just a few guidelines. You would mainly coordinate topics so we are not doubling up in any one area. Weekly, you would report to the management group the planned upcoming articles and relay back any concerns. We meet on Thursdays at one o'clock at the Arizona Biltmore Resort."

"Can I attend a meeting before making a decision, meet the other leaders, and get a feel for their vision of this group?" Mitch asked.

"I would have it no other way. Can you come this Thursday?"

"Sounds good."

* * * *

Mitch drove home, thinking about the lunch conversation. Something didn't seem quite right, but he thought it was potentially a great opportunity. They had not talked actual money, but Paul had said they would Thursday if Mitch agreed to sign on. He found it interesting Paul and John had discussed his family, with Paul knowing his oldest was a year away from college. He also thought it a bit ironic that Paul was wearing a Notre Dame pin. Even with these small questions, Mitch struggled not to build this possibility into something it wasn't, as the proposition was quite exciting. To be in on the beginning of what could become a nationwide movement—that would be very rewarding. He wasn't concerned about writing more articles each week; his wife often joked he was way overpaid for the amount of time it took him to do his work. She worked her tail off as a marketing manager for a manufacturing company. He also was not that concerned with coordinating numerous other writers, as each state and region of the country had plenty of issues to ensure no duplication of topics would occur. Mitch assumed if this new venture grew large enough, he would add some staff. The more Mitch thought, the more excitement he felt. There was still something at the back of this mind that did not seem quite right. He ignored that thought as he drove.

Mitch pulled into the driveway as a cablevision truck was pulling away. He walked in the door off the garage and kissed his wife hello. Guessing at the quizzical look on his face, Marie explained.

"First time I ever heard of a cable truck in the area the minute we call to say the cable was out. The technician said there have been several issues in the neighborhood in the last few days, and he had just finished a repair when they got our call."

"Well, at least Jane can still watch her *SVU* reruns," Mitch joked.

"I kicked her off the television—told her no more until she had practiced her dance and completed all her homework. How did your meeting go?"

"Interesting—I've been asked to be part of a conservative movement."

"I thought you *were* a conservative movement," Marie said playfully.

"Yeah, yeah. Seriously, it sounds really interesting. It's an organization called the Liberty Group. They are just starting, and they plan to have organized sections of their group in every state. They want me to submit weekly articles as well as to basically lead their team of writers for what they publish on their website."

"Is John organizing this group?"

"No, he was the intermediary. John introduced me to some guy named Paul Gregory. Paul laid out the specifics. I'm meeting with the leaders of the organization on Thursday. I told them I'd see what they had to say and make a decision from there."

"You wouldn't be leaving the *Republic*?" Marie asked, concerned about what her husband was agreeing to.

"No way, this is additional work and additional pay," Mitch added quickly. "How was lunch with Steph?"

"Oh, fine. Just catching up on things. You're interested in their offer, then?" Marie asked, bringing the conversation back to the Liberty Group.

"I am, though it seemed a little strange. For instance, Paul had obviously talked with John about me prior to this, and John hadn't mentioned that. But, still, I am very intrigued by the opportunity. We'll see what we learn on Thursday."

"How much additional pay will it be?" Marie asked.

"We'll talk about that on Thursday, if I agree to join them. They initially brought it up, so I'm sure it will be enough to make it interesting."

"Did you get your next article done for the *Republic*, or do you need to work on it yet this weekend?"

"What are you, my editor now?"

"Just asking. So, did you?"

"Yes, it's done. I addressed some global warming concerns."

"Anything imbedded for anyone?"

"Maybe—we'll see."

"Will they figure it out?" Marie asked.

"I don't even know if Mark still tries. Todd may be too upset by what I wrote to even make an attempt. As for Al—he always figures it out."

Chapter 3

Al Miller walked into work and turned on his computer. He liked coming in to the office a little earlier than everyone else—it allowed him to get a few things done before the e-mails started coming in and phone started ringing. Al was the controller of a midsized, family-owned manufacturing company in Fostoria, Ohio. He was tall and slim, with red hair and brown eyes. Like his friend Mitch, he had taken pride in keeping himself in shape and worked out several times a week. He didn't mind coming in early; Al enjoyed his job, knowing he was very fortunate to work for a successful company and with wonderful people. He felt especially fortunate with what had been happening in the economy recently.

Al worked in the finance building of his company, which meant he was across the street from the main plant and office. The finance building was one story, about the size of a nice ranch-style house. Al had a corner office, with windows on two walls, overlooking a portion of the manufacturing facility as well as the parking lot. The owners of the company made sure the offices and landscaping were well maintained and comfortable for their workforce. Al loved his office. The air conditioning was configured such that his was the coldest office in the place, and that suited Al just fine.

He checked his e-mail quickly, deleting the nonsense he had received during the overnight hours. It seemed every accounting publication sent out a request to sell him some report every night. As Al went online to check his company's daily cash report from their bank, he remembered this was Wednesday—the day Mitch's online articles were usually in the *Republic*. He clicked the preset link in his favorites to go to the paper's Web site. Mitch and Al had been friends in high school and became college roommates, living four years together at Bowling Green State University, better known to alumni as BGSU, which was a midsized college in northwest Ohio. They had also rented an apartment together their first year after graduating until Al got married. After the first two college years living in dorm rooms, the two of them moved to an apartment, adding two additional roommates, Todd and Mark. Even though they now were spread across the country, all had remained strong friends. Al enjoyed Mitch's articles immensely, tending to agree with him on most points. Mitch always said Al should be the one writing the articles, but Al was more cut out for accounting. Ironically, it was Al who was editor of their high school newspaper (although Mitch was a writer as well), and it was also Al who had initially started as a journalism major at BGSU before switching to accounting as a sophomore. He and Mitch had both graduated with accounting degrees; Mitch just decided later he had had enough of numbers and followed his journalistic calling.

For the better part of the last year, Mitch had begun encrypting a message in his articles for his former roommates. Once Mitch had tipped them all to look for a hidden message, the fun had begun. Al always figured Mitch was too smart for his own good, and he assumed it was just too mundane to write a simple article; Mitch had to script it in a manner that resulted in a puzzle for his old buddies to decipher. Sometimes, Al would get Todd or Mark on the phone, and if none of them had read the article, they would review it at the same time to see

The Liberty Group

who could come up with the message first. Al usually won, so the others stopped playing. They often didn't even try to see the message. These other two roommates at BGSU didn't necessarily see eye to eye on the issues with Mitch as much as Al did.

Al clicked to the opinion page of the *Arizona Republic* Web site and found the article. He glanced at the clock. *I've got time to read this before our Wednesday staff meeting*, he thought.

Beyond Dispute and Clear Facts

Our president, before he officially took office, gave a speech to the state governors in November 2008 saying how "few challenges facing America—and the world—are more urgent than combating climate change. The science is beyond dispute and the facts are clear. Sea levels are rising. Coastlines are shrinking. We've seen record drought, spreading famine, and storms that are growing stronger with each passing hurricane season." He indicates that a reduction in carbon dioxide in the atmosphere will save the world and that humans are to blame for these issues. Do you know how much carbon dioxide is currently in the atmosphere? Well, my research indicates there are about 384 parts per million of carbon dioxide. Now, I am no mathematician, but friends, that's 0.0384%! Of this total, 95% is naturally caused by items such as the decaying of trees occurring today, not man-made pollutants. That statistic should tell you all you need to know.

The global warming alarmists I researched, as well as the Al Gore fear machine, have based much of the so-called certainties they "know" will happen on the effect of increasing CO_2 levels in the atmosphere. The award-winning An Inconvenient Truth movie showed dire results due to increased levels of CO_2.

Our president says the science is beyond dispute. One man, the lead author of the 2001 Intergovernmental Panel on Climate Change report, disputes the "science." This veteran climatologist won't accept research funding of any kind from the oil or auto industry. His name is John Christy and like many of the "disputers" he gave the opinion during a Fortune Magazine interview that the efforts to battle this climate change result in "all cost and no benefit." In a further interview with CNNMoney.com, John Christy stated that it was his expert opinion that initiatives put in place to lower U.S. greenhouse gas emissions by 80% by 2050 would "affect the global temperature by only seven-hundredths of a degree ... We wouldn't even notice it."

Answering this business about all the facts being clear as to the real causes of temperature change and what actual role man has played, here is a study I hope and pray that the president and all members of Congress will read before proceeding with any form of the current cap and trade proposals. All I ask is to agree to review it. A team of researchers from the Scripps Institute of Oceanography went through the very detailed exercise of analyzing ice core data from the Antarctic to obtain atmospheric carbon dioxide levels and air temperatures before man existed— for the past 240,000 years to be precise—a time frame that includes three ice ages (which I know man did not cause) as well as the obvious warming periods that followed. I hope the alarmists don't get too upset, but the research indicates air temperature increased well before any increase in CO_2 levels. (I know—preposterous!) This study found the lag in time of carbon dioxide increase was 400–1,000 years. This should stop Gore supporters in their tracks. It opposes the assumption that increasing carbon dioxide leads to temperature increase. If carbon dioxide increases lag temperature increases, all of Al Gore's computer models based on the opposite can be thrown out the window. Do the facts still seem clear?

How about the possibility that the source of our heat can vary over time? Is it just possible that the activity of the sun can result in a small increase in temperature over a period of, say, one hundred years? One theory (without going into great detail, but it is available in a ten-minute Internet search) is that sun activity varies over time, changing the amount of magnetic activity and solar wind, which in turn leads to changes in low-level cloud activity (varying the amount of heat reflected away from the earth) leading to changes in climate. Also, NASA scientists have written about the "melting" of the ice caps on Mars and that the temperature on Venus has risen from 470 degrees to 513 degrees in the short period that data has been gathered. If Mars and Venus are warmer, would it not make sense that the Earth is warmer, and would be with or without the presence of humans?

Let's use the legal system our country has established in a hypothetical situation. Let's say that humans are on trial for causing global warming. The prosecutors have put up all their witnesses and statistics that the temperature is higher and has risen during the last one hundred years, when humans' industrial output has been at its peak. They have shown the correlation even if they cannot prove the causation. Now, the defense team has listed several of the items I have previously mentioned and added that we had ice ages and warm-ups long before humans walked the Earth and that Greenland is named such because at one point it was green (hence, the temperature was much warmer than today). With all these arguments would you, on a jury, say that the science is beyond dispute and the facts are clear that humans caused the temperature increase, or would you say a reasonable doubt exists about this claim?

Is my point that we should we do nothing? Of course not. Let's continue to develop technologies that use less of the earth's precious, limited resources and more of the renewable sources. Let's recycle, let's encourage the auto industry to manufacture more efficient autos (without mandates—let capitalism work), let's even paint our roofs white if we so choose, and let's be good stewards of our environment. Let's not allow a government to hamstring our businesses into unrealistic energy changes that result in the biggest tax increase in the history of the world, *increased electrical rates beyond comprehension, huge jumps in gas prices and natural gas rates, and the loss of an unfathomable percentage of manufacturing jobs in the United States. That would truly be catastrophic! The current proposal of the American Clean Energy and Security Act of 2009 would result in all of those things. The dire consequences this legislation would bring are definitely clear and beyond dispute.*

Al sat back and heaved a sigh. *Well, Mitch—that was written with a little more edge than usual,* he thought. As always, though, Mitch was debating a point using solid examples, without any personal attacks. It was all issue based—something most editorials lacked. Al knew Mitch had picked on a powerful movement and that quite a bit of hate mail was headed his friend's way. But it was a movement based on a lot of hyperbole and emotion. Al was definitely in agreement with Mitch on this issue, being an accountant for a manufacturing company not withstanding. Al knew the dissenting opinions Mitch would receive came with the territory though. He set to work trying to find the puzzle within the article. He was looking for the key—Mitch always included a decoder—the key to solving the puzzle. He had just started rereading the article when his phone rang.

"Hello—Al Miller."

"Hey, A—did you read Mitch's article?" It was Todd. Most of Al's college buddies called him "A"—something Mark had started. Al was slightly surprised that Todd was calling this early. Todd Kelnar was a popular culture teacher at the University of Arkansas in Little Rock. It was an hour earlier there than in Ohio, making it about six in the morning.

"You're in a little early, aren't you?" Al replied.

"Never mind that, what is this trash he wrote? How can he deny what is happening?"

"Oh, I'm fine, thanks for asking," Al replied sarcastically. "I didn't see much in his article that I had a problem with. Or are you talking about the message for us—I haven't had a chance to look for it. Did you solve it already?"

"No, I haven't even looked for the stupid message. Do you really believe this? Al—you're the reasonable one. How can you deny what we are doing to our environment?"

"Todd, we have this discussion every few months. You and Mitch do not agree on most political issues. His articles are going to rile you; you know that. And you know what? That's at least three sentences you said without quoting a movie." Todd had an insane love for films and usually threw in movie quotes every chance he had, most often using *The Princess Bride* or some *Star Wars* reference. There was a time in college when Todd would award points to his roommates for getting the name of the movie he quoted, the character name, the actor, etc. You earned bonus points if you could continue the quote or the conversation of the characters from the movie. It really was no wonder that he had become a popular culture teacher. "Unless, of course, you are quoting Al Gore's movie—I refused to watch that one."

"Well, you should have," Todd retorted. "Maybe you would care a little more about what is happening to the world."

"Relax a little, Todd. I think you have been hanging around your liberal college friends a little too much. Mitch was giving his opinion; do you really think he is totally off base? He had some good points in there."

"Sure, the point about the sun activity is a little hard to ignore. But so many scientists are in the human-caused global warming tent. I can't ignore them either."

"Well, why don't you call Mitch? He obviously has done some research. Or you could do your own research and write him a rebuttal. In the meantime, seriously, how is everything with you? Your undergrads getting eager for summer break?"

"Things are going well. The weather is really getting warm. Proving my point, I guess."

"Whatever, we still on for later this summer?" Al asked. "I'm really looking forward to us all getting together."

"Me, too. Listen, I came in early to get my exam ready for the students. I should get going. How's that gorgeous wife of yours? She hasn't become bored with an accountant yet, has she?"

"She's fine, thanks for asking—and thanks for calling. Take care, Todd."

Al hung up the phone. He had been working on a reunion of sorts with their little college group and their families for later in the summer. As with most planning, the more people involved, the more complicated it had become. They had finally settled on a week (in late July - early August) and a place, back in Bowling Green, naturally. Todd was the easy one to schedule; twenty years since graduation and he remained unmarried and had the fewest schedules to plan around.

Al went back to his computer and started reading the article, looking for the indicator Mitch had left behind. If readers weren't looking, they would never find the message, but Mitch usually made it somewhat easy if you knew there was something to find. The cipher oftentimes had something to do with a number. Al looked for any references to numbers, and a quick perusal turned up 384, 95, 80, 100—too many without another key of some sort. He started rereading the article and a sentence in the first paragraph stuck out: "That should tell you all you need to know." This sentence could be pointing the direction to the clue. Mitch usually had some sort of clue to the key within the text. The "that" in this case referred to a statistic: 95% of the 384 parts per million of carbon dioxide in the atmosphere were naturally occurring, not man made. Could that be it—95% of 384? Multiplying that total resulted in a rounded 365. That didn't seem right—too big a number. How about using the actual percentage, which would be .000384 multiplied by 95? It was obviously too low.

He reread the article one more time and was convinced that the code had something to do with 384 and 95. "*Of this total, 95% is naturally caused by items such as the decaying of trees occurring today, not man-made pollutants.*" Maybe Mitch was pointing to the much smaller portion, not the 95% but the remaining 5%. Al multiplied .05 by 384, which resulted in a round 19. The key could be pointing to every nineteenth word. Al scanned the first few sentences and determined that the nineteenth word was "how." Starting at the sentence after quoting the president, Al counted another nineteen words, deciphering "are" as the next clue. Al knew to skip direct quotes (Mitch was good, but not that good), and he also knew to count numbers, whether spelled out or left in numerical form, as one word. "How are" so far. Al continued diligently assembling the message, skipping a few other direct quotes along the way, and he came up with the following:

> *How are my friends today? I know movie man won't like this opinion; business man will agree. Exercise man, I don't know.*

The nineteenth word after "know" was "stop," one of the many terms Mitch used to signal the end of the message ("stop," "end," "finish," etc.). This one was fairly brief and tame. Many times, Mitch would poke fun at his friends or make a sports prediction of some sort. As to the message, Mitch had to be referring to Al as "business man," while Todd was "movie man." "Exercise man" was Mark. Al clicked over to his e-mail and sent Mitch a quick note thanking him for the message, criticizing him on how easy it was to solve and indicating things were fine in Ohio. He mentioned he had already talked to Todd and that Mitch was correct; movie man did indeed have issues with the article. He ended the e-mail saying he would call him this weekend. Al then sent another e-mail to Todd and Mark—this one had only two words: *Solved it!*

* * * * *

Mitch was scripting his next article at his desk at the *Arizona Republic*

Thursday morning. He was putting the finishing touches on it so he could turn it in to John when Brian interrupted his work.

"What are you doing for lunch?" Brian asked.

Brian Maddox had worked at the *Republic* a few years less than Mitch. He was a sports reporter, covering a variety of items, but baseball was his forte. He had pitched in college but tore some ligaments in his arm, ending his career as a sophomore. Mitch surmised Brian had put on a few pounds since his playing days, though his 6'6" frame dispersed his weight well. Brian was African American and a confirmed bachelor; at least for now, Mitch always reminded him.

"Hey, Mads," Mitch responded (everyone called him "Mads"). "I'll have to pass on lunch. I've got a one o'clock meeting today, so I'm working through the lunch hour."

"Maybe tomorrow then," Brian said. "The D-backs have an afternoon game; we could make it a businessman's special. Take the afternoon and watch baseball. It would be work for me. You could talk to a few fans about the state of the economy. Or, even better, since we are playing the Dodgers, you could find some out-of-town fans and ask them about the sorry state of the Californian finances."

"We'll see," Mitch chuckled back.

"What's your meeting about?" Brian asked.

"About doing some moonlighting on the side; John knows about it, though. He kind of set it up."

"Sounds as if he's trying to get rid of you," Brian joked. "Maybe he is tired of your politics."

"I hadn't thought of that. I don't think so, though. He needs me too much."

"Maybe so. I don't think we could find another conservative writer very easily. You guys are few and far between right now."

"Tell me about it," Mitch replied. "From what I have heard so far, though, this meeting may be the start of turning that around. At least if these guys are as organized and well financed as they claim."

"Interesting—I'd love to hear about it when you're done." Brian walked away looking for someone else to join him for lunch.

* * * *

Gus walked into the room he had reserved at the Arizona Biltmore. Gus loved the Biltmore. Advertised as the only hotel in the world with a Frank Lloyd Wright–influenced design, the Biltmore opened in 1929 and quickly earned the nickname "the Jewel of the Desert." The designers used indigenous materials and molded blocks on site (Biltmore blocks) that included a geometric pattern that was said to represent a freshly cut palm tree. The resort included eight swimming pools, one of which sported a ninety-two-foot water slide, a wide array of spa treatments, and two eighteen-hole adjacent championship golf courses, and Wright's at the Biltmore was Gus's favorite restaurant. Gus had plans, when this was all over, of spending as much time in this great resort as possible.

Gus went to the hotel early to ensure he was the first one there. He had wanted to discuss what was to be said to Mitch. He waited for Paul and the others and thought about how he had arrived at where he was. There had been difficulty in finding the individuals he had now trusted. Even though he liked his team very much at this point, he had lied to them about certain aspects of his life and had yet to reveal his full plan to the some of the others. Gus knew it was drastic, but he felt this was the perfect time to accomplish his ultimate goal. Karen knew just enough to keep moving forward, with Paul and Charlie knowing a little more. All three of these individuals walked in at that moment.

"Thank you all for coming today," Gus began. "We have been working together for over a year now, and the plans are coming along in a most wonderful fashion. Paul and I have contacted Mitch Bartter, and we believe he can be convinced to join our team. It is imperative he remains in the dark on the, shall we say, more drastic aspects of our cause. He will be joining us here in a few minutes, and if all goes well, he will attend every Thursday from now on."

"I met with him the other day," Paul said. "He seemed pretty excited about the opportunity, as we presented it to him anyhow. I think he will jump in with both feet. My first impression is that he is pretty sharp. We will have to work to ensure we keep him ignorant of certain aspects, as Gus said."

"And if we don't make another mistake—like in California," Gus interjected. "Charlie, we can't have another screw-up like that. Speaking of which, how is our little problem in Sacramento going?"

"It is being taken care at this very moment," Charlie replied definitively. Charlie Davis was a tall, beefy man in his early fifties, with dark black hair (obviously dyed) and heavy eyebrows. His once muscled body was transforming into fat almost daily. He was the vision that came to mind whenever the term "security thug" was used.

"I didn't know of a problem," Paul said, hoping to hear more about this situation.

"No need to go into specifics," Gus said. "It is being handled. And Charlie will be much more careful with his e-mails from now on. Let's discuss Mitch Bartter, as he will be the most important key to our ultimate success. It is imperative that he knows only what he needs to know. I don't want any misunderstanding on this point. We need someone like him for the national appeal of our plan, and I don't want to waste anymore time with mistakes."

"Understood," Paul responded for the group. "He will be here shortly. What are we telling him today?"

"We just introduce ourselves; he hasn't met Karen or Charlie, or even me for that matter," Gus explained. "We will let him ask the questions from there. If you are unsure how to answer, then let me do the talking."

"Are we sure about this guy?" Karen questioned. Karen Simmons was in her late forties, was medium height and shapely, with a look much younger than her biological age would suggest. Her blond highlights stood out attractively against her well-tanned skin, and her face seemed to be in a perpetual smile. Charlie had trouble keeping his eyes off her and was continually pestering her with romantic advances.

"I've researched him just a little, and Mr. Bartter has done his share of investigative reporting. I'm concerned that he will try to find out more if he feels we are withholding from him. Also, his wife is a professional market researcher—are we concerned about that at all?"

"I explained all this before, Karen," Gus replied impatiently (and with a hint of frustration in his voice). "Mitch's message and his personality are perfect. He will attract the other writers. Our use of him will not last long enough for him to cause too much trouble. Just answer the questions he asks, deferring to me if necessary. As for his wife, she does mainly corporate research. She doesn't pose any threats."

"I don't know," Karen replied. "My contacts tell me she is damn good and as bright as they come."

"It's under control," Gus replied confidently.

The four of them helped themselves to some of the refreshments that Paul, as always, had ensured were made available as they waited. At a little before one o'clock, Mitch walked in, and Paul got up to meet him.

"Good to see you again," Paul said. "Let me do the introductions." The others also stood and formed a semicircle around Mitch.

"Here we have Karen—she's our treasurer and CFO, and over here we have Charlie—he's a vice president in charge of research and public affairs, and this is Gus—our fearless leader."

Mitch shook each of their hands in turn.

"I'm glad you're considering our offer," Gus began. "Paul has filled us in on what you discussed over lunch the other day. Hopefully, we can satisfactorily answer any questions you have and welcome you onto the team."

"Can I get each of you give me a little of your backgrounds?" Mitch began.

Karen started. "I'm a CPA. Started my career with a large public accounting firm, and after ten years, I decided to start my own firm. Gus and I met when he served on the board of a client. I've now worked with him on various projects in the past, and when he explained what he wanted to do, I eagerly joined the team."

"Were you an auditor or tax preparer before you started your own firm?" Mitch asked.

"You talk as if you were once in public accounting," Karen stated.

"I was an accounting major in college, and I have friends who have worked for some of the larger accounting firms," Mitch replied.

"Well, I started as an auditor and really enjoyed learning about so many different businesses. I worked my way up through the firm and assisted in some of the consulting aspects as well. After a while, I had some disagreements about how our local office of the firm was being managed and decided I could do better on my own. I met someone else, a real tax guru, who had a similar feeling in his firm, and we started our own little business. We now employee over fifty professionals. Business has been very good." Karen gave the slightest of nods to Gus as she said this.

"I've always respected her business acumen!" Charlie said enthusiastically. "As for me, I've held a variety of jobs in the past. I've worked for several companies as a corporate consultant. That's how I met Gus. He asked me to join this little party of his."

"What type of consulting?" Mitch inquired.

"General business. I motivate management. I assist with workout plans for troubled companies. I also have a background in relocation issues."

"Sounds impressive, but I still have no idea what you do," Mitch said sarcastically.

Charlie narrowed his eyes briefly and then broke into a hearty laugh. "You're right—I know it sounds cryptic, but Gus has always liked my results."

"He's right," Gus chimed in. "Charlie has always done a bang-up job for me. As for my background, I was fortunate enough to inherit a considerable sum of money when I was very young. I made some excellent financial decisions and transformed a small fortune into an incredibly large one. I'm not trying to brag, just saying it like it is. I invested very wisely and benefited greatly during the market run-up of the 1980s and 1990s. For certain circumstances I won't go into, I switched a considerable amount of my investments to real estate and enjoyed that boom. Once again, I fortuitously was gradually reducing my real estate holdings over the last three years and managed to retain most of my investment value when that market busted. So here I am, funding a large part of this venture."

"And why is that?" Mitch asked.

"Why am I funding this—didn't Paul explain it fully the other day?" Gus replied.

"I'd like to hear it from you."

"Understandable. I believe in capitalism. I believe in the ideals laid out in the Constitution. I have immense appreciation for the number of individuals who have died and sacrificed to keep our country free. Now I see those beliefs being trampled. Some in this country have been trying to get us on a slow road to socialism for years, and now in my opinion, with the makeup of the White House and Congress and with what has happened over the last six months, we are now entering the on-ramp of the highway to becoming a socialist society. I feel the need to do something. I have contributed millions of dollars to organizations that are trying to prevent these changes, but I feel compelled to do more. I'm a fighter. I'm going to fight for what I believe."

Mitch took in what Gus had said as he looked around the room. "So the rest of you agree with Gus here?" Paul spoke for the other three.

"We obviously have not put in the cabbage that Gus has, but our fundamental beliefs are the same. We feel our freedoms are slowly being taken away, in favor of an overreaching and intrusive government."

"And Gus, besides financing the operation, how else are you involved?" Mitch asked.

"Isn't financing the project enough? Just kidding. Actually, over the years, my wealth has brought invitations to join numerous boards for major corporations. I have extensive backroom contacts throughout the country. I am working to keep the money flowing to the group. I've procured corporate sponsorships of rallies to be held, concerts, various forms of advertising, etc. I want this to be huge—but I want it to come out of nowhere. No one knows who we are right now, but in a few months, everyone will know the Liberty Group! I think people are more willing to jump on something that is new—look at the Obama mania that occurred. I'm convinced it wasn't so much his message as it was his 'newness,' if that is a word. His was a fresh face. I want our group to be new and fresh in the same way. I am working on putting many things together that will happen in quick succession—making a big splash, if you will."

"And what are your expectations of my involvement?" Mitch asked.

Again Paul spoke. "As we discussed the other day, we would hope at a minimum that you would contribute articles and set up a network of writers who would assist us in providing informed opinions to help sway the American public away from the path we believe the country to be on. You would organize the receipt of articles and topics. The goal from there is to have individual state issues highlighted in articles with links to each state, but that obviously will take time. For now, you would focus on setting up your contacts in different regions, getting them to agree to write articles, and submitting articles yourself. We could even reprint some of your past work for the *Republic*, with their approval, of course. Our Web site will be our big weapon—that is where people will go daily—it will be like nutrition for them, hopefully providing them information everyday on how they can help or how they can refute arguments opposing our ideals. This is a very important responsibility. From there, hopefully, this turns into a truly dynamic opportunity, with new challenges as issues come up. You would be the Web site front man, organizing all political content."

"Hold on," Charlie said, waiting for this moment. "Let's not get ahead of ourselves. I've read some of your articles. Why are you not more critical of the president's background? He has some real character issues—you should push those more if you write for us."

As Gus scowled at Charlie, Mitch responded thoughtfully.

"I try to take all things that have happened in the past with a grain of salt. I think we all could be conceived to have character issues. If it is a vote on an issue or a public stance, then it is fair game, and I discuss it. If it is speculation about someone's affiliations in the past, or what that person did in college or even some minor indiscretions, then I try to ignore it as best I can. If I was not in the room when the person supposedly said something or met with somebody, how can I cast aspersions about the subject matter?

"I maintain the belief most people in public office are trying to do the best they can. If I do not agree with how they are doing their specific jobs, then I discuss it. Truthfully, I always felt the issues happening in the present will ultimately decide how I judge a situation. We've all made mistakes in the past. We were all young once, and we all continue to do the wrong things at times—at least what some people would consider wrong. For example, Charlie, if you decide to throw a party at your personal residence, and you get sloppy drunk, some would consider you should be judged harshly for that behavior. However, you were on your own property, and as long as you didn't harm anyone or break any laws, why should you be judged? Would you want everything you did twenty years ago to dictate how potential employers or business contacts view you today? We are all probably weak on some personal issues for which others will want to criticize us. I don't see it as my responsibility to highlight those items. I believe it is my job to offer alternative ideas to liberal points of view—to educate those willing to read my articles on how certain economic and political situations in the past can teach us what might be helpful today." Mitch stopped briefly, thinking to himself, before continuing his rant. "We have become too fractured in today's society, because of issues like what you just asked about. There is always someone looking to tear down the individuals in power, no

Eric Myerholtz

matter what the actual truth may be. I will not do that or be a part of it. I will emphasize conservative viewpoints and argue against decisions I believe direct this country down the wrong path. Quite frankly, as liberal as this president has appeared thus far, if I cannot debate him in a civilized fashion on the issues, if I have to rely on his pre–public life days and personal relationships, then I have already lost."

Gus was preparing to bring this session to an end. He liked Charlie but knew the man's mouth could get him in trouble sometimes. However, Paul beat him to the punch with another question.

"And from where does your philosophy stem? What path brought you to be the conservative idealist that you are today?"

"Interesting question," Mitch responded thoughtfully. "As with many people, I'm certain it was a combination of factors. I grew up in what I will call a confused household. My mother was raised Republican but usually voted Democrat, and my father was raised a Democrat and usually voted Republican. I always was interested in what was happening politically but not emotionally involved. As I finished my high school years and continued into college, I began reading more about our country's founding fathers. I was curious what motivated them and where their ideas came from, and began trying to apply their thoughts and writings to today's world. I read Thomas Paine's *Common Sense* and one line crystallized my thinking: 'Society in every state is a blessing, but government even in its best state is but a necessary evil; and in its worst state, an intolerable one.' I also remember, during my formative high school and college years, Reagan saying something to the effect that every government program is a step away from freedom. Some are necessary, but we should strive to have a few as possible. I guess you can trace my fundamental believes to those things mostly."

"Are you saying the founding fathers were all conservative?" Karen asked. "I kind of assumed that they were more radical."

"I know we just met, and please do not take this as condescending, but that is a common misperception, in my mind, anyhow. I believe the founding fathers were conservative in that they believed in a limited central government, individual freedoms, and that certain rights were bestowed on them by their 'Creator.' Think about those limited government concepts today, as we debate how high taxes should be, as our central government fires the CEO of a major corporation, as it takes control of much of the banking industry, and as it attempts to put many in the energy industry out of business."

"I like that answer," Karen said. "But do you think the thoughts and actions of the founders are still relevant today?"

"Still relevant?" Mitch asked. "I think they are even more relevant than ever."

"But the world was so different 230 years ago," Paul interjected. "They couldn't have contemplated the form of the earth we live on today. The amount of poverty and the concentration of wealth. I just don't see how we can use those thoughts today. Don't get me wrong, they were great people in their time and did fantastic things, but projecting those beliefs in today's world seems almost ludicrous."

Mitch was not surprised by Paul's statement. He had argued this point before, but he always had an ace up his sleeve for a response.

"Do you know who influenced the ideas that the founding fathers put to practice by writing the Declaration and establishing the Constitution? Any ideas?"

"I really haven't studied that," Paul said honestly.

"Remember that there obviously was no radio or television back then; there were books and newspapers, though. Reading was what most educated people did, and they read all the time. They were able to read about history and to learn from it. The founders based much of their conclusions and the final products of their work on the Englishman John Locke, who had lived a hundred years earlier, and on Montesquieu, theories a full fifty years earlier. And, of course, Cicero, who lived only 1800 years earlier. If Cicero's thoughts could be relevant enough almost two millennia later, then I think we can still use these relatively young two-hundred-year-old ideas."

"Excuse me," Charlie chimed in, "but who on God's green Earth was Cicero?"

"Marcus Tullius Cicero was a Roman orator and attorney, and is considered by many historians to have been one of the most brilliant minds of the ancient Roman Empire," Mitch said. "John Adams said that throughout time, no greater philosopher or statesmen had lived. The founders borrowed much of their natural law philosophy from Cicero."

"What do you mean—'natural law'?" Paul asked. This was turning into History 101, Mitch thought. Fairly heavy stuff for his first meeting with these people.

"Natural laws would be considered universal. Laws that are the same regardless of any situation—laws of appropriate behavior as deemed by the Supreme Creator. Cicero stated that true law is 'reason in agreement with nature.' The inalienable rights of the Declaration would be considered natural laws."

Gus had had enough. He was not the most patient person once a meeting had seemed to lose its purpose. It was time to give Mitch the hard sell.

"Mitch, all this talk is very interesting, and we will have many more meetings to continue our debate. We're a small group right now but a smart one. We have a map of how to get where we are going. We've done our research, and you are the guy we want. Being based here locally, you can give us your input on any of the issues we are deciding, and you can have your finger on the pulse of relevant items in other states through your reporter contacts. We realize this will be quite an increase to your workload, but what truly rewarding opportunity doesn't include some sweat? Isn't that one of the aspects that has made our country great—hard work pays off in the end? As I explained, this will all come together very quickly, and we want you there to help make it happen."

"When will the Web site be active?" Mitch asked, feeling more excited every minute.

"We have some basic information right now," Gus explained. "We have been advertising that greater things are to come. Next week, we want to start populating the site with articles. I have already contacted some people to contribute a few pieces, but overall, it will be a very basic site for now. We will have a list of goals and beliefs—hopefully an article by you and an outline of where we will be taking this venture. The Web site itself will take a few months to get the hits we want, but that is the planned time frame for the bigger splashes as well. The bottom line, Mitch, is we need you, and we think you will fit right in with what we will accomplish. We could talk all day about why we are doing this and time frames and ultimate goals, but I think you have the basic premise. Can we count on your support—will you join us?"

Mitch thought for a few moments; this really was a hard sell. He did like everything they had said, and they all seemed to be genuinely passionate about the cause, although Mitch questioned Paul's inquiries, and Charlie had not talked very much. He really did like the idea of being there at the beginning and contributing to a new organization that was working to improve the country; not to make too much of it, but when Gus had just asked, "Can we count on your support?" Mitch had heard, "Will you help your country?"

"As John Adams once wrote to his wife Abigail—*'We live, my dear soul, in an age of trial. What will be the consequence, I know not.'* Yes—I'm in—and thank you for asking me to be a part of this. I am very excited. Who is organizing the Web site?"

"That would be me and Paul," Charlie said. "I have a small staff, I will put you in touch with them, and they will give you the particulars of posting your articles. You will work with them as we add more states' links. Ultimately, you will be taking over complete responsibility."

They exchanged e-mail addresses and cell phone numbers.

"Paul will send you an e-mail list of the individuals in our group and any other details of the basic information. We will meet here every Thursday at one o'clock to check our progress," Gus finished.

"Excellent, is there anything else?" Mitch asked.

"You were our only agenda item today," Gus said. "I think we are good, and we look forward to your first article and to hearing about your progress with other writers."

Mitch shook everyone's hands again, thanking them for including him. As he walked out of the room, he felt energized, ideas running in his head already.

* * * *

"What was the deal with that question about criticizing the president?" Gus demanded of Charlie after the others had left.

"Relax, Gus; I just wanted to put him on the spot for a second. See how he reacted. We had been kissing his butt since he walked in. I wanted him to feel slightly uncomfortable. He seemed a bit cocky to me."

"Fine, but I would have appreciated a heads-up. We were following a script. You ad-libbed a bit there."

"You pay me to ad-lib at times, like in Sacramento today. But no harm done. He's on board, and our plan can continue on schedule."

Gus gave him a hard look. "Sure—no harm done. But the Sacramento issue is something I don't want to repeat. Make sure your team has no more slip-ups like that again."

"Believe me, there won't be," Charlie said confidently.

"Along those lines," Gus replied, "did you see the e-mail Mitch got from some guy named Al? It said thanks for the message. Were we aware of a message?"

"Yes, I saw that. It must have been a message Mitch sent before our surveillance was online. He got that note from Al a day after we started. I think we are good."

"Make sure we are good!" Gus replied.

* * * *

Denise Broadbeck sat at Starbucks trying to enjoy her iced venti non-fat chai tea. She was bothered by several strange instances recently and was replaying them in her head. She had been introduced to a guy named Charlie last month (through an business acquaintance), and Charlie had asked if she would be interested in joining a conservative group who wanted to do some "exciting" things, as Charlie had put it. Charlie had really pushed hard to get her to write some articles and to try to bring other of her contacts into the group, as writers or just by donating to their cause. It sounded like a great opportunity, but Denise was just slammed with too many other things at the moment. After a few days of contemplation and research on the group, she decided to say no. Charlie continued with the hard push, in an almost threatening manner, which was very disconcerting.

Denise was director of sales for a large insulation manufacturer. She had also contributed numerous opinion pieces to the *Sacramento Bee* and even had one published in the *Wall Street Journal*. She was very intrigued by this offer, but didn't get a good read from Charlie at all. Her research on the group had not turned up much information aside from what Charlie had told her already. She had talked to several of her friends about the group, but none had really heard of them either. Charlie did say that this was a movement that was starting from the basics, so maybe it made sense.

Then there was the follow-up call she received from Charlie. In an attempt to show him that she might change her mind, Denise had pressed him for some other names associated with the group, but Charlie deflected her with the request to come to Phoenix and meet the leadership. He had explained that she would submit her articles to a lead writer, but he didn't offer a name there either. Then Charlie asked if she had talked to anyone about their conversation, which she thought very odd. Of course she was going to talk with others, but the way he phrased the question made it seem as if he already knew whom she had talked to. It was almost like a test, and he wanted to see if she was telling the truth, but how could he know whom she had discussed this with?

The final straw was receiving two e-mails from Charlie in quick succession. The first e-mail was a summary of what they had discussed as well as a request for confirmation that she was on board. The e-mail came to her home computer address, which she never gave out—how did he get it? Denise was positive she had provided her work e-mail; it was a business card she had given him, for heaven's sake. There was no way he should have her home e-mail.

The second e-mail was even more disturbing. Sent right after she received the first one, this message was obviously not meant for her, but was to some guy named Gus and talked how her coming on board was a done deal. It also included references to "the plan finally coming together" and "people paying" for the harm they had done. It was all very cryptic but quite unsettling. It obviously was not to be seen by her; she was sure Charlie had just absent-mindedly hit her address again. Either way, she called within an hour of receiving both e-mails and told him that she would have to respectfully decline the invitation. Denise made it clear that this was her final decision and that she did not wish to be contacted again about the matter. Charlie seemed very disappointed, bordering on angry.

Denise looked at her watch and realized that she had a meeting starting in a few minutes—she should walk back to her office. As Denise stepped outside, she looked into her briefcase for her sunglasses. She didn't notice the dark green Toyota Corolla driving by with its window down slightly, nor did she hear the shot that came from the car, due to the silencer on the weapon. Denise did feel a pain ever so briefly as the bullet hit her heart. She collapsed instantly as the Corolla drove away without the slightest hint of wrongdoing. People around Denise scrambled to her to see what was wrong, but no one had noticed the shot. As several of them dialed 911 on their cell phones, the Corolla turned a corner and was out of sight, and Denise drew her last breath.

* * * *

The Liberty Group

Mitch started making phone calls when he returned to his office. He had talked several times with a Boston reporter he felt would contribute greatly to this cause. He also had a contact in Florida, and he had a hunch his friend Al would be interested in trying an article or two. Gus didn't say it had to be well-known authors. They basically wanted insight from the grassroots level—at least, that was how Mitch had interpreted it. They already said they had a California reporter, and Mitch had contacted someone from Dallas. He wanted someone from New York, but getting a conservative from New York might be tough, at least within New York City. Mitch always found it intriguing how much of the state of New York actually voted Republican, but New York City with its vast population controlled the results of the whole state. This phenomenon was not unlike the entire country, where most of the counties within the states voted Republican, but the large cities outweighed those votes to swing in the favor of the Democrats. Mitch had yet to understand this. In the twenty or so years of his adult lifetime, it seemed the large cities, and much of the underprivileged in those cities, continued to vote for Democrats, yet their situations never improved. They remained the underprivileged. Only the few times when conservatives controlled the Congress and bills were passed to lower tax rates across the board did the standards of living increase. As Jack Kemp had said, "a rising tide raises all boats." Yet, the Democrats had a monopoly on the voting habits of these people. Mitch could only conclude that the Democrats had better salesmanship, helped of course by much of the mainstream press. Just recently, an editor of *Newsweek*, in an interview on MSNBC with Chris Matthews, had referred to the president as "sort of God." He was not even questioned by Matthews after making the statement. A news magazine editor making a statement that the president was sort of God on a news show, and he was not even called on the carpet about it. *What ever happened to being a journalist?* Mitch thought.

Anyhow, he had five writers he hoped would contribute immediately. Mitch would reach out to some less familiar contacts after the first few weeks. He wanted to verify that the paperwork was all in place and that he understood what needed to happen to ensure compensation for these writers, knowing positively they would ask about that before committing.

Mitch's final call was to Al.

"Al Miller," his friend's voice said when he picked up the phone.

"Can I please speak to Grady Sizemore?" Mitch asked. Grady Sizemore was the centerfielder of the Cleveland Indians, Al's favorite baseball team. Mitch knew Grady was injured and liked to constantly remind Al the Indians were jinxed and had not won a World Series since 1948. Heck, the Arizona Diamondbacks had only existed for a little over ten years, and they already had one World Series championship under their belt!

"I'm sorry, Grady is unavailable to take your call," Al replied. "He's busy planning the pennant run for the Tribe."

"Good luck with that," Mitch said. "How are you, A?"

"I'm fine. How about you—how're Marie and the kids?"

"Everyone's doing fine. Hey, I'm in a bit of a bind, and I need your help."

"Anything for you, pal. You know that."

"I want you to rekindle your journalistic spirit. I've got an opportunity for you."

"What are you talking about?" Al asked with a confused laugh.

"I've been asked to head up the opinion pages of a new conservative group's Web site, and they want articles from all over the country, from writers who will use national as well as state-specific topics," Mitch explained. "Naturally, I thought of you."

"Naturally. I mean, when I need a good tax preparer, I always call a newspaper writer. Don't you know other *actual* writers across the United States?"

"Of course I do, but they have given me some free reign with this, and I think it would be better to get the opinions of some who are living through the problems, not just writing about them. When we talk, you always have some good points, and I know you have never fully quenched that journalist thirst of yours. Come on, it will be fun. I can also pay you for your articles. A nice little stipend for each submission. Plus, as important as Ohio has been in the last two election cycles, your articles could really help the conservative side."

"You should have been in sales," Al retorted. "I haven't tried to write anything since college. You don't even know if I would be any good. I might get you fired from this assignment."

"No way. I tell you what, write one article, and I will proofread it. If I say it's good enough, you're in. Will you at least try that for me?"

"Okay—I'll try one article—you want something Ohio specific?"

"That would be great. You're going to enjoy this, believe me."

"Do I have a deadline?" Al asked.

"Just get me something when you can. I'm going to be adding writers constantly. I already have some on board, and I will be contributing as well. I should have plenty of material for the first few weeks our site is up."

"You're still writing articles for the *Republic*, right?"

"Oh, yes," Mitch replied. "The proverbial 'don't quit your day job' situation. I don't know how this opportunity will end up. I just met the management team today, and they all seem motivated and bright. They have some moneybag financing it so far, with the hopes that advertising and ultimately selling different membership levels will finance it further. They want to grow very quickly in order to help significantly influence the 2010 elections."

"It sounds a lot like the Heritage Foundation," Al said. "I go to their site all the time—it is full of excellent information. They have teams of researchers. I wonder why your rich guy financier didn't just hook up with that group."

"I asked something along those lines. This guy is a bit of a control freak. I think he wants to determine the direction they take, who they ultimately endorse, who they support financially, etc. I also think he wants his name front and center."

"Why you—why didn't they ..." Al hesitated on how to finish his question, but Mitch bailed him out.

"Why didn't they select someone more well known?" Mitch said.

"I guess that was where I was going," Al said, slightly embarrassed.

"Hey, after twenty-five plus years of being friends, don't worry; you can't offend me, you stinkin' mediocre accountant. I actually asked that same question. The answer was basically they wanted fresh names, untainted in the liberal media. People that are unknown. They feel the unknown masses can better lead a widespread movement than well-known figures who, despite their brilliance, are dismissed as right-wing extremists."

"All right, Bartter, I'll send you an article. Get ready to be impressed. You better not show your editor at the *Republic*; he may realize there are others who can do your job."

"I'm not too concerned," Mitch joked back.

"Are you going to ask Todd for articles, too?" Al asked.

"I don't think Todd would write articles we are looking for. It would be fun rejecting them, though."

"So you feel comfortable who you are getting on this trip with, right?" Al asked.

"What do you mean?"

"Just that you are committing a lot of time based on a meeting you had with four people. Have you at least checked into these guys?"

"Well, I suppose that would be a good idea."

"Why don't you put your wife to work on it," Al suggested. "She's smarter than you anyhow; she'll find anything you need to know."

"Good idea," Mitch agreed. "I'll ask her when I get home. By the way, I've got another article coming out in the *Republic*—have fun with it."

"Talk to you later, Mitch—thanks for thinking of me for this project of yours. I'm very flattered."

"I'm sure you'll do me proud," Mitch said as he hung up the phone.

Chapter 4

On Friday, Gus and Charlie met to play golf at one of the six championship courses at Desert Mountain Golf in Scottsdale. The two played golf quite frequently as Gus liked the privacy of conversations on the course. The fact that this one was designed by Jack Nicklaus in the middle of the desert made it even better. After hitting a sand shot to within two feet of the cup and putting in for par, Gus asked Charlie if the surveillance of Mitch seemed to be completely in place. Charlie reported a team would follow him everywhere from that moment on, recording every place he went. They would also log all contacts possible. The electronic surveillance devices were also working properly.

"Yes, he got right to work on making contacts with potential writers for the cause when he got back to his office yesterday," Charlie said as they walked back to the golf cart.

"Anything unusual?" Gus questioned.

"Nothing really, mainly different opinion columnists here and there, although he did ask an old friend to lend a hand in Ohio. They went to college together. This guy's an accountant for a manufacturing company."

"Do we know anything else about him?"

"Nothing yet. He was a little inquisitive about our management group. He suggested Mitch have his wife do background checks on us. Do you want me to look into him further?"

"I don't think so," Gus replied. "Mitch mentioned yesterday that he was an accounting major in college—we knew that. It is only natural that he would reach out to some of his friends. As for checking into us, I'm guessing Mitch would have done that anyhow. He's a bright guy. Besides, his using an accountant doesn't worry me. You know what accountants use for birth control, don't you?"

"What?"

"Their personalities."

"Funny, but that doesn't apply to Karen—I wouldn't mind her balancing my books," Charlie said slyly.

"I keep telling you you'll get nowhere with her; she is out of your league," Gus said, shaking his head.

"You saying that just makes it that much more of a challenge," Charlie said as they teed up their next shots.

* * * * *

That afternoon, Mitch was finishing up at the *Republic* when John called him, asking to have a word.

"What's up?" Mitch asked as he entered the spacious office overlooking Central Avenue.

"I was curious how your meeting went yesterday with Paul and the others," John inquired.

"Extremely interesting," Mitch responded. Remembering Al's advice on learning more about the Liberty players, he followed up. "How well do you know Paul?"

"Like I said before, we have been on some boards together—that's it. I believe he is an attorney. He called me about you a few days before

I introduced you. Most of what he said at the restaurant was all new to me, too."

"Well, he was joined by three other people, and they went into more detail on the basics that Paul laid out at our lunch. It does really sound quite fun. I have already contacted several other people around the nation to assist with the articles. They are all pretty excited about it. I plan to investigate the website a little closer this weekend and make sure I understand how that all works."

"This isn't going to conflict with anything around here, is it?" John asked, raising his eyebrows slightly.

"John, you know me—Mr. Get It All Done."

"Yeah, I know you, Mitch. You get it all done, sometimes even with a minute or two to spare. Can we have the agreement that I can pull you off this detail if it becomes a problem?"

"I promise it won't be a problem," Mitch replied. "Don't you already have my article for next week?"

"Yes, I do. I just want us to be on the same page."

"John, I will do as you say; if my work suffers here, you can pull the string on this other venture. I've been a loyal *Republic* employee for ten years. That won't change now."

"Good enough," John replied. "Good article, too, by the way."

"Aren't they all good?" Mitch joked back.

* * * * *

Mitch pulled in his driveway feeling very good on Friday evening. He was energized by this new project, but he was also excited, as he was surprising his wife with an anniversary dinner tonight. Their actual anniversary wasn't for a few days, but it fell on a Monday this year, and the weekends are always better to celebrate. Also, to surprise someone, you have to go a day or two ahead of time. Mitch and Marie had married soon after she had graduated, being a few years younger than her husband. He had proposed in college, though. Marie had originally decided to attend Kent State University, which was also in Ohio, but it was about a two-and-a-half-hour drive from Bowling Green. For numerous reasons, most of which she claimed did not involve Mitch, Marie transferred to Bowling Green State after a year at Kent. She graduated a Falcon a few years later.

Mitch was rather proud of his proposal. Being an avid golfer, he had invited Marie to play a round on a course near where they grew up (and where Mitch had worked during high school and college). He had a little help from some of his friends at the course with the set up, but basically, he and Marie played the first hole, and Mitch made sure that Marie putted out first. When she reached into the hole to pull out her ball, she discovered a little jewelry box there. Mitch kneeled on the first green and asked Marie to marry him. She of course said yes.

He shook himself from his reminiscing and walked into the house.

"Hey gorgeous—happy anniversary," he said to Marie when he saw her.

"Happy anniversary?" she questioned as they gave each other a hug and kiss. "You're a little early for that."

"Well, that may be, but we're starting the celebration tonight!"

"Do you have anything planned?" she asked.

"Do I?" Mitch responded enthusiastically. "The kids haven't said anything to you yet?"

"I haven't seen Lynne or Jane, and Ed says you told him he could spend the night at Nathan's."

"Well, Ed's right, and Lynne and Jane are staying at friends as well. We have reservations for dinner at the City Grille in about ninety minutes."

"Well, at least you gave me some warning—I'd better get in the shower then!" Marie said enthusiastically. Two hours later, Mitch and Marie were toasting their eighteenth anniversary.

The Liberty Group

"Thank you for being my best friend—I am so lucky," Mitch said as they set their glasses down, and he leaned in and kissed her gently.

"I'm the lucky one," Marie replied. "You do so much for me and for our family. We are truly blessed!"

"So, in a couple years, we'll have our twentieth—let's make it huge—what do you want to do?" Mitch asked.

"I was thinking of a cruise through the Greek Isles," Marie said without hesitation.

"Were you? And how long have you been thinking of that?"

"Only about fifteen years, and remember, we talked about a cruise for our tenth anniversary, but we weren't able to make that happen."

"True," Mitch replied. "Are you thinking with or without the kids?"

"Well, that depends on our financial situation a little. It would be fantastic to take the kids, but it would be wonderful with just the two of us as well."

"Maybe this additional project of mine with the Liberty Group will give us the additional income to take that cruise and still put money in the college funds," Mitch said hopefully. "So the Greek Isles, huh? You know, Al and Lisa went to Italy for her fortieth birthday last year. They said it was incredible. Would you want to spend a little time there as well?"

"I'll tell you what," Marie said. "You make enough doing this extra work, and we'll take three weeks—ten days in Italy and ten days on a cruise in the Adriatic and Aegean."

"Oh—you've got it all planned out now, don't you?"

"I'll start my Internet searching tomorrow! You know the search is half the fun."

As the food arrived, they continued to dream about the Mediterranean excursion.

* * * *

After a wonderful dinner and some scrumptious desserts, Mitch and Marie were in the car on their way home.

"So—anything exciting happen today?" Mitch asked his wife. "We were so involved in our talk of Italy and Greece I never really asked you."

"Not really. I worked on a few projects regarding some new products and talked with some sales reps about a dispute they are having with a customer. How about yours?"

"Nothing out of the ordinary—I made contact with some more people to help with the Liberty Group. Did I tell you, yesterday after the Liberty meeting, I called Al and asked him to help as well?"

"Really?" Marie asked, somewhat surprised.

"Remember, he started at BGSU majoring in journalism, and he was editor of the high school newspaper."

"Oh, yeah, clearly he's almost overqualified," Marie replied sarcastically.

"He'll do fine. I had to do a little convincing with him as well. He actually had a fairly good idea about checking into this management team that I am getting involved with. I was contemplating doing that anyhow, but since John was the one who hooked me up with them, I wasn't sure it was necessary. Al suggested that you assist me with the research. Said something about you being smarter than me."

"Well, he obviously has that right. Of course, he has known me longer than you have."

"That's right—I forgot you two grew up about ten houses apart," Mitch replied.

"Maybe he will provide a good article or two. How are Lisa and the kids?"

"They doing fine—he said they are all looking forward to getting together later this summer! So, you'll help me with these background checks?"

"Sure, and I'll send you a bill, too," Marie said.

"How about if I prepay with a nice long, relaxing back rub?" Mitch said as they pulled in the driveway.

"I usually don't let clients pay that way, but just for you, I'll make an exception," Marie said, and they went in the house.

Chapter 5

Al awoke on the following Sunday and let his dog out. Al's family was slightly smaller than Mitch's—he and his wife Lisa had only one dog to go along with his two children. His kids were similar in age to Mitch and Marie's; his son (Michael) had just finished eleventh grade, and his daughter (Savannah) had just finished eighth. As it was the first Sunday of the summer vacation for his kids, he decided to allow them to sleep in while he went to the early service at church. Sunday school had ended for the summer, and it seemed the older his kids got, the more resistant they were to going to church. Al still made them go most of the time, but today, he didn't feel like the debate.

Al was Lutheran and loved his congregation. The pastor was in his early sixties but had a trim physique and an energy that belied his age. Al loved the pastor's sermons. He used no notes and always had a good message. The sanctuary itself was in the shape of a cross, not unlike many churches. Al and his wife had recently traveled to Italy (in celebration of his wife's fortieth birthday), and they had seen innumerable churches and cathedrals of renown. Obviously, a modern-day church in Bowling

Green, Ohio, wasn't going to compare, but this was Al's church home, and he wouldn't have the setting look any different.

Al settled into a pew near the front as the service was about to begin. The first reading was the story of Eve, Adam, and the serpent in the Garden of Eden, and the pastor's sermon was about this reading. "Temptation is universal," the pastor had said, "but most people want to deflect the reason for giving in to someone else. They want to blame." Al couldn't have agreed more. He also passed into thought on some of Mitch's articles, and how too many times, the politicians blamed each other, even though they all were involved in governmental decisions. That was one of the things that Al really respected about Mitch—his ability to comment on the issues, without passing blame.

"We are on the hook for the choices we've made," the pastor said. Al could only think, *How I wish everyone felt that!* After the service as he drove home, Al thought of some way to incorporate the themes his pastor had used into the article Mitch had asked him to write.

* * * *

Marie walked into work on Monday morning feeling refreshed after the very relaxing weekend. She had a light morning scheduled, so she thought she would start checking into these people that had her husband all jazzed up.

She began with Gus Reed. She found the sad story of his daughter and some brief information of his days as an attorney—a public defender, actually, which Marie found surprising. His name was on several corporate boards, which she attributed to his money as it seemed that once you made a few contacts among the upper echelon in the business world, you most likely were asked to join a few boards. She expected to find quite a bit about him, but there was surprisingly little overall on the Web. He wasn't on a list of any political donors, nor did he seem to have ever held a job since his inheritance. Marie just assumed someone as driven as Mitch had described Gus to be would have either started his own business or joined someone else's in thirty years. She also could not find anything about him prior to the inheritance. He seemed to have just materialized out of nowhere at that point. She was puzzled, as Marie considered herself an expert at Internet research.

Figuring she would come back to Mr. Reed, Marie moved on to Karen Simmons. Most of what she found on Karen related to her work as a CPA with Arthur Andersen, later renamed Andersen. Prior to the entire Enron debacle, where one office of a global firm managed to bring down the accounting giant, Karen had risen quickly within its ranks, becoming one of the few female partners and an expert in oil and gas refining. In 1999, after almost fifteen years with Andersen, she and another Phoenix CPA started their own firm. Marie surmised that the two had worked quite hard to cultivate small business customers in the Phoenix area, as their firm grew quickly and now employed fifty professionals performing mainly audit and tax compliance work. Karen had never married, at least not that Marie could find. She made a note to talk to Al about Karen; Al had worked for Andersen as well, but she knew it was a long shot that the two had ever met.

Marie then looked up Paul Gregory and found several hits on the boards he served. Paul was an attorney and actually had worked for several liberal groups. Marie thought this was strange but assumed anyone can change. Reagan had been a democrat in his younger days, and what was the Winston Churchill quote she had heard her husband say so many times? "If you're not a liberal when you're twenty, you don't have a heart, and if you're not a conservative when you're forty, you don't have a brain." That's how she remembered it, anyhow. She noted that Paul and Gus served on some of the same boards, guessing that Gus was instrumental in adding Paul. Paul was divorced, with no mention of any children. Not a whole lot was discovered about Paul's professional life in the last decade or so.

Charlie Davis was even more of a mystery. With the little background Mitch had given her, Marie couldn't even figure out which of the twenty

Charlie Davises in the Phoenix area was the Liberty one. None of the ages/backgrounds she found seem to match. She began to wonder if it was his real name. Marie's phone rang. Her assistant indicated that a marketing meeting had been scheduled just that morning—she had about fifteen minutes to prepare an outline of the company's latest market research. Marie jotted down some of the possible matches for Charlie and figured she would try again later. Just as she was pulling her presentation together, the phone rang again.

"Marie Bartter."

"Happy anniversary!" Mitch said on the other end. "On the right day this time."

"Happy anniversary to you, too. How are you this morning?"

"Doing great—sitting down ready to write my article—I hope it's not too *taxing*. Get it—taxing. I write about taxes."

"It wouldn't be an anniversary without one of your hilarious puns," Marie quipped, rolling her eyes. As she finished the sentence, a large bouquet of flowers was placed on her desk.

"I've just had a delivery—thanks for the flowers—they are beautiful!" Marie exclaimed. Mitch usually sent flowers to her at work several times during the year, and obviously, their anniversary was one of those occasions.

"I'm glad they came so early today. I hope you have a fantastic day—I love you, and I'll see you tonight."

"I love you, too," Marie answered.

* * * * *

Mitch was eager to see his article in the *Republic* the following Wednesday morning. He had spent a good part of the previous two days making additional contacts across the country as well as gathering the necessary information on them to give to Karen (payment-related items such as social security numbers, addresses, etc.). He was thankful he had completed this article ahead of time. This one had some points that he repeated often. Taxes were one of the topics Mitch hammered over and over again. Mitch debated the level of taxation in the United States with most of his more liberal friends. His brother-in-law, Doug (married to his wife's sister), had once stated that he believed U.S. citizens were under-taxed, and Mitch was just dumbfounded.

"How much is enough, then?" Mitch had asked.

"Well, that would depend on how much you earn," Doug surmised. "I would say that the top tax bracket should approximate 50 percent for federal purposes."

"Do you realize tax revenues to the government can increase when individual tax rates go down?" Mitch replied.

"That has more to do with overall employment than with the rate of taxation," Doug retorted.

"You are absolutely correct, but aren't those two items related? Have you have heard of or seen the Laffer Curve?"

"I've heard of it, but I'm struggling to recall what it relates to," Doug replied.

"Well, let me ask you, if the tax rate was 0 percent, and let's say your total income is $50,000, how much in taxes would the government collect from you?"

"Well, that's easy—zero dollars at 0 percent," Doug answered.

"Excellent—now let's use the same scenario, only changing the tax rate to 100 percent," Mitch continued, laying his trap. "How much would the government collect?"

"If I made $50,000 and paid 100 percent in taxes, then the government would collect $50,000," Doug responded.

Mitch frowned. "Let me ask this another way—would you work for free?"

"No way."

"Okay, but isn't that what you are doing if the tax rate is 100 percent—your company pays you and you pay the government and you end up with nothing."

"Now I see; sure, at 100 percent tax rate, the government collects nothing because no one would work."

"Right, now, if the tax rate was 90 percent, some would work but most wouldn't. The government would collect something, but not much. Similarly, if the tax rate were only 5 percent, the government would get something, but not much. As you continue with both examples, coming down from the higher rates or increasing the lower rates, tax revenue increases until you reach the maximum revenue point. Plotting this on a graph, you end up looking at a semicircle, basically. The point is that if the current tax rate is somewhere above the maximum tax revenue rate, the country would collect more tax by lowering the overall rate. Now, this is an overly simplistic explanation. A large part of the theory is that as more people are able to keep a larger portion of their own money, instead of paying it to the government, they will spend more. Corporations will reinvest more, creating more jobs. The job creation leads to more taxes collected overall even at lower rates."

"Sure, but as you say, that is just a theory," Doug argued.

"Well, when Kennedy, Reagan, and George W. lowered rates across the board, government revenues increased," Mitch stated. "That is a fact, not a theory."

"Whatever," Doug had said at this point. "You're not going to change my mind on this. The rich are rich and therefore should bear a large brunt of the tax burden." He walked away as if this were the final word.

Mitch brought his thoughts back to the present day and reread his article. He hoped that he had given more of a challenge to Al and the others on deciphering this one.

When Does It End? The Taxing of America

Last year during the presidential election process, the IRS released data about the individual and corporate tax burdens paid in this country. Obama was campaigning on the statement that, if he were elected, 95 percent of

Eric Myerholtz

Americans would not see a tax increase of any kind. He claimed that only the rich would pay more taxes; they obviously can afford it. Joe Biden went as far as to imply that if the rich didn't want to pay more taxes, they were unpatriotic. Well, just how much do the rich pay? (Please bear with me—I need to provide some statistics to make this argument. Reading statistics is as enjoyable as reviewing the tax code, section by section, alpha to omega. Please stay with me, though—I end up at a good place.)

This argument begins with the recently released data for the 2006 tax year. The top 1% of wage earners accounted for 22% of the total adjusted gross income but paid over 40% of the federal income taxes. Mr. Biden, is that patriotic enough or not? Do they need to handle 50% of the bill for everyone for your definition, or does patriotism start at 75% for these individuals in any given year?

For the top 5% of wage earners, 60% of the tax burden fell to you, while your group only accounted for 37% of the total adjusted gross income. Starting to see a trend here? Let's skip to the largest group—the bottom 50% of wage earners—one half of all income tax filers accounted for next to nothing of the income tax burden. In this real life game of Survivor, basically one half of the players are providing the benefits for the whole tribe.

Fans of this progressive system, it gets even better when you look at the quintiles. The bottom 20% actually received payments equal to 2.9% of tax revenues from the government in the form of the earned income tax credit (which means the top 80% of wage earners actually pay 102.9% of the net income taxes collected). The second lowest 20% also get a net payment, this time of 0.9%, which conversely requires the top 60% of wage earners pay for 103.8% of the net taxes. Let's now look at the middle 20% (I guess what we could call the true middle class)—they pay 4.4% of all income taxes collected. So that means that the bottom 60% of wage earners pay a net of

68

0.6% of the income taxes collected, and the corollary to that is that the top 40% pay 99.4% of the income taxes. These statistics are not imaginary or plucked out of the air—this is directly from the nonpartisan Congressional Budget Office. Really!

Enjoying these statistics yet? (I'm almost done with them.) So, 40% of the income earners in this country pay 99.4% of the income tax bill. Please remember the earned income tax credit was Ronald Reagan's idea and tax policies he championed and managed to get passed have basically eliminated the tax burden on the bottom 40% of wage earners all-together. With that knowledge, I ask again—do the rich pay enough? Hopefully, for many of you, this information is not new.

Liberty from paying taxes has been accomplished for a great many, yet when any tax decrease is proposed, the protest is always that it unfairly benefits the rich. Tax cuts obviously benefit the people who actually pay tax, so please, don't fall for this argument. These top taxpayers are also the job creators in this country—they are the entrepreneurs that take their ideas and invest in them. Letting them keep more of what they have earned will continue to create more jobs. It has happened in the past, and it will happen again if we just let it work.

Looking at our current administration, their policies indicate a belief that government is the entity that should be in control of the jobs, and those paying the taxes now do not pay enough. I have a difficult time not coming to the conclusion that the administration does not see our money as ours—they see our earnings as government property, and they get to dictate what portion of it we should be allowed to have. While still a senator and campaigning for our country's top office, President Obama made the following statement about estate taxes and their possible repeal: "Let's call this trillion dollar giveaway what it is—the Paris Hilton Tax Break. It's about giving billions of dollars to billionaire heirs and heiresses at a time when American taxpayers just can't afford it." This statement indicates the president's mindset on the money and property you have managed to save and collect over your lifetime after paying your income taxes each year! (I'll discuss the ridiculousness of the estate tax in a later article; for now, let's move the individual income tax debate forward.)

To properly fix this, where do we start? There are several plans that would tax consumption (the more you spend, the more you pay) or that would establish a flat rate. I will detail more of these ideas in future articles as well, but I encourage anyone reading this to do a little research of their own—see what other economists have proposed on the topic. I know we will not change the tax code overnight, but a good start is opening our eyes to the entire picture, truly seeing!

Everyone hopefully agrees the first step is to lower tax rates, including corporate rates. This gives long-term incentive for individuals to earn more and for companies to reinvest more. Research has indicated for every dollar increase in corporate taxes, between seventy and ninety-two cents comes from employees' pay. Governmental stimulus packages only borrow from future income and will result in increased tax rates (we'll have to pay back what we have borrowed). Please, call your congressional representatives to tell them that you want tax rates to go down, and also, look at the Liberty Group Web site—some excellent tax information can be found there as well. The bottom line right now is that fewer and fewer people are already shouldering the tax burden. Mr. Biden, the rich are quite patriotic. Stop attacking them—just stop.

Mitch reread the article one more time. He always liked the tax debate, as he truly believed he won it every time. It also gave him an idea of how to involve his friend Al on the Web site to a greater extent.

* * * *

Al had been fortunate enough to play in a golf outing during the day, so he was unable to review Mitch's article until later in the evening. When he returned home, Lisa related a very stressful day she had experienced, and Al was in no mood to cook. The Millers headed out to a Chinese restaurant.

"Tell us about the engagement dinner," Savannah demanded, having heard the story several times. "Every time we eat Chinese, I think of it."

"What engagement dinner?" Michael asked.

"Oh, you've heard it before," Lisa said.

"No. If I have, I don't remember it," Michael replied.

Al had proposed when he was a senior in college and Lisa was a junior. She had finished her undergrad at BGSU during the winter semester (in just three and a half years) after Al had finished in the previous May. They were married a year and a half later. His proposal, as he looked on it now, was fairly lame. Al spent a good part of that day decorating the apartment he shared with Mitch, Todd, and Mark for Christmas—he purchased a tree from the grocery store parking lot, trimmed it, and placed other decorations around living room. He hoped the festive decor would add to the ambiance. Lisa came over that evening as planned to study for their upcoming end-of-semester exams. After an hour or so of studying, Al had excused himself with the pretense of going to get something in his bedroom, where he changed into a suit and tie and came back out to the kitchen with a ring in his pocket. He poured himself a glass of wine with a very shaky hand and took a drink.

"How are you doing?" he asked her.

"Fine," she managed to half-laugh back to him. "What's going on?"

Al then got down on his knee and proposed, pulling out the ring that Lisa had basically pointed to in a magazine a few weeks earlier. She said yes immediately, and no more studying was accomplished that night.

People were always surprised when they related the story of how they met. As with most universities, Bowling Green had certain weekends that were always block-type parties. Toward the end of the spring semester each year, East Merry Madness was held, named after the street where several apartment complexes always grouped together to purchase kegs with just about the entire student body arriving to enjoy the party. Mitch, Al, Todd, and Mark had an apartment on East Merry and contributed to the cause, usually providing two or three kegs. They all invited their friends, and an acquaintance of Al named Sandee had brought Lisa to the party that spring. Al and Lisa talked quite a bit that night, but Al was still seeing another woman, so he did not ask for Lisa's phone number at that point.

Luckily for Al, the following fall semester included East Merry Mania—same party, different time of year. Sandee once again brought Lisa with her, and this time, Al talked to her all night. He did not hesitate to call her the next day, and they became engaged a short two and a half months later. Al always gave the theory that when you're in college, you see each other every day, which meant he and Lisa had had an estimated sixty to seventy dates prior to his proposal. This explanation fell on mostly deaf ears, especially to Lisa's parents. They were concerned that if their daughter was married, she would not go on to graduate school. Al could remember, now with humor, the first dinner his parents and Lisa's parents had enjoyed together. This was just days after Al had proposed. They were in a Chinese restaurant, and Al recalled that Lisa's father asked a question somewhat along the lines of whether Al would be the kind of husband that would allow Lisa to go to graduate school. Al's mom jumped in, slapping her hand forcefully enough on the table that the silverware clinked against the plates, causing more than a few people to turn and look.

"Wait just a minute," Al's mom began. "Al was not raised in a house where the husband 'allows' the wife. The wife is her own person and does what she wants. The husband and wife are a team and make decisions accordingly!"

Al remembered the dinner being quite uncomfortable from then on. Nineteen years of marriage (and one PhD for Lisa) later, Al hoped her parents now realized that they had nothing to worry about.

Al related most of these events once again to Savannah as they waited for their entrees, with Michael losing interest two minutes into the story. After dinner, the family returned home, and Al headed to his computer. He pulled up Mitch's article, enjoying every bit of it. He then set to work on the message. After twenty minutes of playing with some of the numbers, he was still at a dead end. Looking through the article for the fifth time, he noticed a phrase a little out of place: "alpha to omega." Beginning to end. The words prior to this were "section by section." Was this referring to the article—the beginning and end of each section, or paragraph? Al started writing down the first and last word of each paragraph, deciphering, *Last place this year for Tribe fans. Really enjoying new Liberty work. Looking forward to seeing everyone. Stop.*

"Nicely done, Mitch," Al said to himself. "You managed a dig at my baseball team in your message." Al checked his e-mail next, and a message from Todd told him the Arkansas professor had apparently beat him to solving this one.

Chapter 6

Mitch walked into his first official Thursday meeting excited to hear more about the overall group and the progress the others were making. Karen and Paul both talked in depth about the Web site as it was fully functional now; several graphs and charts had been placed on it related to governmental spending and taxing. They praised Mitch's articles as well as the ones from the other participants that Mitch had handpicked. Mitch reported that he now had seven writers committed to contributing articles, from various parts of the country.

"I know one of the heartland writers is lambasting the House of Representatives for passing the so-called Clean Air Act. I sure hope that dies in the Senate!" Mitch stated as he completed his report.

"Really?" said Karen. "I read your article a few weeks ago in the *Republic*. You really believe all that stuff you said. How can you disregard what so many experts have confirmed and not believe humans are causing global warming?"

"The same way that you apparently believe humans are causing it," Mitch replied. "I thought I laid out some pretty persuasive arguments."

"Well, I'll admit that I am like most of the members of the House of Representatives and have not read the bill. I do care deeply for the environment, and this is probably the one issue I may be in disagreement with you guys. I think we need to do something, and this bill is a start."

"I'm a little surprised you are part of this group with that belief. Not so much on the climate side of it but on the business side. This bill is incredibly flawed. It will require the country to have the same stringent residential housing requirements that California currently uses. Have you looked at the state of their economy lately? It will expose new construction to extremely higher costs. It also requires people selling their existing houses to bring them up to the same standards when they ultimately sell them. This will hurt an already ailing housing market.

"Where in the Constitution does the federal government have the right to demand what is required of a house? That should be left up to each locality," Mitch stated. "This is the point that is continually swept under the carpet—there is really no federal authority for any of these audacious freedom limitations the government is imposing."

"You're correct; I am more on the global warming side of the issue," Karen replied. "I did not realize that it had those requirements."

"No one realizes it—not even most of the representatives who voted for it," Mitch argued. "This 1,200-page bill was rushed through the process, including a 309-page amendment that was added at about three o'clock in the morning on the day of the vote. How could these elected officials read all that and vote intelligently on it? It is criminal in my mind, considering the long-term ramifications. James Madison actually warned us that people will no longer trust government if the elected officials write laws that are incoherent and so voluminous that they cannot possibly be understood. I think we have reached and surpassed that point. We need to return to a more basic approach on all of these issues."

"I was referring more to your article—you seem to be a global warming denier," Karen retorted.

"I don't seem to be; I am, at least as it pertains to human-caused global warming. There is as much science against the man-made argument as there is for it. You just hear more about the man-caused science because that is what the liberal media wants you to hear. Recently, an EPA representative was reassigned off his duties because he wrote a lengthy report refuting the man-caused argument."

"It is just common sense; the earth is warmer—that is a fact," Karen stated.

"Warmer since when—the Ice Age?" Mitch responded. "Yes, it is. It all depends on your perspective and the time frame you want to choose. It used to be common sense that the earth was flat. Greater knowledge leads to better conclusions. My article's purpose is to bring awareness to the issue—to encourage others to perform their own research, not just to believe what an Al Gore supporter says. Either way, this bill is terrible. It won't make any difference in the carbon dioxide in the atmosphere; it will just raise energy rates. Greenpeace didn't want it passed because it didn't do enough, in their opinion. As I said, I just hope my article gets people to do some of their own thinking and maybe contact their congressional representatives."

Gus decided it was time to bring the meeting to a close. "A spirited debate to be sure. I'll think we'll save more for later, though. Thank you all for coming. I appreciate the updates. I have a little surprise for you. I am arranging a fundraiser for the Fourth of July to be held at Rustler's Roost. You and your spouse—or a date, I should say, as Mitch is the only married person here—are invited. There will be plenty of food and drink, maybe even a few celebrities and some musical entertainment. Please, come if you can! I'm also trying to arrange another big splash between now and then—maybe mid-June. I'll keep you posted. Karen, I need a word before you go."

"And Karen," Charlie chimed in, "I'd like a date before you go."

"Same answer as always, Charlie," Karen responded in an exasperated tone.

As they all got up to leave, Mitch was first out the door, admiring the wonderful lobby area of the Biltmore as he passed through. He was out in the parking lot when a voice called out.

"Hey, Mitch!" Mitch turned around and saw Paul coming toward him, half jogging. "I need to go over a few more things with you about other states we want to focus our attention on, but don't have time right this second. Can you meet me after dinner this evening, say nine o'clock at Majerle's downtown?"

"I think I can make that work," Mitch responded, smiling.

"Great—I'll see you there."

* * * *

Mitch arrived at Majerle's and ordered a beer at the bar. It was about 8:55. He had been here a few times. Dan Majerle was a basketball player who had played for three NBA teams, mainly with the Phoenix Suns, retiring in 2002. However, Mitch always remembered Dan Majerle from his college days. Dan played for Central Michigan, a rival of Bowling Green in the Mid-American Conference. Their junior year, Mitch, Todd, Al, and Mark, along with a few other classmates, had gone to the conference tournament to watch the Falcons. Majerle lit them up for what seemed like fifty points, in Mitch's memory, anyhow. He always felt an old college connection in this place.

As Mitch looked up at the ballgame on the television and sipped his beer, a very attractive blonde sat down next to him, ordering a gin and tonic.

"It's been a lousy day," she announced to no one in particular. Turning to Mitch, she said, "I always feel better after a bad day if I do something for someone—like buying him or her a drink. Can I get you another beer?"

"No, thanks, I'm good for now," Mitch responded.

"Rachel Schafer," the woman said, holding out her hand. She seemed to be about thirty and had startling blue eyes to go along with her other attractive features.

"Mitch Bartter," Mitch replied, shaking her hand and turning back to the game.

"What do you do, Mitch?" Rachel asked.

"I'm a columnist for the *Republic*. How about yourself?"

"I'm the IT director for a small manufacturing company. I'm always amazed how every employee in the world thinks computers should solve every problem they have. It has just been one of those days! I'm going to let that go now." Rachel closed her eyes and let out a deep, cleansing breath.

"What does your company manufacture?" Mitch asked, trying to be polite.

"Oh, some parts for copy machines. What do your columns cover?"

"I'm a conservative columnist—I write opinion pieces."

"You know, I think I have read some of your stuff," Rachel replied almost too enthusiastically. "Didn't you have a global warming piece recently?"

Mitch glanced at his watch—9:10.

"Yeah—that was mine," he said while looking around the bar for Paul. Still no sign of him.

"Do you travel much with that job?" Rachel asked.

"No—not really."

"Me neither—I wish I would more. Where would you go if you could go anywhere?" She was trying to keep Mitch's attention on her.

"Well, my wife and I were just talking about a cruise through the Greek islands," Mitch responded.

Rachel frowned slightly at the mention of Mitch's wife. Mitch looked around the bar again.

"Are you waiting for someone?" Rachel asked.

"Yes—I was supposed to meet a business associate tonight, but he appears to be a no show."

"Why don't you have another beer? He may just be running late," Rachel suggested. Mitch supposed Paul could have been held up. He tried Paul's cell phone but there was no answer. He ordered another beer, figuring if Paul didn't show by 9:30, he would head on out. Rachel also ordered another drink and downed it quickly.

"You a sports fan?" she asked.

"Definitely," Mitch responded. "Baseball has always been my favorite. How about you?"

"Not much of a fan, although I have watched some baseball over the past several years. I do remember when that really tall pitcher hit the bird with a pitch. Didn't he used to play for Arizona?"

"Randy Johnson—yes, he helped lead the D-backs to the World Series title."

"Who's winning tonight?" Rachel asked.

"Arizona has a two-run lead," Mitch answered.

After watching a discussion the manager was having with the umpire, Rachel tried more conversation.

"How did they rule that pitch that, what did you say his name was, Johnson hit the bird with?"

"I think they said it was a fowl ball," Mitch joked. It took a second to register, but then Rachel laughed loud enough for a few customers to turn toward her.

"Very quick with that pun," she said. Mitch didn't think it was that funny. Rachel kept trying to engage him in conversation, but if Paul wasn't going to show, he would rather be home with his family. He checked his watch again—9:28. He tried Paul's cell again—no answer. He threw some money on the bar.

"It was nice to meet you, and I hope you have a better day tomorrow," Mitch said as he stood up and turned to go.

"Sure you don't want to stay and wait a little longer?"

"No—I'm going to take off. It looks like my friend's had something come up."

"Please—as I said, I had a terrible day, and I don't want to go home to a lonely apartment," Rachel pleaded. "I just want some nice company for a while. You seem like the kind of person who would like to help."

"I'm tired. I'm sorry about your day, but I am going to head on home."

"Come on—stay," Rachel said as she stood and moved in close, brushing her body against his. "I'll make it worth your while," she whispered in his ear.

Mitch was taken aback. Did he really just hear her right?

"You seem very interesting, and I am quite flattered, but I am going to go. Have a nice evening." He turned and left before she could say another word. He got in his car, started driving home, thinking of how strange the last thirty minutes had been. Mitch didn't hang out in bars and definitely had not had anyone other than his wife come on to him that strongly in a long time—probably in his entire life. *What in the world happened to Paul?* he wondered, blaming him for the awkward moment that had just occurred.

* * * *

Mitch pulled in the driveway feeling almost guilty about what had happened. He walked in the door to find Marie had already retired to the bedroom. Lynne and Jane were watching a movie; Ed was in the basement. He told his kids he was tired and kissed them all goodnight. Marie was lying on the bed watching television as well when Mitch walked in.

"How are you?" he asked.

"Fine—a little tired. How was your meeting?"

"Never had it—Paul never showed. I tried him twice on his cell but he never picked up. Anything exciting happen while I was out?"

"Nothing. I talked to my parents for a while."

Mitch had decided on the way home to tell Marie what happened. She wasn't an overly jealous person (he was much more insecure when it came to that), and he knew delaying telling her would only increase his feelings of guilt.

"Strange thing happened while I was waiting for Paul. This woman sat next to me, struck up a conversation, and then came on to me pretty strong when I got up to leave."

"Really?" said Marie in a half-believing tone. "You sure you didn't just misinterpret anything?"

"You don't misinterpret a line like 'Stay—I'll make it worth your while.'"

"She didn't say that! How old was she?" Marie was visibly flustered.

"I don't know, about thirty, I would say."

"Attractive?"

"Actually, yes, quite pretty."

"And she told you to stay?"

"Almost begged, actually. She said something about not wanting to go back to a lonely apartment—needing some company."

Marie stood up and paced the room a bit. "Are you making this up, Mitchell? It's not very funny if you are!"

"No—I just thought I should tell you. She didn't come on really strong until I was leaving—but I got out of there the minute she said that."

"Don't go back to that place. You didn't get her name, did you?" Marie was half-joking but sounded a little hurt.

"Rachel Schafer I think is what she said." Marie gave him a piercing look. "As I said—I left the minute she made that comment. You know I would never jeopardize our life together! I love you more than anything, and I would never hurt you like that!" Mitch pulled her next to him on the bed and gave her a hug.

"All the same, if Paul wants to meet you somewhere again, you pick the place from now on—and tell him your wife might show up with you," Marie said defiantly.

*   *   *   *

"So, how did it go tonight?" Charlie asked.

"Miserably," Russell replied. Charlie had two lead people on his staff that handled the messier parts of his job—Russell and Joe. They also employed about six others for security operations.

"Seriously?" Charlie replied, shocked. "I handpicked that girl myself. She's gorgeous."

"I was in the bar the whole time," Russell explained. "It wasn't for a lack of trying. Rachael did all she could. Mitch just wasn't going to take the bait."

"Okay—I'll call Gus. I'm sure we'll try something else soon. Thanks, Russ."

Charlie hung up the phone and cursed. He owed Gus a hundred bucks. Gus had told him that getting some dirt on Mitch wouldn't be that easy. He dialed the phone after checking his watch—10:05—Gus should still be working in his home office.

"So—the verdict is?" Gus answered when Charlie's named popped up on the cell phone screen. "Given that it is only slightly past ten and you are calling me already, Mitch either didn't take much convincing, and we already have what we were after, or it was a total failure. I'm guessing it was the latter."

"You were right—Mitch didn't go for it."

"I told you. We will need to take a much more subtle approach. We'll get some leverage on him."

"Sorry," Charlie replied. "I'll get something quickly."

"Don't worry about it. I expected you to fail when you told me your plan. Remember—I researched Mitch fairly extensively. I knew he had a little more integrity than to go off with some woman who tried to pick him up in a bar. The only thing to be sorry about is losing a hundred dollars to me."

"Yeah, yeah—I'll pay you tomorrow."

"Okay," Gus said as he hung up the phone. Gus was certain Charlie's suggestion would not work, but he secretly had been hoping it would. Gus felt his selection of Mitch was right for its ultimate purpose, but predicting human behavior was always difficult, at best. Gus knew he might need to have something to hold over Mitch, and the sooner he had that leverage, the more confident he would be. Gus believed in contingency plans, and he needed one if Mitch learned too much, too quickly. He smiled as he plotted how else they could get the upper hand. Charlie, on the other hand, was not wearing a smile. He hated letting Gus down, and he knew that sooner or later the animal instinct in Mitch would win out. He'd get him.

* * * *

"Mitch—it's Paul. Sorry about last night; I got held up. I was going to call you, but I realized my cell phone was out of juice. I'll get back with you later." That was the message on Mitch's work phone when he arrived at the paper that Friday morning.

You're darn right you're sorry! Mitch thought to himself, still a little miffed about what had happened the night before. He had just settled behind his desk and was about to check the Internet for news when his phone rang.

"This is Mitch Bartter," he answered.

"Greetings from Arkansas," said a familiar voice.

"Todd—how the heck are you?" Mitch asked. It had been about a month since they had talked.

"I'm great—it's summer and 104 degrees here in Little Rock," Todd said sarcastically.

"If you're looking for sympathy about the summer heat, you shouldn't call someone in Phoenix!" Mitch retorted.

"Hey, I was wondering if I could come for a visit?" Todd asked. "I've got a break for a few weeks—I thought I might come out and see Marie, maybe say hi to you, too."

"Funny—of course you can visit. We have no plans until the reunion in August. When did you think you might come?"

"Maybe Memorial Day weekend. I've got some things in Little Rock to take care of, but I'd love to fly out and see you. I know we'll see each other in August, but I'm feeling the need to get out of town for a little while. Sound good?"

"Sounds great!" Mitch said. He had not seen Todd for almost two years.

"I'm online right now—I think I'll book a flight to come down next Friday and fly back home on Monday, if that works for you guys."

"We'll make it work—I can't wait."

"See you in a week then!" Todd said enthusiastically.

Chapter 7

Karen got up that morning feeling as though the last thing she wanted to do was to go to work. She hadn't slept well for months, and last night was no exception—Karen tossed and turned for hours. The partnership she had started ten years ago with William Jensen was going through some trying times. Jensen was a tax expert and had cultivated that side of the business, which was doing fine. It was the audit side that was suffering, having lost several clients to competitors and a few others going belly up in the last several years. Karen and her other audit managers were not doing a good job of replacing this lost revenue. As the partner in charge, it was up to her to ensure that the money stream kept flowing, and it was this pressure that led to her joining Gus's team. She was not going to allow her business to become a failure.

Gus was a board member for one of Karen's larger clients. She had received a call from him a few days after her year-end audit presentation to its board of directors. Gus had told her how he respected her presence in the board meeting and how she handled herself with the board's questions. He mentioned he had an opportunity for her, outside the normal compliance work. Gus was starting an entity, and he wanted a take-charge CFO but really would only need it on a part-time basis. He thought she would be the perfect person to easily put together a small staff to handle payroll and financial reporting issues as well as provide any tax assistance.

Karen responded that she seemed terribly overqualified. She wasn't trying to sound conceited, but it seemed that for what he was talking about, Gus could get by with someone less costly. Gus liked her and was willing to pay for someone with solid experience. He didn't balk at her $450 hourly rate, and Karen believed Gus was a gateway to other new clients, with his extensive contacts. She had agreed to work for him, but first, he had to resign from the board of her client. Karen did not want any independence issues with how she ran her firm. She definitely would not allow herself to work for someone who appeared to have influence over the opinions she rendered on financial statements. Gus resigned immediately.

After assisting him in setting up the entity and putting in place the procedures for payroll reporting, he had enticed her further, as she had hoped, by setting up meetings with some potential clients, who ultimately awarded her firm their business. This helped Karen immensely for a while, but she was yet to learn of the full power Gus wielded.

About two months later, Gus explained the basics of his plan (leaving out some of the final crucial details), believing that he and Karen were of a like mind. Gus miscalculated, and Karen told him she would have nothing more to do with his Liberty Group. Gus gave her a brief, maniacal smile, saying, "I don't think you will be leaving us."

"I will not be involved in what you are planning!" Karen responded defiantly.

"Oh, I think you will. You see, I choose my participants very carefully. Your end of the partnership has been floundering for some time now. I know it, and you know it. In fact, without the few bones I threw you in the last couple months, you would be folding within a year; I'm sure of it. You probably haven't heard, but Jensen has had several offers from other firms to move his tax practice. He has not done so yet, I can only assume, out of respect for you.

"Now, with all that being said, I did choose you for a reason. I can help you tremendously, not just with clients but with pure cash. If you stay on through the entire operation, I will give you a million dollars. I reward loyalty."

"Sounds more like you purchase it," Karen replied vehemently. She wanted absolutely no part of this.

"You'll be making a big mistake," Gus warned. "I have more resources at my disposal than you can possible imagine. And I know you care for the fifty or so employees working for you. It's a tough time to be out of a job right now. *You* might be able to latch on somewhere with your public accounting connections, but what about the others? I'm sure most of your employees have families, too, so are you prepared jeopardize the well-being of I'm guessing 250 to 300 people by turning down easy money? Not if I've calculated right."

Karen knew in that instant that Gus was not to be reckoned with, and she was right where he wanted her. She acquiesced at that point, with the hope more time would provide a way out. So, here she was, a few months later and in deeper than ever. No magic solution had presented itself to eradicate her relationship with Gus's group. She continued to perform the tasks asked of her. Her guilt from knowing the basic plan was losing the battle with the feelings of responsibility she had for her employees. Gus made no secret to Karen that she would be closely watched and would be implicated in anything he was, so her telling others of his plan was no good. Additionally, as nothing had been done yet, Karen would be unable to provide evidence of illegal activity; all she had was idle chitchat. Unfortunately, Karen knew better.

She walked in the door to the firm on this Friday in mid-May, grabbed her mail, and turned the corner toward her office. The layout of the building was basically a square, with a larger conference room in one corner, Karen's spacious office in a second corner, and her partner's office in a third corner. The fourth corner was a supply room, and the center portion was the copy room, break room, and library. Along the walls were additional offices and cubicles for all the staff. To get to her office, she needed to walk halfway around the square, passing her partner, who was already at work.

William Jensen was a few years younger than she was—early forties—and impressively built at 6'3", with slim but well-toned features and sandy-colored hair. Karen was amazed that he had never married and seemed to date very little. She assumed he was too engrossed in his job to find the right person. She had thought about asking him out herself at one point, but reconsidered given their business relationship. Karen and Will had met at a one-day business conference in Phoenix. They both worked for large accounting firms at the time and shared a coffee after the conference, commiserating over some of the aspects they liked least of their respective jobs. They had joked at the time they should join forces and run a firm the right way. Weeks later, Will tracked Karen down and asked her if she had given any more thought to what they had discussed. She actually had been considering it. It was quite a difficult decision, leaving a very good job with a stable firm to start over. In the end, it was the excitement of the new opportunity that persuaded her. Will never seemed to hesitate about his choice.

Will Jensen had worked tirelessly through his early career to learn every facet of the tax code. He prided himself on knowing more than anyone else about it. He did think it was ridiculous how much the code had evolved over time to the behemoth it was now. Will was eternally in a good mood (one of the traits Karen liked most), and Karen had never seen him get riled, even with the numerous tax deadlines they were up against at times, most of which were caused either by the clients themselves not providing all the information in a timely fashion, or because of inexperienced associates not pulling their weight at crunch time. He always kept his cool.

This was nothing next to his creativity and knowledge of his clients' businesses. She had seen him save hundreds of thousands of dollars for some of their larger clients. Karen was almost ashamed of how much of the success of the partnership was attributable to him and how little, she felt, was due to her own efforts. Karen had thought about confiding to Will her issues with Gus. So far she had not—telling herself that the fewer people who knew, the better; that she was protecting him. Deep down, she probably didn't tell him for fear of losing his respect.

"Good morning, Karen!" Will greeted her enthusiastically as she passed his office door. "I wasn't sure if I'd be seeing you in this morning. It seems most of the office is either at a client today or off on vacation. I think it is just you, me, and a few of the younger staff studying for the CPA exam."

"Good morning, Will," Karen managed to respond. "I just have a few things to review, and I'm taking off. I'll be in my office if you need anything."

"Could I have a word before you leave today? I want to run something by you."

"Sure, no problem." Karen continued to her office, sat down, and took a sip of her Starbucks coffee. She reluctantly grabbed a file from one of the nonprofit organizations the firm audited and began her review. Two hours and three files later, Karen decided she had had enough. She packed up and started to head out, reaching the front of the office before remembering Will had wanted to talk to her. She turned back and knocked on Will's door.

"Come in."

Karen walked in to an impeccably organized office. He had a phone, computer, and adding machine on his desk, and nothing else. Not one credenza had a stray folder or extra scrap of paper lying on top of it. He was just putting away the file he had been working on, and Karen heard a Bare Naked Ladies CD playing on his computer.

"Thanks for stopping by—I hope I'm not keeping you from anything?" Will asked.

"No, I'm just going to head home," Karen answered. "I may go work out later today, but other than that, I have nothing planned. So, what did you want to talk about?"

"Well, at the risk of sounding like a parent, I'm worried about you. Are you feeling all right—is anything bothering you?"

"I'm fine," Karen lied. "Why do you ask?"

"Is it the firm—are you concerned about business?" Will probed, ignoring her question. Karen's expression gave her away. Will moved from behind his desk to sit next to her in the other chair on the opposite side. Karen continued looking down, not meeting his eyes.

"Don't worry," Will stated. "It will work out. We'll get through this little rough patch. You have done a great job bringing in a few new clients recently. I'm sure you'll continue to work your magic. If we need to cut back on some staff in the short term, we'll have to, but we'll come through the downturn stronger than ever. We both know that the business environment is extremely difficult right now, and Washington isn't helping us any." Karen looked up and stared Will in the eyes. She had never noticed how kind his eyes looked—a beautiful brown shade. He was beginning to get some age lines at the corners, but they only seemed to enhance the friendliness of his appearance.

"I need you to give me a truthful answer," Karen began. "Have you had offers to take your tax practice to other firms?"

Will hesitated for a minute. He was guessing Karen was in an emotional state, and he did not want to add to her burdens, but he also wanted to be honest.

"Actually, yes, I have had a few people call me. I have rejected their proposals outright. We have a good foundation here. I have no desire to move somewhere else. I love what you and I have built together. This firm is my proudest achievement."

The affirmation of what Gus had told her months ago seemed to unlock the barrier to her emotions and tears starting pouring out. She tried to gain control of them, but was unable to.

"Hey—it's going to be fine," Will said, trying to calm her. "The firms that called can't hold a candle to what we have and where we can go. We always talked about how we liked the ability to control the size and the speed of growth. We're doing things the right way here. Every business goes through difficult times. We'll make it."

"It's not that—well, it is that, ultimately," Karen sobbed. "I'm into something that I cannot talk about."

"You can tell me anything," Will replied sincerely. "I'll help in any way I can."

"You're doing all you can already to make us successful," Karen said, regaining her composure. "I know the tax side has been carrying us for a few years. Hopefully, I'll be able to have the audit side contribute more very soon."

"Karen, what can I do? What are you involved in?"

"I'm just dealing with some personal stuff that I would rather not burden you with. You are very kind to offer, but I'll be fine. You've already helped, letting me cry on your shoulder like this. I'm going to get going."

Will stood as she did, taking her hand in his. "If you change you mind about talking or if you need assistance with anything, please call me." He gave her hand a gentle squeeze.

"Thank you again," she said as she left.

Chapter 8

Todd's airplane left for Phoenix at 10:00 am on the Friday morning before Memorial Day. Todd liked traveling and had been to many parts of the world. Similar to Mitch, he was also tall with a little more meat on his bones but had sandy blonde hair and deep blue eyes. In college, Todd was always the one the girls would go for when the four roommates were all out together. Mitch and Mark were both fairly attractive as well, but Todd was clearly the top choice among the females. Al wasn't even in the running—the red hair and freckles not being in the classically handsome category. However, by their senior year at BGSU, Mitch, Mark, and Al all had serious girlfriends who ultimately became their wives, and Todd had yet to be in a serious relationship.

As Todd settled back into his seat on the plane, he thought about some of the parties they used to throw back at Bowling Green. Becoming a college professor meant Todd had remained perpetually in a similar setting he and his roommates enjoyed, and he often thought about their time spent living in the apartment on Merry Avenue. He closed his eyes as the plane gained speed down the runway and replayed one of the scenes he remembered with fondness.

"Hey, Mitch—how you holding up?" Todd asked as he finished off another beer. The party had been going on for hours and about forty people were packed into their apartment. Luckily, they lived on the bottom floor.

"I'm awesome!" Mitch yelled over the music.

"Really—you seem like you've had quite a bit, even for you."

"No really—I'm great. I'm about to get another one right now."

"Where's Marie?" Todd asked.

"I think she is in the bathroom. Can I get you a piece of pizza?" Mitch asked, holding out a rather small slice.

"Nope, nope, nope, nope, nope. I want a big one!" Todd responded, in his best Jimmy Stewart impression, holding his arms wide apart.

"*It's a Wonderful Life*—George Bailey—in Gower's store buying a suitcase," Al chimed in, having walked up to the table right after Mitch and Todd.

"Very good, Al," Todd said, reaching into the box of Pisanello's pizza and finding the biggest slice there. "But, I knew you would get it—I don't know that Mitch would have known that one. I didn't see you there."

"Lisa needed another beer," Al said.

"I've been meaning to ask you—how did you ever get her to agree to marry you?" Todd asked incredulously. "She's flat-out hot! And she's settling for a dweeb, red-headed accountant! Who would have thought that?"

Al knew Todd was joking, but he also knew that the level of alcohol in Todd's blood was working somewhat like a truth serum, turning off some of the normal social filters. Al had always known that Todd was attracted to Lisa. "Shh—don't tell her I'm an accounting major; she thinks I'm pre-med!" Al joked back.

"That would explain it," Todd said. Mitch had been downing his own piece of pizza as Todd turned on him now.

"So—are you going to marry Marie? It sure seems like you are heading that way."

"If I'm lucky enough to call her my wife someday, that would be incredible. It seems a little premature to think about it, though."

"Premature—you've been dating over a year longer than Lisa and I, and we're already talking China patterns," Al said.

"Yeah, well, of all the people I know, I thought you were the most reasonable and would be the most patient when it came to getting engaged," Mitch responded.

"I was patient—I knew after a month that I was going to marry her—or at least try anything I could to get her to marry me! I waited an entire additional month and a half after that to ask her. By the way, you'll both stand up for me at my wedding, right? Mark and you two, along with my brother—agreed?"

"Well, I don't know," said Mitch. "What's going to be the gift for the wedding party? Get back with us on that, and we'll let you know."

A very inebriated Mark then joined the group, throwing his arms around both Mitch and Todd.

"How many beers have I had? I think I've had sixteen or seventeen beers! A—how many have you had? Ooh—pizza. Give me a slice!" Mark was about three inches shorter than the other roommates, with a stockier build. He had played football (running back) at Ashland College for a year before transferring to Bowling Green and meeting Mitch, Al, and Todd in the dorms. Mark was from northwest Ohio as well, and Mitch had remembered Mark as an opponent in basketball—their high schools were in the same league. Al had played basketball, too, more of a benchwarmer than a player, though. He had no recollection of Mark when they first met.

"Al here was just asking us all to be in his wedding," Todd said to Mark.

"Great, man—I'm in!" Mark replied.

"Thanks, Mark," Al said, wondering if Mark would remember any of this the next day.

The music suddenly became even louder, and the four of them turned to see another friend, Bill, turning up the stereo, grabbing a beer from someone else's hand, and putting his arm around Robin, Mark's girlfriend.

"Got to go," Mark said, and he turned to head in Bill's direction. The other three looked at each other.

"I think we better make sure Mark doesn't do anything stupid, and we should make sure Bill doesn't provoke him," Al said.

As they started through the crowd, Mitch had the clearer path, even beating Mark to the spot, and he stayed between Bill and Mark while creating the space for Robin to move toward her boyfriend. Mitch steered Bill back through the throng of college drunkenness and out onto the cement step, shutting the door and deafening the noise just a bit. Bill was another accounting major that Al and Mitch knew from a few classes, but not very well at all.

"Bill—how much have you had to drink?" Mitch asked.

"Not enough yet," he replied. "What are we doing out here? That girl is hot! Let me go back."

"You might not have known, but that girl is our roommate's girlfriend. He's drunk as can be and probably doesn't have the patience he should for another drunken SOB hitting on her."

Bill looked crestfallen. "I'm sorry, Mitch—*my* girlfriend broke up with me this afternoon, and I'm not dealing with it very well. We had been together for two years. I thought I saw that girl in there staring at me, so I was just seeing if she was interested."

"I can tell you she is head over heels for Mark. You probably saw what you wanted to see. We've all been there. I'm sorry about your girlfriend."

"I think I'll head home," Bill said sadly.

"You don't have to go. I'll talk to my roommate—he'll understand. You'll just need to stay away from Robin—that's her name." Marie opened the door and stepped outside, followed quickly by Todd.

"What's going on?" she asked.

"My fine accounting friend and I were having a little chat," Mitch replied. "I was just inviting him back inside."

"No, thanks," Bill said. "I'm going home. You're right—I think I've had enough."

"We'll walk you home," Mitch said, nodding at Marie and Todd, pleading with his eyes that this was something he thought they needed to do.

"That would be great," Marie responded. "I need a break from the noise, and I could use some fresh air."

"Suit yourselves," Bill said, shrugging his shoulders. They turned to walk south down Thurstin Street, which was the western border of the campus, toward Bill's apartment. Mitch could now hear in the distance Mark leading what sounded like most of the apartment in a group sing of Bad Company's "Feel Like Makin' Love."

After walking a block or so, Marie started up the conversation.

"Are you sure you're okay, Bill?" she asked. He seemed distraught as they walked.

"I'm actually feeling lost. I really thought I was going to marry the woman who said some very mean things to me today. Now, I act totally inappropriately to someone else. That's not me. I'm just—I don't know." Bill shook his head, obviously embarrassed.

"Listen, Bill, I know we accountants will always be in demand from the ladies," Mitch joked. "If it is meant to be, you two will find each other again. I'm convinced of that. I know there is someone special for you. But you have to be positive. That makes all the difference!" They had arrived at Bill's apartment and knocked on the door. Bill's roommate answered.

"There you are, Bill. I was wondering about you." Bill went to the kitchen to look for some food.

"Do you know Bill and his girlfriend broke up today?" Mitch asked the roommate.

"I just found out. I called her apartment looking for him, and she told me."

"You're going to be here all weekend, right?" Marie asked.

"Yeah, why?" responded the roommate, confused.

"Because he needs a friend all weekend—he's down and he's hurt," Marie responded forcefully. "He really shouldn't be alone. Promise us you will stay with him."

"You got it. You're right. I won't leave him alone at all."

"Mitch—give him your phone number," Marie said.

"Good idea—call us if you need to go do something," Todd added. "We'll help if necessary. Bill, we're leaving."

"See you later," Bill responded feebly. He had overheard the entire conversation and was completely humbled by the kindness these people were showing for his well-being.

Todd smiled as the airplane captain came on to tell them how high they would be flying and what they might see on the way to Phoenix. He closed his eyes and thought more of his own college days, eventually drifting off to sleep.

* * * * *

"So, give me an update on Mitch," Gus demanded. Gus, Paul, and Charlie were meeting together; Mitch and Karen had not been invited.

"Well," Paul began, "he has been doing everything we have asked of him. He has ten different writers now contributing, and these are good articles. He takes care of getting all the pertinent information for payroll, and things seem to be working like clockwork. He keeps trying to expand the information and the number of states. Mitch is working much more quickly than we anticipated. He has been great."

"That's good," Gus said almost absentmindedly. "How about obtaining some leverage—how is that going?"

"We haven't tried anything else yet," Charlie said. "We've scoured his financial records as well. Pays his taxes on time. He has a little credit card debt, but nothing abnormal for someone with three kids and a mortgage. I don't think we will get financial leverage. Mitch does have a friend coming into town today. I've got something planned to see if we can't lure the friend and have him bring Mitch along as well."

"Is this the accountant that is writing articles as well?" Gus asked.

"No—this one lives in Arkansas," Charlie responded. "He's a college professor—from what we have picked up, he's a bit of a free spirit, though we haven't done any serious digging. Do you want us to?"

"No—let's see what happens on his visit. You continue to have Mitch followed, correct?"

"At all times—just like you said."

"Gus, why so close a surveillance on this guy?" Paul asked.

"He is the one major person we are using that has the least knowledge of our ultimate goal. We want to keep it that way for as long as possible. As you guys said before we brought him in, he is a smart guy. If he starts catching wind that we are using him for an ulterior motive, I want to know immediately. You know how I hate surprises."

"And that is why you are so determined to have an ace up your sleeve in regards to his participation, if necessary?" Paul again questioned.

"Exactly. The timing is starting to come together. This summer is going to be a blast—but it has to be set up right. He can't know anything too soon, and if he does, we need to be able to convince him to keep things quiet. Is that understood?" Gus may have phrased his comment as a question, but the others took it as a command.

"Of course," Paul and Charlie answered together.

* * * * *

Mitch picked up Todd at the airport, and they headed toward Mitch's house.

"Good flight?" he asked.

"It was fine—I slept most of the way," Todd answered.

"So—what did you say on the phone—you're here until Monday; is that right?" Mitch asked.

"Yeah, just a few days—sorry it is so short, but we will have August, too. I need to head back on Monday for several reasons."

"Well, what would you like to do while you are here?" Mitch questioned. "We have never taken you to Sedona—it's a gorgeous area."

"I'm up for anything—Sedona sounds good. I always enjoy a baseball game, too," Todd said.

"Unfortunately, the Diamondbacks are up in Oakland this weekend, but maybe we can catch part of game on TV or at a sports bar," Mitch said enthusiastically.

"Got any time for golf?" Todd asked.

"I can always make time for golf. Why don't we plan on Sedona tomorrow, golf on Sunday, and maybe even tonight catching the game somewhere. I will need to finish a few work-related items at some point. Have I told you about my recent additional project?"

"No—but Al mentioned something when we talked. It was in your last message, too. Sounds interesting, but let's not get too much into politics right now."

"No problem," Mitch said, smiling.

Mitch and Todd became fast friends at BGSU. Mitch and Al had roomed together as freshman in an older dormitory on the east end of campus, and then again as sophomores, but moved to the newer Offenhauer Towers, where they met Todd and Mark. They all lived on the same floor and ultimately rented an apartment together for the last two years in college.

Mitch was always more of the athlete and Todd more of the academic, especially when it came to popular culture. Todd was constantly bringing a new type of music or an obscure movie into the apartment and forever asking trivia questions to his friends. And of course, there was the endless quoting of movies. Mitch could not believe the amount of useless knowledge Todd stored in his head, although

Todd thought the same thing about the sports statistics that Mitch could rattle off. Mark had no use for either of these things, while Al was able to hang with both Todd and Mitch, no matter the senseless topic being discussed.

The two spent the afternoon at Mitch's house, catching up with Marie and the kids. Todd admired the changes to the house since his last visit, but had a hard time comprehending how old the kids seemed.

"That happens—kids grow up and change," Mitch said matter-of-factly. "They are almost twice the age they were when you last saw them. "

"I know—it just doesn't seem that long ago," Todd replied.

"Believe me—it doesn't to me either," Mitch said.

Early in the evening, Mitch and Todd headed out to BW-3's. As they pulled into the parking lot, they were oblivious to the dark sedan pulling in behind them. They headed to the bar area, and Mitch ordered a Sam Adams while Todd opted for a Bud Light. They had just put their order in for some wings when two very pretty young women came in and sat at the bar near them. Todd noticed them immediately, but knew that his time was to be spent with Mitch. Besides, these women seemed quite young for him, maybe just out of college, if that.

Mitch reached for his beer while looking at the television screen, accidentally picking up Todd's Bud Light. Todd wrapped his hand around Mitch's wrist and pointed a finger in his face.

"Is very bad to drink JoBu's rum. Very bad," Todd said in a Caribbean accent.

"*Major League*," Mitch said, a little uncertain if it was the correct movie. "And sorry about that."

"Very good," Todd said. "So—you're here in Arizona for the long haul—going to retire here?"

"Retire—that seems a little bit away. But overall, yes, I think we have built enough of a life here to call Arizona home now. How about you—you staying in Little Rock for another twenty years?"

"No way. I like my position and the university, but you know me, always looking for something different. I have actually been looking into the possibility of teaching overseas."

"Really—where?" said a soft voice on Todd's other side. The two young women he had noticed in the bar area had now positioned themselves on either side of Mitch and Todd. "And what do you teach?" asked the same voice. She had blonde hair and deep blue eyes. As she was closer now, and since he saw co-eds almost every day at work, he knew she could be no more than twenty-one.

"I teach popular culture. Thanks for asking. Are you here with your parents?" Todd joked.

"Do I look that young? I tell you what—let me buy your next drink and that will prove that I am old enough to purchase alcohol at least."

"No—you won't be buying me a drink," Todd said, looking at Mitch and smiling. "I will be happy to buy one for you and your friend, but my buddy and I have not seen each other in a long time, and we are just catching up."

"We'd love to hear about what you guys do," said the woman on the other side of Mitch. She was a brunette, shorter than her friend, but with high cheek bones and a brilliant smile. She flirtatiously batted her eyes as she said this.

"Would you?" said Mitch. "Well, I write for the *Republic*, and when I'm finished with that, I go home to my beautiful wife and three kids."

"Now, why did you have to go and spoil our fantasy?" said the brunette.

"Your fantasy—what, to see if you could embarrass two middle-aged men?" Mitch asked sarcastically.

"No—you two are very attractive," replied the blonde. "We noticed you the minute we came in and couldn't help coming over to see you. Where do you teach popular culture?" She had noticed that Todd did not sport a wedding ring like Mitch.

"Actually, in Arkansas. As I said, I just got in today, and Mitch here and I were trying to catch up." Todd was torn. He did like to flirt, although he knew that he was not going to act on any of this with someone so much younger. He had had a few situations with undergrads before and had come dangerously close to making some decisions that would possibly have cost him a job or two. However, he had never slept with a student, and even though these women were not Razorbacks, he was not going to be tempted.

The waitress set their wing orders in front of them.

"We'll let you eat in peace and catch up," said the blonde, motioning to her friend.

"Thanks—we appreciate that," Mitch said.

He and Todd had a fun dinner reminiscing about BGSU, talking about old friends, and discussing their respective stages of life. Todd never was looking for a companion, being perfectly happy with his carefree lifestyle. He was serious about teaching overseas.

"I'd love to learn a new language, while maybe teaching English in another country," he said.

"Have you picked out the country—or do you have a list of potentials?"

"I haven't sent any correspondence yet, but maybe Italy."

"Have you talked with Al? He and Lisa spent about ten days in Italy last fall," Mitch reminded Todd.

"That's right—I'll bring it up with them next month when we are all back at BGSU. Do you know if everyone is coming?"

"I know Mark and Robin will definitely be there, with their boys; obviously you; and, of course, Al and his family. What about your old roommate—Dave Tellman?"

"You know, I haven't talked to him in years."

Mitch excused himself to go to the bathroom. As he was the driver, he had switched from Sam Adams to Diet Coke after the first beer, but the order of blazin'-flavored wings had kept him downing glass after glass. The blonde approached Todd again after Mitch had left.

"Your friend seems like he could use a little fun," she said playfully. "Convince him that we should all go do something."

"He told you he was married," Todd replied.

"We don't care."

"Maybe I do—how do you know he's not married to my sister?" Todd asked.

"Is he?" she asked, calling his bluff.

"Well, no, but she is a good friend of mine. He's never going to go out with you two, and besides, we're too old for you. Go find some younger guys to flirt with."

"We want to flirt with you two."

Mitch exited the bathroom and headed toward Todd. He could see the blonde was up close and personal. He did not see the brunette come at him from the side.

"Are you and your friend all caught up?" she asked. "Ready now for some fun?"

"Boy, am I," Mitch responded. "I think I'll go home and have some fun with my wife."

"Come on, don't be like that," the brunette said as seductively as she could.

Mitch could not believe this was happening again. He walked past the brunette and away from Todd to the front of the restaurant. He found their server, paid the bill, and returned to get his friend.

"Come on, Todd—we're going now," Mitch commanded.

"See—I told you," Todd said to the blonde.

The two men left the restaurant, getting into Mitch's Honda. He tore out of the parking lot.

"I can't believe that just happened again!" Mitch exclaimed.

"I know," agreed Todd. "You would have thought they had got the message before we ate."

"No—I mean someone tried to pick me up a few weeks ago, too."

"Was she as hot as they were?" Todd asked.

"She was beautiful—a little older though, maybe thirty," Mitch answered.

"Maybe I'll rethink my Italy plans and move here," Todd responded.

"It's not funny, Todd—it seems awfully coincidental," Mitch pondered. "Twice in a couple weeks."

"Oh, tonight was just because you were with me," Todd joked. "I can't walk down a street without a few twenty-something-year-old women throwing themselves at me."

"Right, Casanova. Whatever. I, however, at least up until the last few weeks, could go anywhere without that happening, and I like it that way. It's just really strange."

* * * *

"What—*again?*" Marie said when they got home and told her about the evening's events.

"And, Marie—they were smoking hot!" Todd exclaimed.

"Watch it, Todd!" Marie said to Todd, knowing he was joking to rile her.

"I'd say they were every bit as hot as those girls that lived around the corner from us on East Merry," Todd said convincingly.

"We lived around the corner from you on Merry Street!" Marie shouted.

"Right—your neighbors," Todd said, unable to repress a laugh.

"Todd—you …" Marie cut off, starting to laugh, too. "Well, that settles it—I guess I am just going to have to come with you from now on whenever you go out to eat."

"Okay—but then you're going to have to develop a taste for wings," Mitch retorted.

"Maybe I will risk you still going out on your own," Marie joked.

*　*　*　*

The next morning, Mitch's family and Todd all piled into the mini-van and headed out early. Sedona, often called Red Rock country, offers unbelievably beautiful views of rock formations in the Arizona desert.

"How often do you guys go up to Sedona?" Todd inquired.

"Not very," Marie answered. "Usually, only when we have visitors who have not seen it. I don't think we have been up there since Al and Lisa were here."

"When was that?"

"When Al ran that marathon out here—I don't know—five or six years ago."

"So, what's special about Sedona?" Todd asked.

"Wait until we get there," Mitch replied. "You did bring the camera, right, Marie? I want to make sure I get a picture of Todd in a pink Jeep." As they turned onto I-17 North, no one in the car noticed the black sedan trailing about two hundred yards behind.

"So, any of you want to come to Arkansas for college?" Todd asked the kids.

"Never really thought about it," Lynne answered. Lynne was taller than most of her friends, about the height of her mom but shorter than her younger sister. She had long brown hair and had just finished up her junior year in high school, so college choices were definitely starting to swim around her brain.

"Where are you considering?" Todd asked, eager to learn more about Mitch's kids.

"Well, I am of course looking at the programs of the larger schools here in Arizona, but I ultimately want to be a lawyer, so I'm still deciding what my undergraduate degree will be."

"I'm going to Arizona State University," Jane said confidently.

"You know that already?" Todd asked.

"I spent a week there last summer at a science camp—it was great!" Jane answered enthusiastically.

"And what will you study?" Todd questioned.

"Archeology. I'm going to Greece to be an archeologist," she responded matter-of-factly.

"You have it all figured out, don't you?" Todd said, smiling. "How about you, Ed?"

No answer. Todd turned around to see Ed with his earphones in listening to his MP3 player. *Oh, well, I'll ask him later,* Todd thought.

After a couple of hours, they pulled into Sedona, found a public parking lot, used the restroom, and headed for the Jeep tours.

"We'll take the tour—it is about two hours long, and then we'll get some lunch," Mitch said.

It wasn't long, and they were heading out of town into the desert. Todd was still trying to take in the beauty. The views were truly breathtaking on this sunny day. The black sedan had found a parking place as well, and its two occupants had followed the group at a safe distance. They had known the group was going to Sedona, so the shadows had dressed casually.

"Do you think we should follow them, Joe?" Russell asked.

"You've never been here before, have you?" Joe replied. "They have to come back here anyhow. We'll just wait. The tour will last a few hours."

Mitch, Marie, Todd, and the kids had taken the Broken Arrow tour. This option included views of Submarine Rock and Chicken Point, although Todd about lost his cool as the Jeep descended the Road to Nowhere. He thought for sure the vehicle would flip back over front, as steep as it seemed. The views were spectacular, and the guide was very knowledgeable about the area. The two hours flew past in a whirl of picture taking and soaking in the unbelievable vistas.

Upon returning from the Jeep tour, the group settled themselves at the Oak Creek Brewery and Grill for some lunch, still discussing what they had seen. Mitch and Todd ordered some microbrews, and they all enjoyed the Earl of Steak Sandwich, except Marie, who opted for the spinach salad. Mitch was just finishing off his meal when he noticed two gentlemen who looked familiar to him.

"Do you remember seeing the guys at that table anywhere before?" Mitch discreetly asked Marie. The kids were listening to a story Todd was relating about some of the excuses college students had given him as to why they had missed an assignment.

"No—I've never seen them before," Marie answered.

"I'm sure I have seen them—together," Mitch said, puzzling where it had been.

"They look like tourists to me—I suppose they could be from Phoenix, though. Maybe they eat at B-W's, too—you're in there enough."

Mitch laughed. "I guess—maybe." Mitch shook off his thoughts of the strangers, and they all enjoyed some chocolate fantasy dessert—again, Marie opting for a healthier alternative.

* * * * *

Mitch and Todd stayed up late that night, sitting by Mitch's pool talking about college while drinking a little more than normal.

"Beer seems to taste just a little better under the Arizona sky," Todd commented as he opened another bottle. "Of course, it could just be that I'm enjoying the conversation and the company."

"Thanks for the compliment—and thanks for coming, Todd. It really means a lot."

"What do you miss most about college?" Todd asked.

"Oh, I think most people would say they miss the carefree days—deciding what you want to do and, for the most part, when you can do it. I miss hanging with you and Al and Mark most of all."

"Aren't you sweet?" Todd replied sarcastically.

"How about you, Todd; what do you miss most?" Mitch turned the question on his friend.

"Everything. I loved college. I loved the feeling that the campus was its own separate world. And now, being in my early forties, I love being surrounded by youth. It actually makes me feel younger. But, truthfully, I miss the friendship we had—sharing everyday experiences together—all of us—Al and Mark and the numerous other people we saw on an everyday basis. I think that is ultimately why I became a college professor. I wanted to stay in the college world."

They sat there in silence, gazing up at the brilliant star-clad desert sky, contemplating what each other had said. Todd started the conversation back up a few minutes later.

"What scares you most, Mitch?"

"What do you mean?" Mitch responded.

"I mean, what keeps you up at night? What bothers you most?"

"Getting very deep tonight, aren't we? I guess I worry most about the health and safety of my family. Time goes by so fast, and we have these precious few years together. Tragedies happen every day. I don't know how I would cope if anything happened to Marie or the kids." Todd could see that Mitch's eyes had misted over a bit.

"I am also concerned," Mitch continued, "that I am not being the best husband or father. Now that my kids are older, everything seemed easier when they were toddlers. You could read them a story, or play tea party or Little Bear with them, and everything seemed fine. Now, they spend so much time away from us. And of course, I am so lucky to have Marie—I need to ensure I am tending to what she needs."

"What do you mean?" Todd asked.

"I know you are not married, but I see so many couples that take each other for granted, and after a few years, they stop doing the little things for each other. I believe that's how people start the growing apart process. I have told myself that I will never let that happen."

"That's a much better answer than I thought you would give—here I was anticipating you would say something about Obama and the current Congress scaring you. You're right about one thing, though—

The Liberty Group

you are lucky to have Marie—she's as good as they get! I don't know why she picked you."

"It's a mystery," Mitch agreed. "Anyhow—I guess more immediately, I am concerned about the kids' college education. I want them to go wherever they want, and I know they are willing to work for it, but I want to provide as much of that as I can. You live in the world of academia—you know how much out-of-state tuition is. Anyhow, enough about my fears. How about you, Todd; what scares you?"

"I asked you because I have given this some thought. I guess my biggest concern right now is not knowing when I am successful—does that make sense? I cannot define my version of success."

"I'm not quite sure I'm following—sounds like you are doubting what you are doing," Mitch said.

"Well—how do you define success?" Todd rephrased the question.

"I would say if I am happy, then I am successful. I am happy if I know I am doing a good job at work and at home," Mitch replied.

"That's pretty black-and-white description. You seem to have it all figured out."

"Are you happy, Todd?" Mitch asked straight out.

"That's it—I don't know. I am as happy as I have ever been—I just don't know if I am as happy as I can be."

"You are quite philosophical tonight."

"It must be the beer," Todd said. The two friends sat quietly together, thankful for this brief time together.

* * * * *

Mitch and Todd awoke early on Sunday morning, enjoyed a round of golf at the Raven Golf Course at South Mountain, where Mitch shot twelve strokes better than Todd, had a late lunch after the round, and headed back to Mitch's. The remainder of the evening was spent playing games with the kids and enjoying a wonderful meal that Marie had prepared. Todd headed back to Arkansas the next day, wishing he did not have to go.

"You could always move out here, Todd," Mitch suggested. "We have universities in Phoenix, too, you know."

"I'll consider that. Maybe that is the missing ingredient. Who knows? See you in about a month—BGSU again—I can't wait!"

"Neither can we—travel safely, Todd," Mitch said, giving his friend a hug as he dropped him off at the airport.

Chapter 9

Gus had set a special Monday meeting of his upper management of Liberty Group without Mitch. Specifically without Mitch. He wanted continual updates on what Mitch was doing, where he had been going, and how Charlie, Paul, and Karen felt the selection of Mr. Bartter was progressing thus far. The general discussion was that everyone liked Mitch and thought he was perfect. They reviewed his articles as well as the number of hits the Web site was getting. The money for advertising and selling memberships (allowing greater access to additional information and research) was coming in much faster and in greater quantities than anticipated.

Conversation turned to the tactics being deployed in Mitch's surveillance, as well as the information that had been learned thus far. Charlie provided the report and gave details of the conversations overheard as well as the second failed attempt at luring Mitch into some offense worthy of blackmail.

"Have you thought that this guy might just actually be a decent person, and maybe he loves his wife?" Karen asked, still not comprehending how far into this situation she had come.

"Or maybe he prefers gentlemen—he wouldn't be the first to have a wife and kids, yet swing from the other side of the plate," Charlie hypothesized.

"Not everyone acts like you do, Charlie!" Gus spat at him. "Either way, I think it was recklessly foolish to try the same tactic twice. I expect better out of you. Mitch is smart—he might see a pattern developing—putting two and two together. These incidents start happening at the same time he joins our group. We need to do something different. Still haven't found anything in his background that we can use?"

"Nope—he got married right out of college, went to work, started having kids, coached their little league teams, helps out at their schools, was treasurer of his church for awhile, no signs of affairs, no unethical dealings at the paper, nothing. This guy should run for Congress." Charlie shook his head.

"Well—think of something and run it by me this time before you try it," Gus demanded.

"Do we have to have anything?" Karen implored. "Why is it necessary to bring down a good guy? He's doing all that we are asking of him. Isn't he playing the role you want him to? You haven't told me the final details of the plan, so maybe I do not understand everything fully, but I can't see why you feel it is necessary to be able to destroy this guy's world." Her disgust for this group was growing by the second.

Gus's eyes bored in on Karen, slanting slightly. "Karen—we have been over this—I like to have contingency plans. I will have my leverage. I will not allow an unfortunate turn of events, like Mitch getting wise to us, to put a stop to our objectives."

"Our backyard ears did pick up a conversation he had with his friend Todd a little over a week ago," Charlie offered. "Mostly sappy friend stuff, but at one point, Mitch discussed being concerned about the financial obligations coming up with his kids approaching their college years. Maybe a bribe or financial windfall scheme will trip him up."

"We're bugging his backyard now?" Karen asked, a look of disdain on her face.

"His backyard and certain rooms in his house," Gus answered sternly. "Karen—let it go. Obviously, sex isn't going to work—so, yes, attempt another tried and true tactic—good old-fashioned greed. And let's consider a little trap for his wife, too."

Karen rolled her eyes but said nothing. The revulsion she was feeling was becoming harder to ignore. She had to find a way out of this situation. Paul noticed her body language and made a mental note to talk to her later.

* * * *

The idea had been brewing in Mitch's head for awhile now, and he was curious if his friend would be interested. As he was finishing up his workday on Monday, Mitch give Al a call.

"What are you up to, A?" Mitch asked when Al answered.

"I'm waiting to pick up Savannah. She had a drama club meeting at the school tonight. To tell you the truth, I just finishing talking with a congressional representative."

"What? Who?" Mitch asked in quick succession.

"Bob Latta—he's our district's representative. He was here waiting to pick up his daughter, so I thought I would talk to him a bit about what is happening right now."

"Can I ask what side of the aisle he calls home?"

"Staunch conservative," Al replied. "Hey—it is Bowling Green. Seriously, he is new to Washington, but I do not think you would have any complaints about how he has voted thus far. What are you doing?"

"I wanted to talk to you about an idea I had. Your articles are being received well. Have you followed the comments on the site?"

"Thanks, Mitch—yes, I have perused a few of them," Al answered.

"But I've written only a few articles. It all seems very strange. You put some thoughts down, and people love to respond to them."

"Welcome to the world of blogging. I did see that quite a few people liked your latest article about John Kasich."

"Do you remember him from his days in the House?" Al asked. "He was part of the Contract with American group. I think he will be a great governor for Ohio! It should be a fun election season. By the way, you won't believe what the Ohio government did this week. Talk about taking a page from the federal book. They passed a 3,000-page budget just eight hours after receiving the document. Our State Representative Randy Gardner said it best. 'There's no doubt that when government does something this big this fast and not in public … clearly, there will be mistakes, and problems that come to light over the next days, weeks, and months.'"

"That is good," said Mitch. "Listen, I don't have a lot of time. Here's my idea. I would like to try something on the Web site. I want to advertise a few days ahead of time that you will be live on the Web site in a debate over taxes with a selected liberal. You two will go back and forth on the individual income tax issue. You seem to have a great grasp for it."

"Me—are you sure I'm you're guy?" Al asked apprehensively. "You know as much if not more than I do. Your article a few weeks ago was fantastic."

"That's part of the plan—I will play the other side. I will try to give all the liberal arguments I've heard over the years. This will be great!" Mitch was very enthused about this brainchild of his.

"I don't know—sounds a bit like a setup," Al questioningly replied.

"Not at all—well, I guess maybe a little. But I will try to refute everything you say." After a little more explanation, Al thought he had the general gist of the situation.

"So, let's see if I totally understand. We pick a time to have a live chat on the Liberty Web site about taxes, specifically individual income taxes. I will start with a statement about the current system, and you will come in with questions and comments, and it will go from there."

"That's right—I won't even give you any more direction than that," Mitch continued. "I think I know where you stand. You can take it in whatever direction you want, and I will give my best liberal discussion with you."

"When would you like to have this little talk?"

"How about next Monday, say around one o'clock your time? Can you do that from work?"

"If I come in early and work through the normal lunch hour, I'll just take my lunch later. Is an hour enough time?"

"That should be more than enough. I'll put a note on the site that a 'businessman from Ohio' will be having a discussion with a liberal volunteer regarding taxes at that time—I'm sure we'll have more than a few comments when it is all done. Just log on next Monday and go to the discussion page. We'll shut out all others from the actual give and take and allow their comments after."

"Sounds fun—I'll get preparing," Al said as the friends ended their conversation.

* * * *

Mitch wanted to do a little preparation work himself, not only for his online discussion about taxes, but about a few other articles he had been considering. The family had just finished a dinner of pesto chicken he had prepared, and the kids were working on their homework. Marie had jumped on her laptop and was immersed in whatever she was surfing, so Mitch began the outline for an article.

"Dad—you should have heard our teacher today in current events," Lynne said from across the room. She was sitting in the family room studying while Mitch was at the bar counter in the kitchen.

"Yeah, what was that?" he replied, not looking up from his own computer.

"She said that Republicans should have the donkey symbol because they are a bunch of ..." Lynne hesitated.

"Jackasses?" Mitch said, finishing the thought he had heard from several other people before.

"Well—yeah, that is what she said."

"Did she say this to class in general?" Mitch asked.

"No—in fact, I don't think she knew any student heard her say it. Another teacher was in the room, and I walked in as they were talking."

Mitch just smirked a little and turned back to his work.

"You're not going to comment on that?" Lynne asked, slightly surprised.

"Did you say anything to your teacher?"

"No—I acted as if I hadn't heard."

"Do you agree with your teacher?" Mitch probed further.

"You know I don't. I just don't pay enough attention to what either side says right now. A lot of my friends are Obama supporters, though. Still, I thought you would be upset that a teacher would say something like that."

"If she were to make that comment to the class as if it were the only way to think, then, yes, I would have a major problem. If she was in a private conversation with someone else, then she has every right to express her opinion. As I have tried to convey through my articles, we must as a nation get past feeling offended by the opinions of others, especially in politics. This Internet world of blogging and Facebooking has led to so much division and rancor. Everyone is entitled to an opinion. I encourage intellectual dialogue on the issues, just not blind name calling. Most of my articles always stress everyone doing their own research—forming their own conclusions. I will always strenuously defend someone's right to his or her own opinion, even if it is the exact opposite of mine, especially if it is an informed opinion."

"It did get me to wondering, though, why the donkey and elephant are the political symbols," Lynne said, almost in the form of a question.

"Did you look it up?" her father responded as he typically did when any of his kids asked questions of fact like this.

"I didn't wonder *that* much."

"Ironically, the donkey did refer to a jackass," Mitch stated. "I believe it was Andrew Jackson who was labeled with the slur, and if memory serves, he embraced it and put the donkey symbol on his political posters."

"Andrew Jackson?" Lynne said. "But he was, like, a really early president."

"Like, yeah, he was. Jackson was elected in 1828. Anyhow, quite a few years later, a political cartoon by Thomas Nast depicted a donkey in a lion's skin scaring animals in a zoo, with the elephant labeled 'The Republican Vote.' Both the donkey and elephant stuck as the symbols from then on."

Mitch looked up to see that his daughter had returned to her homework. He wasn't sure if she had listened to the end of the conversation. Shaking his head, Mitch went online himself, sending an e-mail to Al, Todd, and Mark repeating much of this conversation with Lynne about the "jackass and the teacher" and telling them about the "ignoring" they had to look forward to when their kids were older. ("If you ever have kids, Todd," he added.) He finished some more work for both the *Republic* and the Liberty Group and headed to bed.

Chapter 10

Mitch pulled into the parking area of the Biltmore, eager for his Thursday meeting. He was surprised at the energy he felt working on this project—the past month had really been fun. Also, given his conservative views and the perceived assault on those views by the current leaders of Congress as well as the administration, Mitch really felt his work was rewarding right now. He was doing what he could to assist his country. He truly thought of it in those terms. Mitch was able to reach a much wider audience on the Web site than he ever could at the paper.

After everyone had arrived and selected some of the snacks provided, they all sat around the table, and discussion ensued regarding their progress. Paul reported that the Web site hits were growing at twice the rate they had anticipated, and membership sales were very popular. Mitch had contributed additional benefits for members, including receiving daily e-mails of bullet point information detailing what was happening in Washington as well as other state legislatures. Membership also included letters from the Liberty CEO and full access to all articles historically posted on the site. The information right now was still fresh, but after a few months, the articles would begin to be purged. Paul lauded praise on Mitch for his quick action at procuring the numerous writers and also at putting together the daily bulletin.

"That's great!" Gus said emphatically after listening to Paul's report. "Are we keeping a database of those who are contributing?"

"Of course—that information will be invaluable," Paul agreed.

"Mitch—what big topic is up next for our Web site?" Gus asked.

"I thought I would discuss the presidential obsession with appointing czars," Mitch said.

"What do you mean?" Charlie asked.

"Don't you follow the news?" Mitch asked. "The president continues to appoint different czars to numerous positions. It's getting ridiculous."

"I don't think many people understand what the czars do or what that means," Paul said.

"I just assumed it was another person working on a problem—like the drug czar trying to help stem the rising drug problems," Charlie added. "Heck, didn't Reagan appoint that czar first? Haven't all the recent presidents appointed czars?"

"You guys are proving to me that some information on a public site regarding this topic is necessary," Mitch said. "Yes, Charlie, the recent presidents have used the 'czar' title for several positions, but usually only one or two people and the most was five, until now. President Obama, at this point, has named eighteen czars. The problem is these people answer to no one but the president, and the practice has always been constitutionally questionable."

"And why is that?" Paul asked.

"Well, the Constitution was written with a little concept called checks and balances," Mitch continued. "All government officers given significant authority by the president need to go through a confirmation process in Congress. These officers include not only the department heads of the cabinet, but many other levels of executive appointments, including assistant secretaries and deputy undersecretaries. Congress has the right to call these people before them to justify any actions they take."

"And these czars don't fall under these same conditions?" Karen asked.

"No, they do not. They are an extension of the presidency and therefore not subject to congressional review. The president, of course, is allowed to have as many advisors as he or she wishes, but they are not to set policy as these czars are doing. In my opinion, it is a way for this president to become more powerful than his predecessors. I can't say that is his goal; it just will be the result. Similar, I guess when you think about it, to what FDR attempted with his court-packing plan."

"Court-packing what?" Charlie asked, finding it hard to keep up with Mitch, wishing the writer would just shut up.

"This was definitely aggressive." Mitch began his history lesson. "It was dubbed a court-packing plan by opponents. In 1937, FDR was concerned that the Supreme Court was too powerful. Similar to today, he worried about the court asserting its power by ruling laws passed by the Congress and state legislatures to be unconstitutional. He even went as far as to say that the Court had been acting 'not as a judicial body, but as a policymaking body.' FDR decided the best way to ensure that the Supreme Court would enforce the Constitution as it was written, and to save the Court from itself, was to add justices. Federal judges at the time, as they are now, were appointed for lifetime terms or until they chose to retire. FDR's solution was to appoint a new member to any federal court when one of its members had reached the age of seventy and chose not to retire. He claimed that by doing this, the judicial system would continually be refreshed with new ideas, and the wisdom of the older judges would be intertwined with younger individuals who might have more practical experience with the issues of the day. He even said in one of his fireside chats that his plan would save our national Constitution from hardening of the judicial arteries."

"Wow," Karen replied, interested in this little bit of history. "That had to be a radical concept back then, let alone how it would be perceived now. I'm sure allegations of ageism would be leveled against that concept today. How would that have affected the Supreme Court at the time?"

"Well, there were six justices over the age of seventy at that point," Mitch answered. "In his proposal, Roosevelt said that there would not be more than fifteen justices. Ever since the Constitution was ratified, Congress has determined the number of justices, not the president, with totals ranging from the original six up to ten. In 1869, Congress set the number back to nine where it has remained since. So, in theory, FDR could have added six justices."

"So, what happened?" Gus asked.

"The legislation failed. If I remember correctly, the Senate majority leader at the time passed away during the debate of the issue, and this was a key blow to getting the bill passed. The Senate voted to recommit the proposal to the Senate Judiciary Committee, and when they recommitted it, they gave strict instructions to strip the bill of the court-packing language. It wasn't Roosevelt's finest moment."

"Man, you know your history," Charlie said, impressed.

"Well, we seem to be repeating it now. Between this czar fetish and the census power grab, I feel this White House is doing more to circumvent the Constitution than it is to uphold it. I realize that every administration has acted in ways that might not be strictly constitutional, but this White House, in a mere six months, has flouted our basic government foundation to new extremes."

"You're being a little harsh, aren't you?" Karen asked.

"As I have said before, I try to believe the best of intentions. I still think that President Obama is attempting to do what he thinks is right—and what is best for the country. He just is doing it at the expense of the Constitution, in my opinion. I have a fundamental disagreement with the president on this issue. And this is not the only thing he has done. Here's another example …" Gus cut him off, though, indicating that Mitch had given a considerably lengthy answer to the simple question of what was next for the Web site.

Eric Myerholtz

"We need to wrap this up," Gus concluded. "Any other major points of business for our group?"

Karen whispered to Mitch, "He needs to wrap it up because he has a massage scheduled in ten minutes at the Biltmore spa."

Mitch chuckled as Gus formally adjourned the meeting.

* * * * *

As everyone was packing up after the meeting concluded, Paul grabbed his things and followed Karen out to her car. She was getting into her black Lexus when Paul called out to her.

"What is it Paul? I really need to get going," Karen said exasperatedly. She always wanted to get away as quickly as possible from these meetings she loathed so much.

"I just want to make sure you are okay—you seemed a bit tense in there on Monday when we were discussing Mitch."

"Paul—it is no secret that I do not agree with everything that is going on. I am a member of this group for my own reasons. I just don't like the path we are taking to get where we want to be. Maybe it would help if I knew where this path was leading."

"I guess it is an ends-justify-the-means thing," Paul responded, trying to allay her concern. "You can't get too caught up in the details. Just keep the accounting side of things straight, and it will all work out in the end. I promise."

"And how many good people will suffer because our means?" she asked.

"Again—don't worry about the details—leave that to Charlie and Gus for the most part."

"It's not that easy—I do have a conscience," Karen said scathingly. "I just don't see things as black and white as the rest of you do. Or maybe I should say as green."

"It will be worth all the effort—please hang in there. Call me if you ever need to talk."

Karen drove away, her mind reeling with questions of what she should do.

* * * *

As Mitch was heading out of the meeting, he decided to wander around the Biltmore a little more since he had never spent much time there. He took in the architecture and strolled around one of the pool areas. He made his way back across the hotel, through the lobby area, and into the parking lot, where he passed Charlie loading some items into his car. Mitch noticed that Charlie was heading back in, not leaving the hotel.

"Thought you left already," Charlie said to him with a smile.

"Just admiring the resort a little bit."

"It is beautiful. I try to gaze around the pool as much as possible, if you know what I mean."

Unfortunately, Mitch did. "We ended a little abruptly in there—can I ask who is providing the information on legislation that is available with the memberships?" Mitch asked Charlie.

"You'll have to talk to Paul about that—I really don't know," Charlie responded. "I'm sure it's no jackass teacher, though." Mitch stood on the spot, replaying the sentence Charlie had just uttered in his head.

* * * *

Karen started to head back to her office after the meeting. She was still trying to figure out what she was doing. She felt her heart was in the right place, but there had to be a better way. As she pulled into the parking garage, Karen realized her concentration level would not allow her to give the best of efforts to her work right now. Although it was quite warm, she felt the need to get some air to try to clear her head. One of the perks of being the boss was no one would question you if you needed to take some personal time. She walked downtown for most of the afternoon, stopping in shops with no real point to her wandering. Karen came around a corner and saw the Ruby Room. "Time to get out of the heat," she told herself, and walked in, sat down at the bar, and ordered a glass of wine. She had a headache from thinking about how to quit the Liberty Group.

Out of the corner of her eye, she noticed that someone had sat down beside her. She did not look up, but she definitely was not in the mood for any conversation.

"Can I buy you a drink?" the man's voice said.

"I have one, thanks," she answered curtly without moving her gaze off the glass in front of her.

"That's too bad," the man answered. "Here I thought we might drink a little, talk a little, and then start an accounting firm together." She glanced up, and Will was sitting next to her.

"It's you—how did you know I was in here?"

"I just came out of a bookstore a few blocks from here when I saw you walking down the street. I was trying to catch up to you when you came in this place. You okay? I know you don't usually go to bars without a reason." He started looking around the place. "Are you meeting someone? I didn't mean to intrude."

"No—not meeting anyone—just trying to gain some focus on a few aspects of my life right now," she answered before she thought about it. Will always put her at ease.

"Anything you want to talk about?"

"No—I don't want to burden you."

"It's no burden. How about we grab some dinner? I'll even do most of the talking if you would like. I can spin this tax code into some really magical conversation—you'd be surprised. However, if you want, I'll be here to listen as well. Heck, if we talk enough about our firm, we'll write dinner off as a business expense."

"Sounds good—but not too much business," she suggested. "I could use a relaxing dinner."

"No problem. Let me make a call."

Although he tried to be discreet, Karen had the distinct feeling that Will had broken a date to take her to dinner.

"I hope you didn't make any change to your plans on my behalf."

"Not at all—none I didn't want to make anyhow," he answered truthfully. "You seem like you could use a friend tonight."

He couldn't have been more correct. She felt a little guilty, but not enough to let it bother her too much. Will and Karen headed to a place called Pizzeria Bianco. It was still pretty early on a Thursday evening, so seating wasn't a problem. After ordering drinks and an appetizer, Will decided it was time to try to figure this out.

"Karen—what has been going on? Something is on your mind—I can tell."

"Can you? I know I have never been very good at keeping my emotions in check. I am involved in a situation that has me very concerned." Karen stopped, not really wanting at all to go into more detail. The silence hung there for a few moments as Will waited to see if she would continue.

"Maybe I can help," he offered. "Tell me what you can, and let's talk this through together."

"I don't think that would be a good idea. Suffice it to say that I got myself into the problem; I'll get myself out."

"There is no shame in accepting help from someone willing to give it," Will explained. Karen gave no answer but was looking at him. He took the hint and did not want to push too hard. Will continued, smiling. "Fine. I'll keep my comments to general specifics. I usually find that when I'm in a predicament, in my mind, I am making the problem bigger than it really is. I imagine the worst, but in reality, it is not nearly as bad as it seems. When I step back, clear my head, and focus on the issue at hand, there is usually a solution. It sometimes takes a little thought, but the answer presents itself eventually."

"Forgive me, but I don't think you have ever had a problem," Karen retorted, almost laughing. "You are always so calm and in control."

"Oh, I guess my acting skills are pretty good then. But we all have issues. We humans can be a frail bunch. There was this one time in college … well, we don't need to go into that. Anyhow, I always find that a positive outlook gives hope, both to ourselves and those around us. That is a motto I try to follow every day. Positive Mental Attitude!"

"The power of positive thinking—are you serious?" Karen asked, dumbfounded. "You're coming at me with that?"

"How well do you know Scott Mason?" Will asked, totally out of the blue.

"You mean the tax manager you hired a few years ago? I obviously interviewed him, but I haven't spent much time with him beyond that—just professionally at a few client meetings. He seems to know his tax code. He hasn't attended our annual Christmas party or golf outing, though."

"You're right, he's a first-rate tax advisor. But he has a horribly negative attitude. He hasn't attended those events because he minimizes their importance. And you know who frequently calls in sick and complains the most about how much work he has? Scott. I personally attribute that to the lack of optimism in his attitude. I'm not saying he is not really feeling ill when he calls in; I'm just saying that his poor outlook runs him down."

Karen smiled and shook her head unbelievingly. "You really think his immune system is weaker because he complains all the time? Do you have any medical studies to back that up?"

The waitress had brought their drinks and the appetizer. They ordered their entrees.

"So, answer my question, Dr. Sunshine," Karen said playfully.

"Of course I do not have medical facts to support my theory, but is it impossible that the body reacts to feeling good by producing more of whatever keeps your immune system strong? Don't people talk about some euphoria after a great workout, or some athletes talk about that runner's high where the body just feels unstoppable? Can't some of that be connected to positive brain waves, too? Well—that's my theory, anyhow. And it works for me."

"What do you mean?" Karen asked.

"How many times do you hear someone say, 'I think I'm coming down with something?' And sure enough, in a day or two, they have either a cold or the flu. I cannot count how many times I have had a tickle in my throat or an achy feeling you might get at the start of an illness, and I have *willed* myself not to get sick. I know—it sounds crazy, but I just think positively that I am not going to be run down—drink some extra water and keep going about my day. It works for me."

Karen respected Will tremendously and knew he was very intelligent, but this seemed a little too child-like. Will could read in her eyes that she was surprised by what he was saying.

"Karen—I want to help you with whatever this problem is, but you seem reluctant to share any of the details with me. I am offering a different approach to the problem. This could really help—clear your mind and think positively that you can solve this. I know you can do anything—knew it from the first time we had coffee after that conference years ago."

"Thanks, Will, I appreciate the confidence in my abilities. I will think about what you said. You have helped already—more than you know." Karen was touched by her colleague's kind words.

They enjoyed the rest of their dinner talking about a few of their clients and mapping out how best to grow the firm in the struggling economy. They talked well into the evening, ending it with Will walking her back to her car.

"Thanks again for everything," Karen said. "I really needed this tonight." She leaned in and gave him a quick hug.

"Anytime you need something—just let me know," Will said,

closing her car door. He watched her drive away, wishing she would let him help her more.

* * * * *

Fridays at the *Republic* for Mitch were usually reserved for working on the articles for the following week. He was doing just that as well as keeping up with some other national news, but his mind kept going back to Charlie's comment. "Jackass teacher." That was so strange. He knew he had sent an e-mail to his friends about his conversation with Lynne, but he hadn't mentioned it in the meeting. Could it be a coincidence? That term seemed a little too specific to be coincidental. He decided to let it go—he was just being paranoid.

* * * * *

Karen awoke that Friday morning feeling renewed. She took what Will had said to heart and realized that she was letting her perceived failure at keeping her business in the black too personally. She had always been someone who took control and was confident in her decisions. Karen had allowed too many other factors break her confidence, and her actions over the previous year or so had been the result of that.

"No more!" she said defiantly to herself. "Now—how can I get out of the Liberty Group?" She set her mind to finding the answer.

* * * * *

Marie's Saturday once again included lunch with her friend Stephanie. Marie had made many friends out here in the desert, but Steph was definitely her closest. Marie, Stephanie, and Stephanie's husband,

Patrick, had all worked together for a nonprofit when the Bartters first moved to Phoenix. Stephanie still worked there, but Marie had moved on to her current job, and Patrick was now a professor at Arizona State University. Stephanie was a few years younger than Marie and had a beautiful five-year-old daughter to whom Marie was godmother. They enjoyed getting together at My Big Fat Greek Restaurant, usually on a Saturday, although they would meet for dinner occasionally, too.

Marie had a few errands to run first and said goodbye to Mitch and the kids about 10:30 that morning. The restaurant was located near the Chandler Mall, and Marie could take care of most of her to-do list there. She paid no attention to the old green Ford Taurus following her.

As she exited her car, the sedan pulled a few spots away. Marie went about her tasks, enjoying herself as these mainly involved shopping. She loved to shop, but finding an incredible deal was what Marie relished most. She found some great things for the kids at Nordstrom's and Dillard's. She returned the book she had purchased for Mitch at Barnes and Noble (he had already read it—some time ago). She also picked up a few new sheets for the guest room at Linens-N-Things. As Marie went about these errands, she was oblivious to the man following her, snapping her picture left and right. He managed to get many different angles of her and numerous head-on shots.

He got his best picture as Marie was coming out of Fuzziwigs Candy Factory. She always tried to pick up Mitch a bag full of Boston Baked Beans, his favorite candy, whenever she was at this mall. After placing her purchase in her handbag, she looked up and the man, at a distance, clicked at just the right moment. As Marie headed to the restaurant, her photographer double-timed it in another direction. He knew where she was going and arrived at the Mediterranean place about a minute before her and walked up to the hostess.

"I will give you a hundred dollars to seat me at a table next to a woman who is about to walk in," he whispered.

"What—I ..." the hostess began, but the man could not take the time to explain.

"Fine—two hundred dollars," he said, cutting her off. "It's for a surprise—please."

The hostess grabbed the two Ben Franklins from the man's hand, and he retreated, standing against the wall. Stephanie had been walking up just as Marie reached the restaurant door—they entered together.

"Two, please," Marie said to the hostess.

The man against the wall gestured toward the hostess as well, mouthing, "Next to her." The hostess took Marie and Steph to a table, and about five minutes later, seated the gentleman at a table next to theirs. The women enjoyed the lunch and catching up. They concluded by setting a date for the four them, Mitch and Patrick included, to all go out to dinner. Once they left the table, the man, having placed a latex glove over his right hand, discreetly grabbed the water glass Marie had been using and deftly placed it into a plastic bag.

Chapter 11

Mitch came into the *Republic* the next Monday morning excited for his online chat with Al. He continued his research for his next article as well as reviewing other information for the Liberty site. After a few hours of work, his mail arrived. He had reached a decent breaking point from his current subject and started going through the pile that had been set on his desk. He had several letters from readers, mostly pointing out some differences of opinion with recent articles. This wasn't an unusual occurrence—readers loved to give him feedback. After reviewing about five letters, he came to a plain brown package with no return address. He opened it, discarding the box and finding a folded manila envelop inside. Upon opening this envelope, Mitch found a large sum of cash along with a note.

> *Keep up the excellent work. Write an article attacking Speaker Pelosi on her many inconsistencies. I'm sure you can come up with quite a few. There is plenty more where this came from if you do a few of these articles for me.*

There was no signature. Mitch sat there and reread the note. This was definitely new territory for him. He pulled the box out of the garbage and set everything on his desk. He then dialed his boss and asked him if he had a few minutes. Mitch didn't touch another thing until John came over.

"What is so urgent, Mitch?" John asked.

"Look at this," Mitch said, handing John the short note. John read it quickly and looked at the cash on Mitch's desk.

"How much is there?" John asked.

"I don't know—I haven't even touched it except to remove it from its packaging. I want the paper's attorney here right now."

"What do you mean?" John asked, although knowing Mitch, he assumed he knew what was coming next.

"I'm not accepting this. As there is no return address and the note leaves no evidence of the identity of who sent it, I can't just send it back. I want an attorney to record when it was received, that I notified you and the attorney straight away, and the money put in escrow until we can ascertain who sent it. I want no control over it. The damage to my credibility, and the paper's for that matter, is at stake. I can't believe some idiot would do this." Mitch's anger was rising.

John reached over and started counting the money. "There's $15,000 here. Man, someone likes your writing."

"No—someone wants to control the opinion pages of the *Republic*. That will not happen." Mitch's agitation caused several heads to turn in his direction.

"Relax," John said, placing his hand on Mitch's shoulder. "I was just making a statement. Okay, I'll get the lawyer."

A half hour later, a representative from the *Republic*'s attorney's office had shown up, been brought up to date on the situation, and had asked several questions. The attorney was a man in his mid-thirties with a neatly trimmed goatee who hid his early baldness by shaving his head. The attorney indicated that he would take care of the details, and Mitch felt a little relieved but was still upset about the situation.

The Liberty Group

He looked at his watch and realized there was less than an hour until his online conversation with Al. "I'd better get something to eat and try to relax a bit," he thought, shaking the mail from his mind.

* * * *

An hour later, Al took a deep breath, sitting in his office in Ohio, and started typing. He had already followed the instructions Mitch had sent him regarding the format and where to go online.

"Today, I will discuss the tax system. The United States has developed an incredibly complicated and very graduated tax system whereby in recent years the top income earners are bearing more of the burden than ever in recent history."

"How can that be the case?" Mitch responded. "The Bush tax cuts only benefit the wealthy. The richest people must be paying less! We need to spend the money that has been proposed to stimulate this economy and to provide healthcare to all Americans. We will not be able to do that if the rich do not come to the table. As Joe Biden said, it's time for them to be patriotic." Mitch smiled as he played the devil's advocate.

"You don't believe they already come to the table with more than anyone?" Al questioned.

"Maybe they do bring more than others right now, but they are not bringing enough," Mitch continued.

"Have you ever seen the explanation of our tax system by a professor of economics from the University of Georgia? I believe his name was Kamerschen."

"I'm sure I haven't. And if I ever did, I'm sure I forgot it!" Mitch responded.

"It has been circulated extensively on the Internet, so many have read it. I may get it a little mixed up, giving the example from memory, and I will adjust some of the percentages for what is happening today, but I will take a stab at enlightening you a little, using this wonderful example.

"Let's start with the idea that ten people all meet at a bar, say, every Friday, and they all order the same drinks. The bill total is an even hundred bucks. They decide to pay in the same manner that our current tax code is set up. The first four pay nothing, with the fifth person paying only one dollar. The sixth person pays three dollars, the seventh pays seven dollars, the eighth pays twelve dollars, the ninth pays seventeen dollars, and the tenth, and therefore the richest, pays sixty dollars."

"That is not how our tax system is set up!" Mitch exclaimed, continuing the mock argument.

"It absolutely is. The top 5 percent actually pay 60 percent of the individual income taxes. In my example, I'm allowing the top *10* percent to pay *60* percent. Everyone always assumes the middle class is getting soaked. The poor don't pay and the rich have loopholes, but the fact is the rich pay well over their proportionate share. Now back to the example. These ten people meet every Friday for a year, order the exact same drinks, and pay in this same manner. Finally, the owner of the bar comes over to them one day and tells them as a reward for their loyal business, he will serve them the same drinks for only eighty dollars. The group still wanted to pay their bill the way we pay our taxes, so the first four men were unaffected. They would still drink for free. The other six realized that they could not just divide the twenty-dollar savings evenly among themselves, for the guy paying only one dollar would end up *receiving* two dollars to have a drink. The bar owner, being helpful, decided to suggest a manner that would be similar and came up with the following:

"First four people still drink for free—no change.

"Fifth person now also drinks for free—saving one dollar or 100 percent of what he had paid.

"Sixth person now pays two dollars, saving one dollar or 33 percent.

"Seventh person now pays five dollars, saving two dollars or 28.6 percent.

"Eighth person now pays nine dollars, saving three dollars or 25 percent.

"Ninth person now pays fourteen dollars, saving three dollars or 17.7 percent.

"Tenth person now pays fifty dollars, saving ten dollars, or 16.7 percent.

"Everyone was now better off, with the exception of the first four, who were still drinking for free. So all were happy, right? Well, not quite. The group started to compare how much they were saving. The fifth and sixth person said they were only saving one dollar, while the richest one was saving ten dollars. That didn't seem right to them. Why should he get ten times what they got? The first four people were upset that they didn't get anything at all of the twenty dollars saved. They couldn't believe that could be fair—the richest guy gets ten dollars, and they get nothing! They all pointed at the tenth guy and said that the rich get all the breaks and how unfair it was. So the next Friday rolls around, and they all show up, except the richest guy. They all go ahead and drink, even drinking the tenth guy's drinks, but this time, when the bill for eighty dollars comes, and they all pull out their money, they realize that they only have thirty dollars among themselves."

"That wouldn't happen," Mitch typed. "No one would be upset if they still had to pay nothing."

"You don't think so?" Al asked. "What is said every time a tax cut is proposed? Most democrats cry foul, claiming that the proposed tax cut unfairly benefits the rich and that the poor are getting nothing. That comes up every time—every time!

"Did you also notice in the example that after the reduction, the richest person was now paying fifty dollars out of the eighty dollars—62.5 percent of the bill? His total percent of the bill actually increased, and yet people were upset! This is exactly what has happened under the Bush tax cuts. The upper-end taxpayers have paid a larger percentage

Eric Myerholtz

of the bill. Those individuals struggling to get by and those with lower incomes, who might not pay any tax at all, are always made out to be examples of how unjust any type of tax cut would be. But think about it. I can't stress this enough—a tax cut means those people who pay taxes will pay a lower percentage. You can't theoretically get lower than zero percent. Those paying taxes are the ones who benefit."

"Then we should just cut taxes to the lower level income earners who are still paying taxes," Mitch responded. "They have tried that, haven't they? Aren't those called targeted tax cuts?"

"That is exactly what they have been called in the past, but they never hit their targets. The best way to cut taxes is an across-the-board reduction of tax rates. Everyone who pays taxes benefits, and even those who don't pay tax ultimately benefit from the increased prosperity that tax reductions bring."

"What is your solution?" Mitch asked.

"If our country makes the decision as a nation to tax income, as opposed to taxing consumption, then I am an advocate for the flat tax system," Al argued. "I haven't put pencil to paper to figure it out, but I have to believe we could develop a very simple tax system. It's been proposed in many different forms. Let's say we choose 20 percent as a starting point. Let's also exempt the first $30,000 of income from taxes, to ensure we do not unfairly tax the low-income portion of our nation. Everyone making $30,000 or less pays absolutely no income tax. Our first taxpayer—let's call him Albert—makes $50,000. With the first $30,000 exempt, Albert pays 20 percent of the remaining $20,000 or a total of $4,000 in tax."

"So, he pays $4,000 on his overall income of $50,000, which ends up being only 8% in total," Mitch added, helping the example along.

"That's correct—nice quick math, by the way. Anyhow, let's take someone making twice as much; we'll call her Beth. Beth makes $100,000, and again, we exempt the first $30,000, so Beth pays 20 percent of $70,000, or $14,000."

"So Beth is paying 14 percent, given that she makes $100,000?"

The Liberty Group

"Again correct," Al replied. "Please also notice that although she makes twice as much as Albert, she is actually paying over 3 times the amount of taxes that he does. Now, let's add a third person; we'll call her Cindy. Cindy makes $200,000, or twice what Beth makes."

"Let me do this one," Mitch requested. "Cindy would pay 20 percent of $170,000, since we exempt the first $30,000 still. That would be $34,000 on income of $200,000, or 17 percent."

"You got it. Again, Cindy is paying more than twice what Beth is, even though her income is double. The tax form could be that simple. These percentages and income exemptions were pulled out of thin air for purposes of this example, but the concept is solid."

"Would you phase out the $30,000 exemption at some level of income? That only seems fair. Why should someone making a million dollars get the same exemption as someone making $50,000?"

"No, I would not phase it out. That would only add complexity. Why not just leave it there? Everyone would know what it is with no additional calculations required. Besides, I've shown that the higher your income, the higher percentage you pay—it would just be capped at close to 20 percent."

"What about deductions from income—isn't that where a lot of the loopholes occur?" Mitch asked.

"Many of those deductions came about from our government seeing fit to push social agendas using the tax code. They want to entice you to buy a house, so they make the interest and property taxes deductible. I'll restate what I said earlier. I am a *flat tax, simple tax* advocate. Simple means very simple. No deviations from the basic form."

"Are you at all concerned that people will not give to charities if there is no tax advantage?" Mitch questioned.

"I think people will give more, especially if they are paying less in tax," Al responded confidently. "I don't know how many people pull out their calculators to determine how much of a tax deduction they will receive each time they write a check to charity. I have the basic belief that people are good and that they want to assist in the causes they care

137

about. Whenever a disaster strikes somewhere, such as an earthquake or a hurricane, most communities in the United States gather supplies to send. People are good—they will continue to help. Allow them to keep more of their own hard-earned money, and they will give more to a variety of charitable causes. I have no proof of that, of course, but I believe it to be true. Look at some of the large endowments that exist on colleges and universities across the country. Most of these were established and well funded long before there was an income tax benefit from contributing to charity."

"You have more faith in humanity than I do," Mitch retorted.

"Isn't that the basic difference we are seeing in the two parties right now? The conservatives—and therefore many, but not all, Republicans—believe in the individual and his or her ability to determine the right thing to do for his or her own life. It is a belief in human nature. The liberals—and therefore many, but not all, Democrats—believe that most of humankind should rely on government to make many of the decisions concerning their lives. They believe that government will know what is best, not the individual. The government should determine your healthcare decisions, your investment decisions, how much people should be able to earn, even who should run a car company. The people, or should I say the masses, cannot be trusted to make these decisions for themselves."

"Well, I think you are stretching things a little on that one—painting with an awfully broad brush," Mitch the liberal responded.

"Maybe I am," Al replied. "I do actually believe that most people want the same freedoms that I want, whether they vote for a Democrat, a Republican, or another candidate. I do not think that the current leadership of the Democratic Party reflects this, though. If you try to tell me that those leaders feel everyone should be free to make their own decisions, then we will choose to disagree on that point."

"We disagree on more than that point, but you have given me some things to think about," Mitch typed, effectively ending the conversation.

* * * * *

"Great job!" Mitch said on the phone later that day to Al. There had been an incredible number of people writing comments to the site about the conversation already, most praising Al's assessment and many taking the arguments an additional step or two.

"Thanks—it was actually kind of fun. Although, I must admit you were a bit of a pushover. You let me ramble all I wanted and brought up only top-level arguments against my points. If we ever do something like this again, you may want to find an actual liberal who will argue better for the alternative. Some of those bloggers responding to our conversation are making the liberal case fairly convincingly."

"I'll consider that," Mitch responded. He thought about discussing the package he had received earlier in the day with Al but decided against it. "You have any plans tonight? You should treat yourself to a nice dinner. You earned it today."

"Thanks again—maybe I'll allow myself a Dairy Queen Blizzard!" Al said.

"You and your ice cream," Mitch said, shaking his head. "Have a great evening. I'll talk to you later."

"Hold on," Al said. "I wanted to ask you how the whole Liberty experience was going. I also have to thank you—I have been enjoying the change of pace in my routine by writing a few articles. The extra income is nice, too."

"I'll agree with you on the income part!" Mitch said enthusiastically. "I am almost amazed at how much fun I am having with this project. And you are welcome, by the way—I'm glad you are feeling rewarded. We'll have to talk more when we all get together. Maybe we could even convince Todd to join our group."

"Only if you let him write movie reviews as well—either that or he can be the liberal arguing the cause next time," Al answered.

Eric Myerholtz

* * * * *

Gus was pacing in his study. He had been planning this operation so carefully for so long, and now that the true action was occurring, he was trying to relish every moment. He knew he had prepared for every scenario, and his self-confidence told him he was in total control. He was determined not to fail. His thoughts were interrupted by the sound of his cell phone.

"Gus Reed," he answered.

"I was looking for Nicola; may I speak to him, please?" the voice on the phone asked.

"I'm sorry, but you have the wrong number," Gus replied. "Why don't you check and try it again?"

"I'm so sorry—I will do that," the caller said. Gus hung up, reveling in the completeness of his plan.

* * * * *

Mitch walked in the door that evening, and Sydney came bounding over to greet him. Sage came over as well, just a little slower. She always was more submissive than Sydney. After hugging his kids and asking about how they had occupied themselves during the day, he fed the dogs and went to the refrigerator to see what he could make for dinner. The events of the day—both the bribe and the online conversation—were replaying in his head as he set to making tacos. Mitch was dicing onions and tomatoes when he realized that Ed was talking very loudly to him.

"What is it?" Mitch said, a little too harshly. Ed looked crushed.

"I was just asking how *your* day was, Dad—you didn't answer when I asked the first two times, so I asked a little louder this time."

Mitch, feeling about as bad as he could, set down his knife and gave his son a big hug. "I am so sorry—I had a strange day, and I was replaying it in my head and obviously not paying attention to anything else around me. I am sorry, bud!" Mitch went back to finishing dinner, thinking not only of today's events, but wondering about several of the odd occurrences lately, including Charlie's comment in the parking lot and the bar pickups.

Marie got home a few minutes later, and within a short while, they were all sitting down to dinner together. As Jane said grace, Mitch silently prayed for answers to his many questions. After dinner, the kids all started clearing the dishes and cleaning the kitchen, while Mitch and Marie went up to change their clothes.

"So, did anything interesting happen today at work? You were awfully quiet during dinner," Marie asked, knowing something was going on inside her husband's head.

"You could say something interesting happened," he replied and began explaining the entire morning to Marie.

"How much money was in the envelope?"

"I didn't touch it—John said there was $15,000."

"Wow, we could really do our twentieth anniversary right with that money," Marie joked. She knew immediately that Mitch was not in a mood for comments like that.

"Hon—I am just, I guess 'frustrated' is the word. Too many strange things have been happening lately. This package today is really bothering me."

"Sounds like you did all you could to ensure your integrity," Marie said supportively. "That was really smart to call the attorney and have the money put in escrow."

"Am I crazy to think that these bizarre events—the bribe and the pickup attempts—all started about the same time as my Liberty Group involvement?"

Marie thought for a moment. It did seem a little coincidental, but there was obviously no proof. "Mitch, do you have reason to doubt any of the people you are working with at Liberty?"

"Do I have any reason? Not that I know of. I like Karen, and Paul seems very honest. I don't know that I could ever be comfortable with Charlie, and Gus I just can't get a read on."

"Well—the package today could just be a random person reacting to the high level of animosity and distrust between the two major parties right now. From the way you describe Charlie, it would be difficult to put too much stock in anything he says. As for the pickups in the bars, it was only a matter of time. Most women just stay away because you are with me, and my obvious beauty intimidates them." Marie was smiling at her husband.

Mitch cracked a slight grin. "That much is true. You're right—I probably am reading more into these things than I should."

"You haven't told me how your online chat with Al went today."

"You didn't tune in to it?" Mitch asked, almost hurt.

"Of course I did—I just wanted your take," Marie replied.

"I thought it was great—Al's a natural. We may have to do more of those." Mitch went into some of the better points he thought Al had made, and as they talked, he dismissed his Liberty concerns.

Chapter 12

The following Thursday meant another meeting at the Biltmore. Mitch had put his doubts behind him and was excited to hear more about what was happening. He was also falling in love with the Biltmore almost as much as Gus. This place truly was gorgeous.

After hearing from Gus about more of the corporate sponsors he had procured and the growing balance in the bank account, Paul reported on some general business issues. Karen indicated that thanks to Gus, as well as Mitch's work on the Web site resulting in more positive cash flow, the Liberty Group's twelve-month income projections had increased tremendously. The group then turned to hear from Mitch, who was eager to report his progress as well.

"We now have fifteen different writers, and the site boasts twelve different state links. I am working to add a few more writers—can I get approval to increase my allotment of funds to accommodate up to thirty writers?"

"Thirty?" Gus barked. "That's twice as many as you have now! Are you trying to build an empire?" His tone came across as aggravated, but he was smiling.

Eric Myerholtz

Mitch took a very confident tact. "Just doing what you asked—I really think we are reaching a large audience, based on the Web activity. As Karen just reported, the money has been flowing in. These people are going to be the grassroots organizers in next year's elections. We have state links, several of which are really getting significant hits. I have even thought about setting up a database package that different communities could purchase to allow them to record names, addresses, e-mails, etc.—all with proper permission, of course, for their different areas. This will allow better organization and, in turn, much better fundraising and voter turnout. I also want to add a few technical writers—an economist and someone with past federal government experience. I think they could continue to positively expand our site."

"That sounds all well and good—and believe me, Mitch—you are doing a great job," Gus said genially. "We couldn't be more pleased with the results. Can we cap it at thirty for now, though? I don't want you coming back for another request for more funds anytime too soon. I agree with the direction you are taking this; I just feel it is very important to grow slowly and steadily—if we tackle too much, too soon, I feel the risk of failure is greater."

Mitch was slightly surprised with this reaction. He thought the wider audience was what Gus was after, especially with the additional income the site was generating. However, he was in no mood to argue, and he knew this was Gus's operation. "No problem—I will be at my wit's end managing the ones I get—and thirty is a high estimate—it will most likely come in around twenty-five."

"I do have another question," Gus said, and the change in his tone was obvious. "Why haven't you or some other writers on the site commented on Obama's birth certificate issue?"

It was difficult for Mitch not to roll his eyes. There was always some fringe element trying to pursue a wild goose chase issue. This year it was the Obama birth certificate. Mitch knew that Gus was serious, so he needed to phrase his answer carefully. "I don't think that would be very wise. It is somewhat unbelievable that this is still an issue."

The Liberty Group

"You know, I have only heard a little information about this," Karen said. "What is the deal on the birth certificate?"

"Several groups are clamoring for President Obama to release his actual birth certificate," Mitch began. "He claims he has, and it is on his Web site. My understanding is these groups claim the Web site has what is called a Certificate of Live Birth issued from the State of Hawaii, but this document is not the official birth certificate. The State of Hawaii does not even consider it proof of birth in the state. That is the claim—since he doesn't have his actual birth certificate, then President Obama was not born in the United States and is therefore ineligible to serve as president."

"But his mom was a U.S. citizen," Paul stated, his attorney background providing some knowledge on the subject. "Doesn't that make the point moot? Even if he was not born in Hawaii, his mom's citizenship makes him eligible."

"That is a very good point, Paul," Mitch answered. "However, it is not quite that cut and dry. The Constitution lists as a qualification to be president that one must be a 'natural-born' citizen. The Constitution itself does not define 'natural born.' The Fourteenth Amendment talks about citizenship as well, but does not specifically address Mr. Obama's situation. I did research this topic a little. According to the U.S. Constitution Web site, Title 8 of the U.S. Code details different situations regarding citizenship. A section of the title says that anyone born outside the United States is a citizen if both parents are U.S. citizens, as long as one has lived in the United States. If only one parent is a citizen, it is a little murkier. It mentions if one parent is a citizen and has lived in the United States for five years, a child born to them outside the United States is also a citizen. This title states unequivocally that anyone born in the United States is a natural citizen. All this conjecture is moot if Obama was born in Hawaii, and all evidence supports that he was."

"I can't believe that someone could go through almost two years of campaigning without this being verified," Paul said.

"Exactly," Mitch agreed. "I think, ultimately, it has been verified. That is one reason why I have not really wanted to include anything about it. It is not a policy-based criticism—and I think I have been clear that I debate policy issues, not character assassinations."

"And if he truly is not qualified, according to the Constitution—that is not a policy issue—the flaunting of our founding document?" Gus asked, incredulous.

"In the end, it seems more of a grasping for straws–type ploy. My main question is why President Obama has not produced the actual certificate to silence these groups. In fact, if you believe the information in the mass e-mails these groups send, the president has been paying all sorts of legal teams to prevent a judge from ruling that he has to produce the actual document. One estimate I saw recently indicated he has spent up to $900,000 in attorney fees on this issue. Why is there a need to spend this money if he has the certificate?"

"What!" Karen exclaimed. "That can't be right. Why wouldn't he just produce it? Are these lawsuits getting tossed out of court?"

"Again, I have no verification that he has actually spent that money," Mitch responded. "It may all be rumor. I am pretty sure, though, that as of right now, there are suits in four or five states ongoing. There must be some judges finding merit enough in the case not to just heave it without thought. Again, the question is why he won't produce an actual birth certificate, if he has one and if he hasn't already. That last one is a big 'if.'"

"The one on his site must be the real deal!" Paul said.

"I don't know the Hawaiian law; I just know what the e-mails claim. I can tell you that White House Press Secretary Gibbs was recently asked about this situation. A WorldNetDaily.com correspondent named Lester Kinsolving asked the press secretary something about Obama's claim of transparency, and the secretary cut him off by asking if he was looking for the president's birth certificate. Kinsolving said he was, and Gibbs responded that it is on the Internet. When Kinsolving asked about the actual long form, with the names of the hospital and physician, Gibbs said it was on the Internet, but that form apparently is not. There are also other documents that are being requested but not being brought forth, again, if you believe all the rumors online."

"What other documents?" Paul asked. "There is no way that Obama does not qualify to be president. I can't imagine that someone could reach the final ticket of a major party without that being verified, let alone actually getting elected!"

"Who is supposed to verify that information?" Karen asked.

After a short silence in which everyone was looking at Mitch, he said, "I really do not know. Candidates file information with the Federal Election Commission. I have no idea if they have people who check into such things, or they assume the press will perform some due diligence."

"So you don't know?" Charlie questioned.

"That's what I'm saying—I don't know whose job it is to verify the constitutionality of presidential candidates," Mitch responded.

"Oh, I heard you the first time—I just hadn't heard you say 'I don't know' before—I wanted to hear you say it again," Charlie said, smiling.

Mitch was taken aback. The more time he spent with Charlie, the less time he wanted to spend with him in the future. "I was just answering Gus's question and then providing background on the issue. I do believe President Obama was born in Hawaii. I just do not know why he hasn't put this issue to bed."

"But Snopes.com, or one of the other online fact-checking organizations, probably has," Karen added.

"Actually, I looked on those sites during the election, because certain Democrats were raising the issue about McCain," Mitch said. "McCain was born in the Pacific when his father was in the navy. Of course, he did have two American parents, though, unlike Obama. What's interesting about Snopes is that it does debunk the rumor about Obama, also referring to the Internet-posted certificate as well as to a Hawaiian newspaper listing of the birth. However, Snopes says it is *inconclusive* as to whether McCain is eligible to be president."

"Well, Snopes has usually been known as a left-leaning site," Gus said. "Again, I think we should hammer Obama on this issue."

"I strongly disagree," Mitch repeated. "You just talked about taking it slowly—ensuring our success. If in our infancy we are deemed to be a fringe information site, our credibility will take a big hit. And as I have said numerous times, I like debating the legislative issues, not chasing character attacks."

"And as I just asked, flouting the Constitution of the United States is not an issue worth debating?" Gus argued.

"Of course, any breach of the qualifications laid down by the Constitution would be huge," Mitch agreed. "I would go as far as to say that if this were actually true, it would be the biggest political scandal in history. However, we wouldn't be breaking the story, and we have other more substantive items in process. Why don't we let the ones chasing this issue continue to chase, and we will continue to build on what we've started."

"And if I insist you write a story about this?" Gus asked menacingly.

"I'll walk away. It's a bad move, and I won't be a part of it." Gus stared at Mitch, disbelief written across his face. Very few individuals refused a request from Gus.

"We'll do it your way for now," Gus finally replied. "But remember who is running this operation. Does anyone have anything else to discuss?" The silence in the room was taken as a hint that they all had other work to get back to. "Good enough," Gus said. "We'll meet again next week."

Chapter 13

The next few weeks were relatively normal. Mitch continued to add more Web site columnists, which now numbered twenty-three. He was managing to keep up with his articles at the *Republic* as well. Mitch had also taken the time to add links to each congressional representative's voting record, something he thought was very important for voters to know. It was late in the evening, and Mitch was on his laptop up in his bedroom tweaking several different postings on the Web site. He had not had a recurring feeling of doubt about the Liberty Group—if anything, he was more energized now than ever. He did think at times in the past few meetings he had noticed a knowing glance or an abrupt end to a conversation. He shook these thoughts from his head as he posted some ideas on the site about current events.

He began his post by discussing the recent shutdown of the House of Representatives that Ms. Pelosi had seen fit to author. He could not understand the tactic. House rules state that after the last vote of the day, representatives are allowed to speak freely on the House floor, where they can have one-minute, five–minute, or one-hour segments. This privilege is required to be asked for in advance, and time is then allocated to both parties equally, on a first come, first served basis. This facet of the House protocol is known as Special Rules. The Republicans had applied for their time and were ready to begin their speeches when Speaker Pelosi shut down the House.

Ironically enough, the Republicans were going to talk about the lack of transparency of the Democrat-led House. Too many bills had been rushed through the process, with no time to review what was in them. Mitch recalled Democrats complaining of Republican tactics when they controlled the House as well. He just could not understand why these apparently intelligent men and women had to abuse power so much once they had it. The current example was the amount of legislation being put through at a breakneck pace. Here again, House rules dictated that a bill be publicly posted for three days before it was to be voted on. Some guy named Thomas Jefferson had suggested that rule (back when bills were much easier to understand). However, the Pelosi-led House had, so far during the Obama administration, seen fit to disobey Jefferson's rule for no less than eight different acts, two of which increased federal spending by unforeseen proportions—these were huge bills—one of which was the stimulus bill and the other was the cap and trade bill, known to some as the cap and tax bill.

Interestingly, the House claimed they had to pass the stimulus bill to get the economy going, with not a day to lose. That same bill then sat on President Obama's desk for four days while the president took a weekend jaunt to Chicago. The cap and trade bill included a 300-page amendment added in the middle of the night before the vote, yet members were forced to vote on that legislation before being able to decipher what was in it.

Again, Mitch knew Republicans were not innocent of similar tactics when they had the power, either. They had participated in similar high-handed maneuvers at times as well. *Why not just let the government work the way it was established to run?* Mitch thought to himself. *Why does this "power" lead to so many bad decisions?* He was reminded of the previous night when he had been reading the seventh Harry Potter book to his daughter Jane. Even though Jane was fourteen, she still enjoyed having her father read to her. The Harry Potter phenomenon had not been lost on the Bartters. In fact, Mitch thought he definitely had one of the most Potter-mad families around. All of them except Marie had read the books several times. Mitch had waited in long lines on the nights of the releases for the last three or four books, sometimes purchasing multiple copies so more than one family member could be reading at a time. They had loved the movies as well, usually going on opening night and debating long after the movie had ended why the plots had deviated from the books here and there. Ed had seen the latest film (chronicling the sixth book) at least five times already.

Now that his kids were older, they still loved Harry, and it was one connection Mitch clung to, knowing his kids were now closer to leaving the house as adults than they were to being young kids. He had read to Jane just the night before one of the final chapters in the entire series. In the book, Harry was questioning why his mentor had never sought to be the magical world equivalent of the president, and his response was "perhaps those who are best suited to power are those who have never sought it. Those who … have leadership thrust upon them, and take up the mantle because they must, and find to their own surprise that they wear it well." Mitch knew that too few of the elected officials wore their mantles of leadership well. Was Washington one of the great presidents because power had been "thrust upon him"? Conversely, had President Obama ever stayed in one elected position long enough to make a difference, or was he always determining how to make the next step up the ladder, always seeking more power? He knew he had the makings of an article for the *Republic* of some sort here but couldn't quite get it to flow the way he wanted it to.

"You look deep in thought," Marie said softly as she entered their bedroom and slowly pushed the door shut without turning her back to Mitch.

"I didn't even hear you walk in—just considering a lot of things," Mitch replied. "What are the kids up to?" he asked.

"They are downstairs watching a movie. I told them we were headed off to bed."

"I guess it is that time," Mitch said, looking at his watch and realizing it was past eleven o'clock. Now that their kids were older, they generally were given free reign on their bedtimes in the summer. Mitch started to get up, but Marie pushed him back down on the bed.

"I told the kids we were going to sleep—I didn't tell you that."

"Oh, I love you!" Mitch said as they fell into each other's arms.

* * * *

Mitch worked for a bit the next morning but needed to head to the library for some research. He could usually find what he was looking for online, but every now and then, he appreciated the old-fashioned way—and he loved looking through some of the old books on the founders. He usually had several items checked out at any point in time that he would read before going to bed, usually related to American history.

As Mitch dropped a few books into the return slot, he realized that he had left one in the car. He walked back out the exit and almost ran straight into a thickly built man wearing a suit and sunglasses. The man was bald, but Mitch surmised it was by choice rather than nature.

"Excuse me," Mitch said as he made his way past the gentleman.

"No problem," said the deep-voiced stranger.

Mitch continued to his car while the other man headed into the library. Mitch grabbed the book he had left, not realizing the gentleman had stopped just inside the door and was watching him through the tinted windows. The man realized a little too late that Mitch was not leaving and was in fact coming back in. He turned and headed toward the desk in a hurry just as Mitch re-entered the library. Mitch did notice the gentleman again, and the thought passed through his mind as to why this person had only walked a few paces into the building. Mitch put it out of his head and went about his research. He moved to the computers and found several references he was looking for and went to pull most of his books. The final one was eluding him, and as Mitch came around one of the towering stacks, he nearly ran into the same man yet again.

"Excuse me again," Mitch said pleasantly. "You a history buff, too?"

"No," the man answered, moving away quickly.

Mitch located the book and checked out. He walked back out into the sunshine, loaded his books in the back seat of his car, and began driving out of the parking lot. In his rearview mirror, he saw another car pull up to the front of the library, and the same bald man got in—no books in hand. Mitch was not quite sure what to make of it, but the ordeal had seemed very strange to him.

Mitch went to the *Republic* from the library—his article about the results, or lack thereof, of the huge stimulus bill had appeared in the morning paper. He was met with several dissenting opinions as he made his way through the newspaper office. Mitch had become accustomed to hearing a few choice replies about some of his articles, but anything that criticized the president seemed to bring out a bit more rancor. Obama had come to the presidency with, in Mitch's opinion, unrealistic expectations. No one who had supported him wanted to hear about the lack of success so far. Mitch had just set himself to jotting notes about another article when his cell phone rang.

"Man—can't you give it a little time to take effect?" the caller questioned.

"Todd?" Mitch asked, not having looked at the caller ID before answering.

"Yeah, it's me. Don't you think you are toeing your party's line just a little too much? Think for yourself a little. Didn't Mr. Obama inherit this horrible economic climate? Give him a chance to work it out—see if his programs work."

"I appreciate your point of view, but we have other periods of time that tell us what to do—things that have been tried and didn't work, and things that have been implemented that did work. Governmental spending has not worked in this country in past situations, or in other countries. The United States cannot spend its way to prosperity. If you have too much credit card debt, do you go out and spend more money? Do you know what has happened in Ireland in the past decade?"

"You are always doing that—asking me something totally different to confuse me. So tell me what has happened in Ireland, because I definitely do not know."

"They lowered corporate and individual tax rates, and their economy has taken off. The answer is not more governmental spending—it is less governmental taxing. The key is to let people keep more of their own money."

"So, you don't you think the stimulus is working, and it won't work if given the chance?" Todd asked Mitch.

"I think my article was pretty clear on that. Listen, Todd, for one, the United States is now in the longest recession since World War II. Most recessions last ten to twelve months, with the longest one in the previous fifty years lasting sixteen. We are now into the nineteenth month of this one. The natural ebb and flow of the economy would suggest that any improvement being experienced is happening despite what the Congress and this administration have done. Second, as I just pointed out, the actions taken are the exact opposite of what should have been done," Mitch said emphatically.

"What do you mean—the opposite?"

"Todd, who employs America?"

"Employers," Todd answered jokingly.

"Okay—employers, businesses for the large part. Of course, there are schools and universities, as well as other governmental jobs. But for the large majority of individuals, private companies are the employers."

"Agreed," Todd said.

"So, if you owned a company, would you want the government helping you create jobs or hurting you?"

"Obviously government should be helping—which is what the stimulus bill was all about. Thank you for making my point."

"We will disagree on that—the stimulus bill is a gimmick to gain more control. We can come back to that. Disregarding the stimulus, has government been helping or hurting business?"

"Helping," Todd said, not too confident about his answer.

"Well, I guess it is open to debate. You should call Al—he lives it every day working for a manufacturing firm. I will use cap and trade as an example. Increasing the energy costs to manufacture a product does not help—it is another obstacle to success. The proposal to tax upper-income individuals to pay for the massive healthcare bill will hurt business as well."

"How is that? If we can pay for additional healthcare by taxing a small portion of the society, won't just about everyone be better off?" Todd asked.

"It might provide benefits to some, but what happens when employers, out of necessity, choose to kick their employees into the public option? Another thing you need to realize is that many small businesses have corporate structures that allow the owners to pay the tax of the company on their personal tax returns. These owners are required to report the income from the company personally. Taxing higher-income individuals is an immediate tax on many small businesses—the ones that employ a good portion of America!"

"I don't think most people understand that," Todd said. "You just explained it to me, and I'm still not sure I understand it."

"You're right; most people don't. Unfortunately, most people don't read enough of how the world works. Anyhow, those are just two examples. This government is killing the incentive to grow. They are punishing success—all in the name of taking money from greedy corporations. That's what will come next—vilifying these entities even more." Mitch drew a breath before continuing.

"Let's say I own a company, and I pay my employees on an hourly basis, but I pay them less each hour they work. For example, the first hour the worker makes $15.00; the next, $13.50; and the hour after that, $12.00. Do you think I would have workers staying more than three or four hours? No way!"

"But why would you pay them like that?" Todd asked. "Wouldn't you pay more to the employees to work overtime?"

"Exactly—you give the workers incentive to work longer—earning a higher wage. Now, think of our tax system. The more you earn, the less of it you get to keep. The exact opposite of common sense! It punishes those who have worked hard and climbed the economic ladder. It punishes the entrepreneurs who have created small business and, in turn, created jobs! I would almost contend that the tax rate should be lower the more income you make! I bet job creation would be astronomical!

"Another point to remember is that these business owners are the investors in jobs. They take their profits and build their companies larger, creating more jobs. Taxing them more eliminates this incentive to grow their businesses."

Todd was beginning to get a headache and felt as if Mitch were talking in circles. "If you say so—I just wanted you to know that not everyone feels the way you do about the stimulus plan."

"Oh, believe me, I hear enough rebuttals here in Phoenix—heck, I just had half of the *Republic* staff berate me before you called—but I never tire of hearing opinions from Arkansas as well!" Mitch decided to change the subject. "I am really looking forward to getting away from the paper for a brief time and seeing you all—anywhere in particular you want to go when we are back in Bowling Green?"

"I hope we hit a few of the old bars we used to frequent—as well as walk around the campus—have you been back lately?" Todd asked.

"Not in a few years," Mitch replied. "I've been to the area to visit my family, but I haven't been to the campus. Hey—I need to get some work done. Thanks again for the opinions—I'll take them under advisement. Talk to you later."

While he was talking to Todd on the phone, his mail had been delivered. He rifled through the stack, discarding most of it. One envelope was handwritten in a calligraphy-like style. *What—am I getting a wedding invitation here at work?* Mitch thought as the writing was so ornate. He opened the envelope and took out a single page letter to which a cashier's check was attached, made out to him, in the amount of $50,000.

"No way!" Mitch exclaimed, and every head in the roomed turned to look at him. He quickly read the letter.

> *You didn't seem impressed enough with my last offer. Believe me, Mr. Bartter, I am on your side, and I just want to help. Use this money for whatever you think is necessary to further the conservative cause. I would also like an article about the pork projects of many top Democrats. Please consider this, and I will consider sending more money.*

Similar to the previous bribe attempt, there was no signature or return address. Mitch called John immediately.

"Another one?" John asked, shocked, as Mitch described what he had just received.

"Come and see it—I tell you—I don't know how to react at this point. One thing is certain: we need that attorney to come back." Mitch hung up the phone and thought for just a second. He was going to document this all he could, and he reached into his desk. He took out a very small tape recorder, replaced the battery and the tape, and found a strategic spot to put it on his desk. He then quickly called Brian Maddox.

"Brian—I need a favor right this minute—are you available?"

"What—you need a verbal punching bag again?"

"No time to explain, can you come to my desk immediately?"

Mitch's urgent tone was enough to snap Mads to attention. He hung up the phone without answering Mitch's question and made his way across the office. Mitch quickly made a copy of the check and letter before Brian had reached his desk.

"Thanks, man," Mitch said to Mads in a relieved manner. "In a few minutes, an attorney will be here to talk to me and John. I can't explain right now, but I need you to sit in the empty cubicle just over there"—Mitch pointed to his right—"you should be able to hear everything. Call me paranoid, but I want to discreetly have a witness to what is about to happen. Do you have about thirty minutes?"

"Sure—no problem," Brian said

"Write down as much as you can," Mitch said, handing him a pad of paper and a pen. Without any further questions, Mads situated himself where Mitch had asked. Mitch kept his eye on the entrance to the room, and within ten minutes, the attorney showed up with John. Before they reached his desk, Mitch pressed the record button on tiny recording device.

The scene from a few weeks ago replayed itself again. Most of the same questions came from the attorney about what Mitch was doing when he received the envelope, a description of everything that was in it, if he had kept the envelope, etc. Mitch made sure he answered loudly and that he referred several times to the first time this had happened and how he followed the same procedures. He repeatedly instructed the attorney to ensure the money went into escrow until the person sending it was identified so he could return it all. The attorney jotted down all the facts, took the check, and affirmed that he would once again take care of all the details.

"Try to put his behind you—we'll get to the bottom of it," John said comfortingly as he patted Mitch on the back. "Why don't you dive back into your article for next week?"

"Good idea," Mitch said. "Thanks for the help, John." After John had left the room, Mitch walked over to the cubicle where Brian was sitting. Mitch could tell that Mads was in a state of utter shock.

"Did that guy say you received a check for $50,000?" Brian asked, hardly able to keep his voice low.

"Shhh! And yes, he did. Can you believe that? It is just crazy."

"And this is the second time this has happened?" Brian asked, confirming what he had heard.

"Yes," Mitch said again a little impatiently. "Were you able to write everything down? Will you be able to remember what happened?"

"Dude, I'm confused as heck, but I am a reporter. I need to remember athlete's quotes when they don't know what they are saying half the time. If I can remember their incoherent babbling, then I can remember all this. I did get most of the conversation down. By the way, great job being discreet—could you have talked any louder?"

"Just wanted to make sure you could hear me."

"Well, your acting skills could use some work. So, who is sending you money to write about what they want? I'm mean, obviously you don't know, but do you have any thoughts?"

"Not a one—but this isn't the first strange thing that has happened in the last few weeks. I don't want to share too much at this point. I know you are probably full of questions, but for now, let's just keep this between us. Agreed?"

"Let's keep what between us?" Mads responded.

"Great—I'm sure I've kept you long enough. I know I need to get back to work," Mitch said. "Thanks again and I will keep you updated."

Mitch didn't really need to get to work. The appearance of this second envelope brought all his concerns about the Liberty Group flooding back. He was becoming more convinced that all of these strange happenings related to that group one way or another. He wanted to formulate a plan to investigate his new friends a little. Of course, it did occur to him that this money and the incident the other day could be related to his Web site work, but not necessarily the group itself. Either way, Mitch determined at that moment that he was going to find out who it was for certain. His first thought was to arrive about an hour early tomorrow for his next Liberty Group meeting. Maybe he could ask around the hotel to see what some of the staff knew about Gus. Hopefully, that could allay some of his suspicions.

Chapter 14

Mitch was packing up his desk before heading over to the Biltmore when his phone rang. The ID screen indicated it was Al.

"Hey, buddy," Mitch answered, talking fast. "What's happening?"

"You sound busy—I can try you later."

"I am on my way out the door. Later would be great—that would help. I did mean to tell you that I liked the quote from U.S. Rep. Jim Jordan in your latest article on the Web site; where did you see him?" Mitch asked.

"He came to speak at a local rotary meeting. Seems like a very sharp guy. Which quote did you like—when he paraphrased Margaret Thatcher?"

"Yes—about not having the votes to win the issue, but if you win the debate, you are setting yourself up to win the next election cycle."

"Hopefully, that is what we are doing with this little project of yours, huh?" Al responded.

"Exactly," Mitch answered. "Hey—I do have to run—I'll call you later."

The Liberty Group

* * * * *

Mitch had decided to take a cab to the Biltmore today. He knew paranoia was getting the better of him, but he did not want any of the others to see his car there earlier than it would have normally been. He hoped this was all a wild goose chase, but he had to try to determine what was happening.

Mitch arrived at the Biltmore about 11:45, with their meeting scheduled for 1:00. He contemplated how to start asking about Gus without arousing suspicion. He walked up to the front desk.

"I usually attend a meeting at one o'clock every Thursday here in one of your meeting room," Mitch said to the person behind the desk. "Long story, but due to car problems, I had to be dropped off early. Do you know if that room is available until the meeting starts?" The clerk made a call, obtaining the information and taking a while with the conversation.

"Apparently, the person who reserves that room on Thursdays has it from 11:00 through 2:00, although I was just told he usually meets with one group of people at 11:00, they break for lunch, and then reconvene at 1:00 when a few others join them."

"Oh—so they are here now?" Mitch asked, feeling his temperature rise a bit. "Did you see them come in?"

"I do believe I saw the older gentleman—I don't recall who else."

"Thanks for your help." Mitch began to walk away.

"I also found out the same person also has a meeting on the third Thursday of each month as well—later in the afternoon—three o'clock," the clerk said. "That meeting requires some specialized telecommunications equipment."

"Interesting," Mitch said thoughtfully. He walked away, shaking the last bit of information from his current thoughts. Mitch decided he would at least peek into the room right now, assuming Gus, Charlie, and Paul were at lunch. If not, he would use the car story he had just given the clerk. He avoided the restaurant areas, not wanting to accidentally be spotted by any of them. Their room was reserved as usual, and the door was open. Mitch walked in and found no one there, although what he recognized to be Gus's briefcase was sitting next to a chair, and he was certain that the two computers set up in the room belonged to Paul and Charlie, as they were in their customary places. He looked around the room, contemplating what he wanted to do. A quick look out the door proved that no one was about to join him.

Mitch decided to take a chance and went over to Charlie's computer and jiggled the mouse to activate the screen. It was on the startup screen; he hadn't even signed in yet. Strike one. He walked to the other table where Paul's computer was sitting, and luckily, Paul had already signed in, with the screen displaying an e-mail page. He had obviously signed on and accessed the wireless network of the hotel. Mitch scanned the e-mails noting several labeled GReed@LibertyGroup.com. Several had not yet been opened, and Mitch was not about to click on one of those. He did notice some, however, that had been opened and not deleted or sorted into a folder. Mitch clicked one dated June 2, hesitating only to look up to ensure he saw and heard no one then read the e-mail.

> *Paul—please provide an updated list of contributors organized by individual vs. corporate as well as by each state. I do appreciate the database you have designed to maintain this information. The reports you previously sent were exactly as I envisioned. I cannot stress to you enough the importance of this evidence down the road.*
>
> *Gus*

Mitch closed that message and scanned for others. He clicked on another one from Gus, but it was just a meeting reminder. He knew time was probably running out before the other three would return from lunch. Mitch scanned Paul's other e-mails, looking for anything with an attachment from someone at the Liberty Group. He saw one more from Gus with the familiar paperclip attachment symbol. It was dated

May 25, exactly one month earlier. His heart was starting to pound very heavily as his conscience was questioning what he was doing, but the subject line was one he could not ignore. It read simply, "Bartter Project." Mitch quickly forwarded this one to his own account at home without opening it and then deleted the message, hoping that Paul would not miss it. He went into Paul's deleted folder and permanently deleted it as well. He did not want Paul opening it and seeing the notice that it had been forwarded appear at the top.

He exited back to the mail inbox page and walked to the door. He looked down the hall—no sign of the others, but he did not want to risk being found in here too soon. He hurried out of the room and toward the main lobby. It was still fifteen minutes before their meeting was to start. He ducked into a bathroom and tried to calm himself a little. He wanted to show no sign of guilt when the meeting started. Mitch could not wait to get home and read the e-mail, though.

The Thursday meeting was similar to their previous ones. Gus elaborated on his Fourth of July party a little more. When the meeting was over, they all packed up and headed out. In the parking lot, Russell observed Mitch get into a cab as well as Karen's departure. He then came into the Biltmore himself—telling his partner to follow the cab. Paul was just coming out, and Russell flagged him down. Paul had been involved in several other of Gus and Charlie's operations in the past and knew Russell.

"Hi, Russ—giving a report to the big guy?" Paul asked in a cheery manner.

"I actually wanted to talk to you," he responded, all business.

"What about?"

"Did you forward an e-mail to Mitch today?" Russell asked.

"Me—not that I recall."

"It was one Gus had sent you with the subject line 'Bartter Project'?"

"No—I definitely did not send that."

"Funny, because we intercepted it coming into his home e-mail account. We have not let it proceed on as of yet."

"Who would have sent that from my computer?" Paul asked, confused.

"I may have that answer—Mitch arrived about an hour early today by taxi. Did you see him earlier than normal?"

"No—same time as always." Paul's mind was racing—would Mitch really have looked at his computer? He was also trying to remember what was in that e-mail. "Look, I'll go back and tell the others. You can delete that e-mail before it reaches his home—correct?"

"We can."

"Can you alter it instead?" Paul questioned as an idea had just occurred to him.

"We can do that as well. We have no way of knowing if he has already read it, however. The timeline would seem to fit that he may well have seen its content."

"I'm guessing that if he had read it, he wouldn't have taken the time to forward it. I don't think that e-mail was horribly revealing, but I can't take the chance that it was. No—I think it is best if I alter it before he sees it. If he did indeed send it to himself from my computer, then he will know we are up to something if no e-mail comes through. Can I come with you right now and do that? I don't want Mitch heading straight home and getting this."

"You're lucky his cell phone is still a very basic model," Russell commented, indicating that Mitch was unable to access his home e-mail from his phone. "I'm set up in the van outside—you can change it from there. However, we are tailing him as well. He got into a cab, and it appears headed for his office."

"Still—I want to change it right now. Thanks for this information, Russell. Let me go back and tell the others what we have discussed, and then I will be right out."

"No problem." Russell turned to return to his vehicle.

Paul thought for a moment, watching Russell leave the lobby. He had already decided *not* to tell the others despite what he had just said to Russell. Paul was concerned Charlie would overreact, and he knew they were getting close to Gus's more involved plans. The big guy was already on edge. Extricating Mitch at this point would cause a major problem. If he changed the e-mail enough, Mitch would be more comforted than shocked at the content. The more Paul thought about it, the more convinced he was that Mitch had yet to read the message. Better to change it quickly. He waited just a few more minutes and then headed out to the van.

"How long do you think until he gets back to his office?" Paul asked Russell upon entering the van.

"I would guess about five to ten minutes," Russell answered as he typed away at his computer, accessing the e-mail.

"I can change anything I want about this message?"

"I can even make it look like it was sent on a different date if you want."

"Perfect," Paul said as he conjured in his head a new detailed e-mail that would fit the subject heading listed.

Mitch did get into a cab and headed straight back to his office. The ride seemed to take forever. Mitch almost ran through the crowed newspaper office to his desk. He accessed his home e-mail from his work computer and opened the message he had forwarded to himself. He began reading slowly, taking in every word.

> *Bartter Project:*
> *We will ask Mitch Bartter to head up our Web site activities. If he is willing, Mr. Bartter will contact numerous other writers, have daily opinion pieces, and set up as many state links as possible. This position is integral to our success, and Mr. Bartter is our top choice to make this happen. Please research his articles and let us develop an offer for his services. Paul knows his supervisor at the Republic, John Manos. We will reach out to him to see if he would approve Mitch for the job, and if so, if he would be willing to arrange a meeting. This is the best guy for*

our project. He will help us promote the conservative ideas we need to put forth in order to ensure different results in future elections. I trust you will all work hard to impress him, assuming we can bring him in for an interview. Thank you very much.

Gus

Well, that was awfully anticlimactic, thought Mitch. Still, something did not seem right. He reread the e-mail. It was very complimentary to him, but he would swear that when he had looked at the date of the e-mail to Paul in the hotel, it was May 25, notable because it was exactly one month earlier than today. If that was the correct date, then this e-mail was sent over two weeks *after* his initial meeting with the management group of Liberty. Why would there be an e-mail with this information dated after the group had already signed him up? Had he remembered the date incorrectly—was it possibly March 25? No—Mitch was certain that the date had read May 25. After staring at his computer for about ten more minutes with no revelations coming to him, Mitch closed the message and started back to work on his *Republic* article.

Chapter 15

The following day, John, Mads, and Mitch were having lunch together at yet another Buffalo Wild Wings. Lunches at BW-3's on Fridays were fairly commonplace with these three. John could tell that Mitch was bothered by something and used the pretense of lunch to maybe put him at ease and hope to get some information about what was on his mind. Brian trumped him though and started into Mitch on a political issue.

"I didn't like your article today, Mitch," Mads began. "I know—I usually do not like your articles."

"That's too bad—I thought yours was great!" Mitch responded, nonplussed at Brian's comment.

"What is so wrong with the progressive tax system?" Mads blurted out. "You know—we've had this tax system a while now; we have seemed to do pretty well with it."

Mitch could just not stop hammering home his opinion of the unfairness of the individual and corporate tax structure and how much it held back American success and job creation. At least one article every month confronted some aspect of the tax system.

"It's wrong because it punishes success," Mitch began as if this were the clearest point in the world. "Someone will need to make the argument to me of why there should be higher tax rates for higher income earners."

"Well, I'll start with the obvious—they can afford it!" Mads said emphatically.

"I don't share that sentiment. Just because people have more money, they should shoulder more of the tax burden of others? Let's restate this argument in a different manner. Let's say your child does excellent in school and earns 100 percent of the points available in a class. Let's also say that someone else only earns 70 percent of the points in a class—should your child be forced to pay a tax of points so the other child can earn a B? Does that make sense?"

"No—it doesn't make sense, but it is a flawed argument. Points earned in class are not used for anything other than to gauge how well you did in the class. They are not a commodity like money. Money powers the economy. Doesn't logic suggest that if more people have money, then the economy will be more efficient?" Mads argued.

"You can call my school argument flawed if you want, but the theory is sound; you earn points—you earn money," Mitch responded. "It is exactly what we are doing. The government cannot spend one dollar without first taking it from someone else. Let's try another argument. Let's say you practice hard to become a good runner. You are exceptionally fast at long races and can average 5:30 a mile for a full marathon—twenty-six plus miles. Now, someone else has not practiced as hard and can only run eight-minute miles. Should the race rules penalize you, say, one minute per mile and benefit the other runner the same amount? No—but that is what our tax system does."

"Again a failed argument in that running is also not a commodity. Besides, some people have natural running abilities; it just comes easier to them."

"And being successful at a job doesn't come easier to some people? Let's face it: certain individuals have a stronger work ethic. That is not a point for debate. Some people care more about the job they do just like some people try to just get by. Tell me I'm wrong. I don't think you can." Mitch stopped for a moment to contemplate his argument, but started right back in.

"Don't you think that the tax code should be designed in a way that collects the maximum amount of revenue while encouraging economic growth? Economic growth needs investment. And who invests? Those who have money. By taxing the investors more, the government takes away resources that would otherwise be used to create economic growth. Now, besides your original argument that the wealthy can afford it, give me another reason for increasing the tax rates as income increases."

"Well, we need to close this enormous budget deficit somehow," Mads said defiantly. "Average Joe and Jane American sure can't make up that gap."

"Nice try, but taxing the wealthy, in my opinion, will lead only to larger deficits," Mitch replied.

"How do you figure that?" Mads asked, shaking his head.

"Our tax system is not just progressive; it is uber progressive—the top 20 percent of income earners pay over 85 percent of the income taxes. When you have such an unbalanced system, tax revenues tend to fluctuate more as economic activity fluctuates. So, as the economy grows strong, more tax is collected, and as it turns down, like our current situation, tax revenues drop precipitously. If you increase rates on the wealthy and tilt the scales even more against those individuals, this volatility increases even more. Our deficit is due to the unbelievably high level of gross negligence and over-exuberant spending Congress has exercised for the last twenty or so years—both Republicans and Democrats. We had great economic times in the 1990s and for most of the 2000s as well, and tax revenues skyrocketed. Did we use these positive economic times to work down our deficit? No, we did not! Congress unexplainably decided to increase spending by even greater amounts. We need to have fiscal restraint. Spending within our means will bring back prosperity more quickly than any other tactic." Mitch took a deep breath before continuing.

"So, any other reasons the rich should pay so much more?" Mitch asked again.

"Heck, I'm not sure I understood your argument against my last reason. I think you are trying to confuse me. All I know is that if we cut taxes, the people who need the money the least get the most. It's just not fair."

"You're starting at the wrong point of the equation. Sure, the people who get the most from a tax cut make the most money, and that may not seem fair. But you have to start at who is paying taxes. If you start everyone at zero, and then look at who pays the tax revenue the government collects, it wouldn't seem fair either, just in the opposite way. Didn't you read the tax debate I had on the Liberty site a few weeks back? Anyway, if you still think the wealthy do not pay enough, we may have to agree to disagree. You can't get a break from a cut in tax rates if you do not pay any taxes. It is that simple. Tax rate cuts benefit those who pay tax, and currently, almost 50 percent of wage earners do not pay taxes."

"Mitch—it is just common sense!" Brian was almost yelling now. "Who else can afford the additional taxes necessary to make up the deficit?" He was quickly becoming annoyed with his friend's stubborn attitude.

"There it is—the point that ultimately is always made," Mitch said. "Who else can pay? How about no one? I reiterate my point from just a few minutes ago. How about we spend less and tax everyone less? No one even seems to consider that possibility, but that is an option. It is so maddening that just about every politician campaigns on reducing waste, and yet once they get in office, Congress continues to spend more. Both sides of the aisle! They say what the people want to hear while they campaign, but yet, they have difficulty following through on those promises. I don't think it is for a lack of trying, but usually the incumbents in power when the new ones come in do not allow

the reduction in programs and spending. It is the age-old adage—it is near impossible to take something away once it has been given."
"You're getting a bit off topic, aren't you?" John interjected.

"It's all related. The government has done a great job of convincing the public that it is the *right* of the government to allow you, the governed, *to keep* a portion of your paycheck instead of the governed realizing that it is their money being taken. Have you ever listened to the syndicated morning radio program Bob and Tom?"

"Bob and Tom—that's not a very political show," Brian said. "Don't they have comedians on all the time?"

"Exactly. Anyhow, I was driving to work and listening to their show one day. Tom gave the opinion that Election Day should be April 16. His point was that we would all pay a lot less in taxes if we were voting the day after most people had to file their income tax returns." Mitch decided to try to catch his friend off-guard.

"Here is another argument. Mads – —how much do you make?"

Brian looked a little shocked at the question. Mitch responded to his hesitation.

"Come on—John probably already knows, and we're two different types of writers. Just between us friends. How much do you make?" Mitch asked again, carefully phrasing the question in that manner.

"I take home about $2,700 every two weeks," Mads answered truthfully.

"Perfect—that is what you take home, not what you earn, correct?" Mitch asked, setting the trap.

"Right—I thought that is what you meant," Brian answered, confused.

"That is how most people think of it as well—'What it my net paycheck?' This attitude discounts totally what is being withheld from your *real* earnings. I contend that having employers withhold your federal taxes is great for the government. When taxes are withheld a portion on each check, most people don't even stop to add it up. I propose we should do away with withholding, in theory. Let's make everyone write a weekly check or a check every two weeks to the government to cover their tax bills. Where do you think tax rates would be then?"

"These are all great points, but it still comes back to the initial argument. You can't change things overnight, and we have to pay for the programs our government has committed to running. You have to get the funds from someone."

"I'm going to let it drop at this point," Mitch replied. "You will not convince me of your points, and I don't think I'm going to convince you of mine. I will say just one more thing. The total governmental spending in 2005 was $2.472 trillion, while for the current year, it is forecast to be $3.998 trillion. Now, imagine you have a mortgage payment of $2,000 per month. Would you be able to increase your mortgage payment to $3,234 in just four years when your income *decreased*?"

"Of course not; that would be financial suicide," Brian responded.

"That is what our country has done—we are collecting less and spending more. We have not attacked this problem from the spending side. That is imperative."

After lunch, they paid their bills and headed outside. They had walked to the restaurant, and as they strolled back to the paper, John asked Brian to go on ahead. Mitch rolled his eyes, knowing he was about to face a series of questions.

"So, what is going on, Mitch?" John started.

"What do you mean?" Mitch asked.

"Come on—we've worked together long enough for me to know when something is wrong. It's not exactly like you do a good job of hiding it." Mitch knew John was right. People could usually tell if something was wrong. It wasn't so much that he was mean or treated people badly; it was more that he just wasn't his normal self.

"It's nothing—just haven't slept well recently." This was true, but it was more a symptom than a cause.

"Why aren't you sleeping well?" John probed, guessing that Mitch was being evasive.

"Numerous things—concerned about the direction of the country, mainly," Mitch joked. He knew John would continue asking, but throwing non-answers at him might force him to give up, at least for now. Mitch didn't have the proof yet that something was seriously wrong with this Liberty Group. If he expressed his concern to John, Mitch was afraid of the questions that John might bring to Paul in a half-cocked manner, attempting to extricate Mitch from the situation.

"Yeah—the country. Right. Seriously—Marie and the kids okay?" John asked sincerely.

"They're fine—no problems."

"Are you overextending yourself with this Liberty Group involvement?" John continued. "Your work at the *Republic* hasn't suffered at all, so I assumed everything was going fine on the Liberty end as well."

"It's great. It's all great, John. As I said—I'm just a little tired." Mitch hoped his forceful reply would give his boss the hint to let it drop.

"All right—but when you are ready to talk, you know where I am."

* * * * *

Mitch got home that Friday evening, and after a dinner of delivery pizza, Lynne went out with her boyfriend, Jane jumped on her computer, and Ed was watching a *Star Wars* cartoon. Marie had decided to do some Internet surfing as well, so Mitch grabbed the leashes and took his dogs for a walk, hoping to clear his head. The Phoenix evening was still very hot, but his blood had grown accustomed to it after the years he had lived here. He relished feeling the heat on his skin as he, Sydney, and Sage traipsed through the neighborhood. Mitch began to list his concerns about Liberty in his head as he walked.

First, there were two separate times that women had thrown themselves at him since his involvement with Liberty started. There was obviously no direct connection to anyone at Liberty regarding these occurrences, but as it hadn't happened once in the twenty years since college prior to this, he was including it as a concern. Second, the comment Charlie made that seemed too coincidental. Not to mention that he just did not like Charlie at all and didn't trust him. Third, the e-mail. He had thought about it over the last forty-eight hours, and he was certain that the date he saw originally was May 25. Given that he was certain about the date, the e-mail he received made no sense. Finally, of course, the bribe attempts. As he put all this together in his mind, Mitch decided to call Al. Ever since college, if he had a dilemma, he always valued Al's opinion. Mitch pulled out his cell and dialed his friend's number.

Al and his wife had decided to surprise their kids with a quick family weekend getaway to Mackinac Island. Pronounced Mack-In-Naw, the island was situated between Lake Huron and Lake Michigan, just to the east of the Mackinac Bridge, which connected the lower and upper peninsulas of Michigan. The island kept a "turn-back-the-clock" feel by disallowing automobiles. All visitors took a ferry over to the island from either the upper or lower peninsula, leaving their cars behind. Horse-drawn taxis and bicycles dominated the transportation on the island, although most of the tourist areas were centralized, and walking was no problem. The Miller family had just arrived, checked into their hotel, and had walked the short distance back to the center of town to Horn's Bar for a late dinner when Al's cell phone buzzed in his pocket.

Recognizing Mitch's cell phone number, Al answered, "Horn's Bar and Grill."

Mitch knew it was Al's voice.

"Where are you?" he asked, half laughing.

"I told you—Horn's Bar and Grill."

"Well, where exactly is that?"

"On Mackinac Island, just sitting down to dinner." Mitch knew of the island, having grown up in that part of the country.

"I'm sorry to bother you. Can you call me later tonight or tomorrow?" Mitch said, almost pleading.

"Let's shoot for tomorrow—how about one o'clock your time? I'm sure we will tool around the island most of the day, but we are planning to eat at the Grand Hotel for dinner, and I know that we will need to take care of the necessary primping and priming that will occur prior to going out." Al looked at Lisa—she smirked back at him.

"Sounds good—I really need to discuss something with you," Mitch said.

"Everything okay? You sound concerned," Al said, stepping away from the table and out onto the street to give more attention to his friend.

"I'm sure it's nothing—it has to do with Liberty. We'll talk tomorrow."

"Hey—I'll talk now if you need to," Al answered.

"No—enjoy your family time. Tomorrow will be fine. Thanks, Al." Al heard Mitch click his phone off.

"Everything okay with Mitch?" Lisa asked as Al returned to the table.

"I don't know—something's bothering him. I'll find out more tomorrow. So, did you check out the menu while I was on the phone? What sounds good?"

"They have a lot of southwestern dishes—I guess it was appropriate Mitch was calling you from the great Southwest."

"Do you want to split a bottle of wine?" Al asked his wife.

"You must not have noticed—they have Guinness on tap."

"Do they? Well, I know what I'm having."

Lisa had surprised Al several years earlier with a Christmas gift of a trip to Ireland. They had spent a week traveling around the southern part of the country, renting a car, driving on the left hand side of the road, and staying at bed and breakfasts. It was a wonderful trip, and of course, being in Ireland, most places served draft Guinness. Al had really taken a liking to it. Now, whenever they went out, if the place had

Guinness on draft, he usually ordered it. He had even found a place in Bowling Green that poured it in the same fashion as in Ireland, long, slow, and with a shamrock pattern in the foamy head. It had a much thicker taste than most beers and was definitely an acquired taste, but Al loved it now as it always reminded him of the wonderful time he and Lisa had had together.

"So, you're going to drink that tar again?" Savannah asked.

"Hey, I like it—don't bother me."

"Well, I guess it is okay, since we are walking back to the hotel, and you do not have to drive," his daughter replied.

They finished their dinner and walked around the downtown area. Mackinac was famous for fudge, and there seemed to be a sweet shop every other store. Most of the shops were tourist-type businesses, with shirts and snow globes and key chains. Al, Lisa, and the kids enjoyed their evening stroll very much. The next morning, they awoke to mostly cloudy skies, albeit dry. The family went down to the lobby for the hotel-provided breakfast and then headed out again. Mackinac also had a fort that was built at the end of the Revolutionary War. It played a role in both the War of 1812 and the Civil War. Today, reenactments were the main attraction. Al, Lisa, Savannah, and Michael walked up the considerable ramp and toured the historic site, with Savannah taking part in the cannon firing (she held her thumb on a hole as the cannon was cleaned of previous debris). They listened to some history of the fort and toured the numerous buildings. Later, they headed back into town as the rain started to fall. The drops became considerably heavier, and the four of them ducked into a restaurant for lunch. They warmed up and enjoyed the conversation as they ate.

After looking at some more shops and wandering around some of the neighborhoods with huge vacation homes, they headed back to the hotel to rest up for the dinner. Al took the opportunity to give Mitch a call.

"So—what's on your mind?" Al asked his friend.

"It's going to sound strange, I'm sure," Mitch replied. "That is one reason I wanted to talk to you—hopefully, you can be an objective opinion."

"What do you mean—what's been strange?"

"Well—I have had a feeling that this Liberty Group is not all that it seems, mainly due to a few interesting things that happened in the last month or so."

"Like what?"

"Twice I was hit on—that never happens—I mean, come on, I'm in my forties. And these women were gorgeous—way above my status on the attraction meter."

"Yes," Al said, laughing. "Todd told me about the night out you two had. I figured that was a monthly occurrence for you."

"Al—I'm serious, man," Mitch implored. "Something is just not right."

"Is the group treating you badly?" Al asked, as he walked out of his hotel room and onto the balcony, overlooking the lake.

"No—they all seem to love me. They have given me free reign to run the Web site, and I have really enjoyed it. But one guy—his name is Charlie—I have never felt good around him. And he made a comment after one of our meetings that seemed just too similar to something I had said earlier that week."

"So he's quoting you back to you—that probably happens with your readers sometimes," Al responded helpfully.

"That's just it—he quoted me from a conversation I had with Lynne—you may remember I sent you, Todd, and Mark an e-mail about it—that comment about the teacher and the jackass?"

"He knew about that?" Al asked, surprised.

"It sure seemed like it. Then, of course, there are the two bribe attempts."

"Bribe attempts—what do you mean?" Al asked, his concern growing with each comment.

"Twice now, a sum of money has arrived addressed to me and offering more if I write articles as the sender suggests. You know, any one of these situations happening individually wouldn't make me squeamish, but taken together, they concern me quite a bit. I decided to act on those concerns."

"What did you do?" Al asked, not sure he was going to like what he was about to hear.

"I showed up at the last meeting about an hour early, just to ask some of the hotel staff about the leader. I was informed he was already there, with two others, and that they are usually there about two hours before the meeting I attend. They were eating in one of the restaurants at the hotel, so I went to the room, and one of the guy's computers was on and not locked. The screen showed his e-mails, and I read a few and even forwarded one to myself."

"Geez-a-me Christmas, Mitch. What if they had walked in?"

"I know—it seems a little crazy just saying it."

"So, what was in the e-mail you forwarded?" Al continued to probe.

"Nothing really. Its subject line was 'Bartter Project,' but the content just talked about trying to entice me to join them. The perplexing part is that when I first saw it, I remembered the date being May 25—which was a few weeks after I started. It wouldn't make sense to send this out after I had been working with them for a few weeks. I don't know—I'm just confused."

"Mitch, I have always thought that you had great instincts. If your internal warning gauge is going off, there is a definite reason. With that being said, don't do a fool thing like that e-mail caper again! If they had found …" Al's voice trailed off.

"If they had found what?" Mitch asked.

There was silence for a few moments. "Al—you still there?"

"I'm here—I was just thinking." Another few moments of silence. "Mitch—a few of these strange items that have happened are e-mail related, correct?"

"Well—this one is."

"That 'jackass' comment was sent in an e-mail to us, too. Is it possible your e-mail is being monitored?"

"Why would that be happening, not to mention how?" Mitch was taken aback. He had not even considered that. "I really don't know."

"It's just that you are concerned about communications in e-mails—that would be a possible answer to those concerns," Al said.

Mitch thought for a few moments and realized that his friend might have a point. "So, what do I do if that is the case?"

"Excellent question—don't send anything important from your home e-mail, for starters. This may sound very paranoid, but I wouldn't assume your work e-mail is safe either."

"Now you are sounding awfully conspiratorial."

"I know—it sounds ludicrous. But you have also said that this group is very well financed and seems to have unlimited resources. I would be careful. If we start with the premise that your home e-mail is under surveillance, then is it a stretch to think your work e-mail would be, too? You haven't been asked to do anything you're not comfortable with, have you?"

"No—as I said—overall I'm having a blast!"

"Okay—hopefully, we are just two idiotic people who have seen too many movies," Al said. "I'll chew on those bribe attempts a little and get back with you. You know what might help—trying to get to know the other two better."

"What do you mean, 'the other two'?" Mitch asked.

"Well, you have talked to me before about Gus and Charlie. See if you can learn more from the others—Paul, and is it Karen? Maybe set up a dinner with them, one at a time. See if you learn anything more."

"That is a good idea—I'll definitely do that. Thanks, man—I had hoped talking with you would make me feel better. I actually think I'm more concerned, but I'm glad you know what I'm dealing with—that does make me feel better. We'll see what happens. You guys enjoying Mackinac?"

"Oh, yeah—it's always fun to go somewhere with the kids—we are so fortunate to have great kids! I'm sorry I'm not being more helpful with your concerns. As I said, I'll keep thinking about them. How about you—what's on tap for your family this weekend?"

"I'm going to take my posse to see Harry Potter—that will help take my mind off things. Enjoy the rest of your weekend."

"Thanks—you, too."

* * * * *

Al, Lisa, Savannah, and Michael all put on their best clothes for the dinner at the Grand Hotel, which was truly a spectacular site. It opened in 1887 with the popularity of Mackinac as a summer getaway increasing at that time. Its front porch, accentuated with huge columns, was the largest in the world, spanning 660 feet. Two movies had been filmed on the grounds, and beautiful gardens were plentiful.

The Millers boarded their horse-drawn taxi and clip-clopped to the Grand, with Lisa and Savannah not wanting to traipse the mile or so in their heels. They took a backpack with appropriate walking shoes for after dinner. The Grand Hotel had three menus that rotated daily. Each menu consisted of four courses, with several appetizers to choose from, several soups, a salad, and fantastic main courses. Not being guests of the hotel, the Millers paid ahead of time—flat fee for the dinner, no tipping allowed—and sat in the opulence of the 1,000-seat dining room. The chairs were striped green and white, while pastel colors adorned the walls. Of course, the length of the room was windowed, looking over the grounds and out onto the lake. The family enjoyed the meal immensely, which even came with some scrumptious desserts. After dinner, they walked around the hotel and poked their heads into the dance room where a band was playing. The Miller family all jumped on the dance floor and kicked it up for a few songs, laughing and singing along. As usual, Lisa turned several heads. She was tall with short, light brown hair and beautiful eyes. Al always noticed other men looking at her whenever they went out; of course, Lisa did look at ten years younger than she really was. He even chuckled a little as someone at the edge of the dance floor asked Savannah if Lisa was her older sister. Holding hands as they enjoyed the leisurely stroll back to the hotel, Al and Lisa felt so fortunate to have this time together as a family. It was truly a magical night.

* * * * *

"Looks like Mitch might be on to us," Charlie said to Gus.

"What do you mean?" Gus asked.

"I just listened to a call he made to his friend Al," Charlie explained. "You're not going to like this. First, he sensed something was wrong and apparently showed up at one of our Liberty Group meetings early."

"When in the world did this happen?" Gus almost shouted, a stone dropping in his stomach.

"I think last week. Anyhow, he went into our room while we were at lunch, and Paul had left his computer on." Charlie went on to explain the conversation he had been forwarded from his surveillance team. Gus was getting more angry by the minute, his face turning a shade of puce.

"We can always threaten him or his family—scare him if that is what it takes to complete all our objectives," Charlie said.

Gus looked piercingly at Charlie. "You know I do not approve of those types of tactics. I resort to them if it is the only option, but I would rather 'trick' Mitch into a decision that he has to live with as opposed to taking hostages or sticking a gun in his face. I have tried to be nonviolent with this operation. I know your background is slightly different, but besides the Sacramento issue, we have not physically harmed anyone, and I want to keep it that way."

"Okay—you're the boss," Charlie responded.

"Is this friend Al the one Mitch has writing for us as well?" Gus asked.

"It is."

"Hmm. Is it possible we need to keep an eye on him, too?"

"I don't think so. This is the accountant we talked about before. I don't see how he can hurt us, outside of planting more ideas in Mitch's head."

"Continue to monitor their communications—let me know if he suggests anything else about our group," Gus directed.

"But what about Mitch?" Charlie asked.

"Let's do nothing right now. If we react in some manner, we just prove his concerns. If we go about business as usual, he will still be in the dark. Just no slip-ups. We have him monitored pretty tightly. We'll know if he does anything else."

"How about Paul?" Charlie asked hesitantly.

"Get him over here right now."

Chapter 16

Karen was at a client's office on Monday morning, going over some of the work papers her staff had put together. During these trying times, she at least had the solace of her job. Many of her friends did not understand how she could enjoy being an auditor, but she saw herself as a business advisor first. She was a consultant to her clients, helping them in any way she could. She understood that Will's contributions might be more tangible—saving a client $50,000 in taxes was easy to quantify—but Karen was confident she made significant suggestions as well. Karen had helped several clients avoid some fraud situations that potentially would have cost millions. In her mind, she was like the football lineman who makes the block that allows the running back to run for eighty yards. The running back might have the stats beside his name, but without the lineman, those stats would never have happened. Without her advice and consultation, she knew many of her clients would not be nearly as successful as they were today. It was this knowledge and confidence she was relying on to come up with a way out of her Liberty situation. Since her talk with Will a few weeks earlier, she had felt more certain about herself and had pulled out of her funk.

Will had been right, and she was going to figure this out—she knew she would.

As Karen was reviewing some complicated accrual analysis, her cell phone rang on the table.

"Karen Simmons," she answered.

"Karen, it's Rick." Rick was an audit manager in the firm. He was one of the first people she had hired when she and Will had started the firm.

"Hey—I'm at Solar Pyramids, and I was wondering if you had a chance to review the proposal I gave you last week?" Rick asked.

"I did—it looked good but I did change some of the wording. I was going to give it one more perusal. Why do you ask?"

"The CFO here at Pyramid gave me a great lead on a display screen manufacturer in Mesa. They seem to be at odds with their current professional services firm and may be looking to shop their business. Anyhow, I called over, and they asked me to send some information about us. That proposal has a section with the most up-to-date strengths of our firm, and I was hoping to lift some if it to send as an e-mail. Unfortunately, I gave it to you on a flash drive without saving a copy."

"The Internet is down here, and I can't access my office information," Karen replied. Pondering for a moment on how to solve this situation, Will popped into her head. He could access her work files. She could always change her password—there really wasn't anything he was going to see. "I tell you what," she said. "Let me make a call and see what I can come up with."

"That would be great—this guy seems really angry for some reason, and I think we need to strike while we can. From what his friend here at Pyramid says, he's been thinking about changing for some time, and it would probably be about a $75,000 account, between tax and audit. I want to respond today—show him we're serious."

"All right—if you don't have something in ten minutes, call me back." Karen hung up her cell. She dialed the office number and asked for Will. As usual, he answered on the first ring.

"Will—it's Karen."

"How are you?" Will's voice was its customary happy tone.

"Great—we have a lead on a potential new client—Rick seems pretty excited about it. He needs some information that I have, but I can't access it from here right now."

"Do you have it on the system here that I can get for you?" Will asked helpfully.

"I do—but it's on my computer—not on a shared drive. Would you go to my office, access the file, and e-mail it Rick? You need to review that proposal anyhow."

"I'll need your password."

"I know—it's FASB1984," Karen replied.

"Seriously—your password is FASB?" Will asked, laughing.

FASB, pronounced *fasbee* by most accountants, stood for "Financial Accounting Standards Board." The stock market crash of 1929 and the Great Depression led to many financial changes, including the desire for uniform standards of accounting to be used by all companies. Congress passed the Securities Act of 1933 as well as the Securities Exchange Act of 1934, laws that seemed to be leading to a governmental takeover of the accounting rules, but the SEC voted in 1938 to allow the private sector to regulate accounting. The Accounting Principles Board was established and set the standards to be used for many years. However, in the early 1970s, the Financial Accounting Standards Board was created, and the SEC ratified its role in oversight and the establishment of financial accounting and reporting principles, standards, and practices. This board would issue statements to clarify the accounting of many intricate transactions and situations. These statements were usually referred to by number, such as FASB 87 or FASB 119. Of course, most of this was about to change with a codification of accounting rules, but for now, FASB still ruled.

"I thought I had no life," Will joked, unable to stop himself. "This isn't a password; it's a cry for help."

Eric Myerholtz

"Let me guess—your password has something to do with the tax code?" Karen retorted.

Will stopped laughing, hesitating for just a moment. "We're not talking about me."

"Just e-mail the information to Rick and copy yourself on it as well." Karen gave him the file location within her computer and hung up the phone. She went back to reviewing the accrual work paper.

Will first grabbed a diet soda from the vending machine and then went to Karen's office and sat down. As he waited for her computer to start, he glanced around. He had been in here a hundred times but now realized she had no personal effects at all. He knew she had never married, so there were no pictures of the family vacations. Some other single people in the office had photos of friends or pets. There was one particular tax professional who did a great job, but Will cringed every time he walked in the break room and she was there—knowing he was about to get an earful of all the amazing things her dog was doing. She had pictures of the canine everywhere on her cubicle, a rather ugly beast in Will's opinion. Karen's office, however, was completely devoid of any such decoration. Everything on display related to her professional life. Her CPA certificate hung on the wall along with her MBA. A dry erase board covered most of another wall, with client names and notes jotted on it. He wondered what Karen did in her free time—not that she took much vacation. Will assumed that she must have some hobby, though.

Karen's computer had reached the opening screen, and Will typed her name and the password, gaining access to the firm's network. He searched first for the proposal and found it exactly as Karen had described. He then clicked into her e-mail (the firm used Outlook). As he was moving the mouse across the screen to create a new file to send, Karen's office phone rang, startling Will, causing him to knock over his soda and reflexively click the mouse, which opened one of Karen's inbox messages. Will stood up, retrieved some paper towels, and cleaned the mess from the spill before returning to the screen. He didn't realize he had inadvertently opened an e-mail. He was about to close it when a name popped out from the text—Mitch Bartter. Against his internal desire to give Karen her privacy, he read the short message.

> *Karen,*
>
> *The Mitch Bartter plan is going very well. He doesn't suspect a thing, though Gus and I are concerned about your lack of enthusiasm with regard to this. You know there is no other way—and this will help you tremendously.*
>
> *Gus wants to step up the time frame just a bit from what we have discussed in the past. The second and third phases will be brought to a close in the next few weeks, with the final phase about ready to commence ... I know Gus has been reluctant to share the full details with you, but believe me, you won't be disappointed.*
>
> *Please continue your efforts. Mitch is none the wiser, it seems, and that is where he must stay—for his own good. See you Thursday (unless you want to see me sooner).*
>
> *Charlie*

Will was totally confused, punishing himself for letting his curiosity trump his conscience, forcing him to read the message. Still, this sounded very strange. He printed the e-mail, closed it, and then sent the proposal to Rick. Before exiting the program, he scanned her inbox to see if there were any other messages from Charlie, whoever that was. He saw several but resisted the temptation to open them. He turned off her computer and walked back to his office, his mind racing about the message. Mitch Bartter was one of his favorite columnists—could this be the same person, and if so, what was the plan about him? Some plan with phases, whatever that meant.

Will sat down in his own office, rereading the message when his phone rang.

"Yes?" he answered curtly.

"Will? It's Karen," the voice on the other end said. "You okay? That wasn't your usual jovial tone."

"I'm sorry—the phone startled me a bit," Will lied.

"Did you find the file?" Karen asked.

"Yeah—sent it a few minutes ago."

"Thanks—I'm sure Rick will be happy. Make sure you look at it, too—maybe we can add two more clients instead of just one." Karen hung up the phone.

Will's mind had drifted away from business to something much more concerning. He decided to make another phone call.

Chapter 17

Years ago, Gus laid out his plan in phases. When he was in college, Gus and his best friend had devised the original outline or at least the desired outcome and discussed the steps needed to achieve that goal. Over the years, Gus had written out the plan hundreds of times, tweaking everything a little bit. Obviously, as circumstances in the country changed, his strategy would change, but his overall objectives remained the same. Gus had at times put the plan on hiatus, though he never abandoned it. In the last ten years, he focused his energy more than ever toward his project. Everything did seem to be flowing together now, though.

Phase one, the planning and initial implementation phase, was progressing nicely. Gus had cultivated relationships over the last fifteen years that would become critical to the plan's success, but the final part of this portion had started in earnest about three years ago, when he first brought Charlie fully into the fold. Charlie, caring about nothing but himself, was 100 percent on board from the get go. He loved the idea of the havoc the plan would cause but was really after the payday Gus was promising. Things couldn't happen fast enough for him. Patience was not one of Charlie's strong points. It was actually this character flaw of his that had led to the near-disaster in Sacramento. The Liberty Group was ready to launch the site—but it still needed the critical point person. This person would ultimately play the biggest role, or so it would seem.

Gus, Charlie, and Paul debated who best to do this, and they had produced a group of three names. The research into each of these three people was tremendous. What were their life circumstances? How many kids did they have—how long had they been in their current jobs—what type of past led them to where they were today? The three of them pondered all these questions. They wanted someone who would be popular with the public.

The threesome eliminated one of the possible subjects, with the remaining two being Mitch and a woman named Denise Broadbeck from Sacramento. Denise was single and had submitted some résumés around the Phoenix area, so the group assumed she would be willing to relocate. Being single was favored—it eliminated some of the possible complications, although using someone married with children had its advantages as well. Gus wanted to think about it some more, but Charlie had decided to take matters into his own hands. He likened Denise to Sarah Palin, and Charlie thought this woman could coattail the same enthusiasm to their cause that Palin had generated across the country.

Charlie calculated Gus would ultimately decide on Denise, so he went ahead and started the ball rolling by contacting her. She possessed certain qualities that Charlie appreciated most, and he definitely wanted to spend more time with her. Denise seemed quite excited at first but soon became wary of the group. It didn't help that the company she was working for picked this time to offer Denise a larger salary for what she was doing. That was probably the tipping point that made her turn down the Liberty Group. Charlie took it hard, especially when he had made the mistake of sending an e-mail not meant for her. Denise's rejection, plus seeing something she really shouldn't was bad enough, but telling Gus was the worst of the ordeal for Charlie. Gus went ballistic but worked with Charlie to eliminate any complications regarding Denise. It wasn't something Gus wanted to do, but it was, in his opinion, necessary. In all revolutions, some people are sacrificed, he rationalized.

Denise's elimination left only one real candidate, Mitch Bartter. He was local and fairly popular, both items that were optimal to the group. He was married, however, with three kids. Gus determined they would use his family to their advantage. Ultimately, they hoped he would see things their way, and there would be no complications. They didn't know Mitch well enough.

* * * * *

Mitch walked in the *Republic* with his brain feeling like mush—having contemplated his situation so much in past few days. His conversation with Al over the weekend was still playing in his head, and he had not slept well at all, waking an hour earlier than normal. He begrudgingly got out of bed and decided to head into the paper early. He spent some time online catching up on the continuing healthcare debate as well as several other issues, jotting down notes for upcoming articles. Mitch also sent an e-mail to Karen, asking if she would be available for dinner sometime this week—on the pretense of introducing his wife and reviewing some of the paperwork necessary for a few more of the contributing writers to be paid appropriately. After a few hours, most of the staff started filing in. Brian Maddox sauntered over toward Mitch, his Arizona Cardinal coffee cup in his hand.

"Morning, Mitch, enjoying another glorious day in the desert?"

"Yeah—it's a laugh a minute," Mitch responded, with a little more sarcasm than he intended.

"Whoa—what's up, man?"

"Just a lot on my mind right now. I'm sorry if I seem a bit tense. How are you doing?"

"I'm fine—just watching the world go by while I write my articles," Brian replied joyfully.

"I do have a request of you," Mitch said in an infuriated tone as he checked his e-mail and saw several from Brian. "Please stop sending me all these links regarding the healthcare debate. You're cluttering up my inbox!"

"What do you mean—you don't want to hear the other side?" Brian said with a wide smile.

"I'm reading and listening, trying to keep an open mind," Mitch replied.

"An open mind—how about opening your mind to the fact that forty-five million people are without healthcare in this country?" Mads said, obviously ready for the debate. (He actually had been reading several articles about healthcare over the weekend and sought out Mitch this morning. Mitch assumed as much, given the enthusiasm Brian had brought to the conversation.)

"You're going to start your argument with that number, are you? Fine. Are you purporting that our healthcare system, and our government, should pay for any and all healthcare needs of individuals in our county illegally?"

"Yeah, yeah, I know that forty-five million total supposedly includes illegal aliens."

"Not supposedly—it unequivocally does. So answer the question."

"I don't know about that specific question," Brian responded. "I just know that people in pain should get relief, and there shouldn't be that many uninsured in our country, not if we want to call ourselves an advanced nation."

"I agree that people who are hurting need to get the care," Mitch agreed. "There is not an emergency room in the country that will turn anyone away if they have an imminent problem. That large forty-five million figure always quoted also includes millions of people who specifically choose not to pay for healthcare insurance—they can afford it, but decide based on their stage of life and health not to have coverage. Also, if allowed to work, capitalism will take care of this. There is not an entrepreneur alive who would not salivate over a marketplace of forty-five million potential customers, to use your number. Government regulations have hamstrung the insurance companies, for example, from crossing state lines to sell their products. And let's not forget the fraud. Part of the proposal to pay for this behemoth program is that government is finally going to limit the fraud in Medicare. Private industry fraud is about 1 percent. If Medicare is fraught with fraud, how pervasive an issue will it be in an expanded healthcare program run by the government?"

"Good points," Mads replied. "However, if those who choose not to be insured eventually get sick, they still go to the hospital or doctor's office, get treated, and if they can't pay, the rest of us end up footing the bill. Plus, have some compassion for those less privileged than yourself—those without healthcare."

Mitch drew a long, slow breath—he was so frustrated with being branded cold-hearted due to his stance on several issues. He restrained his voice and tried to educate his friend.

"Brian, I'm very compassionate for anyone with an immediate need. However, in terms of long-range planning, I truly believe I am much more compassionate than you. This entitlement age in which we live will be the end of our freedom—look at what has happened to some of the great countries of Europe—look at Greece right now. Here is where we, as a country, have arrived—government must provide a plan for your retirement and for your healthcare and endless welfare programs and so on. These entitlement programs keep so many people living in poverty—and it destroys the incentive to succeed. You can find study after study proving an entitlement mentality develops over time—people just give up trying when things are provided. Yes, a very minimal amount of things—but yet they are provided. Many of these people never go out and find work to fit their skills, or they turn to crime. I don't call that compassion; I call that government programs run amok! All these proponents seem to be making the same false assumption—equating compassion with the amount of governmental spending!"

"Well, I just wish more of the ignorant people mucking up these town hall meetings would learn a few facts and get their arguments straight before asking stupid questions," Brian exclaimed, changing the argument. "These organized groups just trying to cause trouble is frustrating."

"I agree that no one should try to cause trouble," Mitch began his response. "But I also believe that questions should be answered. That is what keeps getting lost in the debate. Many of the representatives as well as some in the press have redirected the story to be about those causing trouble. Speaker Pelosi wants to point at these people and say they are carrying swastikas, and the mainstream media want to believe it is all part of an organized group, but if any of these proponents had adequate answers to the questions being asked, then there would be no story. These are everyday citizens asking valid questions. However, the representatives are even admitting that they do not know what is in the bills that are being proposed. Since they have no answers, they are resorting to name calling and vilifying those asking the questions."

"Come on, Mitch, just like your opinions on other issues, you want to ignore the facts. We have a healthcare issue—it is time for the government to step in."

"Brian, our debates always seem to come to this point, whether it's climate change, taxes, or now healthcare. You seem to have a fundamental belief that it is the obligation of government to solve every crisis in someone's life. I have the belief that it is government's job to get out of the way and let individuals work together freely to solve their problems. The market will find much better solutions than government mandates ever will—provided the market is given the chance." When Brian did not have a reply ready, Mitch continued his argument. "I think Jefferson said it best as it relates to this type of issue: 'If we can prevent the government from wasting the labors of the people, *under the pretense of taking care of them*'"—Mitch added the emphasis—"'they must become happy.' You see—he foresaw a power grab by the government under the guise of taking care of the people—this is nothing new. It's this type of intrusion that led the founding fathers to structure our government the way they did."

"There you go quoting again—how do you keep those in your head?" Mads said, frustrated that he could not quote some famous guy right back at Mitch.

Mitch ignored the question and pressed on. "Most of these large social programs result in unattainable goals at astronomical costs, and usually don't benefit the intended recipients nearly enough. Look at social security. It should have trillions of dollars available to pay the upcoming retirees, but as the government has seen fit to spend that money for current operations, the system is going broke. But let's assume for a second all that money is there. How much does it provide to a retiree? What do people get currently, somewhere between $1,200 and $1,500 a month, maybe $2,000 a month if they are lucky? What's the average age of death in the United States—roughly seventy-three for men? So, after working forty plus years and putting in 6.2 percent of their earnings, as well as the employers putting in 6.2 percent of wages earned during their lifetime, a person gets roughly $18,000 a year for six or seven years? So, we have this huge expense of the government that does not result in nearly the benefit promised. And the government waste is incredible! Not to mention that even if all the money collected was available, the system would still go broke!"

"So, government should do nothing?" Mads asked.

"I didn't say that. But a government program is not the answer. Government programs always cost exceedingly more than projected. Medicare was adopted in 1965, and at the time, the twenty-five-year projections called for a cost of twelve billion dollars in 1990. Any idea what Medicare actually cost in 1990?"

"Well, I'm sure it was more than the projection—probably double or maybe even triple that total," Mads said begrudgingly.

"How about *one hundred* billion—over eight times as much!" Mitch said emphatically. "And we want to turn the entire healthcare industry over to them. The CBO has scored the House bill on healthcare as adding a considerable amount to the already obscenely high deficit, and the CBO estimates historically have been lower than the actual costs."

"This insurance industry needs help—and it need to cover pre-existing conditions ..." Mitch cut Brian off.

"I'm sure you have work to do, as do I. We can continue this another time. Just remember, a government program is not needed to solve all problems that arise. In fact, less regulation at times will do wonders. For instance, my example a few minutes ago of allowing health insurance companies to cross state lines to sell their products—this would increase the competition and choice—words those pushing these huge bills like to throw around—without a government plan. The reason those in power currently want the government option is for control, pure and simple. They want to have the control over our lives more so than they do already. As I keep saying, it goes back to the basic belief in the individual versus belief in government."

Brian opened his mouth to say something, but then decided not to continue. "You're right—I do have work to do—but this isn't over!" Mads said, pointing at Mitch and smiling.

* * * * *

The next few days were fairly uneventful, with Mitch concentrating on what was being published on the Web site and noticing how many more memberships had been sold. The Liberty Group had been mentioned several times on national talk radio shows and on CNN a few times. His own name had even come up once or twice on these national programs. It was definitely gaining the momentum that Gus desired.

Gus himself had set up several events sponsored by the Liberty Group, usually with celebrity speakers or an occasional conservative congressional representative. Mitch wondered how much of a contribution Gus needed to make to have someone from Congress talk at a function. Mitch also wondered why Gus was never in attendance at these public events. In fact, none of the "Big Four," as Mitch called them, were ever taking a front-line role. Paul and Charlie did most of the planning, and Mitch was sure Karen took care of getting the money where it needed to be, but none of their names were listed in any prominent fashion. Any literature distributed at these events or Web site notices only listed the Liberty Group in general. He was hoping to ask Karen about these things when they went out to dinner later that evening. She had responded to Mitch's e-mail earlier in the week agreeing to dinner, but that she would be coming alone.

Mitch walked to his car on his way to a Thursday Liberty meeting as he considered reasons why Gus, Charlie, and Paul did not advertise their Liberty roles. He dropped into his seat and placed the key in the ignition when he noticed the envelope on the seat next to him. In very large letters written across the outside was "DO NOT PICK UP OR OPEN HERE. YOU ARE BEING WATCHED!" He stared at the envelope for a few seconds, unsure of what to do. Mitch finally turned the key and began to pull out of the parking lot. As he drove, he deftly reached behind his seat where he had placed a business portfolio to be used at his meeting. He smoothly moved the portfolio to the front seat and placed it on top of the letter. When he arrived at the Biltmore, he grabbed the portfolio and letter together, holding both against his chest with one hand as he stepped out of the vehicle, the letter sandwiched between his body and the case. He still opened the back door of his sedan and grabbed a notepad, and as he slipped it into the portfolio, the letter was placed inside as well, without the slightest notice of the two people watching him. He walked into the hotel without anyone being the wiser. Mitch headed for the bathroom first, stepped inside a stall and sat down. He took the letter out and read it quickly.

> *The group you are working with is not what you think. I do not have all the details yet, but I know they are planning something big, and you are being set up. That is all I can tell you now, but I will provide more information as I can. Also, your communications are being monitored—assume nothing is safe.*

Mitch closed his eyes and realized that his whole body was shaking. His concerns for this group continued to grow, and now he received an anonymous letter verifying his feelings. "This has to be some joke" was all Mitch could think right then. He folded the letter and put it in his pants pocket. He ripped the envelope to pieces and flushed it down the toilet. The first part of the message did not really shock him—the scenarios that ran through his head during times of questioning Liberty revolved around Charlie and Gus being up to something. He also had guessed that he himself might be playing a role for them, but he hadn't figured out exactly what that was yet. Al had suggested the e-mail monitoring already as well, but could it be more than e-mail? This note confirmed some of his thoughts, but where did it come from? That was the main new item now. Who would know about this situation, and more important, who would want to help him? He thought about the letter several more minutes and concluded the person who left this was definitely trying to help him. Knowing he needed to get into the meeting, he gathered himself together and left the restroom, heading toward their regular meeting room.

After going over regular business, it was Mitch's turn. He gave his usual report but felt very nervous. When Mitch had finished, Gus ended the meeting with a final reminder of the Fourth of July party in a few days. Mitch hoped he had hid his anxiety during the meeting, but it apparently was evident. As he walked to his car after the meeting, Karen caught up to him.

"You okay, Mitch?" she asked sincerely. "You seemed a little preoccupied."

"No—I'm fine—just thinking of a few other articles, I guess.

Hey—we still on for tonight? My wife is looking forward to meeting you."

"Yes, I'll see you at the restaurant."

* * * * *

They met at seven o'clock that evening, and after introducing Marie to Karen, talk began of their individual lives, how they had arrived at where they were, and of course about the kids. The appetizers were excellent, and both Mitch and Marie were being put at ease by their new friend.

Karen started talking politics, and an article from the Web site about social security came up. Mitch wondered if Mads was channeling into Karen here, as he seemed to be having the same conversation as earlier that week.

"The government has proven it cannot efficiently run any type of long-term benefit program; social security and Medicare are two prime examples," Mitch was saying. "Why would we let it run something as large as healthcare?"

"What about those programs?" Karen replied. "Social security has been in existence since the 1930s. It has helped millions of people."

"No argument, except it has been at an expense much greater than was ever forecast, and it is going broke very quickly at this point. Have you researched the history of the program?"

"Well—no, I mean, who has?" Karen replied. "And we have been hearing for decades that social security is going bankrupt, but it hasn't yet."

"You obviously don't know my husband well enough," Marie said. "If it's part of history, he's researched it."

"Well, social security was signed into law in 1935 by Franklin Roosevelt. It originally covered old-age benefits and was expanded in the 1950s to provide disability benefits. Currently, 6.2 percent of

Eric Myerholtz

most people's wages are withheld and sent to the government, and the employer is also mandated to contribute 6.2 percent. That makes a total of 12.4 percent being contributed for each employee currently working."

"Mitch—I'm an accountant—I know how the program works," Karen replied. "The funds collected are paying the benefits of those retired. That is how it has always worked."

Marie was trying not to be bored. She had become accustomed to Mitch's debates and knew it went with the territory—she started people watching at the restaurant, just half listening.

"Actually," Mitch said, "you're right. That is how it has always been. In 2007, about $785 million was collected, and only $595 million paid out. It has been like that for most years; in fact, since 1982, the system has run surpluses every year—more collected than paid out. So, everything would appear to be fine. However, Congress, in its infinite wisdom, created a law that loaning these surpluses to the federal operating budget is mandatory. Congress then spends this as if it is income in that given year. The time is coming when the amount spent for social security benefits will exceed the amount received. That is the point when we are all in for a very rude awakening."

Their dinners arrived, but the conversation continued. Mitch, once wound up on a subject, could just not let go until he had fully debated the topic.

"One more point on the amount withheld: the government promised at the start of this program that no more than 3 percent would be withheld—ever. That was FDR's promise. And yet, here it is at more than twice that amount. If you take the maximum someone would pay in 1950, when the rate was still just 3 percent, and adjust that total for inflation to current day dollars, the maximum amount withheld today would have been $1,630. However, as of 2009, the maximum amount withheld is $6,622. To make matters worse, in my opinion, the president indicated during his campaign he would consider increasing this tax by 2 to 4 percent on individuals making more than $250,000."

The Liberty Group

"Okay—I understand all of that, but I am going to play devil's advocate here," Karen began. "Is it that big a deal if the rich pay a little more so the less fortunate can get their benefits? Really, does someone making $250,000 or more need to receive social security benefits?"

"Are you saying that individuals making $250,000 should pay more but should not get any benefits of the system they are paying into?" Mitch countered. "Does that seem correct to you? Let's say people average an annual salary of $200,000 for forty years; at 6.2 percent, they will have contributed almost $500,000 themselves, and almost $1 million if you include the employer contribution—assuming no limitations on the withholdings. Why should these people not receive any benefits just because they make more? What you are advocating is pure wealth redistribution, in effect a 12.4 percent surtax on a certain income group."

"Yes, I read your little conversation with that Ohio person—about the flat tax and wealth redistribution," Marie chimed in. Mitch looked at his wife and almost laughed. He thought she had not been listening. And to refer to Al as "that Ohio person"—what was that about?

"Well, the flat tax is a topic for another time. I think that social security is going to be a bigger issue than anyone realizes. Within seven to ten years, we will be paying more than we are taking in. By 2040 or so, all amounts paid out will exceed the amounts taken in since the mandatory loans began. Realize that the government doesn't have the money to pay back these loans anyhow; look out in a few short years. Currently, the government owes the social security system at least $2.5 trillion dollars. This is about $8,000 for every person living in the United States, or a family of four would have to cough up $32,000 to allow the government to pay off its debt to social security. Again, that is just the accumulated debt so far, not the continued shortfalls that will occur in the future."

"You seem to have looked into this quite a bit," Karen said.

"This was an issue when we were in college, and here we are—I am forty-two years old now—you look about the same, if not a little younger." Karen smiled at the compliment. "And it is still a problem. Congress—both sides of the aisle—has ignored this issue basically hoping the elephant in the room would disappear. Some have called for reform and have offered ideas, but the issue was never dealt with properly. This is not going away! With that fact drilled into our heads, let's revisit my original point. The volume of spending and scope of issues surrounding social security could not possibly be foreseen by those implementing the program in 1935. How many costs and issues cannot be foreseen by the mammoth healthcare insurance reform a government-run system would bring today? Again, the government has not run a domestic program efficiently that I can ever remember."

The three of them sat in silence for a few seconds, letting Mitch's last sentence hang in the air. The stillness was broken by when the waiter brought the bills. They discussed a few lighter topics before finally deciding it was time to leave. Marie went to use the restroom, and Mitch took the opportunity to question Karen about the lack of public recognition among the top management level.

"That is a good question," she replied, trying to think quickly. "I guess Gus likes to keep a low profile. He is not a glory seeker—he is just trying to support a conservative cause."

"Still, it seems that the information would be published somewhere. Heck—the Web site lists me as the editor and the names of those contributing articles, but no other names are visible there, either."

"I've really never thought about it," Karen replied. "I'm like you—this is not my main job. I'm doing everything they ask, and I like what we're accomplishing. Besides, you are the editor. Don't you want credit for that?"

"It is nice additional income," Mitch said, deflecting the question. He decided to try to go a different route. "Gus must be loaded. I imagine he is paying Charlie and Paul a pretty penny to keep them on standby most of the time."

"They don't get paid by Liberty," Karen blurted out.

"Really? That's a bit surprising." Mitch contemplated what this revelation could mean.

"I know," Karen said. "I thought it strange, too. He must pay them from some other account he has, but it is not included in Liberty's financials. I mean, we have a small manual payroll for you, me, and the other writers. I do know there is an outside processor who does the bulk of all the other people. I guess when you have that kind of money, the sky is the limit—you can accomplish your goals in numerous different ways."

"What other people?" Mitch asked, hearing of this for the first time.

"Gus told me he has a payroll of about fifty people—I don't know who they are, but he has me transfer money to a separate account that funds those payrolls. I suppose Charlie and Paul could be paid from that fund—maybe he doesn't want me to see how much they make. Anyhow, I assume Gus uses the payroll processor for all the related tax filings—numerous states involved, I think." Karen knew she was walking a fine line. She liked Mitch and did not want to intentionally mislead him. She also knew that if Gus had heard her tell all this, he would be quite displeased. However, as she truly did not know who the other people were and their purpose in the whole scheme, she only felt slightly guilty sharing this information.

"All those payments go through Liberty? How do you record those on the statements? I don't recall seeing that anywhere in the financial information you give us."

"It's not there. I have a receivable on the balance sheet due from a related party. Gus only has me report the income statement in our meetings."

"And no payments to Paul or Charlie?" Mitch repeated, his mind racing with these new facts.

"That's what I know," Karen replied.

"Yeah, but ..." Mitch was thinking.

"Are you really bothered by this?" Karen asked, implying it really was not any of his business.

"No, I guess not. It is interesting, though. Thanks again for meeting us tonight." Marie rejoined them. "We'll see you again in a few days—Gus's party—you coming?"

"Oh, I'll be there. See you then."

Chapter 18

Gus's Fourth of July party was truly an extravaganza. There were live bands, incredible decorations, and more food and drink than anyone could desire. Mitch had heard his friends describe Rustler's Roost before but had never been there. The place was huge, and local legend claimed it sat where a hideout for cattle rustlers once was. It was located about fifteen minutes from downtown Phoenix and was a huge two-story building with an indoor waterfall and a slide into the dining room. The large windows on the north side of the building offered an incredible view of the city lights.

Mitch and Marie arrived as a stirring rendition of "Proud to Be an American" was just starting. They watched as the band played several more songs while taking some hors d'oeuvres and drinks from one of the many staff walking around with trays. They were told it was a casual affair, but Mitch suggested they go upscale casual, and Marie switched at the last minute from slacks to a deep purple summer dress in which she always looked outstanding. She was glad she had made the change, given other partygoers' attire. They spotted Paul, and Mitch ushered Marie through the crowd to join him.

Eric Myerholtz

"Paul, I'd like you to meet my wife, Marie," Mitch said.

"Marie, it is a pleasure," Paul replied.

"Nice to meet you, too. Are you the same Paul who stood up Mitch a few weeks back?"

"Yes," Paul said sheepishly. "I am sorry about that. My other meeting that night ran late, and my phone died."

Marie nodded. "What do you do, Paul?" she asked, already knowing the answer.

"I'm an attorney. Currently, I am mainly working on numerous special projects for clients. I work out of my home for the most part. How about yourself?"

"I'm in marketing. I work for a fairly large company here in Phoenix."

"Paul—I'm not sure I have ever asked you—are you married?" Mitch inquired.

"Divorced. I have been dating someone for a while, but she doesn't always agree with my politics and prefers to not get involved in things like this."

"Do you have many of these kind of shindigs?" Marie asked.

"No, not really," Paul replied, surveying the crowd. "Gus throws a party every now and then, but this is a much grander scale than usual."

Charlie came up at this point, drink in hand, and it was obvious from his demeanor that it wasn't his first.

"Hey Mitch, Paul. You must be Mitch's wife." Charlie looked at Marie, smiling. "Mitch, introduce me to this gorgeous woman." Marie almost visibly shuddered at the comment, Charlie's smarmy manner giving a horrible first impression.

"Charlie, this is Marie. Marie—Charlie. Charlie is the, how did you describe it, 'advisor' to Gus—no, it was 'consultant.'"

"That's right," Charlie said, shaking Marie's hand much too long. "I do some consulting for Gus. Of course, I consult on a variety of matters—so if you ever need any help, Marie, you just let me know!"

"Are you here with anyone?" Paul asked, trying to pry Charlie's attention away from Marie.

"Not yet, but I'm working on it," Charlie replied. "Where's your girlfriend, Paul?"

"You know she doesn't usually come to Gus's parties," Paul said with a piercing look at Charlie.

"But she …" Charlie started, but stopped. "Oh, that's right. I was thinking of someone else. Well, enjoy, fellas. Marie—nice to meet you." And with that, Charlie disappeared into the crowd, Paul's gaze following him for a few moments.

"Charlie—always unpredictable," said Paul, trying to cover a bit for his colleague. "I just noticed another client I invited to come—I want to touch base. Enjoy yourselves, you two. Marie—it was nice to meet you."

"You didn't describe Charlie quite right," Marie commented.

"What do you mean?" Mitch asked.

"Oh, you said he was a real jerk. But you forgot to mention how … how … there's no other word but 'creepy' to describe him."

"Yeah—him I absolutely do not trust," Mitch said. If only he knew how true that statement would become.

* * * * *

Charlie walked up behind Karen as she was talking to a group of people. Karen looked stunning in a black dress and with her hair pulled back. She tried not to show her lack of enthusiasm at Charlie's presence.

"Karen, why don't you introduce me to the group?" Charlie said as he stepped up beside her, placing his hand on the small of her back.

"Charlie, this is Ron and Sylvia Johnson, and this is Alex Bonner. Everyone—this is Charlie." Karen edged away from him as nonchalantly as she could.

"How do you know Karen?" Ron asked Charlie.

"We've been seeing each other for a few months now," Charlie joked, unable to control himself.

"Charlie has truth issues," Karen said quickly to her friends. "We are both involved with the Liberty Group. Actually, Charlie and I have a few items to discuss about Liberty, if you'll excuse us." She pulled him away to a somewhat secluded corner of the room.

"Couldn't wait to get me alone?" Charlie asked, smirking.

Karen let Charlie have it. "Don't you ever joke around about me like that again! I don't care how much you think Gus has your back. I will not have you undermine me in this community or threaten my credibility!"

"Calm down. Isn't it flattering that I wish you were my date? Come on; give me a chance. And, by the way, we have been meeting every Thursday for the last six months. We've been 'seeing' each other. I didn't really lie." Charlie cocked his head slightly and smirked.

"I imagine that is the only thing close to a date you can get—pre-arranged business meetings, besides paying someone to go out with you, that is. Stay away from me." Karen stormed off. After spending about fifteen minutes away from the crowd to calm and recompose herself, she walked back out to the party and asked the bartender for a rum and coke. Mitch and Marie were refreshing their drinks as well.

"Karen—good to see you again," Mitch greeted her.

"A pleasure to see you again, too," Karen replied, looking more at Marie than Mitch.

"Are you okay? You seem a little distraught," Marie asked.

"No, I'm fine. I guess it's the same everywhere. If you throw enough people in the same room, one of them is bound to be a big … is bound to bother you. You know what I mean?" Karen stopped herself before she became agitated again. She decided to change the subject. "Anyhow, as I was saying the other night, Mitch has been such a welcomed addition to our group—his work with the Web site and promoting the group in his articles has been invaluable."

"Well, Mitch has sure been energized by the experience," Marie answered. "How long have you been working with Liberty? I don't recall asking you that the other night."

"Gus approached me over a year ago. At the time, he was sitting on the board of one of my larger clients. He asked me to join his group, and I told him there was a professional independence issue—I could not work for him and have him be a board member of a client. He immediately resigned from that board. I have to tell you—I felt pretty flattered that he respected my work enough to do that. So, I agreed to join the group."

"And how about hobbies—what do you do for fun?" Marie continued.

"As you can imagine, running an accounting firm is more than a forty-hour-per-week job. When I do find a spare moment, I generally like to relax by reading. Being single at my age, though, I usually pour my time into my work and my volunteering—at my church and with a small alcoholism agency."

"That's great!" said Marie. "I find I get more satisfaction from contributing to a group that needs the help than just about anything else I do professionally."

Karen noticed Charlie making his way toward them.

"Oh, good heavens. Forgive me, but I am going to end our conversation very abruptly. If *he* asks, point the other way," Karen said, and she was gone.

"What in the world did that mean?" Marie questioned Mitch, but no answer was necessary. Charlie bumped into Mitch as he tussled through the crowd.

"Were you guys just talking to Karen?" he asked, looking Marie up and down again, not at all subtly.

"She just said she was heading for the restroom and went that way," Mitch said, doing as Karen had asked and pointing the exact opposite of her true escape route.

After about an hour of socializing and appetizers—including rattlesnake—dinner was served in old-fashioned chuck wagon style.

The menu included mesquite-broiled steaks, ribs, and chicken served with every imaginable side dish. The dinner entertainment was another well-known band, and Mitch and Marie took their assigned seats, which put them next to no one they knew. After the meal and some wonderful desserts, a person Mitch had never seen rose to speak.

"In a few minutes, you will all see a firework display fit for the celebration of the independence of the greatest nation this world has ever seen. 'Independence' is an important word today. I personally feel that our independence is under assault, and unfortunately, it is under assault from the most powerful people in this very country. The leaders in two of the three branches of our federal government have either suggested legislation or put policies in place limiting individualism. Lest we forget, we celebrate today what others did to allow the individual freedoms we have enjoyed for so many years. And now, those freedoms are slipping through our fingers. When the president can effectively fire the CEO of a private company or take over major banking institutions, then we are losing freedom. When our elected leader calls for a government-run healthcare system that he says will compete with private insurance companies, knowing full well that the government entity will ultimately dictate what type of procedures are allowed to be performed, taking decisions away from the doctors—we are having undue limitations placed on our individual rights. This is a full-scale war on the freedom we know and desire to maintain. Please, I ask all of you to consider what you can do personally to assist in stopping this assault. The Liberty Group is committed to this solitary cause, and I urge you to help us.

"There is someone here who can probably state this more eloquently than I. He didn't know that I was planning to put him on the spot, but I want you all to meet the face of the man whose words you have been reading for years. Mitch Bartter, please come up here!"

Mitch sat next to Marie, mortified. He had nothing prepared, and who was this guy? Mitch was positive they had never met. Marie quickly whispered in his ear.

"Time to pull a rabbit out of your hat, Houdini—go on; you'll be fine." And with a little nudge, she got Mitch moving toward where the speaker was standing, with Gus just off to the right.

"Come on, Mitch, give us some patriotic words!" the man said over the applause of the crowd.

Mitch reluctantly took the microphone, a quizzical look still on his face.

"Good evening, everyone," Mitch managed to stammer out. He wrote for public viewing every day. Speaking in public was an entirely different matter. "Thank you ..." Mitch hesitated briefly as he did not know the name of the person to whom he was giving thanks. He continued awkwardly. "... for the kind words and for this wonderful Independence Day party. 'Independence Day'—that's a phrase we need to hear more of in these uncertain times. It seems more and more people in our country want to declare some sort of dependence day. As our federal government spends more of our money, reaches farther into our lives, and attempts to claim more power over us, we are becoming a nation of dependents. We must not let this happen.

"We celebrate today the signing and presentation of the Declaration of Independence. Not that it is important today, but as a side note, the Declaration was actually approved on July 2, and John Adams thought that would be the date future generations would come to celebrate. The Declaration those great people signed all those years ago states all men are created equal and have certain inalienable rights, bestowed on them by their creator. It says that governments are instituted among men, deriving their just powers from the consent of the governed. The consent of the governed!" Mitch repeated the line for effect. "Does that sound like how our government is conducting their business today?

"Our president likes to remind us that the United States is currently suffering the worst economic conditions since the Great Depression. I contend that the economic woes of the late 1970s and early 1980s were just as bad, if not worse. Unemployment was higher then than it is now, inflation was rampant, and individuals had mortgage interest rates in the high teens! It was in that atmosphere that Ronald Reagan took office. Did he talk of government stimulus packages and corporate bailouts? Nothing was farther from his mind. Just a few words from that great leader: 'We are a nation that has a government—not the other way around. And this makes us special among the nations of the Earth. Our government has no power except that granted it by the people. It is time to check and reverse the growth of government, which shows signs of having grown beyond the consent of the governed.' Words that ring just as true some twenty-eight years later! Can't we all agree reversing the growth of government is crucial right now?

"Japan, during the 1990s, suffered similar economic ailments we suffer today. They did the same thing we are doing—government spending money it doesn't really have in an attempt to stimulate their economy. It did not work, and now that great pacific country refers to that period of time as their 'lost decade.'

"Even here, in this country, government spending was the answer during the Great Depression. Yet, in addressing the House Ways and Means committee in 1939, FDR's treasury secretary said, 'We have tried spending money. We are spending more than we have ever spent before, and it does not work. After eight years of this administration, we have just as much unemployment as when we started and a large debt to boot.' Our current strategy would seem to attempt that which has not worked for us or for other countries! Why don't we try what has worked! We need lower tax rates, less governmental interference in the private sector, and less government spending!

"So, on this Independence Day, please, remember how this great country became what it is. How *independent* we can be! It is not by letting government control more of our everyday lives. It is by letting individuals be individuals. Please contact as many of our governmental representatives as you can; let them know how you, the governed, feel. It is only through our combined voices that we can make a real difference.

"Thank you again to those who made this wonderful party possible!" Mitch concluded, raising his glass in a toasting gesture toward Gus.

"Thank you, Mitch—fantastic sentiments!" the same unknown man said enthusiastically, relieving Mitch of the microphone. "Always giving a history lesson—that Mitch. He knows everything from the Sons of Liberty to FDR's court-packing plan; I see your looks of confusion out there; you'll have to ask Mitch what that was. Again, please act as a responsible American now—you are responsible for individual freedom. Call your representatives and make sure they know your name. Tell them the Liberty Group told you to call to ensure they knew how you felt! Please continue to enjoy yourselves here tonight and thank you all for coming!" The man turned off the microphone, and he and Gus went off together.

* * * * *

"Nicely done," Marie said as they headed home a few hours later after watching the most amazing fireworks display either of them had ever seen.

"What do you mean?" Mitch asked.

"I mean your speech. I think you are really making an impression on your new friends. Paul seems nice enough, and I really like Karen. Charlie—he's just the backside of a donkey. How many individual discussions have you had with Gus? And you say you do not know who was talking there at the end?"

"No, I do not—and as for Gus, I don't think the two of us have ever talked just one on one. Obviously, we are at the Liberty meetings together."

"So, how many history lessons have you given at these meetings?" Marie inquired, remembering the man's comment.

"You noticed that, too? We have branched off on some tangents of history in our meetings, but I don't recall the Sons of Liberty ever coming up. I did have a brief discussion on that subject with Paul and John at that first meeting, but not with Gus. It was obvious Gus was feeding information to that person; I just want to know why." The strange events just kept occurring, Mitch thought.

"Or Paul told him about it," Marie theorized. "Or he meant your articles. Oh, well, you do like to give history lessons."

"Don't you like how I try to use the history of our great country to help people understand the present? Or do you, similar to our children, see it as a boring lesson, stuff even your teachers didn't want to bother with in school?"

"Whoa, slow down, Mr. Defensive—just having a little fun. I'm proud of how passionate you are and how much you believe in what you write about."

"Thanks—I think what we are all doing for the Liberty Group will ultimately make a difference. We just need to keep getting the message out there. We could really make some people think before the next election cycle." Mitch looked at Marie, and she was casting a knowing look at him.

"What?" he said.

"Nothing—I just enjoy seeing you get excited about your work."

Mitch was excited about what he was doing; he just wished he knew what everyone else at Liberty was up to.

* * * *

Gus sat with Charlie as they enjoyed a cigar on Gus's veranda, having both returned there after the party. It was about 2:30 AM and both men felt satisfied with how the evening had progressed.

"Another successful party, Gus," Charlie said as he sipped his cognac. "Who was the guy that introduced Mitch?"

"Nice touch, huh? He was just someone I hired. You know I like to keep a low profile. Speaking of successful events, how well did our other operations go off today?"

"I've been receiving text messages all evening," Charlie said, checking his phone again. "Sounds like we did what we set out to do. I'll get full reports in the morning."

"Well, it's already two and a half hours into the morning. I think I'm going to turn in. I'll talk to you Monday. Don't try to contact me tomorrow. I won't be around."

"I meant to ask you—how did Paul respond to your little chat about his computer blunder?" Charlie asked.

"As you would expect. He was upset—said it would never happen again. That sort of stuff. I made sure he understood no mistakes can occur—not if he wanted to continue with us."

"Is there any follow-up you need from me on that?" Charlie asked, almost hopeful.

"No, it is too late in the game for any changes. We'll be fine; we're only about two months away. He covered well, actually. His biggest mistake was not telling us. It won't happen again. I tell you what; why don't you send out an e-mail to the three of us, Karen, Paul, and me, indicating that Mitch's progress is going as planned. You could also send that full donor list to Karen and have her update the Web site with it. That will document all those who have contributed to this cause," Gus said with a diabolical smile as he crushed out his cigar and stood up.

"Have fun doing what ever you have planned tomorrow," Charlie said. "I'm going to check in with our other team and maybe give Karen a call, you know, make sure she gets the e-mail and all."

"I don't know how many times I have to say it, but you're barking up the wrong tree with that one. Goodnight. I trust you'll show yourself out."

"Goodnight."

Chapter 19

Mitch awoke on Sunday morning or, more correctly, was nudged by Sydney for their morning walk. He reluctantly got out of bed, moved quietly to the bathroom, brushed his teeth, grabbed his contacts, and walked downstairs as both dogs followed. He let them out in the back yard, filled their water and food dishes, and put his contacts in as the dogs merrily ate their breakfast. Mitch booted up his computer, grabbed the leashes, and headed out with his pets.

Upon his return, Mitch checked the computer to see what was new in the world. Not a whole lot caught his eye, although he did notice that there had been a few disturbances at some of the tea parties that had been scheduled on July 4. Many conservative groups around the country had been organizing what they called tea parties in recent months, an obvious reference to the Boston Tea Party. These tea parties were being held to protest the spending habits of the Obama administration.

He also noticed that someone had tried to hack into the Speaker of the House's Web site as well as the Senate majority leader's. Both attempts had been thwarted, but the individuals attempting the intrusion had covered their tracks very well. Mitch could hear Marie stirring and started her coffee. A few minutes later, she was sipping her morning beverage and reading the paper.

"It's too bad we didn't meet Karen before Todd got here," Marie said without looking up from her paper.

"What do you mean?" Mitch asked.

"I was just thinking that we know two people of similar age that are both single. We could have introduced them."

"Seriously?"

"Well—it just seems to me as though they would hit it off," Marie responded. "Did Todd say anything about visiting again soon?"

"No, he didn't," Mitch replied, laughing. "Maybe we should ask Karen to join us in Bowling Green."

"Now you are just being silly," Marie said. "It was just a thought. So—should we get to know Paul a little better as well?"

"It definitely couldn't hurt." Mitch had not yet told Marie about the package that had been left in his car. He was convinced something covert was occurring—but he was hesitant to discuss too much with Marie yet. He did want to try to determine who else in the group was like him, somewhat in the dark on what was truly happening. He also wanted to know who else was under surveillance.

"Shall I set up another dinner?" Mitch asked his wife.

"Sure, see if Paul and his girlfriend want to join us sometime. We could even have them over here if they want. Or we could invite Karen and Paul for some type of barbeque."

"What—no Charlie?" Mitch joked.

"That guy will never set foot in this house if I have anything to say about it! Whatever he consults on—he must be good. He has to overcome his personality for people to want to work with him."

"You'll get no debate from me on that one," Mitch said, still feeling a little guilty about hiding the information about the package from her.

* * * * *

Karen went into the office on the Sunday after Gus's party, even though it was summer. Public accounting was a profession where overtime was expected, and many late night hours were burned finishing up an audit or tax return. Enterprises required an audit opinion from an independently licensed practitioner for numerous reasons. Any publicly held company was required to have audited statements because the investors relied on those statements. Most private entities had loans from banks, and one of the first lending requirements was usually an audited statement be provided to the bank within a certain time frame after the year's end. Tax returns obviously brought on their own level of deadlines, imposed by the IRS or state authorities.

The summer months were usually the lightest in terms of workload for a public accountant. The April 15 tax deadline had obviously passed by then, although many companies and individuals extended their returns. Most private enterprises had a calendar year end, although many chose a fiscal year end that was different from the typical January through December time frame. An October-September year was not atypical for manufacturing, while many retailers used a fifty-two-week schedule to always end on a Saturday or Sunday.

As it was mid-July, Karen was at her least hectic time but was still finding reasons to stay in the office. She was reviewing some items for a few upcoming client planning meetings when her e-mail box appeared. Another one from Charlie.

This better be all business, or I swear, I'm going to throttle that man! she thought to herself. She clicked open the message and realized it was not only to her, but to Gus and Paul as well.

> *Gus, Paul, and Karen,*
> *Just wanted to keep you up to date on the surveillance. Mitch continues to work on his portion and appears to be none the wiser. We were concerned when he showed up at the Biltmore early a few weeks back, but Paul seems to have deflected that nicely. Since then, there has been nothing unusual about his movements—he and his family continue*

to follow their normal routine. Mitch's speech at the party was excellent—anyone there will be convinced he is the master behind these plans. Gus—stroke of genius having him called in front of the group on the fly!

Gus is setting phase three into motion in the next few weeks, with phase four to begin just weeks after that. I understand Karen is unaware of these details. You'll love it. Please forward any Mitch questions to me.

Karen—I am forwarding to you the most up-to-date donor list. Paul and Gus have reviewed it, and it all seems in order. Please document these into their different levels and post on the Web site. We want these individuals and businesses receiving their proper credit.

Charlie

That definitely wasn't the worst e-mail Karen had ever received from Charlie, but every message was a reminder that she was still in this dangerous game. Away from Liberty meetings, Karen could put those issues in the back of her mind. She knew things were going to come to a head soon—and she wanted out before they got there, or did she?

"Maybe I could try ..." she said aloud, pausing to think. She got busy with a plan.

* * * * *

The week following the Fourth of July party was relatively quiet for all Liberty individuals. Gus felt the time was getting much closer to press the button for the full plan. He had been so patient for so many years; now that the end was just weeks away, he could hardly contain his eagerness. Gus, Charlie, and Paul had arrived for the Thursday morning portion of their meeting, reviewing some financial information Karen was not privy to.

"How about all this fallout over healthcare?" Paul asked Gus, breaking the silence of the three men working. "Is this disrupting your plan? The stories seem fairly close to what you describe."

Gus hesitated for a second, looking curiously at Paul. "Who do you think is behind much of the hyperbole over healthcare and the blame going around?"

"You mean you are the organizer the left keeps complaining about?"

"No—of course not. Come on, Paul, think about it."

Paul contemplated what Gus could mean for a few seconds. He thought of the intensity of the protests against the proposed healthcare insurance reform. He thought about how the press had covered it and how the Democrats had reacted. Nancy Pelosi had indicated that those speaking against the reform were carrying swastikas. She and Steny Hoyer had collaborated on an article published in *USA Today* calling those speaking at town hall meetings against the House plan "un-American." Paul, even though he had somewhat enjoyed the escalation of this debate, thought these congressmen and women to be out of line. Then it clicked.

"You have people under your control working for these congressional representatives!" Paul exclaimed as understanding dawned on him.

"Now you're getting there," Gus said. "It's all part of the plan. I couldn't have planned it any better—this healthcare issue is priming the pump!"

"I am continually amazed at your foresight as well as your dumb luck!" Paul chuckled. "Now that I think it forward, this is beautiful. It will help set the stage perfectly. Here I was thinking it was ruining things, when in actuality, it is laying a wonderful foundation."

"That's right," Gus agreed as a maniacal smile crossed his face, making him look ten years older. "It will come together, and it will unfold as I wish. I will achieve what I want. The years of planning and scheming are finally coming to fruition. I just have to keep myself from trying to push it all together too soon."

*****

Al printed Mitch's article as usual from the *Republic* Web site and read it through just for its pure content. Al had been to visit the Alabama location of his company on Wednesday of this week and was too tired the previous evening to even boot up his computer to review his friend's article. He always read the articles in their entirety first to see Mitch's opinion on the topic before looking for the message.

The Easy Answer to Jobs and Energy

The economy has lost how many jobs during the current year? Four or five million (which is, of course, not counting the jobs "saved" by the president, but that little farce is a topic for another article). The Department of Energy was activated on October 1, 1977, in part to reduce our dependence on foreign oil. Here we are, thirty-two years later, and American reliance on foreign oil is greater than ever. Let me be not the first, not the second, but probably the 1,200th person to suggest a logical plan of action that would help both of these issues.

Over 80 percent of the water surrounding our great country is currently off limits to oil and gas exploration or drilling, yet geological studies estimate these areas hold over 18 billion barrels of oil, roughly the equivalent of 30 years' worth of the imports from Saudi Arabia. Just reading that sentence should crystallize the message our government is sending to us. The first argument is always that environmentally, we cannot possibly allow any exploration in these areas. However, oil production can actually lower the amount of oil in the ocean due to seepage. This has been a problem especially in the area of California's Santa Barbara coast. Is it possible to allow the free market to cultivate this resource—allow good old American entrepreneurship to solve this problem by creating jobs and obtaining this oil?

Yet, the current powers that be are doing the exact opposite of this—actually having turned down this idea flat! A backward approach if ever there was one and again proving their message to us. After the stimulus was passed, Congressman Rob Bishop of Utah and Senator David Vitter of Louisiana introduced legislation that would have reduced restrictions on the oil drilling, both offshore and on, including Alaska's Artic National Wildlife Refuge— better known as ANWR. The middle range of estimates of oil in ANWR are about 10 billion barrels. This oil would be found on two thousand of the nineteen million acres in the refuge and would occur during the year when the ground was frozen and therefore at the lowest level of wildlife migration. This legislation would have created roughly 2 million jobs, increased the GDP by $10 trillion over the next thirty years, and lowered energy costs for all Americans. Here's the kicker—this could all be done with no government spending! This does not even touch the oil shale possibility. Conservative estimates put the total recoverable oil in the Green River Formation at three times the proven reserves of Saudi Arabia. To summarize, jobs would be created, increasing the tax base and, therefore, tax revenues, with absolutely no governmental spending necessary.

So, what do we conclude of a government that will not allow the private sector access to these resources? Natural supply and demand would dictate that cultivating these reserves would result in much lower energy costs, in the United States, of course, but also across the globe. Lower energy costs mean more money in the pockets of individuals and private enterprise (which, in turn, leads to more jobs and more governmental revenue, too!). The United States could assist other nations with their energy issues, instead of all being beholden to the few suppliers currently. I ask again—what do we conclude of a government that will not allow this energy to be harnessed? The only logical answer is that the current people in power do not want the United

States to be more energy independent and, by extension, do not want lower energy costs.

That may seem like a ridiculous accusation, but look at this instance. Recently, bills were introduced in Congress to give the EPA the power to regulate hydraulic fracturing. This is a process using pressurized water shot into wells to stimulate the flow of oil and natural gas. Hydraulic fracturing has been in use for over twenty years and is basically required for most of the new wells in the United States. Individual states currently oversee the environmental and public safety of the process, which has an almost perfect record. The bill introduced at the federal level claims there are concerns of drinking water contamination, even though such a problem has never occurred. Why would this bill be necessary, given the facts?

Another bill drafted by the House Natural Resources Committee would add a litany of new regulations to domestic oil production as well as increasing fees on leases already in existence. These actions should cause us all to stop and think. Why else propose such obstacles to the success of so vital a process?

So again, the question is should we be concerned when our country has all these valuable resources, has the ingenuity and intelligence to harness the resources efficiently, and needs to create jobs—very important jobs? Why would we not take this logical step? No one is asking the federal government to assist with the endeavor; the communication to them is to get out of the way of entrepreneurial Americans—that is truly all that needs to occur.

I urge you all to contact your representatives and demand the country harness our own resources, not rely on those of others. We need to work together, monitoring the actions of our elected officials to ensure a brighter tomorrow. Please continue to research this issue on your own as well. This is the absolute best course of action to take; please do not waste any more valuable time. Tell everyone you can

> to read the Liberty information on this very crucial issue. Demand that we do this to improve our economy, increase our jobs, and create a better America!

Once again, Al thought Mitch hit a bull's-eye. This article was dead-on accurate, in his opinion. Al truly believed most of America did want the country to harness more of its own energy. This was not a Republican or Democrat idea. Unfortunately, as with most important issues of the day, the debate deteriorated into name calling and ludicrous allegations. Al would never understand why both sides could not just see the issue for what it was—energy and jobs.

Of course, Al did work for a manufacturing company whose raw material costs were related to the cost of petroleum-based products. However, Al also thought more in terms of the big picture. If more jobs are created, more people at work means more disposable income, which does mean greater tax revenues (even with his flat tax proposal). Al and Mitch had talked several times recently about the growing debt and the amount of borrowing the current administration was adding to the already incomprehensible number. The only way to start whittling this debt down was for tax revenues to exceed governmental spending. Al had thought for years allowing the United States to produce this oil, not only for itself, but for its allies, could be the key to solving the debt problems. How much revenue could be generated by selling the oil to other countries? We could most likely have a revenue stream for a time long enough to allow us to develop other energy forms as well as solve our looming social security crisis. "Enough of such dreams—logical as they may seem," Al said to himself. It was all predicated on Congress not spending any extra revenue, which was truly a pipe dream. Pushing those thoughts from his head, Al channeled his energy into finding Mitch's encryption.

Al reread the article twice more, and the clue was fairly evident. The second paragraph discussed a "message government was sending us." Al assumed this was also referring to Mitch's message. The reference was to 80 percent of the water around the states containing thirty years' worth of imports. Eighty percent of thirty would be twenty-four—every twenty-fourth word this time.

"Geez, Mitch—this was too easy," Al said aloud. He quickly went to work and determined "saved in" were the first two words, but the next three were "ever help drilling." Putting those five words together did not seem coherent at all. Another perusal of the article revealed another reference to a "message" in the third paragraph. Reviewing that section, Al concluded the clue could be "backward." Maybe the words were in reverse order. Still, even reversing the first words, he found "drilling help ever in saved" would not make sense—even if they were in different sentences. This was not as easy as he had originally thought. After chewing on it a few more minutes, Al considered the possibility he needed to start at the end of the article and work backward. Mitch had never done that before with his messages, but Al decided to give it a shot. "Liberty" was the first word under this theory, followed by "is." Maybe this was right. Continuing on, Al put together "Liberty is monitoring all communication very concerned stop." He double checked his counting and was convinced this was the message Mitch meant to convey. It would also explain Mitch's curtness on the phone the past weekend. Mitch obviously did not want to talk much—if he thought his cell phone was being monitored as well. Al thought for a few more minutes then decided to call Todd.

"Todd Kelnar," he answered on the second ring.

"Todd—it's A—listen, did you read Mitch's article yesterday?" Al asked without the customary pleasantries usually exchanged when he called.

"I did read it—I agree with a lot of it, but we have to really be mindful of any environmental impact of ..." Al interrupted Todd at this point.

"Did you decipher the message?"

"I tried for a little bit, but I had a fairly busy day. I was going to get back at it today. Don't ruin it for me."

"Sorry, buddy—but I have to." Al went on to explain what he had found.

"That is a very strange message—to tell you the truth, I have called him three times in the last week, and he has yet to return one of the calls. Maybe he is just avoiding calling so he doesn't have to give anything away."

"Most likely—but since he is telling us he is 'very concerned,' we have to find a way to help him. Did you learn anything about the Liberty Group when you visited him a few weeks back?"

"Nothing really—how about you—you're contributing articles?" Todd asked.

"And cashing their checks, but I know little else. If you look at their Web site, the most information you get about anyone there is Mitch and some of the other writers. Really, no one else is even mentioned."

"Any suggestions then?" Todd asked.

"How about we both send e-mails. Just talk about the getting together later in the month, but mention that you enjoyed his article and thought he had a good message. You go ahead and use those terms, and I will say something a little different. I'll call Mark and have him do the same. I just feel it is important for Mitch to know we all are here for him."

"I agree—I'm typing an e-mail to him right now."

"Great—and let's keep in touch—see if we can't think of another thing to do."

Chapter 20

Mitch went about business as usual for the next several weeks. He had received the e-mails from his friends and knew they had seen his message. Mitch did feel that he had support from them, even if they were halfway across the country. He did not attempt to call them, for fear of letting on too much. He continued his Liberty work with vigor and was enthusiastic at the meetings. Mitch had not yet shared any more concern with Marie, or anyone else for that matter. He made several failed attempts to have Paul join him and Marie socially. Maybe it was his imagination, but Mitch definitely thought Paul was purposely avoiding him.

Mitch and Marie were preparing for the weekend in Bowling Green, getting everything packed and ready. Mitch turned on the news and saw that the Democratic National Party decided to run an ad he just couldn't believe. Congress had recessed, and many of the representatives were holding town meetings in their districts to talk about the healthcare issue. A few of the representatives were confronted with some very passionate voters who felt that national healthcare was flat-out wrong. Living in the YouTube age, several of these heated discussions were captured and played on the airwaves. The DNC concluded that these people asking the questions were hired by special interest groups, and said Republicans were only doing this because they lost the election, lost on the stimulus. The advertisement went so far as to call Republicans the "mob."

Is this really what we have come to? Mitch thought. *How partisan are we going to get? This is definitely not what the American people expect from their chosen leaders.* Mitch was embarrassed by his own party at times and some of their tactics, but to criticize Americans who were voicing their opinions at town hall meetings seemed unbelievable. This tactic would only alienate more people.

But it wasn't just the DNC. Mitch also saw the White House had issued a statement on its blog requesting anyone receiving e-mails that included "disinformation" or anything "fishy" to forward those messages to a special White House site. Mitch pondered how the White House could ask any citizen to be the judge of what is "fishy," let alone to go so far as to report these individuals to a White House Web site. This seemed to Mitch just a continuation of dividing the country, not unifying it. It was as if the White House was telling Mr. and Mrs. America that instead of healthy debate, they should just continue to hate and to turn in anyone who voiced a dissenting opinion to their stance on healthcare. *Ludicrous!* Mitch thought. As far as he knew, the only proposal on the table at this point was the House bill. The administration had not proposed an official health program yet. The House bill was over 1,000 pages long. One Democrat member even admitted he wouldn't read the bill before voting on it, as he would need two lawyers to help him interpret it. "That sure provides a confident feeling that Congress knows what it is doing," Mitch said sarcastically out loud.

His frustration with the "we vs. them" mentality was at its highest point ever. Mitch had great friends who were liberals and great friends who were conservatives, and he had no doubt if they all got in a room, they could come out with progress on issues without calling each other names or making a point by vilifying the other side.

"I'm sure this is not what our founding fathers envisioned for Congressional debates," Mitch concluded. "How can we get back to a more civil discourse?"

These political issues were starting to take a back seat to his personal situation, though. Mitch felt almost as if he were suffocating, knowing his colleagues were up to something, but unable to get more information. He paced his bedroom, looking out the window at the golf course in the distance and contemplating his options. He definitely did not have any evidence to provide to the police. Over the past few weeks, Mitch had written down several lists of possible ways the Liberty Group could be keeping tabs on him. The envelope he received in his car had really flummoxed him; he was as paranoid as he had ever been. Mitch guessed he would be followed all the way to Bowling Green. He now assumed his phone had been bugged, but he didn't want to change phones to let on he was suspecting anything, which was the same reason he had continued to use his home computer as well. At least Mitch would see Al, Todd, and Mark this weekend. He could confide some of his concerns in person. It had been probably fifteen years since all four of them were together. Mitch just hoped he would be able to relax enough to enjoy the time with his friends. Marie knew he was bothered by something more than he was letting on, but Lynne, Jane, and Ed were still oblivious. Hopefully, he could keep it that way.

After a non-eventful flight, Mitch, Marie, and the kids drove their rental car down Interstate 75 from Detroit toward Bowling Green. This was a drive that included absolutely no change in elevation as the southeastern Michigan and northwest Ohio region is one of the flattest areas of the United States. They, as well as Todd, Mark, and his family, had rented rooms at the Hampton Inn. Al and Lisa's house was big, but not big enough to accommodate everyone for four days. Marie and Mitch had grown up in the area, so the drive was still somewhat familiar to them. As they drove, Mitch thought about Al's kids as well as Mark's. It had been so long since he had seen them; he was sure he would not recognize them. As his mind was never too far from his work, he thought of the analogy that seeing someone else's kid after six years of growing would be similar to the founding fathers walking into Washington, DC, today; they would not recognize the government they left. It would have some resemblances, but that would be about it.

As they neared the exit for Bowling Green, they noticed the university golf course as well as the football stadium. Both visions brought back a flood of college memories for the couple. They decided to drive through the campus before checking in at their hotel, since they had a few hours before they were due at Al's for a cookout. The campus was hardly recognizable as well. Mitch and Al had lived on the east end of campus their freshman year, and that particular dorm looked just as it had twenty years ago as they drove by, but that was about the only thing that was the same. Construction of a new basketball arena was ongoing, and the football stadium had added a beautiful facility at the north end. They turned down Ridge Street, which went through the center of campus. The old book store was gone (a sign indicating an arts center was to be soon built had taken its place) and the field where they had played intramural softball was now occupied by the Olscamp Building, named for the president of the university during their college years. The family continued up a little farther, soon realizing that Ridge no longer was passable all the way through campus. A quick U-turn had the family heading back they way they came, but they turned left at the Moore Musical Arts Center and left again on Merry Avenue, driving up to the dorm where Mitch and Al had lived as sophomores. Another left brought them past the McDonald Hall (a dormitory) and a right back on Ridge allowed them to finish their tour down the center of campus.

"Is this campus where you two first kissed?" one of kids asked sarcastically.

"No, but Al and Lisa did actually have their first kiss outside the dorm right there," Mitch replied, pointing at the McDonald building.

"You have to remember that your mom was in high school when we first started dating, and she then went to Kent State for a year." The kids had stopped listening.

The family made another left on Thurston Street and eventually came to a light on the far southwest corner of campus. While waiting for the light to turn, Mitch realized that Mark's Pizza no longer existed. An icon while he and Marie were there, the Student Book Exchange had expanded into its location. He observed a moment of silence. They turned left again, driving the length of the south end of campus back toward the Hampton.

* * * *

Al was manning the grill as Mitch, Marie, and the kids walked through house and out to the back deck. Mark and his family had arrived as well, but Todd was not there yet.

"What are we making?" Mitch asked Al.

"Salmon and steaks—a little surf and turf," Al said as he set down the grilling tool, embracing his friend. Al gave Mitch a knowing look and was about to ask about Liberty, but he could read in Mitch's eyes that now was not the time.

"How was your flight?" Al asked instead.

"How was my flight—how about offering me a beer first?" Mitch responded.

"You're right; where are my manners? What would you like?"

"Got a Bud Light?"

"Sure, but can I suggest you try this first?" Al responded handing Mitch a Shiner Bock. He turned and embraced Marie as well. "And what would you like to drink?"

"Lisa's getting me an iced tea. Thanks."

Mitch and Marie greeted Mark and his family. They all sat on the deck, which, similar to the Bartter house in Phoenix, overlooked a golf course. Al and Lisa lived in a fairly new house they had contracted to be built. They were situated between the green of a par three and the tee of a par four (which required a good drive to carry the water), so if you listened closely enough, you would hear some pretty colorful language as golfers missed putts and shanked tee shots into the pond.

"Todd a no show as of now?" Mark asked.

"He'll be here," Al responded. "You know Todd. He'll probably have some great story of what held him up. I do know he was driving from Little Rock, not flying, so I imagine there could have been some traffic along the way. I assume he broke the drive into a couple days."

The kids had to be re-introduced to each other, but that didn't take long. The Millers had a Wii Gaming System, which is the ultimate icebreaker. Al had also set out wiffle balls, bats, and some bases, and the beginning of a spirited game was taking shape while the adults sat on the deck watching.

"We don't have to worry about the kids getting hit by an errant golf ball, do we?" Robin asked as she noticed some people on the tee of the par three taking aim at what seemed to be their general direction.

"No, we're usually good," Al responded. "Not that I don't find the occasional ball in the yard when I am mowing, but I'm sure they will be fine."

"What the—a surprise party?" called a voice from the side gate. Mitch was about to respond, but Al motioned to leave it go. Todd had pulled in the driveway and walked to the gate. Al knew what was coming next.

"I tell you whose idea was this?" Todd finished the quote as he took off his sunglasses. Al looked at the others; no one said anything.

"*Stripes*—Bill Murray—the end of the movie," Al answered.

"I'm going to stump you yet, Miller!" Todd exclaimed as he opened the gate with a six-pack under his arm.

Mark and Mitch walked into the yard and greeted Todd.

"As usual, your timing is impeccable," Al said as he removed the steaks and salmon to a serving tray. "The food is all ready. We have a buffet-style meal set up on the counter inside. Grab a plateful, and then we'll come back out here. The weather is wonderfully cool for August."

They rounded up the kids to load their plates first, followed by the rest. Todd was about to crack open a Miller Genuine Draft when Al shoved a Shiner in his hand.

"He did that to me, too," Mitch said at Todd's quizzical look.

"And I notice you are on your second one already," Al retorted.

Mitch smiled. "Yeah, it is pretty good. Who turned you on to this?"

"My uncle, he lives in Texas. Went there for my cousin's wedding, and he served this. I was elated when I got back here and found a place that carried it. It must be getting pretty popular, though—now I can buy it in Kroger here as well."

They passed the rest of the evening reminiscing about college and catching up on each other's lives. Talk eventually came to Mitch's involvement with the Liberty Group and how he had roped Al into contributing. No discussion regarding the more concerning facts were made in front of the entire group, though. They began to dabble into a political discussion, and the healthcare insurance overhaul issue was raised.

"Well, I just believe something has to be done," Robin said. She was an advertising executive for a large company in Cincinnati. She had thick, curly black hair, with bright blue eyes. She and Marie had roomed together at Bowling Green, ironically enough. Robin and Mark had dated a little longer than the other couples from BGSU before getting married.

"Do you want the House bill?" Al asked her. "Have you seen what is in it?"

"No, I haven't seen what is in it, and I don't know if that is what I want, but there are too many uninsured in this country not to do something. And, of course, the pre-existing condition clauses are a major problem area, too."

"Agreed," Al continued. "But we can't do something just to say we did something. And why anyone thinks that government running the healthcare system will be better than what we have is beyond me. Obama made that point without intending to the other day—did you hear him?"

"You mean about the post office?" Mitch asked, as he grabbed his third Shiner.

"Exactly, was that comical or what?" Al replied.

"I think I missed that," Todd said. "What about the post office?"

"I think the president was in New Hampshire. He was touting the fact his healthcare plan would include a public option, but you would be able to keep your current healthcare insurance if you so desired. He noted that some people have argued the public option would put the private insurance companies out of business. Obama said he did not believe that would be the case, using mail delivery as an example. He said UPS and Federal Express are doing fine—it's the post office that is always having problems." Al took a breath as a few of the other snickered. "So, tell me again why would we turn over healthcare to the same entity that is having problems delivering mail? Or to an entity that is bankrupting Medicare and social security? I defy anyone to name a major government program that is not fraught with inefficiency and budget deficits. Lisa, the agency you used to work for dealt with Medicare billings. How easy was that?"

"Oh, it was horrible," Lisa replied. "They were far and away the most difficult agency for us to work with."

"My biggest concern," Mitch started, "is the increasing cost of this administration. I know Obama has said healthcare reform will not add to the deficit, but the Congressional Budget Office study confirmed it will increase the deficit considerably."

Robin was not going to back down so easily.

"I think other countries can spend more on healthcare because they do not waste so much on defense spending," she argued. "We should reallocate some of that money to healthcare."

Mitch had heard this suggestion before and had done a little research. "Would you believe me if I told you that from 2000 to 2008, the years W was in office, spending on health, Medicare, income, and social security increased by more than double what defense increased? And total spending on those human welfare items is almost three times what we spend on national defense in total."

"I don't think that can be right," Robin said.

"You're questioning Mitch on the budget—he is a deficit hawk!" Al exclaimed.

"That's right, I am, and we as a country are in the biggest spending storm of our history! Do you realize that the estimated spending for the current year is four trillion dollars! Can anyone even wrap their minds around that figure? Do you also realize that 2002 was the first year federal spending eclipsed two million? We cannot double spending in that short of a time frame without dire economic consequences!"

"Dire economic consequences?" Lisa asked.

"That's right—rivers and seas boiling, forty years of darkness, earthquakes, volcanoes, the dead rising from the grave, human sacrifice, dogs and cats living together—mass hysteria!"

Everyone laughed at Todd's movie quote. Mitch wasn't finished making his point. "Keep laughing, funny guy. You quote movies, *Ghostbusters*, by the way—it must be Bill Murray night. I'll quote one of our founding fathers, Jefferson: 'We shall all consider ourselves unauthorized to saddle posterity with our debts, and morally bound to pay them ourselves; and consequently within what may be deemed the period of a generation, or the life of the majority.'"

"How do you remember that stuff?" Al asked, impressed.

"Continual reading of the works and deeds of the founding fathers," Mitch replied, as serious as he had been all evening. "They really did set us up for the huge success the United States has experienced. We are now floundering it away. Hopefully, it is not too late to right the ship."

"Speaking of too late, I think I'm going to head inside," Lisa said.

She usually stayed out of the political talk and was ready for a change in subject. "You boys are all golfing together in the morning, correct?"

"Definitely," Mark answered. "She's right, Robin. We should grab the kids and go back to the hotel. I need to be rested to wipe the course with the egos of the other three here."

"If you thought tonight was Bill Murray quote night, wait until the golf course tomorrow, the *Caddyshack* references will be flying!" Todd said as they all pitched in to clean up the empty beer bottles and soda cans.

Smiling, Mitch just nodded. "We'll see in the morning, I guess." They all said their goodnights and headed back to the hotel. Down the street, one of two parked cars brought its engine to life and followed the group to the hotel, while the occupants of the other car remained. Mitch did not notice these cars, but in the back of his mind, he assumed someone was somewhere close by.

Golf the next day was at the Bowling Green State University course, also known as Forrest Creason. Al lived on a newer and more challenging course in town, but as this was a college reunion weekend, the group decided to play the course they had frequented several times while living together. The course was laid out on the northeast corner of campus, bordering the baseball field, the football stadium, as well as Interstate 75, which provided a great view of the eleventh hole's elevated green. Mitch was always the best golfer of the group, having played in high school and just missing in his attempting to walk onto the college team.

Mitch awoke that morning knowing he was going to come clean with his friends about the Liberty situation. He needed advice, and there weren't three guys he trusted more to give him some honest feedback. Mitch was apprehensive about involving them in this ordeal any further—Al was already knee deep. He had even thought about contriving some idea to cancel his participation in the weekend activities. However, if his suspicions were correct, the people watching had known for some time about this reunion, and changing plans late may have tipped them off he was on to something, although the Liberty Group would have been the last of his worries had he canceled the trip. Marie would have killed him.

The coolness of the previous evening had been replaced by more typical August weather. They played the front nine on a beautifully sunny yet quite warm morning. The group continued to catch up on each other's lives and laugh at the three balls Al had put in the water so far. Mitch shot a thirty-nine on the front, which was pretty good given how preoccupied he was. No one else was under forty-five. As they made the turn, they all grabbed a drink and something to eat, and approached the tenth tee. This tee box was just off the parking lot, and Mitch scanned the cars looking for any sign of his shadows. He may have been paranoid, but the van in the lot with the heavily tinted windows did not make him comfortable. He would wait until after the eleventh hole to talk to his friends. The tee to the twelfth was also elevated—they would be far from any ears up there.

After they watched Mitch roll in a birdie put on ten, followed by Todd hooking his drive on eleven into the Interstate 75 traffic, they completed the elevated hole and walked to the twelfth tee.

"I have something I need to talk to you all about. From your e-mails in the past few weeks, you all deciphered my message of concern about the Liberty endeavor," Mitch began, and over the next three holes, he described all the occurrences that had led him to his current feelings, fielding his friends' questions.

"Have you mentioned anything to Marie?" Al asked.

"She knows about some of my worries, but not about the information I have discovered lately. I don't want her or the kids involved any more. My plan is to determine what this group is up to for certain, obtain some solid evidence about it, and depending on that evidence, take care of the situation."

"Just that simple, take care of the situation," Al said. "Mitch, I know you are a smart guy, but if your worst fears are even close, you can't do this on your own. Don't you think it would be better to resign, just walk away?"

"No, I don't. If I am correct in my assumption that the date on the e-mail I forwarded myself had changed by the time I was able to look at it, then they know I have seen Paul's computer. I'm sure they are confident I didn't see a lot, but they don't know that for certain. That computer could have been loaded with secrets I'm not supposed to know. If I try to walk away, they will assume the worst. And most likely, respond accordingly."

"Good point," Al replied. "You told us the incidents that have raised your suspicions; how about telling us the overall goal, as you know it, of the Liberty Group? Maybe we can brainstorm as to where this all might be leading."

"Well, I was asked to join this conservative information group. My responsibility was to establish a daily schedule of writers for the Web site as well as populate the state links with articles about those individual states. I have accomplished this for about twenty states. That was the extent. They have used those entering the site as possible donors to the cause, to which many have given money."

"And define the cause," Mark requested.

"Promote conservative ideas and give information to those reading the site on why certain things work and why others don't. Generally, the cause is to educate America. Hopefully, an American better educated on the issues will select the best leadership for the country."

"By 'best,' you mean conservative?" Todd asked accusingly.

"Let's try to resolve this situation before we debate ideology," Al said.

"And what exactly did you find that causes your concern?" Mark asked again, feeling a little behind on the topic.

Mitch related the e-mail situation again, the package he received, the bribe attempts, and, hesitantly, the come-ons from the two women.

"Hey, that second one was because I was there!" Todd said, half laughing.

"That's right; I forgot. Anyhow, then there was the conversation I had with Charlie where he appeared to quote something I sent in an e-mail to you guys. Al and I talked about that—I firmly believe they are monitoring my e-mails."

"And your plan is to continue on, even after this cryptic conversation you had with Charlie, as if nothing has happened?" Todd asked.

"I have to. I don't know what they would do to me if I let on that I wanted out. I don't trust Charlie at all."

"Do you think you are in danger?" Mark questioned.

"Grave danger?" Todd asked. He answered his own question. "Is there any other kind?"

"Even when Mitch is going through one of the most significant conversations of his life, you feel the need to quote movies?" Al said, shaking his head in disbelief.

"Just trying to break the tension," Todd replied.

"What movie?" Mark asked.

"*A Few Good Men*, the courtroom scene when Cruise interviews Nicholson," Al answered.

"Anyhow, are you fearful for your safety, Mitch?" Al repeated Mark's question.

"Yes, at this point, I am. And I am especially fearful for my wife and kids. I can't let them know I'm concerned at all."

"What can we do to help?" Todd asked.

"Just be there for me, I guess," Mitch stated. "As I said, I am pretty sure they are monitoring my cell phone as well, probably Marie's, too. At this point, I am also assuming my home phones have been tapped. If I need to get a hold of you guys, I will figure out something. I know I sound paranoid, but you guys know me best, and I wouldn't feel this way if it were not warranted."

"And you have shared very little of this with Marie?" Al asked, confirming what Mitch had stated earlier.

"We talked about some concerns I had initially, but I have not expressed any of the recent events. I obviously don't want her to worry, and I also want her to know as little as possible about the shadier details until I am certain this group is up to something."

Mark, Todd, and Al all exchanged glances.

"What—you think it wrong not to tell her?" Mitch asked.

"I think you are going to need her," Al responded on behalf of all three of the friends. "She can help you—you know that. See if you can find out additional information, but I would counsel you to include her sooner rather than later."

"Let's keep playing," Mitch said, almost defensively. He knew his friends were just trying to help, but he had been dealing with these concerns a lot longer than they had. He would include Marie when he was ready.

The foursome finished their round of golf under a great cloud of tension. A few more questions were asked and possible ideas thrown out, but no conclusion or magical answer was discovered. The three friends all felt a bit helpless, given what Mitch had said and how he was feeling. After golf, they met their families for lunch at the Panera downtown and then walked to the same Diary Queen they had visited so often during their college days. Large Blizzards all around—Al kept it to one, instead of the two he would order in his younger days. The rest of the afternoon was more reminiscing and catching up with the entire group.

* * * *

"How is everything in Ohio?" Charlie asked.

"Fine, nothing exciting," Joe responded from the lobby of the Hampton Inn. "Mitch played golf this morning and spent the rest of the day with his friends and their families. They are back at the hotel now. It is three hours later here."

"Have you ascertained what is on tap for tomorrow?" Charlie probed, already knowing the answer.

"They are going to some place called Cedar Point."

"It's an amusement park, and from the looks of the Web site, it is a flipping big one," Charlie said. "Stay close enough to know where he is at all times, understood?"

"No problem, although I don't like roller coasters."

"You do what you do for a living, and you don't like thrill rides? Whatever. You should most likely wait at the exit of each ride anyhow. If you get in line and don't ride at the same time, you could lose him. He'll be with the group; you and Russell shouldn't have any problems."

"I'll check in tomorrow when we get back," Joe said, ending the conversation.

* * * * *

Charlie was right; the following day, the reunion crew all went to Cedar Point. Located in Sandusky, Ohio, Cedar Point was a huge amusement park. A trip to northern Ohio in the summer just wasn't complete without visiting the Point. Billed as "America's Roller Coast" (as it sits on the edge of Lake Erie), the park had more roller coasters than any other place in the United States. Given that they lived so close, Al and Lisa usually came at least once a year with the kids. The others hadn't been to the Point for some time, so there were quite a few new rides for them to try.

The group arrived as the park opened and headed straight to Al and Lisa's favorite ride, the Raptor. After that coaster and three or four more, it was closing in on lunchtime. Cedar Point was busy today, but not overly so. Most ride waits were about a half hour. This was almost perfect for the adults, as they could spend more time talking and reminiscing while waiting in line. The kids were allowed to explore the park on their own—as long as they stayed together. Cell phones would allow them to keep in touch.

Everyone met back up to eat lunch at Johnny Rocket's, sitting outside and enjoying a few performances by the staff (the servers sang and danced to the '50s music at certain times). As the day wore on, the adults eventually found themselves in line for a ride called Max Air, which consisted of two huge swings, with seats on both sides. The swings moved in opposite directions, pendulum style. They only thing holding the riders in place was a lap clasp, and although it was very thick, Al hated the fact there was nothing at all to hold on to with his hands. When the swing reached its top height, you either looked up at the sky or you stared straight down at the ground, hundreds of feet in the air. As Al watched the line of riders in front of him, he knew this was not going to be fun.

"I'm going to sit this one out," he said, finally.

"Thank you, I just did not want to be the only one to wimp out," Mitch said appreciatively. "We could try the water ride over there. Anyone else want to join us?"

There were no other takers. Mitch and Al left the line, which looked to have about another twenty-five-minute wait. The two friends had reached the beginning of the line to Thunder Rapids, but actually riding it was not what Mitch had planned.

"Don't ask any questions, but in three seconds, we are going to run full out—you'll see why," Mitch said in a low whisper to Al. "Three, two, one—go!" It took Al a split second to register what Mitch had said, but he took off right behind his friend. They ran for about a minute and ducked into a sweet shop.

"What the heck was that all about?" Al huffed, confused.

"You'll see," Mitch replied, leading his friend to a corner of the store where they could still see outside. In a couple seconds, two more people came running up, looking all around. Joe and Russell searched for a few minutes and then continued on into the heart of the park.

"I thought I would introduce you to my two shadows."

"Have they been following us all day?" Al asked, the seriousness of what Mitch had been trying to explain for the last few days hitting him hard.

"I kept seeing a couple familiar faces as we got off some of the rides.

I was assuming someone was tracking me, just had to flush them out. Apparently, they sent at least two people." Mitch was calmer about the situation than he thought he would be. This proof was almost a relief; he knew he wasn't crazy.

"So, not riding Max Air, that wasn't because you didn't want to ride it?" Al asked, embarrassed.

Mitch smiled. "We're going back right now, and you're getting on it!" The two of them headed back to the rest of the group.

* * * * *

Gus took the opportunity with Mitch out of town to dedicate the entire Thursday meeting to reviewing the part of the plan Mitch was not ever to know.

"Mitch has done a great job, and he really takes to his work," Paul said. "It is almost sad it will all come crashing down on him."

"So, Mitch takes the fall for all of us in whatever scheme you have planned?" Karen asked, obvious disdain in her tone.

"Karen, we have been over this," Gus replied. "You knew Mitch, or whomever we hired for this position, was going to be a patsy."

"I guess I had hoped that it wouldn't have to be that way. Why does anyone have to be to blame? Can't you set this plan in motion without a patsy?"

"There has to be someone to blame; there has to be a bad guy. In this case, there will be plenty of bad guys, but Mitch will definitely be one of them. Now, moving on. Charlie, you're still good with the surveillance?"

"We followed him to Ohio. He is spending his vacation with some old friends in their college town. Joe and Russell are with him. He seems to still be 100 percent on board. He had some concerns in the past month; we picked up a conversation with one of these friends that seemed to indicate that he had an inkling that Liberty was something other than what we had billed it to be, but he seems to have moved past that. With that being said, we all have to pay close attention to what we hear him say versus what we pick up on the listening devices."

"Not a problem for me, as I am not privy to the text of the listening devices," Karen spat.

"Well, come over tonight, and I'll let you hear everything I got," Charlie said, blowing Karen a kiss.

"Charlie, enough of that," Gus warned. "Karen, I know you are frustrated, but I truly believe we are protecting you by keeping you sheltered from everything. You have a job to do—we don't want other aspects of the group distracting you. This way, you are not doing anything illegal. I think you alone of our management team here plan to remain in the area well after our operation; well, I will as well, but under a different name. Trust me, you don't want to have too much knowledge. When the time comes, you will know everything."

Karen wanted to yell at Gus; she wanted to run from the room and never return, but those ideas were not options right now. She just hoped when she did find out what they were up to, she would have enough time and evidence to stop them.

* * * *

As Mitch, Marie, and Mark still had family in the northwest Ohio area, those two families spent the better part of the following few days visiting relatives. Todd's family was about an hour south of Bowling Green, and he, too, had gone to visit them. The plan was to all get back together for one more meal at Al's house before everyone headed their separate ways. It seemed all too soon the Millers' deck was again prepared for this farewell evening.

"What's on the menu tonight?" Todd asked, being the first to arrive, handing Lisa the bottle of wine that he had brought.

"We thought we would give you a taste of Italy," Al said. "Lisa and

The Liberty Group

I spent ten days there last fall, and it was unbelievable. We are trying our best to recreate a meal we had while on one of our day tours in Tuscany." He was putting together a plate of what looked to Todd like raw bacon, only lighter and much thinner.

"What is that?"

"Prosciutto, it's ham," Al answered. Todd raised his eyebrows slightly, wondering exactly what he was about to be fed. He grabbed a beer out of the open ice-filled cooler on the deck and sat down. The sun was still quite high in the sky, with Bowling Green sitting close to the western end of the time zone. Consequently, the sun seemed to stay up longer here than in most places. Todd had enjoyed his time with his family but was looking forward to this last evening with his friends. Lisa came out to join him with a glass of Chianti in her hand. Al remained inside finishing the dinner preparations.

"Todd—how is Arkansas? We haven't really had a chance to talk about what's happening with you."

Todd always liked Lisa. When she and Al started dating, he thought he was falling for her, too. She had that way about her. Todd remembered being stunned by her beauty when they first met. The years, if anything, had enhanced her outward appearance. And once you got to know her, it was impossible not to like her. She was so friendly and really knew how to talk and listen. Todd even flirted with the notion of asking her out before she and Al became too serious, but he could tell she only had eyes for his friend, and she and Al had became very serious very quickly in college. He never had a chance.

"Oh, I like Arkansas well enough," he replied, answering her question, "but I'm always thinking of moving on somewhere else. I do get bored if I stay in one place too long."

"Or if you date the same person too long?" Lisa hinted, catching Todd totally off guard.

"Cutting right to the chase, aren't you?"

"Todd, you know we all love you, and we want you to be happy.

Do whatever makes you happy. I'm sure that you have to feel lonely sometimes."

"You're right; I do. It's hard, especially now, to meet the right person. All the good ones like you, Marie, and Robin are taken. I missed my chance in college."

"I have to think that you still meet some very intriguing people," Lisa said.

"Oh, I do, and it is always exciting when I start dating someone new. I think I just have impossibly high standards."

"Promise me to keep trying," Lisa said positively.

"Try not—do or do not," Todd said.

Lisa stared at him. "If that is some movie quote, you'll be waiting a long time for a guess. You know I don't play that game."

"Okay, I'll keep trying to find someone," Todd said. "It was Yoda, by the way—*Empire Strikes Back*." Their conversation was cut short by the arrival of everyone else. They all caught up on the last few days and how everyone's family was doing. Mark talked about his parents' run-in with some things at their church and how the church had attempted to display a nativity on the courthouse lawn last Christmas but had been turned down. The little town in which they lived didn't want to ruffle any feathers, so to speak, claiming the separation of church and state would prevent them from doing that.

"You know, the separation of church and state was never meant in that way," Al said. Everyone turned to him, and Mark asked the question they were all wondering.

"I'm sorry, but how did Mitch's words get in your mouth?"

"What do you mean?" Al asked, smirking at the comment.

"It just sounds like something Mitch would say. Maybe this writing thing you're doing is turning you into him. Anyhow, go on, what do you mean it was never meant to be like that?"

"Mitch can correct me if I am wrong, but I believe it was Jefferson who first used that phrase, 'separation of church and state,' and he used it to comfort certain religions. You have to remember the United States was still very young, and the memories of other governments were fresh in their minds. Most governments at the time had a strong religious factor, for example the king in England being the head of the church, or the cardinals of the Pope having significant seats in government. The founders realized America had been based on a freedom of religion—*all* religions. They wanted to ensure no government entity within the states ever created or named a nationwide religion. How am I doing so far, Mitch?"

"I think you are doing great. It sounds like you know more than I do on this subject."

Al continued. "Jefferson said a wall of separation must exist to keep government out of the church, not to keep the church off of government property. He even wrote a full letter explaining his intentions with what he was saying. The letter can be found on the Internet. It is out there for all to read. The founders themselves all thought religion played a very important role for humanity and in its success. The first amendment to the Constitution states Congress is to make no law respecting an establishment of religion, or *prohibiting the free exercise thereof.*" Al strongly emphasized the last part of his sentence. "The document places restrictions on government, not religion. Yet, it is now interpreted as limiting what religion can do."

"So, when did it change?" Marie asked, intrigued.

"Sometime in the mid-1900s. All it takes for a change like this is for the Supreme Court, or any federal court, to interpret something differently, setting a precedent for future decisions. I believe it was in *Everson vs. Board of Education* where the Court only took the eight words 'a wall of separation between church and state' into their decision, failing to cite or possibly even consider the context of the letter explaining the meaning. That has brought us to where we are today. Every subsequent ruling uses those eight words and nothing more."

"I do think," Mitch interjected, "and it is just my opinion, if we had a little more religion within Congress and the White House—and I don't mean just the current White House—more doing unto others as you would have done to you, we would have more constructive and less divisive talk, and definitely more compromises."

"Well said—cheers, Mitch," Al offered, raising his glass of Chianti in toast.

Later in the evening, Al discreetly asked Mitch to join him in the basement. Mitch followed Al downstairs and into a back bedroom. Al turned on a radio very loud.

"Maybe you're leading me to be paranoid," he said, putting his face really close to Mitch's ear so he could hear him, "but I don't know if my house is bugged, after what you said on the golf course and what we witnessed at Cedar Point. I have been trying to think about what to do next."

"Join the club; it is getting harder to deflect Marie's questions of what's bothering me," Mitch replied.

"Yeah, well you know where I stand on that. Any further thought on how to get more information?"

"Truthfully, I have been trying to keep my mind free of this business the last few days. A solution will present itself, I am sure."

Al offered his advice. "I would definitely act in front of the Liberty Group as if you do not have worries about them. If they are concerned enough about you to send two guys to Ohio to follow you everywhere you go, then they are very serious about something. I'm positive they would not welcome questions about their intentions."

"Agreed, I plan on acting as exuberant as ever about what I am doing. I just hope to find a way to figure out what they are up to."

"Just remember there is a fine line between curiosity and foolhardiness. Don't do anything stupid."

"Got it," Mitch said, smiling. "Tell you what, why don't you call me every now and then or send me an e-mail asking me how it is going. I can respond with how much fun I am having with Liberty. Maybe it will keep them off my scent, so to speak."

"Great idea, I'll do that. Also, I was thinking, you mentioned in your conversation with the clerk at the Biltmore you learned Gus has another meeting once a month. You should go back to the hotel to see if you can find out anything more about that aspect. Who else is he talking to and why?"

"Good thinking, I will definitely do that," Mitch said, not having considered this possibility before.

"Also, the way you describe Paul, I bet he is the secretary of the management group. He will know most of the details, even the shadier aspects. Karen seems too far removed, and I doubt that Charlie would be trusted with maintaining important documents."

"You have given this some thought," Mitch said, impressed.

"If I am right about Paul, then finding out some more of what he knows, obviously without his knowledge, would be another possible avenue to try."

"I have been attempting to get to know him better. He is avoiding me, maybe intentionally. My boss did introduce us; I could ask him a place to start down that road."

"This game you have managed to get invited to is one where you need information to win," Al concluded.

"Right, I'll start with those ideas. Thanks so much for your help. Maybe we should rejoin the others."

"Hold on, please also take this," Al said, handing Mitch a cell phone.

"What the …?" Mitch asked.

"I had someone from one of my company's subsidiaries get it for me. They sent it overnight, and it is in that person's name, in Alabama. I don't think whoever they are can trace it to you. Keep it hidden, and use it only in an emergency. If the wrong people see you using it, they will know something is up. You may only get one chance, but if you ever need something, call me, and I will do whatever I can, including being on the next plane to Phoenix. I put my number in there already—speed dial number two."

"What did you put in for speed dial number one?" Mitch asked, perplexed.

"The number for this phone," Al said as he pulled out a second brand new cell. "Give this one to Marie. Tell her everything. She will be more important to contact in an emergency and, if this group is as organized as you say, her phone may be tainted already as well. They are just the basic phones, but they are small and should be easy to hide."

Mitch didn't know what to say—he felt gratitude beyond belief, not just for the phones but for the fact he wasn't alone in this ordeal. He had people willing to go to whatever length to help him. He gave his friend a hug and pocketed both phones.

"Now—find me another one of those Shiners," Mitch said, and the two of them headed back upstairs to rejoin the others.

Chapter 21

The trip back to Phoenix was uneventful. The flight was fine, and as the family had flown back on a Thursday, Mitch decided to head into the *Republic* on Friday to clear some e-mails and maybe work just part of the day (he originally had scheduled the whole week off). This way, he could be more relaxed on the weekend, knowing he wasn't heading back a large build-up of messages.

Mitch arrived at the *Republic* earlier than normal. Al's gift of the phones had been wonderful, but it also underscored the possible danger Mitch had managed to expose himself and his family to. He had not slept well in days. Mitch was so preoccupied while driving that he couldn't even remember the turns he had made to get to work as he entered the building. He settled in at his desk, too upset to eat. Mitch grabbed the Diet Coke he had intended to save for later in the morning, went ahead and cracked it open and took a swig. He needed to rewrite a portion of his current article and had just set to work on it when Brian Maddox sauntered over to him.

"What's up, Mitch? You're here really early," Brian said.

"Trouble sleeping, thought I'd get a jump on the day," Mitch said without looking up.

Brian was startled by Mitch's appearance. His eyes definitely had clearly visible bags Brian knew were not there a few weeks early. He also seemed hunched over and appeared to have lost a little weight.

"You okay, man?" Mads asked tentatively.

"Of course," Mitch said, looking up. "I take it I don't look okay. As I said, I am just having a little trouble sleeping."

"Your sleep deprivation wouldn't have anything to do with the current state of the president's economy or anything?" Brian asked, changing tactics. "Did you see housing starts are on the rise and Cash for Clunkers was great for the auto industry? It's looking up, man. It might be time to get on the Obama train."

Mitch chuckled slightly, always reveling in a chance to debate current issues. Maybe Mads was starting the debate on purpose to help Mitch feel better. In any case, Mitch went ahead and entered the fray.

"Mads, I don't have the time to go into all the points I could make about what you just said. I'll stay with just one of the subjects. Cash for Clunkers will result in a drought of car sales over the next six months. The government can point all they want at how many cars were sold, but it was the auto dealers who dished out the money to the Americans turning in the old vehicles. The government has only reimbursed about 7 percent of those payments as of right now. The dealers are the ones hanging high and dry. I was talking to an owner of several dealerships the other day. Of the one hundred requests they had turned in for reimbursement, one had been accepted, one denied, and ninety-eight were still pending. It also took an incredible amount of time to complete each request, and yet the Web sites the government provided kept crashing. I even heard the government needed to reallocate personnel from air traffic control for this project. This was very poor planning. In the end, dealers won't sell any more cars than they originally would have; they just did it in a condensed time frame. And the entity that hatched this wonderful plan is the one you want running healthcare?"

Mitch paused for a moment. This seemed too much like the arguments he continued to have with good people who just wanted the government assisting with everything.

"Brian," he began, "once again, it is all about your personal philosophy. Do you feel that government should be the solution for getting old cars off the road? Is it the federal government's job to assist the car industry to sell cars by actively getting involved in the process? I don't think so."

"But what is wrong with it?" Brian asked. "If it helps people buy cars and it helps people sell cars, isn't that good?"

"How is this program different than giving certain people a $3,500 tax credit on their tax returns for buying new cars? Do you think that would pass Congress?"

"So what?" Brian replied, clearly getting agitated. "It helped get old cars with poor gas mileage off the street. This was good. Are you just against anything President Obama does?"

"Again, my question is should your and my tax dollars go to assisting someone else to buy a car? Is that the purpose of the federal government? My concern, as always, is that if government assumes it can enter the private sector with this type of program, tax dollars funding car sales, what else and where else will government assume it can enter our lives?" Mitch could feel himself becoming energized as he debated with Mads. This was taking his mind off his very real life problems right now.

"I guess I don't make the same leap you do that this is a gateway program to further intrusion into peoples' lives," Brian argued.

"How can you not, when they are trying to take over your healthcare decisions? They already have taken over a major car company as well several financial giants. Can you possibly believe that control is not their ultimate …" Mitch fell silent for a few seconds, apparently deep in thought, then, smiling slightly at Brian, reached into his bottom desk drawer.

"Mads, you should feel very special," Mitch said as he extracted three books from his desk. Brian realized that two of the books were actually duplicates, at least the titles were the same. The third book was different. One of the books looked very old and worn. Its cover was torn in a few spots, and as Mitch had set it down, Brian could see that it had been highlighted throughout. The other two books looked brand new, as if they had never been opened.

"As you can see," Mitch said grabbing the two books with the same title, "these two are the same book—*Capitalism and Freedom* by Milton Friedman. The older copy is one I purchased in college and have continued to read and reread ever since." Mitch put that one down and picked up the other new book.

"This is a new copy of that book, while the other new one is another book by Friedman—*Free to Choose*. I always have extra copies of these in my desk in case I feel someone is passionate enough to care about how things work yet might be slightly misguided. I feel obligated at this point to give you these two incredibly illuminating books. Your passion for debate has earned you these gifts. Please just promise me to keep an open mind as you read."

Brian turned the copy of *Capitalism and Freedom* over in his hand, examining the back.

"It was originally published in 1962," Mitch said, "and has been reprinted twice—1982 and 2002. The copy I gave you is a 2002 reprint. However, I have highlighted one passage within the introduction. Turn to the first few pages. Now, in order to accept these gifts of enlightenment, you must read that passage in yellow out loud, to me, right now."

Brian looked at him and laughed. "Dude, I don't read books, not any that don't talk about ballplayers."

"Trust me, you won't be disappointed. Read the passage."

Brian turned the first few pages of the book and saw a block of yellow. He cleared his throat and began:

> *How can we keep the government we create from becoming a Frankenstein that will destroy the very freedom we establish it to protect? Freedom is a rare and delicate*

> *plant. Our minds tell us, and history confirms, that the great threat to freedom is the concentration of power. Government is necessary to protect our freedom, it is an instrument through which we can exercise our freedom; yet by concentrating power in political hands, it is also a threat to freedom.*

"Now, that is just the first major point of innumerable nuggets of wisdom made in this wonderful book. You should be very excited; you are about to have an education in economics from the master."

"But who is this guy Friedman? I guess the name is a little familiar."

"Hold on, let me show you something." Mitch clicked into a few folders on his computer and the screen came up with a YouTube clip. "This is Milton Friedman," Mitch said as he clicked the play button. Brian watched as a clip of the Phil Donohue show ran. Phil was asking a question about there being so much discrepancy in the distribution of wealth, so few haves and so many have-nots, and he was asking Milton Friedman if greed was a good idea on which to run an economic system. Milton immediately turned the question around on Phil and asked where in the world an economic system was not run on greed. He went into describing some of the great advancements in society and explaining how they were the result of individual initiative, not government mandate. The clip ended before Brian had been able to process all that was being said. Mitch was now clicking to a word document and printing it off.

"Here is a transcript of what you just saw. I typed this up a while ago. Just listen to this section: *'In the only cases in which the masses have escaped from the kind of grinding poverty you're talking about, the only cases in recorded history, are where they have had capitalism and free trade. If you want to know where the masses are worse (worst), is exactly in the kinds of societies that depart from that. So that the record of history is absolutely crystal clear, that there is no alternative way so far discovered of improving the lot of ordinary people that can hold a candle to the productive activities that are unleashed by a free enterprise system.'* This man was a genius. Please read the book."

"Okay, I'll read your book on one condition," Brian replied.

"And what is that?" Mitch asked.

"When Obama is proven right about the stimulus and his other programs, you will stand on your desk and proclaim how very wrong you are about him and his ideas," Mads said defiantly.

Mitch sighed. How many times did he have to say it?

"Please remember that I harbor no ill will toward President Obama. I do believe he is doing what he feels is best. I cannot fault him for that. I disagree strongly with his ideas, and I do feel his programs are exacerbating our current problems. With that being said, I have no fear of being wrong, so I will agree to your condition. In fact, you will have an entirely different attitude about the stimulus after reading these books. I am certain of that. Now, get reading!"

Brian walked away, looking down and flipping the pages of the book in his hand, almost walking into a wall as he headed back to his desk.

Chapter 22

Mitch had decided to take Al's advice on all counts. He did not have a chance to talk with John on Friday, and this weekend had been busy enough with unpacking and getting everything back to normal. He would track down his boss tomorrow and see if someone at the Biltmore knew anything more about Gus this week, too. First, though, Mitch decided it was time to tell Marie his suspicions. He knew she would first think he was over-reacting, but as he would lay out all the reasons why, she would become more concerned. He knew she would go ballistic when he told her his plan to learn more and not withdraw from the situation. Mitch assumed it was dangerous, and Marie would flat-out object. The more he thought about telling her, the more apprehensive he became. Like a Band-Aid, it was better to rip it off and get the pain over with.

After a dinner of grilled burgers, Mitch played a little Wii with Ed and read some Harry Potter to Jane. Marie had retreated early to the bedroom to do a little reading of her own. Mitch came in and sat on the bed next to her. He reached over to the bedside table and picked up his alarm clock radio. He switched it on and turned up the volume to a much too loud level.

"Marie, I love you so much," he began, almost shouting.

"I love you, too," she said, looking at him with her beautiful eyes and almost laughing. She had already changed into her brightly colored pinstriped pajamas. Mitch had made it a Christmas tradition to buy her a set of pajamas every year or two. "What's with the radio? Turn that down."

"I have some fairly disturbing news."

"What's that?" she replied, setting her book in her lap.

"This Liberty Group, I am very concerned that it is not what it seems." Marie looked at him, puzzled, still not understanding the radio. "I thought you were past that feeling and enjoying what you were doing for them, and why don't you turn off that radio? It is so loud!"

"Please bear with me regarding the radio. As for what I have been doing, yes, I have no doubt been energized. I have relished getting in touch with some of my contacts across the United States again, learning about the issues occurring in different states. I like how the Web site has come together. But all that is not the issue. I think something sinister is going on with Gus."

"Sinister? That's a strong word—what do you mean?"

"I mean I think they have been following me; no, I know they have been following me. I also think they are monitoring my e-mail, phones—all possible communications. That's why the radio, sound cover. Don't ask me how; I just know this is happening. And as disturbing as that sounds, it is not the worst, in my opinion."

Marie was shell shocked. What Mitch was saying all seemed impossible. She and Mitch led quiet lives, centered around their kids. What could her husband be talking about? Had he seen too many movies? She found it difficult to suppress a laugh. "Are you positive you are not imagining this? It doesn't make any sense."

"Hon—no, I am not. Here is what has happened. I have been bribed. I have had Charlie tell me things that he had no business knowing, not without overhearing some of my conversations. I've been hit on, and I received this from an anonymous source." He showed his wife the letter that had been left in his car. "I know this sounds all James Bond, but I think the Liberty Group is a cover for something. And if it is, what are they covering?"

Mitch and Marie sat in silence for awhile. Mitch was trying to replay all that had happened in such a short time in his mind, searching for some clue. Marie was thinking of who else might shed some light on the subject.

"Have you talked with Karen about any of this?" Marie asked hopefully. "She seems to be a voice of reason."

"I don't want to talk to anyone at Liberty about it. I don't know how much any of them know or don't know. And I definitely don't want to let on that I am suspicious."

"Just what are you suspicious of? What could they possibly be planning?"

"I don't know, but I am going to find out."

"And how do you plan to do that?" Marie asked, becoming increasingly worried by her husband's tone of voice.

"Al suggested I ..."

Marie interrupted. "Al knows about all this?"

"I talked to him in Bowling Green. He suggested I ask John more about Paul since he introduced us, and Al also thought I should see what more the Biltmore knows about Gus—as he is there so much. That's where I plan to start."

Marie was again silent for a few minutes. "Those are both good ideas. Did either of you geniuses have the idea that you should just resign—say you have a health issue or something? If you are so sure something sinister is happening, I would think you would want to distance yourself from it as much as possible." Marie's frustration was obvious.

"I don't want to do that. One, I'm not sure they would let me resign. If they have attempted to bribe me, it means they want control over me.

Two, this could end up being a great story. Let me stay on to do a little research. I cannot let on that I suspect anything, though. That means you can't let on you know anything either."

"Oh, that will be easy," Marie quipped. "I'm just going to tell myself that you are imagining all this, and you will not find out anything."

"Marie, I know how ridiculous this sounds, but I need you right now," Mitch pleaded. "I feel very strongly about this, and I need to know you support me. You are my rock."

Marie softened a bit. "You're right. I do support you, I just … I guess I hope you are wrong. In any case, how can I help?"

"I'll let you know. For now, keep this with you at all times. Here's a charger." Mitch handed her the phone Al had procured.

"In case your cell phone is being bugged, too—it was Al's idea. Just keep it with you and keep it hidden. It is what I will use if I need to contact you in a Liberty emergency. Other than that, we won't use it. We will continue on as if everything were normal."

Marie took the phone, and they hugged and returned downstairs to their kids, holding hands as they walked.

* * * *

Mitch walked into work revitalized. Talking with Marie did have that effect; he felt a large weight lifted from his burden; what with Al providing suggestions and no longer hiding his concerns from his wife, Mitch believed he was finally on his way to solving this problem. After settling in and working on his article for a few minutes, he could no longer wait. He wanted to talk to John. Mitch went to his office and knocked on the open door just as John was hanging up his phone.

"You got a few minutes?" Mitch asked.

"Truthfully, I do not," John replied. "Got a meeting in just a few. I'm available for lunch, if that works?"

"Lunch it is then. Meet you here?"

"Sounds good." Mitch headed back to his desk and tried working on the article he had started as well as reviewing some of the upcoming posts for the Liberty site. Time seemed to pass very slowly. Finally, it was time to meet his boss. Mitch again walked over to the office and found not only John waiting, but Mads as well. Mitch was really hoping to have this conversation without Brian.

The three found a restaurant, and invariably, John brought up politics during their lunch. Brian and John discussed the merits of the stimulus and several other presidential decisions. Mitch was doing his best not to join the conversation, though it was obvious the other two wanted him to. They liked being able to gang up on him. After about ten minutes, though, Mitch could take it no longer.

"I hate to say this, because as I have stressed before, I like to think that everyone is acting with the best of intentions. But if I am true to myself, I really find some of what this president says he wants to do at odds with the actions he takes. It is like he knows what to say to make people believe in him, but he has no intention of following through."

"What do you mean?" Brian asked.

"Take the budget, for example. Do you remember the president saying he wanted to move the country from being one of spenders to one of savers?"

"Of course, that was I think in relation to the banking industry," Mads answered confidently. "He wanted to encourage people to live within their means."

"Exactly. Then he proposes budgets for the next eight years that do not even come close to breaking even. In fact, some of them create the largest single-year deficits America has ever experienced. Do you realize that this year's deficit hit $1.4 trillion? Is this leading us to becoming a nation of savers? Are we living within our means?"

"Well, he needed to do that this year in order to save us from disaster," John replied. "Would you have preferred this Great Recession turn into another Great Depression?"

"We have different views on that, I am sure. And by the way, who coined the phrase Great Recession? What a joke. Of course I do not want another depression, but I believe that is what these policies will lead to. Rampant government spending did not save us in the '30s, and it won't save us now. Even if you believe the current year deficit was necessary, then why would all future year deficits be necessary? If in fact these policies are saving us and turning the economy around, then why don't we at least have a balanced budget sometime in the near future? Wouldn't these fantastic economic schemes be putting us into an economic boom?" Mitch realized he was talking quite loud as a few other tables turned his way.

"Now, you're just being too sarcastic for your own good," John said, trying to calm his writer.

"No, I'm not; I'm absolutely serious." Mitch turned to look at Brian. "Have you read any of the Freidman book I gave you?"

"I read the first ten pages or so. That's a hard book for a sportswriter to read. Besides, I've only had it for a weekend."

"Okay, here's another example. The president says he wants to create jobs."

Brian chuckled, knowing he was about to push even harder on one of Mitch's hot buttons. "Actually, he said he would create or save jobs."

"Don't get me started on the saved jobs baloney. How do you measure a saved job? He can claim he saved every job in America. I can claim I saved every job in America. How can it be refuted? Anyhow, I do believe that job creation is the most important requirement to move our country forward, and I also believe most people would agree. So why does the president put up barriers to job creation?"

"You're going to have to explain that," John said.

"Let's use baseball. How do you win a baseball game?" Mitch asked.

Brian looked at him. "You win a baseball game by putting together a solid team that ..." Mitch interrupted, shaking his head. "Just the easy, obvious answer—how do you win?"

"You score more runs than the other team," Brian answered.

"Exactly. Now, what if I told you I was going to change the rules a little? Instead of three strikes for an out and four balls for a walk, I say it now takes only two strikes for an out and six balls for a walk. Do you think you will score more or fewer runs?"

"You would score fewer runs," Brian answered. "Logically, outs would be easier to come by."

"How about if I made the bases farther apart?" Mitch continued.

"Again—fewer runs."

"Well, it's my belief what the president is proposing hurts job creation just as my baseball proposals diminish runs scored. How do you create jobs by increasing business expenses, such as the cap and trade bill? By all accounts, that bill will dramatically increase energy expenses, crippling our manufacturing competitiveness. China and India aren't living by such standards, and they are increasing their manufacturing jobs at a very fast rate. You see what I mean?"

"A little—but ..." Brian was interrupted as the waitress brought their food. The three of them ate in silence for a little while. Mitch was wondering how to talk to John while Brian was there, but the situation resolved itself as Mads received a text message.

"Looks like Wizenhunt is holding an impromptu press conference regarding the upcoming season; I'd better go!" Brian said, wolfing down his food and reaching for his wallet.

"I've got it," Mitch said, referring to the check. "Go see if the Cardinals plan on getting back to the Super Bowl!" With that, Brian left.

"John, I did want to talk to you about something."

"What's up, man?" John asked, enjoying his lunch.

"Do you know anything more about Paul?"

"Paul?"

"Paul Gregory, the guy you introduced me to—from the Liberty Group," Mitch replied impatiently.

"Settle down, Mitch, I was yanking your chain. Paul and I are acquaintances and nothing more. I have probably seen him, I don't know, maybe a dozen times in my life. He approached me about you, and I said I would do the introductions. Why—what's up?"

"Nothing." Mitch had thought long and hard about how much he wanted to divulge. He trusted John immensely, but he and Marie both agreed the fewer people involved in this, the better. "I just am trying to get to know my Liberty compatriots a little better. He's a hard one to track down, though."

"You're not thinking of jumping ship full time, are you?" John asked, smiling. "This national attention the group is garnering going to your head? Remember, I knew you when you were just a little conservative reporter."

"Very funny, and I have no intention of leaving the *Republic*. Just thought I'd see what you knew."

"Unfortunately, I cannot help you. If you ever pin him down, let me know, and we can all do something together. I would like to develop that contact better, too. He has the inside track to that Daddy Warbucks you both work for. Maybe he'll want to start a paper next, and I can be his million-dollar-a-year editor."

"That's a good idea. I'll let you know, although I wouldn't hold my breath on the newspaper possibility."

* * * * *

A dead end with John. The next option was determining if anyone at the Biltmore could provide additional information. Mitch went to the hotel on Wednesday with a plan in mind, but he thought he would need to build some trust equity from whomever he talked with first. He walked up to the check-in desk and got the attention of one of the hospitality managers. This was a different person than he had talked to a few weeks ago. Mitch assumed his shadows were outside somewhere, and his venture here today would be reported back.

"Hello—my name is Mitch Bartter. I was thinking of surprising my wife with a weekend stay here. I'd like to look at some of your suites."

"What weekend were you thinking?" the hotel employee asked, clicking his keyboard.

"Oh, I can be flexible about when. I'm still deciding where I want to go, and then I will pick a weekend."

"Do you live around here, or will you be flying in from somewhere? We can pick you up, drop you off, return a rental car—anything you need."

"No, we live close. I just want to do something special."

"Well, why don't I show you a few rooms, and then you can decide. All of our accommodations include luxurious linens and top-quality entertainment equipment. We have beautifully decorated oversized suites with wonderful views of the mountains." The employee was trying to make the sale. "We obviously have wonderful dining here on site as well as every other amenity you could possibly desire. If you want to make it a truly spectacular weekend, might I even suggest our Ocatilla?"

"Your what?"

"Our Ocatilla—our hotel within a hotel. This is a private sanctuary, with a personal concierge attending to your every need. You can have a bath drawn for you, get complimentary drinks in the lounge, start your morning with coffee or tea brought to your room, many relaxing details taken care of."

"I'll consider it, but I think even your regular rooms will be luxurious enough," Mitch said, questioning to himself how much money he would need for all the Ocatilla services. As they walked Mitch through the hotel, Mitch realized he had only previously seen a very small section of the place. He toured a few of the suites and saw the Terrace Garden with its many fountains as well as the cabana area. During the tour, Mitch pulled a picture from his pocket that he had taken while at Gus's Fourth of July party. It was of Gus, Charlie, and Paul talking. The cell phone picture definitely wasn't the clearest of images, but it would suffice.

"Do you recognize these gentlemen?" Mitch asked. "I meet them here every Thursday for a meeting at one o'clock."

"Yes, I've seen them before. The older one has a standing reservation for one of our meeting rooms, and he keeps a cottage reservation at all times here. I can't tell you his name."

"No problem, I was just curious if these gentlemen have any other special meetings here?" Mitch asked casually.

The hotel employee was caught off guard and answered without thinking. "Yes, the third Thursday of each month there is a meeting at three o'clock in the afternoon. It is basically a teleconference with thirty or so people calling in." He then continued talking about the tour as if the question about Gus was asked every day. This was even better information than Mitch had hoped to get, and he thought he had probably pushed his luck far enough.

"I've seen enough. This place is perfect. Let's go back to the desk and see what you have available next month." Back at the front of the hotel, Mitch thought he recognized a familiar form standing off to the side, still wearing sunglasses. Was it shadow number one or shadow number two? He couldn't quite decide.

"Do you have anything available for the weekend of the twenty-fifth and twenty-sixth of September?" Mitch asked loud enough for the onlooker to hear.

"What room type did you want?"

"One of the resort deluxe cottages, if possible?"

"Yes, sir, we do have availability for that. Can I go ahead and book it?"

"Absolutely!" Mitch said enthusiastically and almost too loudly. "My wife will love it. I can't wait to surprise her!" He went ahead and made all the necessary arrangements, leaving his e-mail for the confirmation to be sent to him.

Mitch went home and jotted down all he had learned. So who else would Gus be meeting with, and why did so many others need to call in? These people were obviously not close enough to come to the meeting in person. Could Gus have another business that he conducted from afar? Are these the individuals Karen mentioned were paid through a different service? The more he thought, the more questions came up. He briefed Marie when she got home, and she had no further ideas either. Mitch would have to keep looking.

Chapter 23

Mitch was at the *Republic* the next morning, finishing off some Liberty Web site data. His regular Thursday meeting was in a few hours, and he wanted to be able to report on the total articles in the archives now. They had been organized by topic, with a drop-down menu provided to allow easy browsing. It was still in its infancy in terms of overall content, but the site was very popular nonetheless. Karen had provided some statistics on the finances brought in by all his work. He stood and stretched and headed for the vending machine, time for a Diet Coke.

Upon returning to his desk, Mitch noticed an envelope lying on top of his article, no writing on it at all. He quickly scanned the large room, looking for anyone he did not recognize. Nothing. He turned the envelope over in his hand a few times. Could this be another bribe? As this one had not come in the regular mail, Mitch guessed it was something different and decided to open it right then.

The first page was a copy of an e-mail, with the addressee's name removed. The message discussed the surveillance of Mitch and his lack of knowing anything. It also described a donor list. The names of Gus,

Paul, and Charlie were all referred to, but no mention of Karen. The e-mail did appear altered; Mitch wasn't sure he had the full content. Also in the envelope was the donor list, a quick perusal of which seemed to be a who's who of conservatism as well as some corporate donations.

Mitch returned the items to the envelope and set it back on his desk. He sat back in his chair, placing his hands over his face. Mitch tried to concentrate on what all this meant, but his thoughts kept going back to who had left it.

* * * *

A few hours later, he was in the parking lot of the Biltmore, heading for his Liberty meeting. Karen was walking in as well and called over to him.

"Hey, Mitch—how are you?" Karen looked very professional but quite attractive in her pin-striped business suit.

"I'm good," he lied.

"Did you get that information I sent your way?" Mitch's mind froze for a second. Could she mean the envelope he just received at his desk?

"You know, the data about the Web site?" Karen clarified.

"Oh, that, yes, I did. Thank you so much. It really helped. You'll see here in a few minutes." Mitch's frustration with the situation was intensifying.

The meeting seemed to be the usual information, with everyone excited about what was happening. The conservative base of the country seemed to be rallying against the very liberal agenda of the White House and Congress. Mitch's mind was elsewhere when Gus said his name.

"Mitch, I read the article you wrote on the reconciliation process the Senate might use to push through healthcare. Truthfully, I still do not quite understand it." This brought him back to the moment, and he recovered quickly. Mitch had debated whether to publish the article Gus was referring to in the *Republic* or on the Web site. He had ultimately decided on the Web site, hoping for a wider audience. Mitch assumed not too many people truly understood what some people in the Senate were proposing and how much it went against the spirit of the Constitution.

"What didn't you understand?"

"Why can senators do this, and how does it circumvent the system?" Gus asked. "Also, why does it take 60 percent to pass a bill in the Senate?"

"Well, technically it doesn't; it only takes a majority. That is how senatorial rules are written. However, any senator can filibuster any proposed legislation. The supporters of such legislation can propose cloture, which limits debate, but takes sixty votes to approve. It also takes sixty votes to override any filibuster once it starts. So, we have to begin with the assumption the supporters of a bill feel there may be a filibuster. If they are concerned about that, then they can move for cloture prior to the bill coming to the floor. If cloture is approved, then senators have thirty hours to debate, propose, and add amendments, etc. Once the thirty hours are completed, a vote is held. That is why the misperception of the 60 percent. Senator Robert Byrd once said oftentimes, it is basically the threat of a filibuster that can keep a bill from coming up. It is this threat that results in the 60-percent super majority being necessary."

"Is that how the Constitution drew it up?" Karen asked.

"Oh no—the Constitution says nothing of filibuster or cloture," Mitch responded. "Most people who have seen *Mr. Smith Goes to Washington* envision a filibuster as Jimmy Stewart rattling off speech after speech. The Senate was designed to be the debating house, and there is nothing on length of debate in the Constitution. Most senators are reluctant to start a filibuster, however, as it ceases all action on any other bills pending. That is why it is said to bring the legislative process to a halt."

"But what is reconciliation then?" Paul asked. Charlie was clearly bored at this point, yawning and tilting his head back.

"Reconciliation is a procedure that was established in 1974 specifically for deficit reduction. As we have mentioned, filibusters are started reluctantly, and therefore usually only on highly contested issues. The budget, as well as bills affecting the budget, has been considered very controversial at times. In an effort to streamline the process of approving these items, the reconciliation process was developed. Basically, at least as it relates to the budget, the process is started with Congress passing a resolution instructing all committees affected to get their recommendations to the budget committee of either the House or the Senate, followed by the budget committee putting the recommendations into one single bill. In the Senate, this bill then only gets twenty hours of debate and a limited number of amendments. Since the filibuster process is not allowed, you can see where the party in the majority is favored."

"Has this ever been used for non-budget bills?" Karen asked, astounded again by the depth of Mitch's knowledge of the government.

"Yes, unfortunately, as both parties, once in power, are guilty of bastardizing the system to get their pet legislation passed," Mitch replied disdainfully. "It really is sickening at times. The founding fathers laid out a very good system. Power seems to blind our elected officials of that fact every now and then. In 1996, the Senate adopted the ability to apply reconciliation to any budget-related legislation, not just deficit reduction. Theoretically, any bill that involves spending or revenue could be considered budget related. George W. Bush used the process to get three major tax cuts passed. He even tried to use it to open the Artic National Wildlife Refuge for oil exploration, but those efforts failed. I take pride in laying out my articles in an easy-to-understand manner. I'm concerned if you two did not comprehend my main points."

"Well, after that explanation, I'm surprised you can sit there and think that you could be clear in an article with that subject matter,"

Charlie said out of the blue. "Dude, I fell asleep twice listening to you."

"Sorry to bore you," Mitch answered, his hatred toward Charlie growing stronger. "I thought I was answering Gus's question."

"I'm sure most people understood the article; I just struggled a little with it," Gus said. "Is there anything else for us today?"

"I have a conflict in a few weeks," Mitch stated. "Can we move the meeting to three o'clock instead of one o'clock?" Mitch knew the week in question would be the third Thursday of the month. Gus and Charlie exchanged looks.

"Mitch, my boy, I'm afraid my schedule will not permit that," Gus replied. "If we need to meet without you, then we will. We will be poorer for your absence. Maybe you could send a written report?"

"Will do," Mitch said. The telling glance between Gus and Charlie proved what he had been told by the hotel staff.

Chapter 24

Mitch continued his attempts to meet with Paul individually, but the man just never seemed to be available. Mitch needed to find some way to learn more about Liberty's alternate plans. Several different ideas occurred to him, all equally unappealing. He thought through them and decided on a course of action that was definitely dangerous, but as he really needed additional information, Mitch felt it was worth the risk. He by now assumed his only possible access was either through Gus, Charlie, or Paul, but that was a stretch, as Mitch would not go near Gus's place. Even though he had learned where Gus lived, he also assumed the place had some serious security features. Charlie just plain scared him. Paul seemed the logical choice; plus, Paul most likely had the most organizational information. Mitch concluded he would see what he could find at Paul's house.

The next question was how to lose the people following him. Finding additional information would be of little use if he was caught doing it. The trick would be not letting on that he knew something was up. After some careful consideration, Mitch decided he would need someone's help. Marie was out of the question; she needed to remain at home for the kids, as well as to be able to provide an alibi for him. His friend Brian would be perfect as his assistant tonight. Mitch would call Mads and ask him to drive to the clubhouse of the golf course bordering Mitch's house. His back yard and the entry to the course were both hidden from the view of the front of the house. Mitch would drop Brian off and then just use Brian's car. He would head to Paul's to see if he could find anything that would help. Mitch discussed this all with Marie, and although she was very nervous about it (as was Mitch), she agreed something needed to be done.

Paul mentioned during their Thursday meeting he had a dinner scheduled that evening, so tonight was the night. Mitch gave Brian the instructions that afternoon upon returning from his meeting, and though confused, Brian agreed do as instructed. Mitch put on his swimsuit (followed by a jogging suit), slung a light backpack over his shoulder, walked into the kitchen, and announced to Marie he was going for a swim. He walked into the back yard, picked up the large garbage bag of weights he had prepared earlier, and dropped it into the pool, making a large splash in the hope that it sounded like someone jumping in. He hurried over to the course, slipped through the gate, and ran along the edge of the property all the way to the clubhouse. Mads was waiting for him just as asked.

"What is this all about?" Brian questioned him.

"I don't want to tell you too much; the less you know, the better."

"Yeah, that's comforting. That will keep me from asking more questions. Where to?"

"As I said earlier, wherever you want me to drop you for a while. I will only need about thirty minutes."

"Fine. You tell me where to go, and we'll look for something along the way."

They drove in silence for awhile, the only conversation being Mitch giving directions. Mitch was preoccupied with what he was about to do. He had never committed a crime, and breaking and entering would definitely qualify. As they approached Paul's neighborhood, a BW-3's came into view. *How fitting, that's where this whole ordeal began*, Mitch thought.

"There you go; pull in there." Mitch pointed to the restaurant. Brian parked the car, and Mitch pulled out a twenty. "Go have some wings and beer on me, and I'll be back soon. In fact, I'll text you when I'm about here, and you can just meet me out front. It might not be from my normal cell phone, though. I had to borrow one; mine was not working properly," Mitch fibbed.

"You're not going to tell me anything more?" Brian asked, obviously ticked off.

"Mads, you're doing me a huge favor, and I really appreciate it. I will tell you, just not tonight. Keep your phone close by."

Brian headed into the restaurant, but Mitch had one more precaution to prepare. He reached into his backpack, removing a screwdriver and a spare set of license plates. Mitch pulled behind the restaurant to a secluded area and quickly changed the plates. He got back in the car and continued on his way. This possible plan was developed a week or so ago, but Mitch did not have a chance to drive by Paul's house prior to tonight (and he didn't want to let on to his followers that he was planning a visit to the neighborhood). He turned onto the street where Paul lived and soon came up to the house. He drove right by, just catching a glance. His plan was to park a few blocks away, jog back to the house, hopefully find an open door (if luck was on his side), and see what he could find.

* * * * *

Joe and Russell were at their stakeout location for the evening. Because they had been monitoring Mitch for months now, they had been using several different vehicles and had been changing the location of where they parked around the subdivision, working hard not to arouse suspicion. The stakeout points were obviously always close enough to maintain the closed-circuit video they had of the front of the house. The monitors were all clear. Mitch had announced he was going swimming, and they had heard the splash a few minutes later from the backyard microphones. There had been no other conversation involving Mitch for some time. Marie had helped the kids with their homework and was starting to put them to bed.

Russell and Joe had outfitted their vehicles for maximum comfort over the past few months. They had a beverage-filled cooler plugged into the power outlet, and they maintained a box of snacks that would feed them for days. Russell was just reaching for a candy bar when his cell phone buzzed. It was Charlie with his usual check-in call.

"Hello, Mr. Davis," Russell answered.

"What is the status tonight?"

"All quiet on the home front."

"Mitch and the family are at home?"

"Yes, Mitch is swimming, we think, and Marie is putting the kids to bed."

"What do mean 'we think'? Is he swimming or not?"

"He definitely got in the pool, we just haven't heard him come back in or say anything. He could just be sitting out by the pool reading."

"Call me back when you hear from him."

"Will do, Mr. Davis."

* * * * *

Mitch parked the car, grabbed a glasscutter and flashlight out of the backpack, and slid on the gloves he pulled out of his pocket. He jogged down the sidewalk and turned off Paul's street. As he drove into the neighborhood, he changed his plan slightly. Now that Mitch saw the houses backed up against each other, he thought he would approach from the back, cutting through someone else's yard. He was glancing at the houses, counting them as he passed and turned, sprinting through a yard when he believed he had the correct house. He was right, and it seemed luck was on his side as there were no neighbors outside as he ran through the yard.

Paul's back yard had a pool, a spacious patio, and very little green space. The house was dark, confirming Mitch's knowledge that Paul would be out tonight. Paul had once mentioned he did not own a dog (or any pet); since he lived alone, he knew he could not care for them properly. Mitch checked the sliding door—locked. There was another door that looked like it opened to the garage—also locked. One window, about three feet off the ground, was shut, but it moved when Mitch pushed up on it. *Great!* Mitch thought. He was hoping to be in and out without anyone ever knowing. A cut window would have ruined that. He slid the window open as far as he could and pulled himself into the house.

Paul's residence looked much bigger from the inside. Mitch had entered into a dining area, set off from the kitchen. He clicked on his flashlight, keeping it low to the ground, hoping not to raise any questions from people who might be passing by or from neighbors glancing in the direction of the house. Mitch assumed a study would be here somewhere, and he found it in the front of the house, across from the master bedroom. One wall of the room was completely covered with a built-in bookcase. Opposite the bookcase was a gorgeous oak desk, on which sat Paul's computer. To Mitch's surprise, the screen was on. He clicked off his flashlight and moved over to sit behind the computer. Mitch touched the mouse, and the screen came up to the password prompt. He had no clue or even a logical guess at what the password would be. The computer was a dead end. Mitch started rummaging through the drawers, looking for anything on the Liberty Group. He found absolutely nothing.

* * * * *

Eric Myerholtz

Paul was meeting with his financial advisor tonight. The advisor was unsure what type of client Paul catered to, but over the last year or so, Paul had contributed significantly to his holdings. He now had over $1 million, and they were discussing the allocation of the portfolio over dinner when Paul's phone buzzed. He looked at the number, puzzled.

"What is it?" his financial advisor asked.

"Well, I'm not sure. This doesn't make sense."

"What do you mean?"

"This number is from my home computer, but it only calls my cell phone when I send something to myself, or ..." his voice trailed off.

"Excuse me," Paul said urgently. He got up, walked away from the table, and made a call.

"Hey, Paul." The voice was Charlie's.

"Charlie, I just got a call from my home computer. It was awoken from sleep mode, and I'm not home."

"Is it possible one of your pets bumped the mouse?"

"I don't have any pets!" Paul was almost screaming.

"How far are you from home?"

"About forty-five minutes."

"Okay, I'll send Russell over to check it out. He's at Mitch's, only about twenty minutes away."

Charlie pushed a few buttons to call Russell back.

"Mr. Davis, we still haven't heard anything."

"Okay," Charlie replied. "Listen, Paul's feeling jumpy or something. Could you run over to check out his house? I think you know where he lives. Joe should stay behind to continue monitoring the situation there."

"No problem, Mr. Davis."

* * * *

Mitch was discouraged, finding absolutely no further leads as to what the Liberty Group was up to. He looked all over the study, including pulling a few books off the shelf and flipping through them. Nothing! He was just about to leave, looking at the desk one last time, when he remembered something Todd had once told him. Todd was talking about the movie *Dead Men Don't Wear Plaid* and had mentioned some secret information was hidden by taping it to the underside of a desk drawer. Todd said that was where Mitch should look in Todd's office if anything ever happened to him. It would have all the information Mitch would need, whatever that meant.

"It can't hurt to look," Mitch said aloud to himself. He grabbed the main center drawer, pulled it out as far as he could, and felt underneath. To his great surprise, there was something taped to the bottom. He got on his back and pointed the flashlight up, looking up at an envelope. It had no label or writing, but it was taped with duct tape. Mitch carefully peeled back the tape, pulled the envelope down, and looked inside. There were three pieces of paper.

The first page was titled "Liberty Timeline"; the second, "Liberty Donors"; and the third, "Liberty Contingencies." Mitch laid the three pieces on the desk and took out his cell phone, the one Al had given him. He took a few pictures of each of them. He was lying on the floor replacing the envelope when a set of headlights indicated a car was pulling into the driveway.

As his pulse quickened immensely, Mitch whispered to himself, "Don't panic!" He urgently taped the envelope back to the desk drawer, got up, and moved silently through the house. He noticed a figure approaching the front door as he swung one leg out the window and was very thankful this room was not visible from the entryway. He heard the door open (whoever it was had a key) just as he slid the window back down. Mitch took off into the night, glad that he had thought of wearing all black. He pulled out the black ski mask he had put in his jogging pants and slipped it on as he ran. He was just coming out of the neighbor's yard when he was met by someone walking a dog. The canine began barking, shaking the silence of the entire neighborhood.

Inside Paul's house, Russell heard the barking and walked to the back of the house. He couldn't see anything from this vantage point.

Mitch didn't stop running; he tore down the sidewalk and turned back toward the car. He jumped in when he reached it and grabbed the keys from under the floor mat. Trying hard not to drive too fast when his adrenalin was pumping intensely, he eased toward the BW-3's, passing the front of Paul's house as he went. The light in the study was visibly on, and he could see a person standing in the room. The figure was much bigger than Paul; it had to be someone else. Someone other than Paul knew that something had happened. He stepped on the accelerator and pulled out his phone, texting Mads.

A few minutes later, Mitch screeched to a halt in front of the restaurant, Mads waiting.

"Get in, get in!" Mitch pleaded. Brian jumped in the car, and Mitch took off.

"What in the world is going on, and why are you wearing a ski mask?" Brian asked.

Mitch took off the mask and tried to calm himself. "Again, Brian, I will explain when I can. Please bear with me, and do not tell anyone you were with me tonight. As far as you know, I was anywhere but with you."

"Am I now an accomplice to a crime? Does this have to do with that letter and money you received at work?"

"I don't know for certain, but I would bet there is a correlation between the letter and where I was tonight. Yes." Mitch was talking very fast. "And as for a crime, I entered but did not break."

"What does that mean, and slow down, Mitch; you'll get a ticket. You'll be home in five minutes, man. Take it easy." Just as the words were leaving Brian's mouth, a siren went on behind them. Mitch felt as if he was about to vomit, realizing the officer would most likely run the fake plates. He slowed and pulled to the curb, but unbelievably, the police car tore past them, obviously on a more important mission. Mitch eased the car away from the curb and drove more cautiously, taking a few deep, calming breaths. He and Brian looked at each, laughing at their relief.

* * * * *

At that moment, Russell was standing in Paul's study, wondering why the desk chair had been pushed out of place. The computer had gone back to sleep mode. Russell had never been in Paul's office before, but everything seemed normal. Charlie had taken it upon himself to have keys made of Paul's house, knowing Paul had too much damaging information that may need to be extracted in a hurry. Charlie had given a key each to Joe and Russell just in case.

Russell was now standing where the chair would have been if someone were to be sitting at the desk. He was scanning the room when something hit his foot. Looking down, he saw an envelope that had apparently fallen from the underside of the center drawer. Peering into it, Russell let out an audible gasp and quickly hit a button on his cell phone.

"Charlie, we have a problem."

* * * * *

Mitch pulled into the golf course parking lot, now mostly empty given the darkness.

"I can't thank you enough, Brian! Again, I will explain it all later. By the way, take off the plates I put on the car. The official ones are underneath. Just toss the fake ones in a dumpster somewhere."

"What do you mean?" Brian asked again, totally confused. There was no reply; Mitch had already grabbed his backpack and was tearing across the golf course.

* * * * *

"Joe—this is Charlie."

Joe had been watching video clips on his iPhone when it rang.

"Yes, Mr. Davis."

"I want you to knock on Mitch's door right now. See if he is there. If not, you stay until he returns, understand?"

"Yes, Mr. Davis, but I have not seen him leave. What do I tell his wife if she says he is not there?"

"Tell her you are from the Liberty Group. There is some urgent business that needs attention, and you were told to wait until he arrived."

"What if Mitch is there?" Joe asked.

Charlie hadn't thought of that. He was certain Mitch was getting wise to them and was equally sure that's who was in Paul's house tonight.

"If Mitch answers the door, just say you were doing a check of the neighborhood, there had been some peeping toms recently. If his wife answers, ask if her husband is there. If he is, wait for him to come to the door as well. I want proof he is home! I'm on my way to meet Russell. Call me as soon as you know where Mitch is."

"You got it, Mr. Davis."

* * * * *

Mitch crossed into his yard and heard the doorbell ring. He ripped off his sweat suit, leaving just his swimming trunks on, and dived into the pool. He swam the length and got out, grabbing the towel he left there previously, and ran into the house. Marie was just about to answer the door when Mitch motioned her away. She crept silently back upstairs as the doorbell rang again. When Marie was out of sight, Mitch opened the door, wet from the pool and toweling off. He was breathing very heavy.

"Can I help you?" he asked Joe, recognizing him even without his customary sunglasses.

"I am with a security company who has been hired to check on the neighborhood. We have had quite a few reports of peeping toms. Have you noticed anything?"

"Luckily, I guess, no, we haven't," Mitch replied, still breathing heavily as if he had been swimming for awhile.

"Okay, I was just checking."

A sudden thought occurred to Mitch. "Do you have a card you could leave with us, in case we do notice something?" Joe was caught; he clearly did not.

"I ran out a few houses ago. I will leave one in your mailbox tomorrow."

"Thanks, that would be great," Mitch replied as the man left.

"Who was that?" Marie asked.

Mitch motioned for her to wait, raising a finger toward her, looking through the window as the man walked to the next house. He then took Marie's hand, guiding her out the back door, past the pool, and onto the golf course, picking up his sweat suit as he walked.

"I'm guessing that was someone who works for Charlie. We had a close call tonight. I think they wanted to see if I was at home."

"How close of a call? You said Paul wouldn't be home, and why we are we all the way out in the middle of the fairway?"

"Paul wasn't there, and I think they might have listening devices everywhere." Mitch then went into the entire story of what had happened since he left.

"This is too much; you just have to tell those guys you are done," Marie urged. "Say you can't keep up with your *Republic* responsibilities and their stuff, too. You should also call the police!"

"What would I tell them, that I broke into someone's house? Besides,

I think it's too late to quit. If I ask to get out, they will assume it is because I have found out too much."

"And if you stay? If they think you found out something won't they respond in some manner to that? Don't you think you're in danger?"

"Of course I think I'm in danger," Mitch said, getting frustrated. "I think I've put us all in danger. But right now, they have no idea what I know or who I might have told. Gus is a control freak. He won't make a drastic move until he is sure he has everything contained. Besides, they need me for some unknown reason. I think our best play is not to panic. Look, they sent that guy to see if I was here, and I was. They won't be 100 percent sure of anything."

Marie scowled at him. "I'll give you a little more time, but at some point very soon, you're leaving that group and going to the police."

"Agreed, I just need something concrete to give them." The couple walked back to the house in silence, Mitch never having let go of Marie's hand.

* * * *

"Mr. Davis, it's Joe. Mitch was home, soaking wet from swimming."

"Really? I would have bet money that wasn't the case. You're absolutely sure that no one came or left the house all night?"

"Nobody left and no visitors either."

"Okay, thanks for the update. Russell will rejoin you in a few minutes." Charlie hung up the phone and looked at the envelope sitting on Paul's desk. The three items in this envelope were, prior to tonight, known only to Gus, Paul, and him. Someone had seen its contents, and Charlie needed to know who that was. Had Mitch possibly hired someone to come here?

"Do you think the person is still in the house?" Russell asked. Charlie thought for a moment. He supposed it was possible, but it would have been foolish not to have left at the first hint of someone arriving.

The Liberty Group

"Were your lights on when you pulled in the driveway?"

"Yes, but you didn't say to arrive by stealth. Maybe I should have assumed that."

"Maybe you should have! At any rate, then, no, I do not think they are still here. Your lights would have lit up this whole room. Heck, we don't even know for sure someone was here. All we know is that an envelope taped to the bottom of a desk drawer fell on your foot. It could have been bad timing."

"Yes, but that coupled with the fact Paul was notified his computer awoke from sleep mode would seem to prove someone was here," Russell argued.

"Who knows how sensitive that sleep mode function is?" Charlie retorted.

"Well, we've been in this office twenty minutes, picking things up and setting things down on the desk, and it still hasn't awoken. I really think someone had to move the mouse or punch the keyboard for it to activate and call Paul."

More headlights pointed through the room as Paul pulled in the driveway. Russell and Charlie waited as Paul half jogged into the house and came into his own study.

"So, what happened?" he asked.

"Apparently, someone was in your office this evening."

"I figured that when my computer came to life. Do we know who?"

"No. Not even sure how they got in, since all the doors were locked. Russell checked them. No broken windows, either."

"What did they take?" Paul asked.

"You tell us; look around to see if anything is missing," Charlie replied. "And why do you have your computer send a message to your phone when it comes out of sleep mode?"

"If you had ever met my ex-wife, you wouldn't ask that question. I wonder if she was the one here." It was then he noticed the envelope and its contents sitting on his desk. "Where did you guys get that?" Paul demanded, his face turning paler by the minute.

"I believe it's yours. It fell on Russell's foot when he was checking out the study after you called me. Did you have it taped to the drawer?" Charlie's tone suggested he was enjoying questioning Paul.

"Yes, that's where I was hiding it. I don't have a safe in the house."

"Our belief is whoever was here, if indeed someone was here, saw the contents of that envelope."

"That's not good," Paul said matter-of-factly. Charlie nodded in agreement.

* * * * *

Mitch pulled out the cell phone once he and Marie were up in their bedroom. He had showered and changed, calming himself along the way. He also said a prayer asking for guidance in what had become too incredibly complicated an issue. He looked at the pictures, but could not make out what they said. Marie tried her best as well, but everything was just too small. He knew he could not e-mail the pictures to himself; that would be a dead giveaway. Brian was going to help him again. He quickly punched in Mads's e-mail address and sent the pictures with the text "Do not open until I am with you!"

* * * * *

Mitch awoke early, again barely sleeping, and anxiously headed into the paper. He knew Brian would not be in yet. His coworker had taken a risk in missing a portion of the Diamondback game the night before (the team was on the road), but he still needed to watch the game and report on it. Mitch was certain Brian would have stayed up late working on the article.

After a nerve-wrecking morning of attempting to write a new article, he saw his friend at last. He headed over to his department and got his attention.

"We need to talk," Mitch said matter-of-factly.

"Darn straight we do. What the …"

Mitch cut him off. "Not here, follow me." Mitch turned and walked to the stairway and up a few flights but stayed in the stairwell.

"What was that about last night? I want some answers now!"

"I'll give you some brief summaries," Mitch replied. "I am working with a group who I believe to be up to something illegal. My involvement has all been above board."

"What are they up to?"

"I'm trying to find out, and whether you know it or not, you are helping me. I sent you an e-mail. I want you print off the pictures in that message, but do not look at them. Just give me the hardcopies."

"Why don't you just print them yourself?" Brian quizzed.

"Long story. Can you just do this for me, please? I really need your help, man."

"You owe me a lot of favors, and believe me, I'm going to collect! I'll bring the pictures over to you in a few minutes."

"Thanks, Mads!"

* * * * *

Brian was good to his word, and within a few minutes, Mitch was looking at larger versions his cell phone pictures. The page titled "Liberty Donors" was really not new information to him. Most of the list had been discussed at the Thursday meetings, and this page was similar to what he had received in the last delivery from his unknown assistant. The dollar figures were quite a bit more than he realized, though. The corporate giving combined to exceed $1 million, and the individual memberships added another $500,000.

Mitch reviewed the "Liberty Timeline" page. It was actually sub-labeled "Final Phase."

1. Find core management team: Done, 2005
2. Establish contacts with targets: Done, 2005–2008
3. Find someone to handle finances: Done, 2008
4. Set up Web-based information—online donations: Done, 2009
5. Find Web site lead person: ~~D.B.~~, ~~T.A.~~, or M.B.: Done, 2009
6. Maintain list of donors, amounts, and contacts: ongoing
7. Have J.M. establish contacts at major newspapers, with individual articles ready for Sept. 2009
8. Set traps: January–August 2009
9. First wave of strike: Aug/Sept. 2009; second wave: a few days later; final wave: a few days after that

Sit back and enjoy the fireworks!

* * * * *

Most of it did not make much sense to Mitch. The core management team was obviously Gus and Charlie, most likely Paul, too. The phrase "contacts with targets" was completely foreign to him. The finances—that must be Karen. The Web site and the initials M.B. were easy enough to understand, though it appeared he was their third choice. *Why didn't they pick one of the other two!* Mitch thought frantically to himself. He had no idea who J.M. was (perhaps the man who introduced him at the July 4 party), but traps and strikes were set to happen very soon, with some of the traps potentially already in place. Mitch knew he needed to figure this out quickly.

Glancing at the "Liberty Contingencies" page, Mitch knew in a second it was in code. Whatever this was, people definitely were working hard to keep it a secret. The page was filled with what appeared to be initials next to letters and numbers: "R.B.—S1; S.R.—S2; B.T.—R1," and so on. He would need more information to figure this out.

* * * *

Will had noticed that Karen's overall outlook seemed more positive recently, but she still seemed quite stressed. With the new clients recently added to the firm, he assumed her concerns were not related to the business, but the same issue she had been dealing with. As she was in her office this morning, Will took this opportunity to see if he couldn't find out a little more.

"Hey, Karen, how are you this morning?"

"I'm good, Will, thanks for asking," Karen said, looking up from the paper she was reading, always happy to see him.

"How is that issue you were working on a few weeks ago? Has there been any resolution to that?" Will tried to sound casual. He noticed a small lip quiver, but Karen recovered quickly.

"Yeah, I think I have better control of that right now," she lied. Will wasn't fooled.

"I'm always here, Karen, for anything you may need."

"I know, Will. Really, I have it handled. I appreciate your concern. You're a good friend." Karen was losing a little patience. She did not have it handled, and Gus had been hinting that the final phase would be starting soon. She still was not privy to the full plan, and she was frightened by what it might include. Karen was, however, resolved to ensure it failed; that was her motivation now, to successfully ruin Gus's big plans.

Will walked back to his desk, frustrated. "Why won't she let me help her?" he said out loud to no one.

Chapter 25

Mitch, Marie, and Ed were sitting in the auditorium of the high school, getting ready to watch Lynne and Jane in a production of *The Music Man* they had worked on with a summer performance troupe. Both girls were very interested in dramatics, and Mitch was looking forward to this escape from his other issues. He always enjoyed watching his kids perform, missing the days that too soon flew by when they would play dress-up and put on little skits at the house. Now he was dealing with boyfriends and his own kids driving, not that these were bad things; he just missed his kids being younger.

"You okay?" Marie whispered to him.

"Yeah, looking forward to forgetting about some things for an hour or two. How about you?" Mitch reached over and took her hand.

"I'm good. I can just feel how tense you are." She tucked her arm around his and leaned in to hug him just as the lights went down.

The production was wonderfully performed by kids ranging in age from thirteen to eighteen. Mitch, Marie, and Ed all enjoyed it very much. As the last act was completed, and the lights came back up; they all stood to leave.

The Liberty Group

"Dad—what's this?" Ed asked, holding a letter-sized envelope.

"I don't know, bud. Where did you get it?"

"It was lying in this empty seat beside me, and it's got your name on it," Ed said.

"My name, let me see?" Mitch said, a weight dropping in his stomach.

Sure enough, as Ed handed him the envelope, Mitch could clearly see his name written in large black block letters. Ed was still looking at him, puzzled.

"I must have dropped it when we came in or during the intermission," Mitch fibbed, not wanting his son to worry or be concerned about an envelope being delivered to him here at the auditorium. "Someone gave it to me at work."

Marie gave Mitch the worried look she had all too often lately. "We'll see what it says when we get home," he whispered to his wife. "Let's go greet the wonderful performers!"

After about half an hour of talking with the performers and other parents, the Bartter family made their way home. Most of the conversation in the car was about school starting soon and the drama performances the high school would be doing. Mitch was silent as they drove, contemplating what new information had come his way. He was also trying to determine who kept feeding him these little tidbits. He had received something in his car, at the paper, and now at a function of his kids. Was there a mole within the Liberty group, possibly someone from the people who meet on the third Thursday of each month with Gus? He thought he should probably wait to see what the contents of this envelope were before he determined if its provider was a friend or a foe.

At the house, the kids continued their discussion of the upcoming school year while Mitch headed upstairs, Marie close behind him. They walked into their bedroom and locked the door.

"Let's see what it says," Marie said, in a what-can-be-next tone. Mitch opened the envelope to find copies of three e-mails, again with the address of the recipient and sender deleted. The names included in the text we confined to Charlie, Gus, and Paul. Mitch checked quickly to see if the pages were in chronological order, which they were. All had been sent in the last few days.

The first one indicated that, as mid-August was approaching, so was the time when the final phase would begin. All were to be prepared. One line stuck out to both Mitch and Marie. "M.B. portion proceeding as planned—still unaware." It sounded ominous, but there were no specifics of the full plans.

"At least they are somewhat wrong about the unaware part," Marie commented, trying to be hopeful.

The second e-mail seemed to be directed to one person (again the addressee line had been cleared) as opposed to the first page, which had been sent to several people (terms like "all of you" were spread throughout it). This message had blanks here and there where some names had been removed.

"This one was to Karen," Marie stated confidently. She was right; the subject of the text clearly was financial. It discussed total money in the bank, total committed to several different projects, and asked for five different checks to be written. The last line said, "Continue payment in M.B. account—increase by amount previously discussed starting with last week of August." It also indicated that the current M.B. account was funded electronically.

"They pay you electronically? And how much did they say they would increase your pay?"

"I've actually been getting a handwritten check. I'm not even an employee. I have been paying my own estimated taxes on this income as well as the self-employment pieces."

"What do you mean, 'self-employment pieces'?" Marie asked.

"Well, I have to pay social security and Medicare taxes on all my income, not just what I choose to. Once I reach the social security limit I can stop … What are we talking about this for anyhow? Gus never indicated that my pay would increase, and I've never given them an

The Liberty Group

account to fund. I think this can only mean one thing." Mitch knew his wife would come up with the answer.

"You're being set up. They want to give the appearance of paying you much more than you have been actually given."

"That is my conclusion as well." With that new nugget of information, they turned to the third e-mail. This one almost seemed like more of a teaser than anything else. All it said was "Always make a good first impression, which for our true purpose will occur very soon. The good people of South Carolina will get some excitement—their recent so-called hero will be shown to be the opposite—keep your eye on the *Post and Courier!*"

The couple both sank onto the bed at the same time, Mitch holding the three pieces of paper in his hands.

"Any thoughts?" he asked, turning to face his wife.

"None that will help," Marie said. "It's clear something is being planned, starting in South Carolina from the looks of it. It also appears you will be a part of it, without your knowledge, as you apparently are oblivious to the plans."

"I kind of feel oblivious. I wish whoever felt compelled to provide us with this information would just tell me everything."

"Maybe they are telling you all they know, giving you the information as they know it," Marie suggested as she got up and went into the bathroom. *As usual*, Mitch thought, *she is probably right. That is what the first note indicated.* He lay back and closed his eyes, concentrating hard on all this new data.

"It must be Karen," Marie said from the bathroom. "Why else would her name be blanked out?"

"I just think Karen would come right out and tell me. Why do it secretly? For example, if she was at the show tonight, why not wait till the end and just hand me the envelope? I don't think it is Karen."

"Well, who else gets e-mails? This person is getting the messages somehow."

"I wish I knew." One thing Mitch did know was the *Post and*

Eric Myerholtz

Courier, a Charleston, South Carolina, newspaper. It would take a little research to determine who this hero was. At least he had an inkling of a direction to take.

Chapter 26

It had been a few days since Mitch received the newest packet of information, and he was determined to find out the purpose of Gus's other meeting. Some may have called him obsessed, but with all the information he had been given, he was not going to let this meeting go unchecked. The main question was how to once again do something without others knowing he was doing it. Mitch told his Liberty colleagues that he had been able to free up his schedule and attend the Thursday meeting he had originally announced he would miss.

He had considered the three o'clock meeting was accomplished by phone, but he did not want to risk attempting to get the number. Not knowing the subject matter or who was calling, he would not even be able to bluff his way through. He had settled on trying to leave a small listening device in the room when he left at about two o'clock. It had cost him $500, but Mitch purchased a calculator with a transmitter already imbedded in it. (Actually, Brian obtained it for him—Mitch gave him an envelope with money and the model he wanted, as well as the directions to a store where he would find it.) Brian had then given it to Mitch just this morning. Mitch's plan was to go to the one o'clock meeting, take out his computer and other items as he normally would, only this time, he would pull out the calculator. He would then leave the calculator in the room when he left, on the chair most likely. Mitch assumed if it was discovered later, someone would most likely put it on the table with their own stuff. Whether the calculator was discovered or not, he would still hear most of the conversation.

The catch was to be within 500 meters to hear the conversation. That sounded like a wide range, but he did not want to stray too far. The more Mitch contemplated it, the more he realized he was over-thinking the situation. He would just take a stroll around the grounds after the meeting. Even better, he would have Marie join him for a late afternoon meal. What would Charlie or Gus say to him if he didn't leave? Were they going to physically remove him from the premises?

He had arranged it with Marie; she would show up about 2:30. Mitch would make whatever excuse necessary if he was asked. About 12:30, he walked out of the *Republic* and grabbed a cab. Mitch checked behind and saw the familiar dark sedan pull out and begin to follow. He let his mind wander and envisioned some sort of spy game, where the people following him had a code word for him and everything he did.

The Falcon is traveling—taking a bumblebee, Mitch imagined someone saying into a two-way talking device. He laughed audibly to himself, the cab driver looking at him through his rearview mirror. Mitch shook himself from these thoughts and checked his computer bag for the fifth time to ensure he still had the calculator as well as everything else. The cab dropped him outside the Biltmore around 12:50. He walked in just like any other Thursday, taking his normal seat and preparing for the meeting, including getting all the items out of his computer bag. Paul, Gus, and Charlie walked in a minute later, followed closely by Karen.

"Good afternoon, Mitch, glad your plans changed and you could make it after all," Gus said genially.

"Wouldn't miss these; I'm having too much fun on this project!" Mitch responded, and then went back to setting up his computer.

"What is the heck is that?" Charlie asked, and Mitch thought for a second he was pointing at the calculator.

"What?"

"That tie. That is the ugliest tie I have ever seen. You're usually a little more casual."

"Every now and then I choose to go a little more upscale," Mitch said, smiling. He had actually dressed differently than usual in the hope that his appearance would distract from the addition of the calculator.

The meeting went off like normal, although Mitch felt a new energy in the room—as if they knew the plan was getting closer. He obviously wasn't to know that, and he was still trying to determine how much Karen was involved. Hopefully, his plan for the afternoon might answer a few of those questions. When the meeting came to an end promptly at two o'clock, Mitch started packing his stuff up slowly, placing his computer bag on his chair. He purposely looked up and asked Karen about her firm as he grabbed the calculator and appeared to drop it in his bag—the devise actually falling behind his bag and onto the chair. Mitch found the strap of his bag, still in conversation with Karen, and slung it over his shoulder, simultaneously pushing in his chair. As he walked down the hall, Mitch smiled at his performance, thinking it was pretty darn good. He stopped and sat in the lobby, taking out a book about Ronald Reagan.

Mitch assumed that it would take about fifteen minutes for Charlie to hear from the sedan outside and for him to come see what Mitch was up to. It actually took only twelve.

"Mitch—you still here?" Charlie asked, seemingly on his way out as well.

"Yeah, I've talked so much about this place, my wife wanted to have an excuse to see it," Mitch answered casually. "When my afternoon freed up today, she suggested we walk through and maybe grab a late lunch. She'll be here in a few minutes."

"Isn't that nice." Charlie tried to think of something else to say, preferring Mitch not to be at the Biltmore right now. However, no words came to him that would not raise suspicion. "Well, have fun then." Mitch smiled behind his book, knowing he had aggravated Charlie.

* * * * *

"I don't like it; what if he asks why we are still here or sees someone?" Charlie asked.

"You need to relax," Gus replied. "Mitch has no idea what we would be doing, nor is it any of his business. You, Paul, and I will have our normal call, and no one else is joining us today. Mitch won't be in the room. He is going to be walking around with his wife. He won't know if we are still here or not."

"I still don't like it," Charlie said.

"Did you get the idea that he was lying? We'll know from Russell outside if his wife shows up." Not two minutes later, Charlie's phone buzzed with the text "Wife is here." Charlie shook his head and let it go now.

* * * * *

Mitch got up and kissed Marie. She gave him a hopeful look, and he just nodded, with the slightest hint of a smile.

"So, show me this beautiful hotel," Marie said loudly. Mitch walked her around the basic tour he himself had received a few weeks earlier. After about twenty minutes, they made their way to one of the restaurants, the one closest to their Liberty meeting room. Charlie had sent a text to Russell asking what Mitch was up to and was pleased hear he was eating.

Mitch had already tested the device while he and Marie were walking around Biltmore. The reception in Frank and Albert's would be just fine.

Mitch had placed the receiver on his belt and ran an earphone under his clothes. He made sure he and his wife were seated with their backs to the entrance, in case an unwanted visitor looked in; he did not want his earpiece showing. The couple ordered their food just as the meeting was starting. Gus told Charlie to dial the number. Mitch could not believe how clear the audio was; it was as if he were right there in the room. The automated voice for a GoToMeeting call said they were joining a party with twenty-five different callers already there.

"Let's have the roll call," Gus demanded, clearly taking charge. "And as always, please remember the protocol." What followed was not a procession of individuals calling out their names, but one by one, different voices said "R1," "S1," "R2," "S2," and so on. Mitch was making notes in the pocket notebook he had brought with him.

"What are they saying?" Marie whispered. She realized this was going to be a little frustrating, not being able to hear the conversation.

"Just kind of taking attendance, seeing who is on the call—hold on," Mitch replied. He heard Gus's voice again.

"Last month, you all reported that everything was set and in place, with the exception of I believe five people. I want to hear from those five right now, and it better be good news. I have paid you all very handsomely; I don't want to be disappointed."

"This is R5, and we are all set. I am e-mailing Charlie the particulars as we speak."

"Send those to me," Paul's voice said. "I'll need Karen to transfer some funds to the proper account, unless you are ready to tell her everything, and she can send it herself."

Gus replied to the question. "No, I don't think she is ready. She will be the last one to get that information. Well, besides Mitch." Charlie could be heard chuckling. "I'll tell her to transfer the money."

Four other voices took turns also indicating that everything with respect to their assigned tasks had been completed. The words "all is set" or "ready for you to give the word" were used, but no details were ever uttered. Mitch assumed Gus had not trusted this open line totally, as well as not knowing who might be joining others on the opposite ends of the lines. All the callers had obviously been instructed not to reveal specifics.

"Thank you all—we are very close now." Gus was speaking again. "Your efforts over the past several years will always remain secret but will be viewed as heroic, in my opinion. I need you all to see this through to the finish line, which is right around the corner. We will take care of the final financial details we just discussed. I believe Charlie has already drafted the e-mails you will receive to let you know when the ball is dropping, so to speak. Keep those phones we provided close at hand and fully charged."

Paul quickly chimed in. "Remember, if you haven't already done so, please e-mail us the particulars of where you want to go after you receive the final e-mail. We will have all your flights booked and ready, timed for the different days that the events in your areas occur. Have a bag ready to go; you will not want to be around for the aftermath."

"Are there any questions?" Gus asked. Mitch heard silence for a few seconds. "All right then, you'll only hear from us one more time. Thank you all once more." The phone connection terminated, and Gus could barely contain his enthusiasm.

"Here we go, boys—sometime in the next week. We have finally come to the end of this plan. It is going to be quite a culmination!" Mitch heard Gus slap someone on the back.

"What are you going to do when the smoke clears, Gus?" Paul asked.

"Travel to Europe for a few months and then return here—I love this city. I will look you guys up when I get back. Remember, once everything is done, no communication between us for at least three months."

"No problem here," Charlie said. "I plan on taking the money you're giving me and setting up shop on some Caribbean island—basking in the beauty of the beauties."

"Spoken like no one else could," Paul said. "That was not a compliment, by the way."

"Yeah—what's *your* plan?" Charlie spat back.

"I've already purchased a house in Seattle. I'll practice law up there, when I feel like it."

"Yeah—real exciting. Have fun with that." Charlie was not sure why anyone would work after receiving the large payments they had.

"The next time we talk, I'll bring the champagne," Gus said.

Mitch could hear them picking up their things, and it was quiet for a little while. He left the earpiece in just in case they came back, but he started filling in Marie on all that had transpired in the room. They sat quietly, picking at their desserts more than eating them. Mitch paid the bill, and they walked through the hotel and out into the parking lot, trying to look like they were still having fun. Mitch opened Marie's door for her when they arrived at the car, and they started driving home, his mind racing about the predicament. Although he had been told by his secret informant several times he was being set up, hearing it from Gus's mouth made it seem more real. This, coupled with the fact that Gus had said "next week," meant Mitch's time was running out to solve this puzzle. He needed a better plan than anything he had come up with so far. When they got home, Mitch wanted to take a walk.

The couple paced through the neighborhood holding hands, though the tension in the air was stifling.

"So, what are you going to do?" Marie finally asked.

"What do you think I should do?"

"I want us to get in a car and drive somewhere until all this—whatever—happens. But what I want and what we should do …" she cut off for a second. "You realize that something bad is about to happen, and your name is going to be all over it?"

"I picked up on that, yes."

"You have to try to stop it. See what else you can find out. Any idea what 'R1' and 'S9' and the rest would stand for?"

"Maybe a little more theory. Since they are calling in, they must not be all here in the Phoenix area. Remember the page of the Liberty Contingencies from Paul's home office—R1, S1, and so on—those were the codes of the individuals calling in. The voices were both male and female, and they all sounded fairly young, in their late twenties, early thirties maybe. I don't know."

"Well, I think our best chance is to keep prying, although it sounds like Karen is almost as much in the dark as you," Marie hypothesized.

"She knows more than I do, but not the important pieces. She controls a big part of the money; they would have to give her some information about that. She is probably under their thumb as well, getting a large payoff," Mitch said, a little more upset with Karen right now.

"I don't think she would be a part of that. It's even possible she is getting set up, too. As I said before, maybe she's your secret informant."

"Yeah, I know you still think that, but if it was her, she would have had plenty of opportunity to give me information in an easier way. No, I'm certain it is someone else."

"So, figure out who it is, get him or her to tell you the full plan, and stop it. It is just that simple."

"Thanks for clearing that up for me." Mitch laughed. He loved his wife, and he knew her strength would see him through this ordeal. It was, however, the last good laugh he would have for a while.

Chapter 27

The next day, Paul and Charlie took care of the remaining details. Gus called Karen personally, and she transferred the money with no questions. As it was Friday, Gus assumed it could take a few business days for the money to be in the proper accounts. That meant Tuesday, maybe Wednesday of the following week. The weekend seemed to last forever to Gus, although he played golf three times and booked his trip to Europe. Paul received confirmation on Tuesday that everything was in the proper accounts. Gus decided to wait one more full day in order to ensure everything was properly set for the following week. He spent Wednesday evening relishing the beginning of the end that would occur the next day.

Gus awoke Thursday morning feeling fantastic. After a full breakfast at the Biltmore, he began to make the necessary phone calls. Within a few short weeks, his plan would come to a glorious finale. He was almost sad to see it end. The careful planning, the months spent selecting the right people for this job, having them placed where necessary, based on the years he had spent developing contacts and cultivating business relationships. Everything was finally in place. *Would it be enough?* was the thought that kept running through his mind. At this stage, it had to be enough; there was no more waiting to be done. Gus was certain he had thought of everything.

"Charlie?" Gus said after dialing his phone.

"Yes, sir."

"It's a go!"

"It's a go, meaning today?"

"Today—set the wheels in motion, and meet me at the Biltmore." Gus clicked off his phone and walked over to his liquor cabinet. This called for a celebratory drink; who cared if it was 8:30 in the morning.

* * * *

Charlie smiled. He and Gus and set this moment up months ago. When the time was right, Gus would give the signal, and he was to call Paul and then send out a mass text message to the operatives on phones they had been provided by Liberty. Paul was to meet them at the Biltmore as well. Charlie took care of these pieces, wishing he could see the expressions of some of the team members he had hand selected. He then went to his computer, as it was time for Karen to learn the final phase and to let her know it was starting right now. As she was still unaware of the details involved, e-mail was more efficient than explaining it all on the phone. Charlie had written a document in the previous weeks to give to Karen when the moment was right. He typed a quick e-mail message to her adding an ending typical for him as well as attaching the document. Karen had been placed under surveillance in the last few weeks, given her less than enthusiastic attitude, so Charlie was fully aware she was at the firm this morning. He knew she would be reading the e-mail in a matter of seconds.

* * * *

The Liberty Group

Karen had been pacing her office more than usual this morning, knowing the Liberty shoe was about to drop. She was still determined though, no matter what the consequences, to stop whatever was planned. At that moment, she received the message from Charlie.

> *Karen,*
>
> *Please read the attached document. Today will begin this final phase. Our hard work is finally going to pay off. Please come to the Biltmore with all financial information of Liberty as soon as possible. Pack a bag if you like—you can keep it in my room.*
>
> *Charlie*

"What a pig," Karen said aloud. Hesitantly, she opened the document. As she read through it, disbelief washed over her face, and by the end, she realized her grip on the mouse was so tight she was amazed it didn't shatter.

The plan she had formulated in the previous weeks to stop Gus was incomplete, as she did not know *what* to stop. Now that she had the information, would she have enough time and know-how? Karen had already duplicated all financial records onto a separate computer; it had taken quite some time, but at least she could prove what had happened. It was her assumption that Gus and Charlie would destroy all records of their involvement in Liberty.

Going over Liberty's detailed plan in her head, her quick mind started formulating several different ideas. As she reread the information in the attachment, she knew it was now or never. Time was of the essence, and Karen took a deep, calming breath as she contemplated a course of action. How best to stop this? Finally, several thoughts clicked, and she acted quickly, first forwarding the e-mail to Mitch, regretting she had not given him more of a warning earlier. (She was also hoping they had not already grabbed him.) Karen then forwarded the document to a client contact who she knew to be an advisor to Senator McCain.

"Please send this to the senator as quickly as possible. As you will see, this is of utmost importance. I will try to hold it up as long as I can." Karen knew the client would be confused by her message, but she trusted the information would get to Senator McCain. Finally, she replied enthusiastically to Charlie's e-mail, saying she would be over as soon as she could break away from the office.

Now what to do? One choice was to run and hide, not show up at the Biltmore, and that choice was very appealing. However, given what she just learned, Karen concluded that being on site might prove more valuable to preventing this diabolical plan. More was at stake than she imagined. Karen had also reached the assumption Gus and Charlie were concerned about this possibility, which explained why they had not shared the final plans with her until now. But in order to try to stop it, she needed to go to the Biltmore. Karen kept all the Liberty information on her laptop and in a few file folders. She placed the duplicate computer and files in a closet in her office with a note on top to explain what it was. She then grabbed all the originals and her laptop and started out the door.

"Karen, where are you going?" Will asked as he walked down the hallway.

"I've got to go now, Will. I'll see you tomorrow—personal business."

"Don't go. I'm sure it's important, but I've seen this look in your eyes before. This still has to do with that same situation, doesn't it?"

"Will, trust me; I know what I am doing."

"No disrespect intended, but I don't think you do. You have graciously not accepted my help in this, but now I must insist. If you go somewhere, let me come with you."

Several staff members of the firm had walked past during the conversation, and Will and Karen both knew that discretion would be better.

"Let me at least walk you to your car," Will requested.

"Fine," Karen said, frustrated as they both headed out the door. Karen wanted to accept his offer, more than he could possible know, but she cared too much for Will to risk his safety as well.

"Is this dangerous, this stuff you're involved in? Don't answer that—I'm sure it is. Please let me come with you!" They arrived at Karen's vehicle.

"I've involved you too much already; I will not let you become part of it. Will, as my friend—actually, my best friend—please trust me on this." Karen had a tone of finality.

"Can you at least give me a call in an hour or so, let me know everything is all right?"

"That much I can do," Karen said, getting in her car. "Talk to you then." Will headed back to the office; he had plans of his own.

* * * *

Mitch was sitting at his desk, working on his article for next week's paper, as well as cultivating ideas for future topics. From his eavesdropping escapade, he knew something was going to start this week, and he was just waiting for the first volley of Gus's plan. Concentrating on his job was very difficult, and Mitch stood up to stretch when his e-mail notification dinged. Mitch clicked to his inbox and noticed the address of the sender—Karen's firm. He opened the message, which was a forward of an e-mail from Charlie to Karen. He read the short message and then opened the attachment as well. Mitch wished what he was reading would have come as a shock, but he had been mentally preparing for the worst possible scenarios for the last few days. He sat back for just a few seconds and then started the only plan of action he felt he could at this point. Mitch quickly calculated, based on the information he had just read, he had about a day, maybe two, before the stuff truly hit the fan. Mitch pulled up another article he had written in the last few days; it was one he was quite proud of. He altered it just enough, hoping his friends would get the message. He sent it to John with the note he wanted it published online today. This was not all that unusual, as over the years when something big was in the news, Mitch would submit extra articles for the online version of the *Republic*. John would usually acquiesce to his request.

Mitch then pulled out the phone Al had given him and made a quick call to Marie. Lastly, he walked to Brian's desk; thankfully, he was there. He whispered a few things in his friend's ear and handed him a note, and then walked away, leaving Mads with a quizzical look on his face.

* * * *

Karen entered the Biltmore prepared to act eager at first with the plan while trying to find some way to sabotage it. She walked past the front desk, smiling slightly at the clerk, and headed for the familiar room. A man she had never seen before came up from behind and grabbed her by the elbow.

"Excuse me!" she said nervously, trying to jerk her arm out of the man's grasp.

"Ms. Simmons, just keep walking," her captor said in a business-like tone.

"Who are you? We've never met."

"No, we haven't, but we have some mutual acquaintances," he answered while ushering her toward the same room as always. They walked in to find Gus and Charlie. Paul's computer was there, but he was absent.

"Karen," Gus began. "I can't begin to tell you how disappointed I am in you."

"What are you talking about?" Karen replied, starting to feel sick to her stomach. "I received Charlie's e-mail this morning. Thank you for finally including me on this plan. Was I later in arriving than you had hoped? Are we getting closer to the final pay-off?" Karen asked coolly. She knew that the others would be suspicious if she acted too much into the plan.

"Nice try, but we know what you did," Charlie said.

"And what did I do?"

"Those e-mails," Gus began. "Paul told us he was a bit concerned about your commitment to our group. When I selected Paul and Charlie, I was confident they would not cross me; I was less certain with you. When Paul expressed his concerns as well, I felt it was time to monitor you more closely. You should have known how thought out this was. Did you really think I would allow you to tell someone else our plans? Why do you think I kept it from you for so long?"

Karen's mind was racing. They knew about the e-mails she had sent. Where was Mitch? They wouldn't let him have that information. Thank heavens she had stopped Will from coming. What were they going to do with her? She summoned every ounce of internal fortitude she had.

"I knew that might be the case," she lied. "It was a chance I had to take. I have been your puppet too long, Gus. I needed to strike back. At least now others do know, and they will stop you. I'm glad I was able to be a part of that! You, Paul, and Neanderthal over here"—she indicated Charlie—"will all get what you deserve in the end!"

"Karen, Karen, Karen," Charlie began. "Just as you were wrong to reject my advances, you are wrong about this. Do you honestly think we were unable to stop those e-mails? They never reached their intended recipients. I'm afraid neither Senator McCain nor Mitch knows the full plan. Thirty or so people know bits of it, but none of them can trace it back to us. We four are the only ones with the full information." His grin was enough to bring Karen to physical violence. She resisted the temptation to swing her computer bag at Charlie's head.

Joe entered the room, a look of concern on his face.

"What is it, Joe?" Charlie asked, taking his eyes from Karen.

"I need to talk to you; it's urgent," Joe stated calmly, but Charlie assumed it was a problem if Joe was going to interrupt their meeting. The two men walked out of the room. Karen and Gus stood staring at each other for a few seconds, the voices in the hall growing louder, finally hearing Joe say, "I tell you it did not come from Karen. I know I stopped that! All I can tell you is somehow Mitch received the e-mail. I can show you every e-mail Karen has sent in the last few days; this one is not on there. But our monitoring of Mitch's e-mail shows he received a message, the same one you sent."

Charlie stood mortified for a few seconds. He would not have been stupid enough to make that mistake again. He knew there was no way he sent the message to Mitch.

"Can you track where it came from?" Charlie asked.

"Our surveillance was set up to receive a copy of everything Mitch received and to get a copy of everything he sent out. This one was sent protecting its sender's identity. We can put a tracer on it; it will just take some time."

"Let me consult with Gus, although I think I know what he will say." Charlie came back into the room, still looking with satisfaction at Karen.

"Karen, Joe here is going to escort you to another room. We'll talk very soon, believe me." Karen decided not to argue or rebut him at this point; maybe she would have a few seconds to think now. She began to leave with Joe.

"Hold on, Joe, take her purse, computer bag, and I think I should probably search her," Charlie said with a horrible grin on his face.

"Charlie, good idea on confiscating her stuff," Gus said calmly. "Make sure her phone is in the bag, but no search will be necessary." He turned to her and began to talk in his most grandfatherly voice. "Karen, we selected you because we liked you. Working with you all these months has done nothing to change that opinion. A chain of events has been set in motion that you cannot control at this point. Please reconsider your attitude. This can still all work out very nicely for you financially. Or, conversely, it could all work out very bad for you legally. To me, there really is no choice. Now, Joe here is going to take you to a very nice room. Again, please reconsider." With that, Joe escorted her down the hall. *At least I kept copies of all that information they just took!* Karen thought to herself as she left.

Charlie explained to Gus that Mitch had in fact received the same information Karen did. Gus did not respond at first, deep in thought.

"Is he still at the *Republic* this morning?"

"Yes. I confirmed that fact while I was in the hall. Russell is on him today, with instructions to call me the minute he leaves. I don't know how he got the e-mail." Charlie felt compelled to add the last statement.

"At this point, it does not matter how he got. We will deal with that later. What matters is what he does with this information. I am deciding between bringing him in as we have Karen and holding them under wraps for a while or letting it stew a few hours. I think it best to bring him in; we cannot have a wild card out there. Call Russell." As Charlie reached for his phone, it buzzed. Russell's ears must have been burning.

"Perfect timing," Charlie answered. "Please escort Mr. Bartter to the Biltmore."

"He just left the paper, but I'm tailing him. I'll grab him when he stops."

"The Liberty Group mastermind Mitch Bartter will be here shortly, Gus," Charlie said as he hung up his phone.

* * * * *

Mitch had spent the days since his audio surveillance determining a plan of action. He had been piecing together the little bits of what he remembered from meetings and from what was provided by his yet unknown assistant. Mitch had given up trying to determine who was helping him; he thought maybe it was Paul, but came to the conclusion that he just didn't fit. Whoever it was did not know everything, or else he or she would have shared it with him; Mitch was confident of that. He also tried to determine who the recent hero in South Carolina could be. From Gus's inference, this target was the first of many to come. If Mitch could prevent the first one, that would at least be a good start. Internet searches had not turned up much, but on a whim, he checked some political offices of the state. Surprisingly enough, on Jim DeMint's Web site, Mitch noted a section about the senator that he had rallied against big spending in Washington and stopped 10,000 wasteful pork projects after the 2006 elections. Washington legendary reporter Robert Novak had hailed him a *hero*. It was the best lead he had on that end of the mystery.

Knowing something was happening very soon, Mitch realized he needed his own contingency plan to counter Liberty Group's. He and Marie had talked extensively about what they should do, and Mitch was even a little proud of what they had plotted. He thought it was amazing what the mind can devise, the clarity one develops, when pressed into a situation such as his. Mitch and Marie had determined to be prepared at a moment's notice for whatever.

It was, in general, a simple plan. Mitch had packed bags for Marie and the kids and loaded them into the back of Marie's car. If he were ever to call her on the phone Al had provided, this would indicate it was time to put their plan into action. Marie was to calmly round up the kids from wherever they might be and head out of town. Her sister lived in San Diego, a drive Marie could make in less than six hours.

Mitch had also discreetly brought a small backpack to work, hidden in his computer bag, the day after his eavesdropping. Each of the next several days, he took in some clothes and a few other items in case he needed to leave in a hurry. These things were stashed under his desk. He had prepared a note to give to Brian or John, though Brian was his first choice. Today, when he left the building, he was carrying nothing; his shadows would think he was going to lunch. Mitch got in his car and headed toward South Mountain Park, saying a prayer while he drove, asking the Lord's assistance in keeping his family safe and asking for guidance to solve his problem. He also managed to pull off his pants while driving, leaving him in his jogging shorts. He had been wearing a pair under his pants all this week, as he assumed this day was coming. As Mitch made his way down Twenty-Fourth Street, he pulled off his tie and shirt. He reached over and grabbed his running shoes off the floor of the passenger side, another item he had stashed ahead of time.

He reached the Mormon Trailhead parking area. This was something he had thought of a month ago, the day after he broke into Paul's house. If he ever needed to ditch his followers again, he would head here. It just required someone else's assistance. South Mountain Park is close to downtown, allowing for easy access, but also has numerous trailheads and parking areas. Mitch figured it would be perfect. He parked his car and got out, stretching for a few minutes, as much to see if another car would pull up soon. He was not disappointed. A sedan with a single driver pulled and parked about fifty feet from him. The man who got out was tall, with sunglasses. Even from this distance, Mitch knew it was the same man he had seen several places, including the library. Mitch started jogging, with no real sense of urgency.

* * * *

Russell was more than a little surprised to see Mitch in full jogging attire when he got of his car, regretting now he hadn't parked a little closer to him. Russell started to walk toward Mitch, but his prey began to jog. Russell began to run a little himself, but was ill prepared for it and thought better. He almost called out to Mitch, thinking of drawing his weapon, but as there were a few other people about, Russell decided against that as well. Mitch would need to return to his car at some point, and Russell had noticed Mitch did not take any water with him. *He won't be gone long*, Russell thought to himself. He returned to his air-conditioned car to wait.

Mitch began running the Mormon Trail. As this was desert, there was very little cover (and absolutely no shade), but he assumed the surprise factor would be enough to give him an advantage. After about two minutes of jogging, he turned to verify his pursuer was not following. Mitch was almost a little disappointed. He had hoped to lure the big man out into the desert, run a few circles around him, and watch him collapse in the heat. The Mormon Loop was a little over a mile, but Mitch had no intention of returning. He took the trail about halfway and then turned onto the Pima Canyon trail, going the short distance to its trailhead. At that parking area, Brian was waiting, and Mitch jumped in the car.

The note Brian had received from his friend that morning indicated he was to grab a backpack stashed under Mitch's desk and drive to this location. Brian had come through yet again.

"Thanks, man," Mitch huffed.

"A hot day for a run," Brian replied.

"That's no lie." Mitch reached into the backpack and took out the bottle of water he had put in there not an hour ago. The backpack also contained a pair of pants and shirt, his wallet, both of his phones, and a few other minor items. He had also been withdrawing small amounts of cash for several weeks, accumulating over a thousand dollars at this point.

"No rattlesnakes along the way?" Brian questioned, half joking.

"Not this time, although that could have made it more challenging." Rattlesnakes were somewhat common on the trails.

"Where are we heading?" Brian asked.

"The airport, please, and crank up the AC!"

* * * *

Russell had waited about twenty-five minutes when he started to be concerned. He was beginning to think Mitch had succumbed to the heat. Russell was about to go looking for him when Charlie called.

"Do you have Mr. Bartter?" Charlie asked, sounding upbeat.

"Slight complication. When Mitch stopped it was at South Mountain Park. He took off jogging before I could get him. I decided to wait for his return."

"You are sitting by his car?"

"Exactly. It's been about half hour. I expect him any time now; he did not have any water with him."

"He's been out of your sight for thirty minutes!" Charlie screamed into the phone. "You idiot. He's not coming back."

"What do you mean; how do you expect him to return to work?" Russell did not know why Charlie was so upset.

"Stay there. I'll send Joe as well, but I think we lost him."

Gus was in earshot and only heard the last sentence. "Tell me you did not lose Mitch."

"It's not confirmed yet, but that is my concern. I need to call a few more of my staff—someone needs to babysit Karen while I send Joe to help Russell." Charlie quickly dialed a number while Gus's eyes bored in on him.

* * * * *

Will was unable to get any work done after Karen left. He watched the clock constantly and kept returning to the same page of tax code he was reading. When an hour came and went and he had not heard from Karen, he was worried. It was now ten minutes later, and he finally pulled out his phone and gave her a call. It went straight to voicemail; she had turned it off. She guaranteed him she would call within an hour. Knowing what he knew, he could wait no longer.

Will would go to the Biltmore; he had made up his mind the minute she left, if he didn't hear from her. He had discovered the group she was working with was meeting at the resort. Will hurriedly shut down his computer and headed to his 2004 Accord, and in fifteen minutes, Will was sitting in the parking lot of the famous hotel. Now, what was he going to do? Will decided to start by just walking in and asking about her, seeing if the front desk clerk might know her by name. What could that hurt? He got out of his car and walked quickly inside.

"Excuse me, but do you know Karen Simmons? She has a meeting here every Thursday at one o'clock," he asked the clerk behind the desk. It happened to be the same person who showed Mitch around the hotel a few weeks earlier.

"That seems to be a popular meeting. I don't know all the names of the people involved, but the woman who attends that meeting is here this morning. She went to the same room as always."

"What room is that and what direction?"

The clerk at this point started to get hesitant. Will definitely did not want to raise any alarms, so he told the clerk not to worry about it; he would wait for Karen out here. He sat in the gorgeous lobby for a few minutes, but then eventually decided to see if he could find her. After wandering for a few minutes, he turned a corner toward the business meeting rooms, and he saw Karen down the hall with a very large man.

"Take your hands off me. I can walk myself!" Will heard Karen say. He was about to tear down the hall after her when her escort started talking.

"Mr. Reed wants you treated well. Please, just cooperate, and you will not be harmed."

Will could also see the handgun strapped to the gentleman's side. He retreated just a bit, having not been seen by either of the two. He followed at a distance and learned what room Karen was led to. He then went back to the lobby and out the door. His cell phone rang as he stepped into the open air.

"Will Jensen."

"Will, it's Annette. I thought I should let you know something that just happened here at the office." Annette was one of several support staff of the firm.

The Liberty Group

"What was that?"

"Four men with CIA identification showed up to search Karen's office. They left within five minutes, taking the computer off her desk, as well as one from her closet. They took some files, too. I tried to call Karen, but there was no answer. Do you know where she is?"

"No, I don't," he lied. "Thanks for letting me know. I'm not sure if I will be back in today or not. I'll keep you posted. Try not to worry about what just happened; I think I know why it occurred. It does not affect the firm at all." He hung up, positive he had done a very poor job of settling Annette down. He climbed in his car and sat there. Will needed time to think about his next move.

* * * *

Mads dropped Mitch off at the airport and headed back to the *Republic*. He went to his desk and started jotting notes down about things Mitch had said, and he even opened up the computer file he had made of the conversation he recorded between Mitch and the attorney during the bribe incident. John approached him.

"Brian, have you seen Mitch? He turned in an article for online publication, and I need to ask him a few questions about it."

"Let's go to your office," Mads responded, following John and closing the office door when they arrived. Hesitantly, Brian began to tell the editor what had transpired earlier in the morning and also told him Mitch was headed to Charleston.

"Wait a minute—slow down. Mitch thinks this group is after him for some reason?"

"Mitch has kept me fairly in the dark on the whole thing. All I can tell you is today he received an e-mail, wrote me a note, and had me pick him up at South Mountain Park. He gave me the keys to his car and asked me to get it for him, but not until he calls me to do that. He then had me take him to the airport, said he was going to Charleston."

"Did he buy a ticket for Charleston?"

"I just dropped him off; I did not go in. I don't know why he would lie about that, though." Brian was surprised by the question.

"Okay, thanks for telling me. Did he ask you for any other help? Is there anything I can do?"

"No, he didn't ask for anything else."

"Hopefully, he calls soon, and we can sort this all out. I'll call Marie and see if she needs help with anything."

"I'm sure Mitch would appreciate that," Brian said as he left the office. He thought about mentioning he had the bribe conversation recorded, but John knew all about that already, no need to mention it again.

* * * * *

Gus's temperature was rising by the minute, and it had nothing to do with the Arizona heat. Word had come back from Russell and Joe there was no sign of Mitch at the park. The fact Mitch knew the plan was bad enough, but breaking his surveillance was totally unacceptable.

"Get the tracks going on his credit cards; we need to find him now!" Gus demanded.

"Already doing that," Charlie responded. "We'll have him soon."

"I don't want him soon; I want him now! How about having someone pick up his wife or kids, and we'll use them to get him in here!"

"They are not home either. We had always tracked Mitch each day, leaving his wife on her own. We put a man at the house now, but she and the kids have not returned. We've also tried to call Mitch on his phone, but he is not answering."

"Did Mitch contact his family before heading out of the paper?"

"No, no calls made at all."

"None? Interesting. If he received that e-mail and knew the plan, it would follow he would contact someone for assistance, and he would at least let his wife know." Gus stood there, puzzling the facts in his head.

"Maybe he panicked. Possibly he is lying out in the desert—suffering from exhaustion. But I think not. Mitch is more intelligent than that. He is hiding somewhere. You're right; we will find him. I do not believe he can jeopardize our plan, even with what he knows." Charlie's cell phone buzzed to life as Gus was thinking out loud. It was a text message, and the news was not good.

"I'm afraid I am going to have to disappoint you slightly, sir," Charlie said, still looking at his phone.

"What do you mean?"

"We just got a hit on one of Mitch's credit cards. He just bought a ticket to Seattle. He's obviously on the run. The plane leaves in thirty-five minutes."

"Get someone over there right now to stop him!"

"Gus, there is no way. He would already be through security. By the time someone got there, bought a ticket, and also went through security, the plane will have left. We will have better luck with someone meeting him when he arrives. Do you know anyone in Seattle or Tacoma?" Charlie's background had dealt with these types of situations before, and he was thinking more clearly than Gus for once.

"As a matter of fact, I do." Gus said. "Let me call …" He broke off. "Hold on a second." Gus left the room, taking his phone out of his pocket as he stepped into the hall, returning a few minutes later.

"Why would he go to Seattle?" Gus asked. "That really does not make sense."

"He got the e-mail, he knows what we have in store for him, and he's running," Charlie responded matter-of-factly. "Maybe he knows someone in Seattle."

"How many plane tickets did he buy?"

"Just the one, according to his credit card."

"No, he wouldn't run without his family. Plus, we've been tracking him for months, and he hasn't been in contact with anyone in that area. He is going somewhere he thinks is on our target list. My instincts tell me he's going to Charleston."

"Instincts? Gus—how can you be so sure?" Charlie thought Gus was sounding paranoid. "How would he know DeMint was first on the list? The e-mail he read listed twenty-six congressional representatives, but no timeline. I still say he his trying to hide."

"We've known Mitch for a while now. Charlie, you know me. I pride myself on the ability to judge character. Does Mitch strike you as someone who would run away, or is he someone, who upon finding out what is in store for him and others, who would work to stop it? Where does he have to go first to prevent the damage? Charleston." Gus stood confidently, staring at Charlie. Everything Gus said made sense, but it would mean Mitch knew about being followed, and he was trying to throw them off. It meant Mitch had planned for this day. Charlie was not prepared to admit his team had been discovered, but he did decide to play along.

"So, if he is heading to Charleston—do you know anyone there?" Charlie suggested. "Perhaps the person working in Barret or DeMint's office?"

"No. That won't work. I don't want either of them compromised for any reason, not for a few days anyhow. You don't know anyone in South Carolina—or even close?"

"No, not my part of the country. May I suggest that Russell and Joe get on the next plane? Mitch will need to stay somewhere, and once he uses plastic again, we will get him. Unless, of course, you want to get on your Lear, and we could be there even before him."

"No, I'm going to enjoy things from here. Go ahead and get your guys on the next plane."

"Can I also send someone to Seattle?" Charlie asked hesitantly.

"Forget Seattle; trust me, that is a dead end. Go ahead and send Joe and Russell to Charleston. Put someone else at the house for when the family returns. I will call a few people who may be able to lend some names to assist us in the field in South Carolina as well. Let me know when we have the family back on the radar."

Chapter 28

Al was at work especially early, getting a jump on the next month-end close. Most accounting departments work hard to get the numbers out as quickly as possible after the end of each reporting cycle, and Al's department completed as many tasks as possible in the final week of the month (today was the second-to-last business day in August) in an effort to streamline the reporting process. He had spent most of the morning and part of the afternoon working on some of this analysis when he took a quick break to see what was in the news. Out of habit, he hit the *Republic* link from his list of favorites, and as he reviewed the site, he noted another article by Mitch. Al was more concerned about Mitch every day, and they hadn't talked in over two weeks. He was a little relieved when he saw another article had been posted just today. He started reading it with enthusiasm, hoping a reassuring message had been included.

Estate Taxes—Stealing from the Dearly Departed

Anyone who has read my articles long enough knows what an anathema I believe the estate tax to be. For some, this may be eighty-ninth on a list of eighty-nine items to be worried about; for some, it may the fifty-fifth or thirty-fourth, but for me, this is probably the third top tax priority (after implementing a reduced flat tax and reducing corporate rates). This egregious tax is so ridiculous; I do not know where to begin. Let's start with this scenario. A person is walking down a major street, minding his own personal business, whistling a happy tune. A car loses control, jumps the curb, and hits the pedestrian, killing the person instantly. Someone else walking by approaches the now lifeless body, takes the wallet out of the person's pocket, and walks away. I believe most of us would consider this behavior treachery, a reprehensible act. I ask you—is it really any different than the government taking a portion of people's estates just because they have died? I personally don't see a difference. Why should, at the time of death, the government generate a tax bill?

The common argument is the estate tax only affects the liberty of a few lucky individuals who have too much money, a select group. Think about that—a Washington bureaucrat is going to determine which people to tax, from Charleston (either South Carolina or West Virginia) to Nome, Alaska. These actions are justified because they only inconvenience a few select people? Does that mean it is okay to steal, as long as you only steal from a few rich people? Also, for that argument to work, some oversight group has to determine how much is too much wealth to have. My point is the estate tax is wrong on principle, so it should not matter who is affected. It should be permanently abolished, plain and simple.

The estate tax was first used in this country in times of emergency—to fund a one-time major program or objective. For example, money was needed for the Spanish-American War, so an estate tax was levied and then repealed when the war ended. It wasn't until 1916 that the tax became a permanent part of U.S. government revenues. Not long after that, the gift tax was established, as the wealthy had started to give their money away on their deathbeds, and the government could not allow that, at least not without it being taxed. Historically speaking, the estate tax, as well as all transfer taxes combined (gift tax and generation-skipping tax in addition to the estate tax), account for less than 2 percent of the overall tax revenue collected. Does anyone believe we could not find 2 percent in pork projects to cut? I offer this up as another argument against the tax—if it does not alter tax receipts very much, why not abolish it?

Let me give you another scenario. Let's take two people, both of whom earn an average of $100,000 a year for thirty years. They both make $3,000,000 over the course of their working years. Let's say the first person spends his or her money as fast as he or she earns it. He or she rents a lavish apartment his or her entire life, never marries, and spends the money traveling, buying "experiences" such as hunting trips in Africa, throwing massive parties for his or her friends, buying expensive cars, etc. At the end of his or her life, he or she has very little left because he or she has spent it all. Now, let's look at the other person. Let's assume he or she saves as much as possible for the first ten years of his or her working life, takes what he or she has saved, and starts his or her own business. Now, this business takes a little while to thrive, but eventually becomes successful, and twenty years later, it is worth $5,000,000, employing fifty people, all paying payroll and federal taxes. Let's also assume that this person married, purchased a home that has appreciated in value, put his or her children through college, and saved money for retirement. This person and his or her spouse both pass away in their early sixties. This estate would owe a substantial amount of tax, just because the person died. So, the first person spends everything he or she makes and therefore owes no estate taxes at death, while the second person saved money, invested in his or her own idea, created jobs (which in turn created more tax revenue for the government), and he or she is rewarded with a big *tax bill upon his or her death. Should our country punish success in this manner? Please do not misunderstand me. I am not judging the first person in my scenario. Everyone should have the right to spend their money in whatever way they see fit. My argument is simply the government should not tax anybody upon his or her death! Let's remember that both people in my example would have been paying income tax on their earnings every year!*

I've heard more than one of my accounting friends say anyone who ends up paying estate taxes basically failed to plan appropriately. A fair point. However, should these people need to jump through a bunch of planning hoops in order to avoid paying tax when the basis of the tax is just flat-out wrong? Again, I cannot understand the theory of why dying should be a taxable event. Every argument always comes back to "Well, they can afford it, so it doesn't matter." Realize these are the people who have already been paying the largest percent of income taxes. About 5 percent of people dying pay estate tax, so let's say it is the top 5 percent of wage earners at any given time. Currently, the top 5 percent pay 60 percent of the income taxes collected. Aren't these people already paying enough?

We need to remember our roots. This country was founded on the principles of allowing the freedom to do what we want, to work hard, and to succeed. We were not founded on spreading the wealth or on punishing success. That is all the estate tax is—a success-punishing, wealth-spreading mechanism. As W. Cleon Skousen so aptly wrote, "The proper role of government is to protect equal rights, not provide equal things." Please help me to stop this tax— please help the Liberty Group prevent this continual attack on our individual rights.

"Amen, Mr. Bartter!" Al said out loud. "Okay, Mitch, what are you trying to tell us today?" Al began scanning the article carefully, rereading it three times and still not seeing a possible key. *You really buried this one, Mitch,* Al thought to himself. He picked up the phone, and then hesitated, looking at the clock. Would Todd still be at the university? Al dialed the numbers just in case. No answer. On a whim, he tried Mark, too, although Mark didn't seem to look for the messages anymore. No answer on there either.

Al turned back to the article. He looked at the numbers at the beginning again eighty-nine—fifty-five—thirty-four. Al thought it was just too coincidental that eighty-nine minus fifty-five equaled thirty-four. It was the Fibonacci sequence in reverse. Al started at the beginning and counted eighty-nine word (including each number as one word) to find "major," and fifty-five words later, the next word was "treachery." Al continued working the Fibonacci sequence in reverse (twenty-one more words, followed by thirteen, eight, five, three, two, one). The entire message was "Major treachery at Liberty Group going to Charleston South Carolina." Al printed the article and deciphered it one more time to ensure he had the message correct.

Al tried to call Mitch immediately at the paper—voicemail. He then punched the preset number for the phone he had purchased for Mitch. No answer there, either. If Mitch had found something out, and his worst fears were being realized, Al knew his friend was in trouble. Feeling the need to talk to someone, he tried Mark at work, since he didn't answer his cell a few minutes ago. His call rang directly into Mark's voicemail, which indicated he would be in San Diego for a conference this week. Al now remembered Mark mentioning that fact in August. Al dialed Todd's number, and as expected, got his voicemail as well. He left an urgent message and sent him an e-mail with the article. He sat back and thought for a few minutes. Al decided it was time to call in a few favors—these would be big requests.

* * * * *

Todd had been in an all-day popular culture departmental retreat and was finally getting back to his office. He opened his e-mail and saw one from Al noting the subject line "Please read immediately." He opened it, realizing Al had copied one of Mitch's online articles, highlighting certain words and numbers. At the end, Al had provided the decoded message. Todd tried calling Al at work only to find no answer. He opened his cell and hit Al's contact info, dialing his friend.

"Hey. Todd, get my e-mail and message?" Al answered, having noticed Todd's name on his cell phone screen.

"Yes—I got it. What do you think we should do?"

"I'm already to Cincinnati. I'm driving to Charleston right now. I figured if Mitch was flying there, I could probably get there about the same time by driving, depending on when he left. I haven't been able to reach Mitch at all, but I don't think he would have sent that message to us, with the detailed information, if he wasn't asking for our help."

"You think he meant for us to join him in Charleston?"

"Maybe, maybe not, but I'm going just in case. Again, I'm assuming I can't get in touch with him because he is on a plane. I will not allow myself to think it is because of any other reason. Hopefully, I'll talk with him before I get there."

"Say the word and I'll be there. In fact, I'll get in my car right now and head out." Todd started packing up his desk.

"This may be a goose chase. Why don't I be the fool for now and continue to Charleston while you stay in Little Rock. Let's both try to contact Mitch, and reply back to the other when we know where he is. He can direct us how best to help."

"Sounds good. Drive safely."

* * * *

Marie had driven for hours without stopping, thinking of any way she could assist her husband. Mitch had called from the airport to let her know he was heading to Charleston, against her initial objections. Her plan right now was to get the kids to her sister's and to turn right around and head back to Phoenix. Something told her ultimately Phoenix would be the place to be.

They pulled over to have some dinner. Lynne knew her mom was upset about something, and this whole last-minute trip to San Diego, especially when school had just started, seemed very strange.

"Mom, why are going to see Aunt Jennifer?" Lynne asked while Jane and Ed were releasing pent-up energy from the car ride by having a tickle fight in the restaurant booth.

"You know I haven't seen my sister in awhile, and with your dad being sent on a last-minute trip, it just seemed like something fun we could do." Marie had told the kids that Mitch had to leave town to cover a story on the east coast.

"But school, Mom—we've got band and drama rehearsals we're missing."

"It's just a long weekend; we'll be back on Monday," Marie answered, not knowing if that was true or not. Lynne was concerned about what she was missing but also knew something bigger was at play. She wasn't convinced her mother was sharing the entire story.

"Is everything okay with you and dad?" Lynne asked, Jane and Ed stopping their fidgeting immediately. Marie knew she had smart kids, and she truthfully wanted to feel some camaraderie on this trip. She would tell them a little.

"Listen, your father has to take care of some important things for work, and there are some complications with it. This does seem strange; I understand that. You must realize, however, that your father and I have never loved each other more, so don't be concerned about anything like that. But praying your father accomplishes what he needs to in a safe manner would be very comforting."

"What kind of complications?" Jane asked, becoming concerned.

"I don't know all the details," Marie lied, "just that he could be gone a few days. Lynne, order me a salad if the server comes back, and order yourselves anything you want. I'm going step outside and call my sister, let her know when we will be there."

"Can I get a milkshake?" Ed asked hopefully.

"Go ahead, whatever you want." Marie left the table to make a call but not to her sister. Marie and Robin had remained strong friends since college, and she needed someone to talk to about all this. She pulled out the phone Al had provided for her and dialed Robin's number. Thankfully, her friend picked up on the first ring.

"Robin—it's Marie."

"Good to hear from you, how's everything in Phoenix?"

"I really need to unload on you; do you have a few minutes?"

"Of course, let it fly."

Marie talked nonstop for the next ten minutes, telling Robin everything that she could think of. She ended her explanation with the fact that she was now headed to San Diego, and Mitch was on his way to Charleston.

"Mark's in San Diego, you know; he had a conference."

"Do you know where?" Marie asked hopefully. This is what she needed: someone, anyone, to help her. "Do you think he would come to Phoenix with me? I just think that is where we need to be, but I don't want my kids there."

"If it's for Mitch, Mark will go anywhere. He's not really enjoying his conference anyhow. He'd probably love a road trip."

"And you don't mind if he's out here a few more days?" Marie asked. "I'll pay for his ticket back to Cincinnati."

"Don't worry about that; he'll be glad to help!"

Marie gave Robin the number of her new phone, telling her Mark should only call her on that. She would be in San Diego in a few hours, and she could pick Mark up wherever he was. Marie felt much better; at least there was someone to assist in whatever way possible. She went back to the table to find the kids eating mainly desserts.

"You said to order whatever we wanted," Jane said sheepishly as all three looked at their mom. Marie burst out laughing.

"I guess I did—move over and give me a spoon for that ice cream!"

* * * * *

The flight seemed to take forever. Mitch had indeed arrived at the Phoenix airport and quickly purchased a ticket to Seattle, using his credit card. He was hoping it would throw Charlie off the scent. He used a large portion of his cash to buy a ticket to Charleston, changing planes in Atlanta with a very short layover. He was now about a half hour from landing at his destination, where it would be about 10:00 PM. Mitch thought about his plan for the next day. It would be Friday—would he be able to talk to the right people in Senator DeMint's office? Heck, would he be able to talk with anyone, or would they just kick him out as a raving lunatic? Mitch's head felt as though it would explode.

The plane landed uneventfully, and he went to the courtesy vehicle area, jumping on the first hotel van he saw. He checked in, paying with cash and using the name Dan Marsacktin. Mitch grabbed a toothbrush and some toothpaste from the hotel desk and headed to his room, grateful for a bed. He knew he needed to sleep; he just hoped he could shut his mind off. He called Marie on their new phones to tell her he had arrived safely. She was at her sister's and had been in touch with Mark, but she decided against telling Mitch that.

"So, you'll go to the senator's office tomorrow, warn him that there will be an issue, and then get on a plane and come home, right?"

"Well, I will go to the senator's office, and we'll see what transpires from there. I will be on my way home the minute I feel I have done what I can here. How are the kids?"

"Fine. Doug took them to Belmont Park. I'm sure they are having a great time." Doug was Jennifer's husband, Marie's brother-in-law. Mitch remembered Belmont Park as a wonderfully fun small amusement park located right off Mission Beach.

"Have you brought your sister up to speed on all the gory details of our predicament?"

"More or less."

Mitch was hesitant to bring up the next subject. He was sure they had both thought about it but were afraid to discuss it. "You know that whatever is about to happen, I am going to be blamed for it, right?"

"I think that is painfully obvious."

"Are you ready to see my name negatively splayed across the newspaper and on the Internet?" Mitch asked. Marie had not allowed herself to think that far ahead.

"This is going to be a real nightmare." Mitch could practically hear her beginning to cry.

"Hang in there; there is nothing we can't overcome. I'll get it all straightened out; I promise." Mitch was consoling Marie as best he could from 3,000 miles away.

"I'm just afraid … what if they catch up to you, what if we never …" Marie broke off.

"Hey, as Todd would say, 'I'll return to you. What we have is true love—you think this happens everyday?'" Mitch replied, doing his best to quote *The Princess Bride*.

"Stop joking around," Marie said, but Mitch could tell she was half laughing.

"I know it is only about eight o'clock in San Diego, but I am very tired, and I want to be fresh for the morning. I am going to try to get some sleep. I love you, and I'll call you tomorrow."

* * * *

Will had been at the hotel all day, either sitting in his car outside the Biltmore, wandering the hallway near the room he had seen Karen enter, or hanging out in the lobby. He had gone over so many possible plans he was confused and exhausted. It was night, and all he had eaten was an energy bar. Hunger was the least of his concerns right now, though. Will had definitely heard the man say Karen would not be harmed, but the sidearm he was carrying seemed to contradict his statement. Will got out of the car and walked back in the hotel once again, finding the complimentary coffee and buying a few more food items from the gift shop; this was most likely going to be an all-nighter. He was not going to leave until he saw her. If Karen was not out by noon tomorrow, he was going in. Now, how best to go in, should it come to that?

Chapter 29

Mitch awoke at about seven o'clock from a better night's sleep than he would have thought possible. He showered, shaved, and went down to the complimentary breakfast the hotel was serving. Mitch had enough cash left to buy a change of clothes, which he did when the stores opened. He again relied on hotel transportation to get him downtown and grabbed a tourism map from a visitors' center to locate Bay Street, where Senator DeMint's Charleston office was situated. He pulled out his cell phone to call Marie, but it had gone dead. Mitch had neglected to charge it during the night.

As he approached Senator DeMint's office, Mitch recognized Russell right off the bat standing with another bookend just outside the building. *The Seattle bluff didn't fool anyone*, he thought to himself, not that Mitch really expected it to work. Getting past someone in front of the building was a challenge he thought he might have to overcome. Mitch was actually thankful that the obstacle was someone he recognized. Quite a few people were walking this morning, and Mitch looked around for a way to create a diversion. A young woman was walking three different dogs. Mitch got an idea.

"Excuse me, but could I bother you for a favor?"

The woman was a bit apprehensive. "What kind of favor?"

"I know you don't know me, but you see those two guys standing outside the Custom House Building? Could you possibly get them away from the door for just a few seconds, maybe ask them to help with your dogs?"

"Why do you need them to move, and why would I need help with my dogs?" she asked, totally confused.

Mitch decided the truth was best. "They have followed me all the way from Arizona, and I am trying to talk to Senator DeMint; something they do not want me to do. I know it sounds strangely cloak and dagger, but trust me, it is very important."

"Look, I really do not think …" she started to say, but just then, one of the dogs took off in pursuit of a squirrel, pulling the woman and the other canines with it. All three dogs were barking up a storm, drawing the attention of everyone around. Mitch quickly turned and stepped behind a tree, peering out to see the dogs running past the building entrance. The two gentlemen were watching with amusement, and the women yelled, "Could you two help me?" as she passed them. They both ran for several seconds to catch up and reach for the leashes. Mitch did not waste the chance as they had moved about twenty yards from the door. He sprinted quietly up the steps, turning briefly to see they had not turned back toward him. He slipped in the door and waved at the woman as it closed behind him. Mitch walked into the office—a pleasant smile awaiting him from the welcome desk.

"Hi, my name is Mitch Bartter, and I need to talk with the senator or one of his advisors on a matter of utmost importance."

The woman at the desk looked him up and down for a minute. "Where in South Carolina do you hail from?" she asked, friendly as can be.

"I'm from Arizona," Mitch answered. "I write a conservative newspaper column for the *Arizona Republic*." He did not want to share too much for fear of being thrown out of the office by security. Who was really going to believe this? He was hoping his newspaper connection would get him in the door. It was something that could be easily verified as his picture was even on the paper's Web site.

"The senator is always happy to talk to the press. He just respectfully requests you schedule an appointment. Now, I have something available next week on Wednesday." The woman was flipping through a calendar on the desk.

Mitch tried to smile and keep his tone calm. "I really do not want to discuss political issues with him. This is something more of a private matter. Is it at all possible to talk with him today?"

"Do you know the senator?"

"No, I just need to share some information with him. Please, it truly is very important." Mitch must have looked honest enough. The woman let out a sigh.

"I tell you what, I will see if Mr. Dickerson can talk to you. He is a member of the senator's staff." She smiled politely and made a call.

"That would be great," Mitch said, just wanting to get someone's ear. He was told to have a seat, and Mr. Dickerson would be with him soon. Soon turned out to be an hour later.

"Barry Dickerson," the man said, holding out his hand as he approached. Barry was slightly taller than Mitch but similarly lanky with dark hair and brown eyes. Mitch stood up and greeted him. The woman behind the desk looked up, and as they walked past, she commented on how they looked as if they could be brothers. After a security check, Barry led Mitch to a small conference room.

"What is so dang-gum important that you have to see the senator today?" the southern gentleman asked.

Mitch again decided honesty was the best policy. "Do you have about fifteen minutes?"

"I have all the time you need."

"Great. Well, as I told the woman at the desk, I am from Arizona."

"I know," Barry interrupted. "One reason I took a little while to get to you is I was verifying your story. You have more Web hits based on your Liberty Group work, though."

"Exactly what I need to talk to you about—Liberty is a big setup. I know the people behind it, the very people that hired me, are about to ensnare Senator DeMint and many others in a big trap."

Barry smiled slightly. "Son, you are the people behind Liberty. Everything I looked up said Liberty was you, with other writers contributing opinion pieces."

"I know," Mitch said, exasperated. He pulled out the printout of the e-mail attachment. "I received this less than twenty-four hours ago. I don't know who sent it to me, but as you see, there are twenty-six names listed, all Republicans, all with some sort of scandal next to their names. It looks to me as if there are three major plans of attack: eight senators are going to be accused of being part of the same sex ring, four senators and eight representatives are going to have accusations of bribery and illegal campaign funding thrown their way, and one senator and five representatives will be accused of voter fraud and falsifying records. Senator DeMint is included in the bribery portion."

Barry looked at the list. "You could have printed this on your own and showed up here hoping to make the senator look like a fool. I'm afraid we get pranks attempted all the time."

"You said you researched me. Do I seem the type to prank? Did you read any of my articles? Aren't I more in line with the senator's thinking? I'm telling you that this office and twenty-five others are about to be inundated with bad press!"

"Why come here first? Why not one of these other congressional offices?" Barry asked. "If you just received this yesterday, why make a beeline for this office all the way from Arizona?"

"I have additional information this will be the first scandal to break. I'm guessing Gus will have one office for each of these three attacks to act as the domino, leading others to fall as well."

"Who's Gus?" Barry said, concern starting to be visible on his face for the first time.

"Gus Reed, he hired me. He has unlimited resources and contacts across the country." Mitch got up and walked to the window.

"Do you see those two guys out there?" Mitch asked, indicating the two men he managed to slip past.

"Yes, they with you?"

"Kind of—I'm sure they were supposed to prevent me from talking to anyone in this office. As I have said, I was the Web site content coordinator for Liberty, but now, in reality, the group set me up as their face so I would appear to be the one behind all this. I was never informed of the plan, and I only just learned of what was to be done. I also recently discovered Gus has twenty-six people working around the country in some manner; my belief is someone on DeMint's staff has been covertly setting him up by placing key phony documents or establishing bank accounts that will taint the senator."

"Now you've gone too far," Barry said defiantly. "I know everyone that works for the senator, and I don't believe any of them would wrong him!"

"You trust all of them that much? This is probably someone who has been working in the office for years, at least three or four. He or she would have access to quite a bit of information, and I would guess this person is fairly young. I know some serious accusations are about to fly, and it will start with this office!"

Almost as if on cue, there was a knock at the door. "Come in," said Barry, not taking his eyes off Mitch.

"Mr. Dickerson, there is a meeting of everyone in the office in five minutes," said the woman from the front desk.

"There is no meeting scheduled today," Barry responded.

"Emergency meeting. The paper just called, and it's all hands on deck. Get up there now!"

Barry looked at Mitch, who just gave a little nod of his head with raised eyebrows, as if to say, "It's what I have trying to tell you."

"You're coming with me!" Barry said, and he escorted Mitch up a few flights of stairs and into a larger conference room. There were about twenty-five people in the room, and conversation had already started about a bribery charge. The paper had just called to say it was breaking the story, and it would be on their Web site within an hour. They wanted a comment from DeMint's office.

"If this hits their Web site, less than thirty minutes later, it will be on all cable news networks," someone in the room stated. "Can we get the attorneys to delay it?"

"If the paper has a credible source, we really cannot stop them," answered another.

"I think you should all listen to what Mitch Bartter has to say," Barry exclaimed above the general murmuring. The room fell silent, and all eyes turned to Barry and Mitch. "Go ahead; tell them what you just told me."

Mitch introduced himself and began relating the story of how he had come to be in the office. He explained this would be the first of many scandals, all involving Republicans, and all being set up from within their own offices. Everyone listened intently, and there was a brief silence before general questions were yelled out.

"Why don't you go to the paper—get them to stop the story?"

"My name is well known enough that some at the paper will recognize it," Mitch stated, "but the only proof I have is a copy of an e-mail. They will not stop a big headline like this based just on that."

"Well, call the police in Phoenix and have them arrest whoever is pulling all these strings."

Mitch shook his head. "The police won't do anything based just on my word—no proof of any crime can be produced just yet. You do not understand the resources these people have. They could be right out in the open, most likely at the Biltmore Hotel, but I'm sure they are by now all using aliases. If I am correct, they have been paying people for years to infiltrate different congressional offices. Plus, they are funding many bogus accounts with money to give the appearance of impropriety. Remember, the mere suggestion of wrongdoing can be a deathblow to a political career. My suggestion is to call a press conference immediately, pre-empting the release of the story and hypothesizing there is a conspiracy afoot. Predict what is about to happen, and when your prediction is correct, it will give you much more credibility. However, remember, it is very likely someone in this room is responsible for whatever proof the paper has. I also suggest you track the source of funds into accounts related to the senator."

"Why don't you talk at the press conference?" another voice asked.

"Great, I'm willing to do that," Mitch responded. Some more ideas were thrown out, but ultimately, the press conference was determined to be the best. One suggestion was to stage the conference on the steps of the courthouse, and it was hastily arranged. News crews sped over upon receiving the information the senator would make a very important announcement. Security had cleared the area, but Mitch was still very apprehensive about being seen so openly in public. He could not find any trace of Joe or Russell. Within twenty minutes of the meeting breaking up, they were all outside, a podium set up, and Mitch had even talked briefly with Senator DeMint, apologizing all he could for not discovering this plot sooner.

Mitch stood near the bottom of the steps when a commotion to his left caught his attention. Two men were running toward him, men he did not recognize. He stood for a split second but then burst through the crowd, instinct taking over. Security managed to grab the two guys coming at him, but as Mitch turned to see this, Joe and Russell appeared about a block down the road, running toward him with two additional people. He realized at that moment the first two were to scare him away from security, and it had worked perfectly. Mitch was now exposed and cut off from getting back. He turned and ran as fast as could, heading toward the historical downtown area of Charleston.

* * * *

Charlie received word that Joe and Russell were camped outside Senator DeMint's office, and there was no sign of Mitch. Charlie's two employees had been joined by four others, local mercenaries hired through one of Gus's many contacts.

"Mitch is a no show so far, but he could have called in to warn them," Charlie told Gus, both back in their command room at the Biltmore.

"I think we have to assume he has done at least that; I take it we have no activity on his cell phone?"

"None. No contact with his family, and his wife has not used her phone either. I think we can safely surmise we underestimated him a bit. He probably deduced the cell phones were bugged. It's very possible he knows much more than we thought."

"Come to that conclusion finally, have you!" Gus retorted angrily. "Mitch was necessary for this all to work, but he was the one element we had to control. I think we are covered overall enough that the plan will still be a success. But you need to review your entire process; see where it broke down. I am feeling the need to dock your final payment more and more."

"Don't worry; we'll get him," Charlie replied, though incensed by Gus's remarks. He felt Gus was as much to blame as he was. Charlie had pushed for tighter controls on Mitch from the start. Gus had headed him off on bugging the entire house and on following Marie everywhere. Now, Mitch's family had disappeared, so that leverage was lost as well.

Charlie turned on the television in the room. He glanced at his watch—8:00 AM—it should be starting any time now. He flipped over to CNN. Was it happening already? Jim DeMint was on television about to make a statement.

"Gus, get over here."

The senator started talking of a story that was about to be reported involving bribery and his office. As the scene was unfolding on television, Charlie's cell phone went off.

"What is happening there? Where's Mitch?" he demanded when the caller ID was Russell.

"We are chasing him right now. He got by us into the senator's office, but we'll have him soon. He is in sight, on foot." Charlie hung up, so disgusted he didn't want to hear any more.

"Are you listening to this?" Gus said. "Mitch obviously fed them information."

"He must have done it by phone," Charlie lied, not ready to face more of Gus's wrath.

"This was smart, pre-empting the scandal. It won't work, though. It will be seen as a gimmick. We have the money in the account, and it will appear as if it was accepted. Stopping Mitch is imperative, though. Find him; you hear me, Charlie? You find him!"

"Do you think we should delay the other aspects of the plan?" Charlie asked. "At least until we have Mitch back in our control?"

"Absolutely not! Besides, it's far too late for some of it anyhow. The information has been sent to the different media outlets. Today was just DeMint, but tomorrow, Federal Express packages will be opened, detailing the transgressions of more representatives. We might even be able to work this to our advantage. We can include this in the story we leak about Mitch, showing how much he was eager to embarrass Congress, even showing up at their offices."

"If you say so. I would much rather have him here and shut him up."

"Well, get that accomplished then!"

* * * *

Within an hour of the DeMint press conference ending, the story of the senator receiving bribes was reported by the local paper on their Web site, which was picked up very quickly across the United States. The facts were laid out with precision, with account numbers, dollar amounts, and a list of favors the senator had allegedly taken care of in return for the cash. His office was in full defense mode now.

* * * *

Will had been in and out of the Biltmore five more times that morning and had been keeping his eye on the entrance when he was outside. Karen had not yet been allowed to leave. He had a foolhardy plan, but he had to try something; anything was better than waiting in his car all day. Will quickly went to the kitchens and procured a hotel employee outfit, paid someone to let him use a serving cart, and wheeled it up to the room Karen had been forced to. He knocked, very nervous.

"Who is it?" answered the gruff voice.

"Room service," Will answered.

"We didn't order anything," the voice answered back.

"It says here to deliver to this room."

"Are you stupid—take it back and stop bothering us."

"I will need a signature saying that you did not order this; it's a three-hundred-dollar meal," Will said as confidently as he could. He reached into his pocket as he heard the footsteps approach. A few clicks of the lock and the door swung open.

"What do I have to say to get you to …" the man stopped talking, shook convulsively, and fell to the ground. Will pocketed his hand-held Taser and entered the room.

"Will!" Karen exclaimed, utterly shocked. "How the …" Will motioned to her for quiet, placing his finger to his mouth.

"We'll talk later; for now, just come with me," Will said, talking quickly. "I have no idea how long the effects will last! Get under the cart." The room service cart had a drape that concealed the lower section. Karen sat with her knees to her nose as Will calmly pushed the cart back into the hall and closed the door.

"Hold on," he whispered, beginning to walk back toward the

elevator. They passed several people in the hall, but none of Charlie's gang. Will pressed the elevator button, and after several seconds, the doors opened. A surge of panic seized him as two of the men he had seen on and off the past twenty-four hours stepped out and headed around the corner toward the room he and Karen had just left. He hurriedly pushed the cart into the now empty elevator and punched the lobby button.

"Karen, come on, hurry!" Karen stood up and Will uncovered a few of the dishes on top of the cart, revealing a black wig and a gray sweater.

"Throw those on," Will said as he was quickly removing the kitchen apparel he had been wearing over jeans and a T-shirt. He also produced sunglasses for both Karen and himself.

Karen did as he said, still not sure how he knew where to go or if this was even the smartest move. The elevator reached the lobby just as Karen straightened the wig and put the sunglasses on. Will wrapped his fingers around hers and whispered in her ear. "They have someone stationed down here. I'm guessing the goons upstairs have discovered their incapacitated friend by now and have alerted the guard here in the lobby. Just pretend as if we're on a weekend getaway or something. We'll soon learn if our disguises and acting can get us out of this." Sure enough, they noticed someone by the door on a cell phone, looking around frantically.

"Let's walk slower, more casually," Will suggested, as he released his hand from Karen's and placed his arm around her shoulders. "Put your arm around my waist and smile. Maybe even laugh as though I told you a joke. And let's just keep looking at each other as we walk, not at him."

It seemed to Karen as though the guy at the door was staring right at them the closer they got, but she continued to look at Will and smile. He started talking about Sedona, as if they had been there yesterday and how lovely it was. Karen was sure the guy was going to stop them, but they waltzed right by him as he continued to scan the lobby.

"Don't move any faster; just keep doing what we are doing," Will said as they hit the parking lot, leading her in the direction of the car. "Your room had a view of this direction. The others are probably watching for you. If we start running, it will raise suspicion." It was all Karen could do not to sprint the minute she breathed the fresh air, but she heeded her friend's advice. They calmly got in Will's car, and he slowly drove away, as if they did not have a care in the world.

"Will, how on earth did you know where I was and that I needed help?" Karen asked once they had driven a few miles away from the Biltmore. This was the part he was dreading. He had no idea how she would react. She may never talk to him again, but he was going to tell her the whole truth.

"Do you remember that day you asked me to access your computer to send the proposal to Rick?"

"Yeah, I guess. A few months ago, right?"

"Exactly, well, I unintentionally opened an e-mail from some guy named Charlie. It was one of those things, you look up to see what you did and a name stuck out from it: Mitch Bartter. Once I saw the name, I kept reading. I am really sorry about the invasion of privacy. Anyhow, this was after you had confided in me you were dealing with something, although you would not let me help. I made the logical conclusion that Mitch and your issues were related. I also did not get a good feel from the e-mail."

"Understandable, don't worry about that, but how did you know about me being at the Biltmore and …" Karen asked as Will raised his hand, indicating he had not told her everything yet.

"Karen, please forgive me. I went a step further after that day, all in an effort to help!"

"What do you mean?" Karen asked. Will was driving toward downtown Phoenix, not quite sure where they should be going.

"You have to understand that Mitch Bartter is someone in whom I have a significant interest. My concern was for the safety of both of you. I called Art as well as another friend of mine." Art was the firm's computer expert. "The two of them managed to tweak the e-mail system so anything coming in from the same person, this Charlie character, would be routed to me as well."

He could not read Karen's reaction. She was silent, looking straight ahead, and she still had on her sunglasses. "They set it up so only e-mails from the address Charlie was using would be routed to me—no other ones!" Will added quickly. "I understand this was a huge invasion of privacy. Please do not be too upset with me. I was really just trying to help. Anyhow, I received the same e-mail you did yesterday, with that same attachment. I knew where you were going. When you did not call me within the hour we had agreed on, I drove straight to the Biltmore. I have spent the better part of the last day trying to figure out how to get you out of there." Karen remained quiet a few more minutes as Will drove. Finally, she removed the sunglasses he had given her, and Will realized her eyes were full of tears.

"Again, I am so sorry ..." Will started, but Karen turned to look at him, and he quit talking.

"Will, I know I should be angry with you. Not too many people could do what you did and not have it seen as an intrusion." Karen's voice was cracking with emotion. "But knowing you as I do and knowing the kind of person you are, I have no doubt it was done with my well-being in mind. I just didn't know that people would go to such lengths to help me." She wiped a few tears from her eyes. "Besides, if you had not done this, who knows where I would be when the smoke clears." She managed a laugh as she said this. Will's feelings were such that he could not stop himself.

"Karen, I am more selfish than you think. It wasn't just your well-being I had in mind; it was my own as well." Will was mustering all the courage he could.

"What do you mean?"

"Hasn't it been obvious? I've been trying for almost a year to tell you how I feel about you; I just couldn't make the right words come out of my mouth. Karen, I'm in love with you. This probably isn't the right time, but if I'm going to be straight with you, it's going to be about everything. When you're in love with someone, you help that person no matter what, and sometimes, you do not think too clearly. I know we have a firm to think about, and I know you've been through a horrible ordeal the last few months, but I had to tell you."

"Will—I don't know what to … I wish you would have said something … the reason I didn't want you to help was because …" Karen was fumbling over her own words now. "I didn't want you to get mixed up with this group; I didn't want to put you at risk because … I think I love you, too!" she finally blurted out. "Here I am trying to protect you, and you go and get involved anyhow." They both laughed out loud.

"Where to from here?" Will asked.

"Give me your cell phone. I've been thinking about this for a few weeks, and I should have made this call before I went to the Biltmore yesterday; I just thought I would have more time. Those guys will not get out of there; trust me." Will handed Karen the phone, and after a brief conversation, she instructed Will where to go.

Fifteen minutes later, they arrived at the restaurant Karen had indicated to head toward. They got out of the car and embraced, Will slowly putting his hands around her face and gently kissing her.

"This Liberty situation is not over," Karen said. "Gus has unlimited resources, and he took my computer with all the records. He will come after me because I know the full plan. Luckily, I have copies of everything in my office. And we have to contact Mitch; he's in real trouble."

"You're right that this is not over. And I am pretty sure that your copies are gone." Will explained what had happened at the office the day before.

"How did they know?" Karen asked, more in general than expecting an answer. She shook this off and continued. "Either way, it is time to change tactics. I have a friend meeting us here. I'll tell her everything.

She'll be able to help; she's a police officer, and I think she'll trust me enough to at least follow up with the facts."

"Excellent," Will responded. "As for Mitch, I sent him the e-mail you received. If he opened it, he is fully aware of the plot. Mitch had been copied on some of the stuff you received from Charlie, so I had his address." He added the last sentence in response to the quizzical look on her face. "Plus, I have been staking out that hotel for almost twenty-four hours, and I haven't seen Mitch. They don't have him yet."

"Oh, good, I guess," Karen said. "They are monitoring all of Mitch's incoming e-mails. They will know he received it. I tried to send it to him, too, but since they were monitoring mine as well, at least recently, they knew what I had done, and they said they stopped it."

"Well, maybe mine got through."

"Where did you get that Taser, by the way?" Karen asked.

"You would be surprised at all the purchases clients try to deduct on their taxes. I make mental notes along the way. I knew where I might be able to borrow one."

"Who would think they could deduct a Taser?"

"Don't ask."

Chapter 30

Mitch stepped outside of Hyman's into the sultry Charleston air. He had finished his buffalo shrimp, downed his final Diet Coke, and used the restroom, splashing water on his face to clear his mind as much as possible. What was his next move? He thought about a hotel, but as he had very little cash left, and he did not dare use a credit card, he put that idea out of his head. Mitch hoped Senator DeMint's press conference would soften the blow until his innocence could be proven. That goal seemed a pipe dream standing here in the middle of this street with about seventy-five bucks in his pocket, nowhere to stay, and no means to go anywhere. His best idea was to try to go back to Senator DeMint's office; maybe they could at least find him a place to stay, although they had enough of their own problems right now.

Mitch turned right out of the restaurant and headed back toward the historic area of the city and toward the bay. He wandered the streets; following tourists and overhearing several of the ghost walk tours as he moved. Should he catch a cab to the airport? A return to Phoenix would not be wise. They would trace his credit card purchase of the tickets and know what flight he was on—they would catch him before he could get to cab. He briefly thought of Marie and the kids, hoping they were safe in San Diego. Mitch almost wished he had followed through on purchasing standby tickets for all of them to Denver, where Marie's mother lived. *The farther from Phoenix, the better*, he thought. When Mitch first broached this idea to Marie, she questioned if he had truly lost his marbles, thinking he had reached the ultimate paranoia. But as it turned out, his foresight had definitely saved his family from this fiasco. Hopefully, in a few days, this whole issue would be solved, but Mitch did not see how.

As he walked the Battery, not really paying attention to those around him, a voice whispered in his ear. "Good to see you again, Mr. Bartter." It was Russell. Mitch kept walking at his same pace.

"I wish I could say the same," he replied, cursing himself for leaving his hat back at the restaurant.

"It was foolish of you to think you could escape us. Nice move back in Arizona at the park. I should have run to grab you then."

"You should have tried; judging from your size and build, I would have given you heat stroke in about seven minutes."

"You're right," Russell said, laughing while he eased his hand around Mitch's upper right arm. He turned serious again. "Mr. Reed is very displeased with your actions." They continued to walk along the water.

"Mr. Reed is a fool. He thinks his actions will be the end of conservatism. I saw his plan. He is a terrorist, plain and simple. Maybe not in the terms most people think, but that is what he is." Mitch assumed since Russell had not led him into a car yet, one was definitely on the way. Russell and the others must have fanned out across the area where they last saw him, and Mitch was stupid enough to walk right into the trap. Mitch wanted to keep talking, hoping to take Russell off guard. Given their weight difference, Mitch would definitely need to surprise him with an attack. He continued his thrashing of Gus Reed.

"Reed is a complete idiot. When I tell the authorities who is really behind much of what has happened in the last few days …" Russell cut him off.

"I am afraid you will never get that opportunity. We have other plans for you, which include—ahhhhh."

Mitch had taken his left hand and sucker-punched Russell square on the nose. The blow caused him to loosen his grip on Mitch's right arm enough that he jerked it back and quickly drove his knee into Russell's groin. Russell doubled over but managed to pull the gun out of his holster. Mitch quickly kicked it out of his hand. Several of the tourists had stopped to watch the melee. Russell raised up and took a swing at Mitch, who dodged it by ducking and turning simultaneously so now his back was against Russell's front, with Russell's arm outstretched past him. Instinctively performing a move he had seen hundreds of times in Ed's judo classes, Mitch grabbed Russell's outstretched elbow with his left hand, reached up, and got a hold of his opponent's upper arm and shoulder with his right hand, threw his right hip into the midsection of the big man, knocking him off balance while simultaneously pulling with all his might on the man's arm. Russell tumbled over Mitch, hitting the cement hard, flat on his back. Hearing several of Russell's bones crack at once, Mitch took off running up Broad Street, not looking back at all.

As he reached the first intersection, he saw the dark sedan he had noticed at the window of the restaurant heading toward him. Mitch tore off to the right and heard the car turn to follow him. Apparently, its occupants had noticed him, too. He had about half of a block lead on the car as he passed a group of tourists being led across the street by a guide. The screeching of the tires behind him told him he had gained a little time. He turned down an alley and then jumped a small fence and ran through someone's yard, hoping to throw off his pursuers. As he exited onto another street, he turned and ran the opposite direction he had been running down the alley.

He stole a quick look behind him and saw the car two blocks down the street. He ran full bore, not knowing if they had seen him yet, just as another car screeched to halt beside him, its passenger window down.

"Mitch, get in quick!" It was Al. Somehow, miraculously, it was

Al. Mitch jumped into the car, and Al took off. Mitch looked out the back window, but the sedan was not coming up quickly. It appeared to be driving very slowly, looking at each property it passed. They had not seen him.

"Drive slower; I don't think they know I got in the car. Let's not raise any alarms." Mitch was trying to catch his breath. "What are you doing here?"

"From your article, it was pretty obvious you were coming to Charleston."

"Right. I didn't mean for you to come, just wanted you to know where I was. I assumed you would decipher the message quickly. How did you know I would be down here by the water?"

"Finding you was just dumb luck," Al said as he turned and headed out of the historical district. "I got in town late in the night. I've been looking for you all day. I was driving around hoping to spot you. I tried the phone I gave you, but it kept going to voicemail."

Mitch pulled out his dead cell phone. Luckily, the charger was one of the few items he kept in the small satchel he was carrying with him. He plugged his phone into the car's power outlet. Checking it quickly, he noticed no text message from Marie. *Good*, he thought to himself. Mitch had told Marie to text him the code ".adg" if she had any trouble (the characters that came up first when punching 1-2-3-4 on the phone). Mitch looked at his surroundings, realizing the car was a brand-new Charger.

"Sweet ride," he said. "Did you rent this? The group may be monitoring the other Web site writers. If you put this on a card, then ..."

Al interrupted. "I borrowed it. This car belongs to a very dear friend of mine, Leonard. We worked together for about five years right out of college and have stayed in touch ever since. Remember when I went to the Cleveland Indians Fantasy Baseball Camp a few years ago? This is the guy that went with me." Al chuckled slightly. "The poor guy bought this car last week. When I decoded your message, I decided I would drive down right away, but I didn't want to take my car in case, as you just said, the group was monitoring me as well. I used a co-worker's cell phone and called Leonard, briefly explaining the situation. Although he was confused, he agreed to meet me at a mall in Toledo. We parked at different ends of the shopping center and left the keys in our respective cars. We then walked across the mall through the crowd; I actually saw him as we were walking. He glanced at me, and I literally did the forefinger across the nose, ala Newman and Redford in *The Sting*. I'll have to tell Todd—he'll be very proud. Anyway, I got in his car, and he got in mine. It may have all been for naught, but I didn't want to take any risks."

"Impressive. So we get to break in this guy's new car. He must be a good friend!"

"I did have to agree to pay for another trip for him to fantasy baseball camp. I kind of hope he was kidding about that! That is some serious coinage! So, what is the plan—where am I driving?"

"Good question. Let's get out of town; I guess head north toward BG for now. I'm not sure what I want to do next." A thought occurred to Mitch at the mention of Bowling Green. "Where are Lisa and the kids?"

"It's a good thing I work for such a great company," Al began. "I explained the situation to my boss, and he authorized a pretty darn nice cash advance to me. I gave Lisa half the money and told her to take the kids back to Cedar Point and to stay at a hotel there, using cash to pay for everything. I told the kids I was going to Alabama for work so they wouldn't worry."

"Great, you have cash! Thanks, man, for coming to my rescue. Did you touch base with the others?"

"Mark is actually in San Diego at a conference. I talked with Todd briefly, and he wanted to come, too, but we decided it would be best for him to wait to see what was going on. We actually could head to Arkansas. Put all three of our heads together."

"That's a bit far; plus, they may consider that a possible destination," Mitch replied to his friend's suggestion. "Let's see if Todd can meet us on the way back to northwest Ohio. You'll need to get back there eventually anyway. I can catch a plane to wherever I need to go next from there. If we drive all night, we can have you close to home midday tomorrow. We probably should not go to your house either, though."

"Good enough, but we're sticking together until this is solved. So, what else have you learned about this group?"

"Let me call Todd and get him on the way. We're going to be driving all night. I'll fill you in as we go."

* * * *

It was all Gus could do to remain calm when he learned that Mitch had slipped through their fingers yet again in South Carolina. His plans, so carefully reviewed, with every step drawn out in meticulous detail, were unraveling before his eyes. He had called Charlie and Paul into the Biltmore meeting room when they received the news from Joe that Mitch had escaped, and Russell was in the emergency room with some cracked vertebrae.

Gus had learned several hours earlier that Karen was no longer at the hotel. The shockwave this sent through the room was frightening enough, but now Mitch's escape was even worse. Two people on the loose, both of whom apparently knew way too much about the events planned for the following week.

"I'm not going to ask how this has happened," Gus began in his calm but obviously fierce voice. "Somewhere along the line, we allowed Mitch too much information, and he put it all together. Worse, he managed to determine all this without our knowing it, or at least us catching up too late. You both have failed me in this." Charlie and Paul looked at each other.

"We have been on him from the start!" Charlie exclaimed. "He had to be getting inside information. We had him monitored as tight as a drum!"

"And yet, he has escaped and is not here in this room with us. How do you explain that?"

"As I said, someone on the inside helped him!" Charlie replied confidently, looking at Paul.

"Hey, I haven't said one thing to him. Everything I have done has been according to the plan." Paul felt compelled to defend himself. Charlie smiled, as he knew Paul had taken the bait.

"Including leaving a window unlocked in your house? Including not informing us right away of the e-mail Mitch forwarded to himself from your computer?"

Paul looked crestfallen. "I don't see how that had anything to do with this. That was a few months ago, and Mitch was none the wiser. I fixed the wording of the e-mail, and we don't know it was Mitch who broke into my house. It's not like he stopped doing his work at that point."

"It has to do with you being a good soldier! You do not keep that type of information from me. I had Charlie's people get me a copy of the original e-mail and the altered one you sent to Mitch. Do you realize you changed the date?" Anger flashed in Gus's cold eyes.

"I had to, based on the content I wrote in the new version."

"And if Mitch wrote down the date he saw when he was alone in the room and then looked at the date on the one you sent, don't you think that might have raised a red flag?" Gus's sarcasm was dripping from every word.

"He wouldn't have done that. I'm sure he was feeling under the gun about sneaking in there anyhow."

"I do not see how we can rule anything out as he was obviously aware of us somehow!" Gus yelled. "We have failed—*failed, failed, and failed!* And because of our failure—excuse me—*your failure*," he exclaimed, pointing at both of them, "Mitch is out there with most of the information that can destroy this whole thing!"

"My guys will find him and shut him up permanently!" Charlie yelled back.

"No, they won't," Gus said, slowly calming his voice. "They will find him, but they will bring him to me first. Then the authorities can have him. I told you I would have my leverage, and so I obtained it."

"You have his family?" Charlie asked hopefully. "Did you have another team tracking them?"

"I explained a while ago that those types of tactics would be entirely unnecessary. No, I have something much better. Mr. Bartter will awake tomorrow morning, whether in our clutches or not, to find out he is a wanted man, with not only charges of conspiracy attached to his name, but also campaign financing law violations and maybe some computer hacking charges tacked on, too. You two didn't realize it was Mitch who made those attempts back on the Fourth of July?"

Charlie and Paul just looked at each other. Charlie decided to go in a different direction.

"Fantastic! His credibility will be shot. I still think he got help from the inside, maybe from Karen. They seemed to buddy up a bit in the last month or so. Do you think she gave him more information than she should have? I know we had a tracer on her e-mail, too; we would have seen anything she sent to Mitch or received on both sides of the equation."

"I do not believe she would jeopardize this, but I am not 100 percent certain. Why don't we bring her back in here and discuss it? Oh, that's right; your team let her waltz right out of the place. Now we have no idea where she is." Gus's anger was rising yet again.

"I've stationed someone at her house and at her office. I'm working on getting her credit cards linked in to our surveillance as well, although we have her purse," Charlie quickly offered as a means to make up for this blunder. "And to be fair, how could we have expected a hotel staff member to Taser our guy out of nowhere?" Charlie regretted it the moment he said it.

"I thought that's what they were paid to do—know where the obstacles are!" Gus chided back. Charlie knew when to stop. Gus continued in a lower, more subdued tone. "Fortunately, nothing is lost yet. Senator DeMint is under the gun today just as planned. More will happen tomorrow. Let's get Mitch and let's get Karen and we will move forward. And gentlemen, no more foul-ups!"

Charlie and Paul put their heads together to try to determine where Karen might go. They both realized very quickly neither of them had learned nearly enough about her. Paul at least had the foresight to suggest sending someone to her business partner's house.

* * * * *

After Will and Karen's escape, they had talked with Karen's police acquaintance for a few hours the previous afternoon. Without any direct proof, outside their statements, it would be difficult to do anything of an official nature. Will suggested he could return to his office at the firm and print off the e-mail, but the officer thought that would not be wise.

"If I were them," she had explained, "I would expect Karen to try to go to her office to get some sort of evidence, whatever she might have. They probably have the place staked out."

"I'm sure she's right," Karen agreed. "So, is there anything we can do?"

The officer thought for a few moments—she seemed to be mulling through a thought, trying to determine if it was a good idea or not.

"Karen, I trust you completely. If you tell me these guys are doing something illegal, then I believe you. They clearly held you against your will for awhile. Again, nothing of an official nature can be done, but I know a few guys who might be willing to join me in an unofficial training exercise, if you will. Why don't you let me make a few calls, and maybe we can set something up for the morning. I've got a fairly large place that can accommodate all of us tonight, so you two should stay with me. That group might not have your place on their radar, Will, but there is no sense in taking that chance." Will and Karen had no objections, and they followed the officer to her spacious house.

Eric Myerholtz

* * * *

Mitch and Al pulled into a Cracker Barrel just south of Cincinnati early that Saturday morning. Todd had been glad to hear from them and jumped in his car as soon as he learned the plan. He made the drive from Little Rock in a little less than eight hours. He got a little sleep in his car in the parking lot of the restaurant after texting his friends that they could find him there. Todd awoke in time to gas up his car and get a paper before his friends arrived.

They all went in to eat. Todd ordered the strongest coffee the place could muster, but the waitress raised her eyes a little as Mitch and Al said "Diet Coke" in unison.

"So, what should we do now?" Todd asked. Mitch took the time to fill him in, as he had Al during the drive, laying out the details of what had transpired the last few weeks as well as the plans in the coming days for the Liberty Group.

"Well, this won't make it any easier," Todd said, spreading the newspaper out on the table. A front-page headline read, "Arizona Columnist Wanted."

"What the …" Al exclaimed.

"I figured," Mitch responded calmly. "Once I learned what some of Gus's ultimate plans were, I assumed I would be part of the fall group. Am I the only one? I had hoped that Karen was not involved with their overall plans, not that I want her to be framed either."

Al was scanning the newspaper.

"I didn't see anyone else mentioned, but I was pretty tired when I read the article," Todd responded.

"No mention of anyone else." Al began reading a portion of the article out loud.

Mitch Bartter, writer for the Arizona Republic, is a person of interest in connection with the bribery allegations against Senator Jim DeMint of South Carolina. Mr.

> Bartter established the Liberty Group, which posed as a conservative nonprofit organization whose stated aim was to educate Web site visitors about conservatism. An accusation of fraud is now also following Mr. Bartter, as funds collected from selling Web site memberships are in question.
>
> Mr. Bartter seems to have personally funneled funds to several other congressional representatives as well, violating campaign finance law. Unconfirmed reports indicate that Mr. Bartter received large payments from an unknown source, deposited those funds into an account under his own name, and then transferred the money to three senators, all in excess of amounts allowed under campaign financing rules.
>
> Additionally, a computer found at the Arizona Republic belonging to Mr. Bartter was used to attempt to hack into the database of both the Speaker of the House and the Senate Majority Leader.

"It goes on from there to describe some of the work done by Liberty and some of the individuals and companies who have been contributing to the group," Al said, finishing his reading.

"Man, you have been busy, Mitch," Todd joked.

Mitch was silent, staring off into the almost empty restaurant. Todd and Al looked at each other, not knowing what to say. Almost a full minute had passed when Mitch perked up as if he had been poked in the ribs.

"Let's order, shall we?" Mitch said brightly, rubbing his hands together. "I'm famished."

"You okay, man?" Todd asked.

"I'm fine. No such thing as bad publicity, or something like that—isn't that the Hollywood motto anyhow?"

"Mitch, I'm sure we'll get to the bottom of all this," Al said consolingly.

"Oh, I know we will. First of all, the Web site was established long before I joined. I don't know how they will lay the entire work of the group at my feet. My boss, John, will back me up on that. They contacted me through him, and he is well respected in the newspaper industry. I'm sure quite a few of the contributions predate my work as well. Second, it will take an awful lot of forgery to tie me to anything they did. Third, according to Gus's plan, the worst is yet to come, and I will have both of you for my alibi. Last, I accepted no money, if it is the money I think that report is referring to. I even documented the money sent to me; we called an attorney and put it all in escrow. Tell you what, order me some scrambled eggs and bacon when the waitress comes back; I need to use the restroom."

Mitch left the table, and Todd and Al looked at each other. They agreed Mitch was acting very level headed about the situation, but they needed to solve the mystery quickly. The two started discussing how best to inform the authorities about what was to happen next. Mitch, on the other hand, tried to call Marie from the bathroom. If she had seen the headlines, he was sure she would not be as calm about the situation. Unfortunately, she was not answering; it was very early in San Diego, actually still the middle of the night. He sent a quick text, telling her to remain calm no matter what she read.

As they ate, the three friends determined the best thing to do was to head north toward Al's. Al suggested calling the owner of the company he worked for—Al knew him to have some political connections that could possibly be used to warn others of what might be coming. Mitch agreed enthusiastically with this idea, so Al headed outside to make his call.

"Mr. Rellim—it's Al Miller. Sorry to bother you on a Saturday morning."

"No problem, how are you, Al?" the man asked genially.

"I'm in a bit of a bind, and I'm hoping you can help." Al went on to explain the situation with Mitch and the information they had at this point.

"Al, let me make a few calls, and I'll get right back to you." The owner hung up the phone. He was true to his word; Al's phone was buzzing within twenty minutes.

"Here's what you are going to do," Mr. Rellim explained. "You and your two friends will drive here to Fostoria, and I will personally escort you on our corporate jet to Washington. I have talked with both a senator and a representative this morning, and after the news about DeMint, they are very eager to get to more information about who is behind this."

"I'm guessing we are about two and a half hours away from Fostoria right now," Al replied.

"That's okay; just get here as soon as you can. I'll have the pilots file the flight plan and get the plane ready."

"Thank you so much, Mr. Rellim, I really appreciate it. I didn't mean for you to stick your neck into this."

"I'll help any way I can!"

Al returned to the table and told his friends the new plan of action. Mitch thought it was great.

"If we can get to Washington today, we may be able to pre-empt a lot of these allegations. I'm sure the tidal wave of them will hit this week!"

* * * *

Joe sent a quick text to Charlie: "Location identified." Charlie did not want a text; he wanted to hear it straight from Joe, who was still in Charleston.

"We got a hit off one of the friend's cards; he purchased gas just south of Cincinnati," Joe began. "Mr. Davis, are you sure this friend will be with them?"

"I'd bet a lot they are together; Mitch is a man who believes in his friends, and from what we have observed, they believe in him. My guess is this Todd guy came to the rescue. I was hoping for better news than a gas purchase. Clearly, they are on the move. The problem now is finding out where they are headed. His other friends live in Ohio, one of them in Cincinnati and one in Bowling Green. How soon can you get to Cincinnati?" Before Joe could answer, Charlie thought better of it. "It will take too long to drive from Charleston. Let me make a call, and I will have you and the others on a private plane very soon. You still have the four others with you, minus Russell, of course?"

"Yes, we're fine, but Russell will be laid up awhile."

"Never thought Mitch had that in him. It is definitely something he will pay for when we catch him. I'll call you back soon." Charlie hung up the phone and went to tell Gus what he had learned. It was still quite early in Arizona, and each of the men (Paul, Gus, and Charlie) had booked rooms for the current week, under different names than they had used up until now. Charlie hoped that the good news of knowing where Mitch was would help put Gus in a better mood. Charlie knocked on Gus's door, but Gus answered with a cell phone to his mouth and motioned to Charlie to give him a minute.

"That sounds like a good plan," Gus said into the phone. "I'll let you know if I need more assistance. You have done marvelously. Have the representative call this Mr. Rellim back to tell him your office has someone who will provide them safe transportation." Gus hung up.

"I have good news; we know where they are heading!" Charlie said enthusiastically.

"Northern Ohio, Fostoria to be precise," Gus answered, sipping a cup of coffee. Charlie was perplexed.

"And how are you sure about that?"

"Don't worry about it. They will be at their destination in approximately two hours—maybe a little more." Gus reached into his wallet and took out a business card.

"Call this man. Tell him you need a team of at least four people, if not more; we won't fail, this time, to be in Fostoria in less than two hours. Tell him Mitch and his friends will be going to the Fostoria airport and are to be taken alive. I have already put a plan in motion that will have a jet ready to leave from somewhere called Fremont, a small town close to Fostoria. Tell this gentleman to have his team take them there. Do you think you can handle that without screwing it up?"

"How do you know all this?" Charlie repeated his question.

"How many times have I told you, I am prepared for just about anything."

"How will these people identify Mitch?"

"I'm guessing not too many people will be heading to the Fostoria airport in two hours. It's a small town, too. They'll figure it out. Now, once Mitch is here, what other issues might we have? We do not know where his family is, but I assume he is contacting them. Of course, they will still think he is out east, so even if they do not hear from him for awhile and contact authorities, they will probably call South Carolina or Ohio first. Well, either way—we'll figure it out when he gets here. I gave your cell number to the pilot in Ohio, and he will call you once he has an estimated time of arrival. You personally will pick them up. No mistakes, understand!" Gus's tone left no question in the matter.

* * * * *

Al made the drive fairly quickly on this weekend morning, Todd following right behind. None of them had contacted anyone else to tell them where they were headed yet. The three had decided to park Todd's car at Al's office in Fostoria, which they did and began to drive the short distance to the airport. As they turned on the country road leading to their destination, two large SUVs turned off a road about a quarter of a mile ahead of them. The SUVs then parked perpendicular to the road as Al's vehicle approached. Comprehending what was happening, Al slammed on the brakes and wheeled the Charger in the opposite direction. Two other SUVs had already appeared out of nowhere and taken a similar position behind them; they were trapped. Al stopped the car.

Four men approached the vehicle slowly, each of them with a drawn handgun. Mitch reached over and put the car in park.

"Let's not try anything stupid," Mitch told his friend.

"How can they know where we were going?" Todd asked. "Al, who knew we were coming here?"

"Just Mr. Rellim, it was his idea."

"The owner of the company set you up?"

"Never, I don't believe that," Al said defiantly. "He had talked to a senator and a representative. He was trying to help."

"I think you just answered the question," Mitch said, quickly putting everything together. Mitch was talking while thumbing his cell phone very quickly. He managed to send two texts, the first to Marie, and after a quick debate in his head among the people currently in Phoenix who could help the most right now, he had sent the second one.

"Mr. Rellim must have unknowingly talked to one of Gus's targets," Mitch continued, clicking his phone shut. "That person probably met quickly with their advisors, telling them more scandals were coming. I'm guessing one of those advisors called Gus. Like I just said, don't you two do anything stupid." Before Al and Todd knew it, Mitch had opened the door and stepped out of the vehicle.

"I'll come with you so you can just leave my friends out of this."

"Nice try, but our orders are to return all three of you," said the man closest to Mitch.

"Exactly to where are you returning us?" Mitch inquired, thinking he already knew the answer.

"Phoenix."

Chapter 31

Gus was feeling slightly better now, though he never considered trying to pull the plug on things for the upcoming week. He had actually set "the governmental portion," as he called it, into motion about three years earlier. Gus had spent too long and had traveled too far down the path to let Mitch's untimely discoveries stop him now.

If all had gone according to plan, Mitch would have awoken in a few days to chaos starting in Washington, his name in the papers, and, most likely, federal agents showing up at his door, combing through the falsified records that had been carefully crafted. *Well, Mitch will still be blamed for it all; it just won't be as much of a surprise*, Gus thought.

The other prong of his attack was scheduled to hit the fan the following day. For several years, he had been selecting individuals (after vigorous background checks and careful observation) and using his money and influence to place them into the offices of dozens of congressional Republicans. Gus was always amazed at what people would be willing to do for a little money. It actually was more than a little; paying off this many people for this long had put more than a small dent in his considerable wealth. He knew it was all worth it, and he was planning a bigger reward for himself down the road: self-satisfaction. Charlie's idea of recruiting so many of these people from liberal groups across the college campuses of the country had been ingenious, a better idea than Gus thought possible of his henchman.

The individuals had been selected several years ago and, one by one, had been placed in the offices of midlevel and senior Republican representatives and senators. They had gained the trust of those around them. They were now in the position Gus had hoped. When he started the Web site phase of the plan, Gus had estimated he needed about another six to eight months. It had actually taken only four as now all operatives had placed their final pieces. Mitch was set up perfectly as the face of the organization, the person pulling all the strings.

The full plan was for numerous, incriminating bits of information to be discovered about all of these Republicans. Gus's operatives of course had cemented the necessary evidence to get these elected officials into serious hot water. A mass resignation of Republican leaders would turn the country on its side. Gus could not help but smile at the stroke of luck the Obama election was to his plan. Not only the election, but the policies the administration had attempted. With the overreaching of power and control the Democratic leadership from Congress and the presidency had achieved, the United States seemed to be leaning heavily back toward the Republicans. Now, all these scandals would break loose, and the American public would have no choice but to maintain the Democrats' power. Gus's ego was being fed each day as he continued to give himself credit for what he saw happening once that goal was achieved.

He had foreseen long ago ultimately what would happen. Gus reached into his wallet and pulled out a very old piece of paper on which he had written the impetus for his long, drawn-out plan. This was over thirty years ago when Gus had been studying U.S. history. Gus theorized the United States had been heading down the socialism road for a while. He discovered a quote by James Madison he read once again now that he was so close: *"that there are more instances of the abridgement of the freedom of the people by gradual and silent encroachments of those in power, then by violent and sudden usurpations."*

At the time he first read it, Gus thought of the many ways the federal government had stepped into the private sector over the years, usually with the idea of helping people. Social security, Medicare, regulations of banks and several other industries, the rules and barriers put up against energy development—even in the 1970s. He knew then the day was coming. The main goal of his plan was to help this socialist society along; he wanted to see it occur in his lifetime.

Gus also determined his plan would be much more plausible under a liberal leader than a strong conservative type. A president similar to Reagan would not mix well with his plot. The way the economy blossomed under Reagan's supply-side economic theories and his stand against Russia was pivotal to America strengthening its world leader position. But more than that, there was a real sense of nationalism under his leadership. People were proud to be Americans. He again laughed, this time out loud. Now, the leader of America had gone to individual countries apologizing for his United States. He knew the time for his plan had come. The liberal president would be a voice of calm when many of the leaders of the opposition party were forced to resign. The press would excoriate anyone with a conservative idea for years. The far-left agenda would be passed without much opposition. Gus knew once additional social programs were established, they would be impossible to take away. The United States already had more debt than it could absorb, and the current government was piling it on. These money issues ultimately would result in more government control over its citizens. Yes, the time was now. It was all coming together.

The last piece to control was Karen; she had been missing for well over a day. Gus shook his head at the incompetence of Charlie's team in this final lap of their marathon. Everything had been so smooth until the last forty-eight hours or so, the Sacramento incident notwithstanding. In the back of his mind, Gus knew Mitch was bright enough to realize something was amiss, but he was certain they would know if that had happened. Gus still had some questions for Mitch he wanted answered. Charlie had convinced him that Karen would be caught soon. They had placed individuals outside her apartment as well as her office and even had sent someone to watch over her partner's house, too. She would turn up soon enough; they had her wallet, phone, keys—everything she could need to get away.

Charlie had called Gus's room about an hour ago from the airport to tell him Mitch and his friends were under his control, heading toward the Biltmore. The mercenary group in Ohio had confiscated all their personal effects before the plane left. Gus would soon be face to face with Mr. Bartter.

Charlie had taken Mitch's phone and reviewed the recently sent messages as they traveled to the hotel.

"Nice, Mitch, warning your wife. And you even correctly assumed we would be at the Biltmore. I guess I will have to stop her." Mitch just glared at him, unable to talk through the gag. Charlie sent another text: "Escaped—call me as soon as you get this."

No call was returned quickly though. They continued on to the Biltmore. Charlie managed to get the three friends into the hotel without raising suspicion, and he told his boss they had arrived. Gus had spent the next few minutes thinking of all he wanted to say to Mitch, and he was now ready. This was going to be fun!

* * * *

Mark was now on driving detail in Marie's car, with her going over different scenarios in her head. She had received Mitch's text: "Caught—send help—Biltmore." She, like Karen and Will, was without evidence. Telling the police she thought her husband was being held against his will did not seem plausible, especially when her husband's name was notoriously all over the papers and Internet. Maybe that would be enough—just tell them there was a Mitch Bartter sighting at the

Biltmore—they would swarm the place. Of course, the Liberty Group would most likely just hand Mitch over, and all the accusations would continue to fly. She knew they needed to stop Gus and Charlie. Mark was not thinking as clearly as Marie.

"We'll go in and get him; it's just that simple," he had said.

"And how will we accomplish that?" Marie asked.

"Just stay out of my way. I'll tackle anything that tries to stop us."

"I appreciate that, Mark, but they will have more than even you can handle. Plus, they will have weapons; I'm sure of that."

"So, what do you suggest? Do you have anybody else we could call? And are you sure that wasn't Mitch texting you?"

"It was stupid. Why wouldn't he just call if he was able to? I think Charlie was hoping I would be so happy to hear from Mitch that I wouldn't think clearly. It wasn't Mitch. And no, I can't think of anyone else. I tried Karen, but she wasn't at her office, and I don't know her cell phone or her home phone."

"Well, I'm driving to the Biltmore anyhow," Mark said defiantly. "Don't worry—I won't do anything that we both don't agree to."

Chapter 32

Gus walked triumphantly into this familiar room at the Biltmore. He had that satisfied look of victory you never want see in your enemy. Most of the work had been done here at the Biltmore; it was only fitting this discussion should occur here as well. Mitch, Todd, and Al had been taken to the airport in Fremont, and as they had been told, a private jet was waiting to take them back to Arizona. They were treated quite well on the plane, although everything they had with them had been confiscated, including cell phones and wallets. The flight did not take very long, and they had landed at a private strip outside of Phoenix, a smiling Charlie waiting for them with five other assistants. They came straight to the Biltmore where it was now late afternoon on Saturday. Charlie whispered something in Gus's ear as he passed, and he came to a stop in front of the three friends.

"Got yourself into a bit of a tight spot," Gus said, looking at the writer. "Mitch, this is so disappointing. All you had to do was continue your work on the Web site. In a few more days, the entire plan will unfold. I had hoped you would wake up one day here in Phoenix with your name splattered across newspapers, all your coworkers gawking at you. I guess we accomplished a little of that; the remainder just won't be as big a surprise for you. But I suppose that is better than being dead. The worst part of your caper to the east is that you dragged your friends Al and Todd here along with you."

"We volunteered!" Al said in disgust. "We'll be wherever our friends need us. You wouldn't understand that, would you! Always about power—guys like you. We jumped at the chance to defeat a terrorist operating from within our own country!"

"A terrorist, am I? Really hadn't thought of it that way. I guess to some I would be considered that." Gus was enjoying himself.

"Gus, just tell us why you set all this up; why go through all the trouble?" Mitch asked, trying to buy time. That was Al's idea, too. Charlie had done a poor job of tying his hands. Al believed he could free himself if given enough time.

"Does it matter, Mitch? Ultimately, the United States will wither to mediocrity, a shadow of the once great country it was. As all the European countries have. That process started long before I showed up; you know that. I'm just assisting the inevitable."

"If it doesn't matter, at least help me to understand. If, as you say, I will be dead, send me to my grave knowing why you needed to kill me."

"Mitch, you misheard me. I said you will *not* be dead, and please, don't take it personally. I needed someone with your literary skills and conservative views, and you were fabulous, right up until you started meddling in my affairs. As I said, if you had just kept to the script, so to speak, your friends here would be much better off. You'd be going to jail either way. Now, it will just happen after we hold you for a few days and let the wheels of my plan spin. However, as we have time to chat, I will indulge your request.

"As you may have surmised by now, Gus is not my name. I am not from Phoenix; I am not even an American. Pulled it off pretty well, didn't I? I began a very long time ago with this plan, maybe not this exact plan, but a plan to help the United States continue down the slow road to mediocrity and even below. This country even made it easy for me. You already had two distinct factions, not fighting with explosive weapons, but still doing damage to each other. I just had to wait until the timing was right to throw the grenades, to find my Pearl Harbor. I thought when the second Bush was elected in 2000, the time was right. The entire debacle in Florida created such an animosity, such hatred and division. I was sewing the seeds of years of planning, but then 9/11 occurred, bringing the country together again. I really thought it would take much longer to get back to a pre-9/11 level of divisiveness, but I was wrong. It only took the most liberal candidate I have ever seen. Then, McCain made it even easier as he selected Palin, and she brought out the worst in Democrats, just as Obama is bringing out the worst in Republicans."

"I still don't quite get it," Al interrupted. "You think the two political parties will bring down America?" Again, Al was as much buying time as anything. He thought he could feel the ropes slackening a bit.

"Not 'bring down,' in your meaning of the word. Just allow it to be distracted within itself, presenting the opportunity for others to take advantage. I really thought I had another year or so, but of course, one must seize the moment when it is presented. The president has been doing too much on his own to bring people together—united against him."

"But what does this gain for you?" Mitch asked. "What is your motivation in eliminating our capitalist ways?"

"It is time for the United States to atone for all its arrogance. Capitalism keeps you strong. I want this country permanently weakened!"

"What do you mean by that? And really, Gus, no one will believe I was responsible for all this." Mitch was conversing in a very casual manner, trying to draw Gus more into the debate. The more time he took, the more time for Marie to help him. "I'm a reporter. I don't have the connections you do. How could I possibly set all this up?"

"My dear boy, people will believe what I want them to believe,"

The Liberty Group

Gus replied, a sinister smile playing across his face. "A good story is hard to forget, and this will be a really good story. You know today's society; the appearance of impropriety is all that is necessary. As the rest of this weekend and next week unfold, more will come to light about you and about dozens of our elected officials, all of whom, ironically, are conservative. Sex scandals, bribes, abuse of power, you name it. The press will do most of the dirty work, finding what I have worked so hard to put in place. The American public will not stand for this; resignations will occur. Republicans not caught in the snare will have trouble getting re-elected. Common, everyday people will of course have even less belief in their elected government overall, which logically leads to the government desiring to control them even more. Oh, I love this country!" For the first time, Mitch noticed the slightest hint of an accent in Gus's voice. He was trying to place it.

"We'll get it all straight!" Al said defiantly. "You'll get what you deserve in the end."

Gus backhanded Al hard across the face. "You seem to talk more than most accountants! That should shut you up! You are nothing—a nobody—soon you will realize that. And as for me getting what I deserve, whom do you mean? Do you refer to Gus Reed, financier? Because, remember, there is no Gus Reed. My real name is known by very few. Your friend Mitch here is the real brains behind the Liberty Group; he is the one causing all this. Those are the facts that will be found, anyhow. As I recall, you, Mr. Accountant, wrote for the group as well; maybe there will be something that points to you, too." Gus continued smiling still more broadly.

"Leave him out of this!" Mitch exclaimed. "Anyhow, the timeline doesn't fit for your little plan. I didn't join the group until a few months ago." Al could feel the ropes slacken a bit more; he would be loose in a few minutes; he knew it. They needed to keep Gus talking.

"I think there will be Liberty employees who claim you were there all along, as well as documents with your signature dated years ago. Don't you realize how much you have done? There will also be plenty of people ready to confess to your long-term involvement." Gus could not help letting out a maniacal laugh.

"Are you talking about Karen? I notice she is not here with us. Are you setting her up, too?"

"Karen, unfortunately, reacted in a similar manner to you. She will have to pay for that. I think her firm and all she has worked for is about to be dismantled. I told you all never to underestimate me. You see, I prefer to inflict pain and suffering much more than a quick death. Charlie, how close are we to having Karen join our little party here?"

"I can't say for certain, but my troops in the field are confident she will be here very soon."

"You see, Mitch," Gus continued, "more of your friends will be joining us. Pity your family can't be here. Where did you send them, by the way? And how did you know about South Carolina so soon and manage to tell your family to leave? I do have to say that I am impressed. You were monitored more closely than I think even you realize."

"I'm obviously not going to tell you where they are." Mitch considered how much he wanted to share in an effort to keep Gus talking. "Al here gave us some phones when we were in Bowling Green. I used mine before I went to the park the other day. As for my knowledge of South Carolina, I'm keeping that private for now as well. But I can't see how you will get past a major flaw in your plan. My boss at the *Republic*—John—he introduced me to this little party of yours. He is a well-respected member of the media; he'll clear my name. Plus, he knows Paul, and will be able to point to him as the catalyst."

With impeccable timing, John walked into the room holding a gun and pointing it at Gus. John had received Mitch's text, sent quickly in the Charger before getting out on the road in Fostoria. Mitch had decided on John over Mads, knowing John had more contacts. Mitch, however, did not think that John would come to the hotel, hoping his friend instead would document facts and send help like the police or someone from the CIA. Why would he be here?

John continued pointing the gun at Gus and walking slowly. Silence filled the room. Gus took a step back, surveying John with interest. Charlie was slowly reaching into his own pocket.

"That will be quite enough," John commanded, entering the room further. Charlie took his hand away from his gun. "This madness has gone way too far. Now you will see who is really behind all this. How are you, Nicola?"

"Wonderful, Bartolomeo," Gus responded. "So good to see you." Comprehension dawning on Mitch, he dropped his head, trying to think of all the ramifications of this revelation.

"What's going on?" Todd whispered.

"I think our potential ace in the hole is actually a snake in the grass," Al responded, as Gus and John exchanged an embrace. With everyone's attention on Gus and John, no one noticed Al had finally freed his hands. He also took this opportunity to reach behind Todd's back and tug a bit on his ropes. They slackened slightly. Todd realized Al's hands were free and started trying to accomplish the same feat.

"You were saying?" Gus said, sarcasm dripping in his tone. "You thought my friend here was going to help you. Mr. Bartter, you are not the only one who has college buddies assisting them today. John and I go way back."

"At least we got his real first name now," Todd whispered to Mitch.

"No, we don't," Mitch exclaimed, loud enough for all to hear. "Unless I am mistaken and there is an ironic twist here, the names they are using to address each other are related to two gentlemen who became infamous in the 1920s, Nicola Sacco and Bartolomeo Vanzetti."

"Who were they?" Todd asked, now buying time as well.

"Yes, tell us all, Mitch," John said.

"Sacco and Vanzetti had extremely radical political views. It was believed that both were Galleanists, meaning they were schooled by Luigi Galleani, an Italian anarchist who advocated revolutionary violence. Most Galleanists were forced from Italy by 1920, and some fled to America. Some were even suspected of bombing the home of the U.S. Attorney General in 1919."

"Your knowledge of history never ceases to amaze me," Gus said sincerely. "Such a waste, though I knew I had picked the right person."

"What did Nicola and Bartolomeo do?" Al asked still looking for an opening. John's arrival now meant there were three opponents in the room. All the other muscle must be somewhere else in the hotel, waiting to hear from Gus or Charlie.

"They were convicted of a robbery-murder in Braintree, Massachusetts, and were put to death. Many blamed the guilty verdict on their political views, and there is still some question as to their culpability in the crimes. Michael Dukakis, then governor of the state, signed a proclamation in the late '70s indicating any stigma related to these names should be removed."

"So, you can see why we chose these names as our code?" Gus questioned.

"I am assuming that you consider yourself anarchists," Mitch answered. "You are hoping to put the United States into a state of chaos—hoping for a revolt of the people."

"Again, being the smartest guy in the room isn't always good, is it Mitch?" John said.

Mitch looked with disdain and disbelief at the person he considered his friend. "Don't you dare talk to me! I can't even fathom how much hatred it takes to be so good at misleading and mistreating people as you have done to me and my family. You know what? It doesn't matter; the United States will continue to be the shining beacon it always has been! Your plot will fail!"

John shook his head and smiled. "Not when a few dozen or so of its trusted officials are caught with their hands in numerous cookie jars. It will be fun to watch! You Americans have taken so much for granted in the last fifty years, and you have become fat and lazy."

"John—calm yourself," Gus began. "If we are to tell it, let us tell it correctly. You Americans have been arrogant for far too long, and while many cannot see it, you began your own destruction, at least in terms of being a world leader, years ago. You are destined to the same fate as all great past democracies. I just wanted to see it happen in my lifetime, so I primed the pump, so to speak. I wanted to see your country get to a point where they can no longer just go into some foreign land and occupy it for a time, take the resources they want, and then leave, offering no further assistance."

"Where are you from?" Al asked.

"All in good time. I have a vision of some other country occupying America for awhile—now, that would be sweet revenge. However, I do not think that will occur before I die. I can cause turmoil, though, so I am. By the time all of what I have reaped comes to fruition, your country will be the laughingstock of the world, more so than it already is."

Mitch sat and listened as Gus spewed his venom in a calm manner. He tried to isolate his thoughts between what his opponent was saying and why he was saying it. Mitch had no idea that his two friends, at this point, both had managed to free their hands.

"John and I met years ago, and though we come from different backgrounds, we shared a kindred spirit in our disdain for many of the past sins of the United States. We talked how the country needed to be more divided, more fractured, in order to cause the chaos we wanted.

"We studied how this country had achieved such greatness. Our conclusion was the individual. This country was founded on the individual and allowing as much freedom to do whatever the individual wanted, with the basic exception of taking away the freedoms of others. Prior societies that tried this, such as the Romans, eventually fell victim to giving too much, taxing too much, and reverting to a much stronger central government."

"So, the question was how do we achieve a 'less free' government?" John continued. "That was what we determined to be necessary to bring the United States down. Let's limit individualism as it only increases output and ideas. Of course, the foundation had been laid, and the United States almost made this too easy."

"And how did we make it easy?" Mitch questioned.

"As I was saying earlier, your two-party system provided the perfect wedge," Gus responded eagerly, wanting to tell this. "We set our goals to assist in making these two parties hate each other as much as possible, creating a civil war climate. Obviously, one party was heading the way we felt necessary, with the perfect agenda of socialism.

"Then, however, the plan was thwarted by the election of Ronald Reagan. He was a great unifier, even though many tried to claim otherwise. Nationalism increased while he was president, and deregulation allowed more individualism to prosper. When the economy boomed with his programs, I knew it would be some time before we could carry out our plan. I even worried that never again would the atmosphere be quite right, such as it was in the Carter years. I was young then, and I have grown much older as I waited. However, slowly, things turned in my favor. Political correctness was our ally. You Americans are always concerned about others; it is a strength and it is a weakness. We exploited the weakness of it. Not wanting to offend anyone has led to many divisive policies and has caused a huge waste of resources." As Gus drew a deep breath, John cut in.

"We could see the time was coming. But we also knew that most of America is still the individualistic and entrepreneurial country it always has been. Your press, of which I was a part, may depict it differently, but deep down, this is true. It is just complacent. I knew, though, if someone were to become the leader that blatantly opposed those conservative ideas, that preached big government and control over the individual, we would have our spark, our own sinking of the Lusitania, if you will. We knew if either Hillary or Obama were elected, we would have our internal civil war. It was actually George W. Bush that helped get to where we are, though. His policies led to the 'change' candidate winning!"

"Yes, but you get ahead of yourself," Gus said. "Let us not forget the technological age in which we live. The ability to post blogs of hatred continued to divide this country, at least among those who care to read about the current issues. Throughout the late 1990s and into the 2000s, the mainstream press also has become more accusatory in its tone."

"And more one sided," John added. "Then, along came W. His policies led to the Democratic control of Congress; we were just fortunate enough the leaders of the Democratic Party were very liberal as well. Once President Obama started pushing his agenda, and Pelosi and Reed jumped on board, we knew a good part of the country would go nuts. Gus here placed many of his operative in the last few years of the Bush presidency, getting things ready."

Gus continued the soliloquy. "We really just accelerated the process. This would have happened eventually. You've studied history, Mitch, and you know democracies always end in tyranny. They last, as some e-mail I read the other day so eloquently pointed out, until the people realize they can vote themselves money from the public treasury. From that moment on, the most votes go to the candidates that promise to provide the most benefits. Sound like our last election? When those benefits ultimately cannot be paid because the tax receipts can't keep up, then the government collapses and a dictator takes over. As your social security, Medicare, and eventually the government healthcare system take over, your American way of life is doomed. Again, we just wanted to see it in our lifetimes.

"Now we will sit back and watch the fireworks. The conservative group financing the illegal operations that will come to light will cast a very poor reflection of individualism. So many people and organizations have contributed to the cause, which of course will only decrease public confidence in general. Since many top Republicans will be on their way to jail or at least resignation, no Republican will be trustworthy. Even though these same Republicans have spent too much of the public money as well, more of them would try to control spending. With the Republicans' credibility shot, Democrats will be the party in power that will continue to spend the country into oblivion and provide social programs that, though not feasible, sound excellent. It won't take long; the 'entitlement mindset' has already sunk in. Good luck getting rid of it."

Todd continued the argument. "I would debate strongly that Democrats would not allow that to happen. Sure, some of the leadership seems motivated to spend too much, but the core values of most elected officials are not that different. They all want a prosperous, independent America. You are basing your conclusions on a very small sample."

"Where have you been for the last twenty years?" John asked Todd. "Haven't you seen what has been happening?"

"Gus," Mitch broke in, "you still have not told us why you hate America so."

"I have told you enough! It's because of your arrogance, your pillaging the resources of other countries under the guise of helping them, your defending countries only to serve your own purpose. How many times does it have to happen—how often do American soldiers have to occupy another land, mistreating the people, impregnating the young women ..." he stopped abruptly, his eyes tearing up.

"Where are you from, Gus?" Mitch asked, repeating the earlier question as things were starting to become clearer. "Hold on; let me guess. I put you between sixty and sixty-five years old—meaning you were born in roughly the first five to seven years after World War II ended. You have done a great job hiding that hint of an accent since I met you, but it has come out a little more as you have been giving your speech here tonight. I'm going to say you are Austrian-born. I believe the United States participated in the Austrian occupation after the war. Your father—an American soldier maybe?"

Gus's eyes narrowed as he said through gritted teeth, "I never knew my father, and it is time for you to shut up."

"Am I right, Austrian?" Mitch continued on, ignoring Gus's command to be quiet.

"Italian, my mother was Italian, but she was living in Austria after World War II." Gus was unable to stop himself as suddenly he felt it was important for Mitch to know this. "I was born in Austria. An American soldier said he loved my mom. He left her, though, 'got new orders,' supposedly. Said he would come back for her, but he never did. Her heart was broken, and she never told me his name. He ruined her life. She was a beautiful woman, but could never find a way to love again. She was the only child of one of the wealthiest men in northern Italy. When she returned from Austria pregnant, she was ostracized by her family, forced to live in poverty until I was ten. Her father passed away, and she was suddenly a rich woman, but still incredibly sad. She died a few years later, and I'm convinced her decline in health was due to her unhappiness over the man who had hurt her so. I vowed, somehow, someday, to find a way to avenge her."

"You have done all this because a soldier broke you mom's heart?" Todd asked, disbelief written across his face. "That is just crazy! You don't know if the soldier was killed—maybe he fought in the Korean conflict—maybe he didn't abandon her!"

"This is not due to just one soldier, you idiot! Do you realize about 2,000 illegitimate children of American GIs were born between 1945 and 1955 in Salzburg alone! How many kids throughout the world grew up like me, a bastard child of a bastard country?" Gus was fuming, angry that his victims could not see the bigger picture. "Your Marshall Plan should have been called the rape and pillage plan!"

At this point, Mitch could see that anger in Gus could potentially be his ally. If he could just give Marie some more time, he knew she would find help. He continued at Gus.

"You're going to criticize the Marshall Plan? Do you realize that the United States paid $13 billion in assistance to Europe in its recovery? The GDP at the time was about $258 billion. To put it in context of today, that would be like providing about $3 trillion in aid using the same percent of the current GDP. Don't sit there and tell me that the Marshall Plan pillaged Europe!"

"Yes, but at what human cost? What human cost, Mitch? You

always forget that with your numbers and your quotes!" Gus yelled at him.

"Human cost! Have you looked at the third world countries of today, all the poverty and malnourishment? Where would Europe be without the plan? There should be statues of Marshall throughout the region! The jobs and economies it created. The Marshall Plan looked forward, not back. It accelerated efforts to modernize Europe. The funding occurred from 1948 through 1952, and by the end of that time period, every participating country had an economy that was operating in excess of prewar levels. Every one! When aggregating all the participants together, the 1951 output had increased 35 percent when compared to 1938. Throughout the 1960s and 1970s, Western Europe enjoyed growth and prosperity unprecedented in its history. For crying out loud, Gus, have some overall perspective!"

"Just like an American to take credit for something that would have happened with or without its meddling. It is of no matter." Gus was calming himself. "My motives are pure; I know that. I hope very soon America will no longer be able to, nor be asked to, go to other countries. You will have spent so much on your social programs that you will be too far in debt; your country will collapse under the weight of the unsustainable promises to your people."

"What about your wife and daughter, Gus? Is this the legacy they would want you to be pursuing?" Mitch was searching for any type of conscience the man might have.

"For someone so smart, I threw that one right by you, didn't I? That was all a hoax, clever though it may be. Do you realize how many doors open to you when you have a tragic story to tell? A few bribes here and there, and I had newspaper clippings and eventually Internet proof. It was a beautiful thing. I never had a wife or daughter."

"So, you're saying you are attacking the American way because of its lack of compassion for other countries when you have relied on its compassion to fulfill your goals of revenge?" Al spat at him.

"Well said, Mr. Accountant. That is exactly what I did." Gus reveled in the irony.

"Can I assume from all you have told us tonight my name has been forged all over the Liberty Group formation documents?" Mitch questioned.

"Yes, John was very helpful in providing numerous items you had signed, and I was able to find someone to duplicate it quite convincingly," Gus responded.

"So, the stories in the papers and on the Internet will attribute the planning, the illegal acts perpetrated by your hired help, the deception all to me. Excellent." Mitch's sarcasm was evident. "And the 'J.M.' on the timeline I saw, that's you, John. You fed the information to the papers on all that is about to happen."

"I have quite a few contacts across the country, and I knew who would publish these items based on accusations alone," John replied.

"And don't forget the money you accepted, and then funneled to political candidates," Gus said, almost laughing. "Such a shame."

"Though he did deftly avoid the sex scandal you attempted," John joked with his friend.

"I knew that was part of this!" Mitch exclaimed.

"That was never my idea," Gus deflected.

"Yeah, that seemed too clumsy for you. Must have been Charlie's brainchild."

"It really is too bad we are on opposite sides here, Mitch," Gus said honestly. "I think you could have been a formidable addition to our team. That mind of yours—pity—it will be a waste to rot in jail. Yes, the country will want a scapegoat. They always want to point at someone and say, 'You are to blame.' You, unfortunately, are in for a long rest of your life, Mr. Bartter."

"You managed to get your family out of harm's way without us knowing it," Charlie said with a diabolical smile, pulling a manila envelope from his briefcase. "That was impressive. However, your pretty wife will not be spared humiliation, unfortunately."

"What do you mean by that?" Mitch asked, his blood beginning to boil.

"Well, as I said, we thought we would know if you were ever on to us. At that point, we were going to use all the blackmail material necessary. As it is, we just get to have a little more fun." Charlie enjoyed himself as he spread the pictures of Marie in front of Mitch, Todd, and Al.

"You're all friends, so I'm sure you won't mind if Al and Todd here see your wife's naked form." The pictures indeed did show Marie sans clothes. It only took a couple glances for Mitch to realize they were obviously doctored. He was just about to say something when Todd's voice broke the silence.

"Those aren't Marie. You just put her face on someone else's body."

Mitch looked at his friend. Todd broke into a half smile. "Relax, buddy. I've seen her in a bikini—no birthmark on these pictures. Plus, look at the picture on the left; her face has a slight shadow on it; the rest of her body should as well."

"Nicely done, Sherlock," Charlie said sarcastically. "That, of course, won't matter. We can also transplant her fingerprints onto these; we already have those, by the way. Once those are found on the pictures, no one will doubt their authenticity. We'll let Mitch's name be the headline news for a few days, and then we will release these little gems—a back story of her secret life. It will be beautiful; you guys will love it."

"So, we get to live?" Todd asked.

"Well, Mitch does," Gus replied, his hand stroking his chin. "But here is what I think happened. Unfortunately, you and Al here figured out Mitch's plan, and you both tried to stop him. Mitch turned on his college buddies and had to eliminate them. Yes, a few dead bodies will add to the overall story. People will believe Mitch capable of anything once that part is discovered. That, too, was Charlie's idea once you went on this little caper to the east. You should have just stayed in Arizona and let it unfold, Mitch. Your friends here would have had a much better life expectancy. Charlie, I think it might be time to separate these fine gentlemen."

"You move too soon," Todd said.

"What does that mean?" Charlie asked, chuckling.

Al had the presence of mind to see what Todd was doing and play along. Todd started talking again, laughably attempting an Arnold Swartzeneggar accent.

"Now the first rule in a crisis situation—you negotiate first and you attack last. You never negotiated."

Charlie and Gus just looked at each other.

"You have no leverage to negotiate. Charlie, get Dale in here to take these two away."

Todd knew that was not a good idea. He liked it better with fewer opponents in the room. He continued the movie quoting.

"You move too soon."

"What?" Charlie said, continuing to laugh. "You already said that."

"The second rule in a crisis situation."

Al broke in. "Uh oh, he's starting that funny talk again."

"If you choose to bluff, you must be prepared to have your bluff called," Todd continued.

Charlie moved as close as he could to Todd's face without touching it. He talked in little more than a whisper. "Believe me, friend; I'm not bluffing. I never bluff. Any more incoherent babbling?"

"Just one more thing," Todd said. "*Now!*"

Todd and Al both reacted at the same time. Todd swung his clenched fist as hard as he could, catching Charlie square across the jaw. The big man fell to the ground in a heap. Al reached out his free hands and pedaled his still-bound feet straight at John, grabbing Mitch's boss and throwing him into Gus. The two of them collided and then hit the wall. Al did not stop, continuing to charge, ramming both Gus and John into the wall again. He pressed the back of his chair against their bodies and worked at untying his legs. Once free, he grabbed the gun from John's holster. Gus had regained his wits enough to yell out for someone, but Al threw an elbow in his gut and stuffed a napkin from the table in his mouth.

Todd stood up with his chair still attached to his backside and planted it right on top of Charlie. His adrenalin flowing, Todd bent down and proceeded to pummel Charlie, altering his right and left fists. Charlie fell unconscious after about six punches.

"Todd, he's out!" Mitch hissed, still bound to his chair. Todd stopped swinging, freed his legs, and relieved Charlie of his firearm. With Todd holding the gun on the two masterminds, Al used his ropes to tie Gus and John together. He then ran over and freed Mitch. Mitch and Todd ensured Charlie was tied securely, and then Mitch went over to the man he had considered a friend for many years and looked John straight in the eye.

"Anything you want to say, pal?" Mitch asked through gritted teeth in a sarcastic tone.

"I'm not worried; it's your name that will be infamous!" Mitch reached back and punched John with every bit of strength he could muster. John fell, knocked out by the blow, and Mitch grabbed his own fist, as it hurt as badly as if he had hit a solid wall.

"What should we do with them?" Todd asked. "Oh, wait, you've got to give me one minute. I can't miss this opportunity." A broad smile spread across his face. He went over to a now conscious Charlie, getting just as close to his face as Charlie had done to him minutes before.

"You fell victim to one of the classic blunders. The most famous is never get involved in a land war in Asia. But only slightly less well known is this: Never go in against a Falcon when death is on the line." With that, Todd grabbed Charlie's head and slammed it against the wall.

Todd turned to face his friends. "So?"

"*Princess Bride*, Vizzini, with the man in black," Al said, laughing. "Although, you did change it slightly."

"I thought the change was warranted. Hey, good catch on the *Twins* movie quote, way to play along."

"Just trying to keep them confused," Al responded.

"That was actually a movie quote? I wondered what the heck you two were doing. How could you possibly be playing that game when they had us like that?" Mitch asked, flabbergasted.

"*Twins* is a great movie—it should be quoted all the time, even when facing danger," Todd joked. "How it didn't garner any Oscars is beyond me. Now, back to my question, what should we do with these guys?" Charlie was squirming all he could, trying to loosen himself. Todd kicked him in the gut.

"First, we keep that gun on them," Mitch began. "Now, let's think. Their security is still around the hotel. We can't just waltz right out of here. Plus, we need Paul. He will have all the information that can set everything right. We still may be able to stop this before it goes too far. Give me Gus's phone—no, Charlie's," Mitch said.

"Why not Gus's?" Al asked.

"I'm guessing Gus has never sent a text to Paul, but Charlie probably has." He confirmed this fact with a quick review of the phone Todd pulled from Charlie. "I'm going to text Paul to get over here right away. I'll make sure he brings his computer, too. Maybe we can pull off a save of other reputations like we tried to do for DeMint."

"Well, let's wait to see who is on the list," Todd said. "There may be a few I don't mind getting in hot water." Todd was smiling ear to ear. Mitch just shook his head, admiring Todd's sense of humor in the tense situation.

Mitch sent the text. The group also decided to split up their prisoners, moving each to face a different corner so they were unable to see each other and so their hands were visible. John was still unconscious, or at least playing that he was. Now, they just needed to wait for Paul.

Chapter 33

Paul had been finishing packing his stuff. Earlier that day, Gus had sent him home to get every scrap of the Liberty Group documentation, as it would be turned over to the authorities implicating Mitch, or it would be destroyed. Paul was not relishing what was coming in the following week. Gus had his personal reasons, and Charlie was letting money guide him, but Paul truly did believe a more socialist society was optimal. Why shouldn't the resources of a country be shared among all the people? It seemed to him what was most fair and what made the most sense. He did, though, have a conscience. He wished no one needed to be torn down to accomplish the goal.

Paul had already decided he was heading north the minute Gus gave him the go ahead. Gus would need him to ensure all the targets were set up appropriately, and all their covert operators were extricated from the assignments. Paul had been the record-keeper since he came aboard. Earlier in Gus's planning, the wealthy man had decided to interview attorneys under the guise of needing one for several of his entities. Gus was really looking for a kindred spirit, asking questions that would reveal certain traits. Paul had been his first choice, and the partnership had worked very well. The two would now say their goodbyes. As Paul was putting some final things in a box, he received the text message to bring all the records to the Biltmore.

Finally! he thought. *I just want this to be over.* Paul had already segregated the records he had been keeping for the Liberty Group over the past three or four years. This included the names of everyone working in the different congressional offices across the county, when they were hired, and several different contracts with security offices. The records also included all the corporate contributions they had received prior to the Web site going live, as well as all the individuals who had contributed and purchased memberships. This data was all kept electronically as well—these boxes contained most of the hardcopies of what had been printed. He loaded everything into his car and started driving toward the Biltmore. *Just get me through the next few days*, he thought.

* * * *

After sending the message to Paul, Mitch rummaged through the bag in which Charlie had thrown all their phones, wallets, etc., and found his cell. He tossed Todd's and Al's each to them as well. Mitch assumed Al would want to talk with Lisa just as he was quickly calling Marie.

"Hello," she answered hesitantly.

"Marie, it's me!" Mitch said enthusiastically.

"Are you all right? Are they forcing you to call me?" Marie was whispering for some reason.

"We staged a coup! Gus, Charlie, and John are all tied up. Are you in San Diego? Have you sent anyone to help us?"

"I am actually about ten minutes from the Biltmore. Mark is with me."

"You're where? Mark? Don't come here! It's still dangerous. All of

Charlie's hired help is around. They don't know we have managed to get control." As he said this, he mouthed to Todd to lock all the doors.

"Mitch, we will be there in a few minutes, and you are not stopping us. Now, what should we do when we get there?" Mitch thought for a few seconds. Then, he realized it just might be perfect. He gave some instructions to his wife.

* * * *

About eight minutes later, Marie and Mark pulled into the Biltmore. They parked where they had a clear view of the main entrance. Mark turned off the ignition, and they waited. After about a minute, Marie noticed Karen getting out of a car with someone that looked vaguely familiar. Mitch had not mentioned to be on the lookout for Karen. Marie hesitated only briefly, but she thought whichever side Karen was on, her entering the hotel right now would not be good.

"Karen!" Marie yelled, stepping out of her own car. Mark got out, too, ready for anything.

Karen turned in Marie's direction, as did the man with her and about five other men and one woman who had materialized seemingly from nowhere. Marie was very concerned all of a sudden.

"That's Mitch's wife; she's okay," Karen said to the others, indicating that they should not do anything. The two women walked toward each other.

"You shouldn't be here," Karen said.

"Look, Mitch is in there with two of his friends. He just called me and said that they have Gus, Charlie, and John tied up in the meeting room, but they know the hallways outside are being patrolled by Charlie's team." Karen motioned Will and the off-duty officers over. Marie repeated what she had just said to Karen, as well as everything Mitch had told her, still trying to place where she had seen Will before. They all agreed to wait in their vehicles as Mitch had asked.

Five minutes later, Paul pulled into the lot. He parked, popped his trunk, and walked around to grab a box. He would carry one in now and get a luggage rack for the others. When he stood up holding the box and turned away from his trunk, he was looking at six men and three women.

"Don't yell anything," Karen said calmly, pointing her finger at him. "Just answer my questions quietly. Who is in charge of Charlie's team, after Charlie?"

"Usually Russell, but now it would be either Joe or Dale," Paul answered, not quite understanding what was happening.

"Do you have either of their phone numbers?"

"No," Paul answered truthfully.

"That's no problem," Marie said, and she called Mitch. Within minutes, Mitch had used Charlie's phone to text Dale and Joe that Paul was pulling in the parking lot and needed help with the records. They were to send some men outside to assist him. This little maneuver worked to perfection as the assembly of undercover officers was waiting when Charlie's gang of four arrived at the car. They were all handcuffed and forced to sit between parked cars in the lot. Joe and Dale were still inside with a few others. Unfortunately, none of the apprehended group was talking, so the total number of men still left was an unknown. Marie called Mitch back, informing him that there were now fewer obstacles inside, but that some did remain.

"Mark is chomping at the bit to come in and get you guys," Marie said. "We asked Paul—he's not sure how many are left."

"Okay. Here's what we do: send in a couple of those police officers; Karen can direct them to this room. We'll come out and see who tries to stop us. And keep Mark back; this could get a little messy."

Mitch, Al, and Todd waited about ten minutes, taking the time to ensure their three incapacitated opponents were tied very tightly. They then slowly opened the door. The hallway appeared empty as the group walked out and started toward the lobby area. They had not gone ten steps when Joe was on them.

"Where's Charlie?" he said, walking toward them, reaching for his weapon. Without warning, Joe was tackled by two individuals hiding in a recess in the wall. Joe dropped his gun—Todd picked it up, as he was closest. The group continued toward the exit. However, prior to reaching the front of the hotel, the remaining four members of Charlie's team jumped them, and the melee continued into the lobby. The two police officers let go of Joe, who was in handcuffs, to resist the four new opponents. Al, Todd, and Mitch helped as best they could, but in the initial altercation, Charlie was separated from the group by Dale and pulled off to the side, with Dale untying him quickly. Hotel guests were scurrying in every direction, and the front desk clerk ducked behind his barrier, reaching for the phone. The fracas seemed to be coming to an end, as the police had three men in addition to Joe under control, with Gus and John also still bound. As they turned around, though, Charlie and Dale each were about to get to their feet. Dale was reaching for a gun in his holster, and Charlie had already grabbed the revolver Todd had dropped in the confusion, taking aim at Mitch.

"You should have left well enough alone!" Charlie spat from his knees, but as he was about to pull the trigger, a blur crossed his vision, and he felt the impact to his face. Charlie landed flat on his back, Marie having kicked him with all her strength. Dale noticed a moment too late that someone was headed his direction as well, and before he could unholster his weapon, Mark had tackled him and was landing blows to his face.

"I told you two to stay outside!" Mitch said, giving Marie a big hug after the guns had been retrieved and the situation seemed clear.

"I wasn't going to let you three have all the fun," Mark said, smiling and rubbing his shoulder where he had made contact with Dale.

"And I was going to make sure you got out safe!" Marie chimed in.

* * * *

It was a tearful reunion that carried into the parking lot as Mitch and Marie embraced for a very long time. The undercover officers had called in on-duty backups to assist with the situation while Mitch and Karen pieced as much together as they could. Will had been standing in the background a bit, ever since the group had exited the hotel.

"Will, come meet Mitch," Karen said. "He has a lot to thank you for."

"What do you mean?" Mitch asked.

"Will is the one who has been feeding you information. He sent you the e-mail a few mornings ago." Will had finally walked over to where they were, and Mitch got a good look at him for the first time. Just like Marie, he was trying to place the face he knew he had seen before.

"Will Jensen." Will was holding out his hand, flashing a bit of a smile. That is all it took to jar Mitch's memory.

"Will—don't you mean Bill?" Mitch said. "Al, Marie, Todd, Mark, get over here! We are not the only Falcon alums here today!"

Will blushed slightly. "My official name is William, but I always went by Bill in my younger days. I moved to Arizona and refocused, you might say. I told everyone to call me Will instead."

The others had made their way over to Mitch, Karen, and Will.

"Do you remember Bill? He was in some of our accounting classes," Mitch asked.

"I remember walking you home after a party one night," Marie said, now recognizing the person in front of her.

Tears filled Will's eyes. "It may sound crazy, but I have never forgotten that night either. You and Mitch showed me some true kindness when I was at my lowest point. Whenever I see someone else in a bind, you two are always my inspiration to lend a hand. I firmly believe you saved my life that night; maybe not in the literal sense, but definitely in helping me find my way."

Karen was moved by her friend's admission. "That's why his name stuck out on the first e-mail you saw," Karen said, putting her hand in his, shaking her head at the irony that these people all knew each other.

"Wait a minute, you sent me the e-mail a few days ago?" Mitch questioned. "Did you feed me all the other information as well—in my car—at the paper—and at the school musical?"

Will grinned a little. "When your life is basically spent doing taxes, you look for any possible way to liven it up a bit. It was a way I could help you without anyone being the wiser. I could tell something strange was happening, and I assumed if Karen knew what I was doing, she would probably jeopardize herself even more. I did the only thing I thought I could: send you information anonymously until I could truly understand what was happening. Of course, that did not happen until this weekend."

The rest of the evening was spent sorting out as much of the story as possible for the authorities. Gus, Charlie, John, and Mitch were all taken into custody, with Mitch still wanted for questioning in the DeMint bribery case as well as the campaign financing items. However, Senator DeMint had called a few federal offices in Phoenix to explain personally what had transpired in South Carolina. Mitch was released that evening, pending further investigation.

Before leaving the police station, he went back to the cell where Gus was being held.

"I felt compelled to talk to you just a minute more," Mitch began. "Your wonderful plot, based on the fractions in America, would never have succeeded. I'm going to use my whole involvement as an example. It was a true team effort to prevent your plan from coming to fruition, and some of my biggest help came from bleeding heart liberals, who happen to be two of my best friends as well." He was referring to Todd and Mads. "That is what will always happen in a crisis here in America; people will come together, not break apart. Everyone wants a free and prosperous United States; we just have debates about how to get there. Sure, some idiot like you comes along every now and then, but your kind will always lose! Most Republicans and Democrats alike will line up against you every day! Chew on those thoughts for a while, a long while, where you are going." Mitch turned and walked out, the vision of the defeated Gus in a jail cell etched in his mind.

* * * * *

A media circus occurred all day Sunday and especially the following Monday morning. Stories came out about prominent Republicans only to be refuted within hours by other news agencies. It truly was pandemonium. It took a few days, but using Paul and Karen's records, all the moles that Gus had used in the congressional offices were rounded up, and most of them confessed all they had done and who they had worked for. Slowly, Mitch's name was cleared in all of those cases. That just left the campaign finance charge. Luckily, Brian Maddox was able to provide the evidence he had gathered, Mitch provided the tape he had made of the second occurrence receiving the money, and John eventually provided the name of the attorney who had been brought in to collect the money and put it in escrow. For most of the week, the newspapers referred to the whole case as Liberty-Gate, with the suffix added as it is to any scandal.

Paul's records also alluded to an incident that had occurred in the California capital, and upon searching both Charlie's and Gus's residences, evidence was found to put to bed an unsolved murder in Sacramento. Additional charges were added to Gus and Charlie's long list.

* * * * *

The group of Mitch, Marie, Al, Mark, Todd, Will, and Karen spent most of these few days answering many questions from different media outlets about what had happened, how it had all occurred, and basically clearing their names. Karen had the most potential for getting swept up with the others, as she participated in some of the planning. For most of that Monday, it appeared she, too, would be going to jail, but in exchange for a lighter sentence, Paul came forward, admitting the blackmail Gus had perpetrated and providing testimony that Karen was unaware of the illegal acts. Paul even provided proof Karen had attempted to contact authorities when she learned the full truth. This was enough to exonerate her of the heavy charges, and Karen was able to keep her CPA license, although she was ordered to perform some community service. Al, Mark, and Todd headed to their respective homes midweek, their friendships stronger than ever.

Chapter 34

Several weeks later, the public fervor had died down, and Will, Karen, Mitch, and Marie were able to enjoy a wonderful evening out together. Will and Karen were explaining to the Bartters the trick of trying to date while being partners in a business.

"At least, you are equal partners in it, no supervisory issues to deal with," Marie said encouragingly.

"That much is true," Will stated. "The issue relates more to the rest of the office—how do we tell them?"

"You don't think they already know?" Mitch asked.

"I'm sure some have guessed," Karen said, a broad smile across her face. "I never told you this, Will, but I had a few people from the office ask me months ago when you and I were going to get together."

"I know; who do you think told them to ask you?" he joked back to her. "Geez, I'd been hinting for so long, but I could never read a response. Thank heaven you got yourself into a life-and-death situation."

"I wouldn't go that far," Karen said, raising her glass of wine. "But obviously, some wonderful things did come out it. Here's to new friendships!"

"Cheers," they all said in unison, glasses clinking.

"You could always just send an e-mail to the office telling them that you two were an item," Mitch suggested. "Or better yet, just make it Facebook official. That will get the office going."

"The bottom line is that there is no correct answer," Marie said wisely. "I would say just be yourselves around the office—no major announcement but not hiding the fact either. Some will ask and others will just assume. Eventually, everyone will be comfortable with it, and you'll move on from there."

"You make it sound easy," Karen stated. "What do you think, Will? Shall we try that approach?"

"I guess, if you don't want to just make out in your office," Will replied, winking.

"So, tell me more about Billy here and his college days," Karen requested, putting her arm around him.

Karen listened as the three BGSU Falcons told stories of their younger days. She also realized she was now happier than she had felt for a very long time. In the matter of a short few weeks, she had gone from dire depression to elation in both her personal and business lives.

As the evening was winding down, Marie suggested they get together again in the near future. She was enjoying this newfound friendship with Karen and wanted to build on it.

"Definitely, let's do it as soon as Will and I get back," Karen replied.

"Get back from where?" Mitch asked.

Will smiled as he responded. "Oh, we didn't tell you. I made dinner reservations at this little place I found a few years back, but it takes a little while to get to it. I really want Karen to see it—they have best menu! We decided to take a little trip."

"What is the name of this place?" Mitch was curious.

"Zsa-Zsa's, it's Italian."

"Where is it?" Marie questioned.

"Florence. I said it was Italian," Will joked.

They parted company, and Mitch walked Marie back to the car. He opened the door for her but pulled her into an embrace before she got in.

"I have a surprise for you," he said, whispering in her ear. "Will you play along for a few minutes?"

"Okay," she responded hesitantly. "What do you want me to do?"

"Turn around." She complied, and Mitch put a blindfold on her.

"What are you doing?" she said, laughing.

"I just really want it to be a surprise." Mitch helped his wife into the car and drove for about ten minutes. Marie tried to think of where they were going based on the turns Mitch was making, but gave up after a few minutes. He slowed down and eased the car into a parking space.

"All right, let me take off that blindfold and show you we were are," Mitch said after helping Marie out of the car.

The setting was a surprise, a big surprise. Although it was beautiful, Marie did not think she would be seeing it anytime soon. "What are we doing here?"

Earlier in the week, Mitch had received an e-mail reminder from the Biltmore Hotel regarding the reservation he had made weeks ago. He had totally forgotten about his investigative excursion trying to learn more about Gus that culminated in the booking of a weekend reservation. It took at least 1.3 seconds for him to decide to keep the reservation and surprise Marie. For all he had put her through in this past summer, it was the least he could do. Mitch was apprehensive about returning to this place, given the memories.

"I have to put those things behind me," he had said to himself resolutely, clicking the confirm icon on the e-mail.

"I didn't think you would ever come back here," Marie said.

"For you, I'd go anywhere!" Mitch said and then explained how he came to have the reservation. "It almost seems fitting that we should put an exclamation point to this little saga with a weekend here."

"So, a little rest and relaxation, huh? I assume the kids are taken care of?"

"Of course they are, and I have a bag packed for both of us. I just really wanted to thank you for seeing me through this whole ordeal. You are my rock. I love you so much."

"I love you, too!" After a long embrace, the couple walked into the Biltmore.